Setting the Stage
for Murder

By Robert W. Gregg

Copyright © 2008 by Robert W. Gregg

ISBN 978-0-7414-5020-3

Cover photos courtesy of Steve Knapp,
www.keukaview.com

Published by:

INFINITY PUBLISHING

Info@buybooksontheweb.com
www.buybooksontheweb.com
Toll-free (877) BUY BOOK
Local Phone (610) 941-9999
Fax (610) 941-9959

Printed in the United States of America

Published December 2012

To my wife Barbara

PROLOGUE

"Professor Whitman!"

"Why must she do that," Kevin said under his breath. He had asked the members of his little summer opera company on Crooked Lake to, please, be informal. No titles, just plain Kevin. Most of them had gotten the point. Not Lisa Tompkins, one of too few violins in the small orchestra. She was either the product of an unusually proper upbringing or derived some perverse pleasure in ignoring his wishes.

"It's Mr. Gerlach," Lisa shouted from somewhere behind the curtain. "He's drunk. I can't get him to wake up."

Harley Gerlach was a far more serious problem than Lisa Tompkins. If he had passed out from too many tumblers of scotch, was hard to imagine that the dress rehearsal would go well. Or en that it would take place at all. Not for the first time, Kevin nd himself regretting his decision to cast the man in the leading e. He had a beautiful voice when he was sober, but he was ly sober and he was thoroughly loathed by the rest of the pany. To say that he was impressed with himself would be a s understatement. And obnoxious? The word could have been ed with him in mind. But it was too late now. The first rformance of Puccini's comic opera *Gianni Schicchi* was due to ake place in four days.

"I'm coming, Lisa. Don't you worry about it. I'll bring him around."

Kevin hurried down through the auditorium, its seats now empty, bounded up onto the stage, and pushed his way through the curtain.

The sight that greeted him was one with which he was now familiar: a barely furnished bedroom which would be the setting for the single act of the opera. In fact, except for a couple of wooden chairs and a handful of knickknacks, the only furniture in the room was a large bed. The bed in which that rascal Schicchi would pull off his little con.

Lisa Tompkins was standing beside that bed and pointing to the bedspread, which looked suspiciously lumpy.

1

"He's there. Under the covers. Drunk as a skunk. I smelled it as soon as I came in."

"Isn't that great," Kevin said sarcastically, as much to himself as to Lisa. It was 5:20 in the afternoon. Dress rehearsal was scheduled for 7:30.

He walked over to the bed and pulled down the spread, something Lisa had apparently been reluctant to do.

"He looks sick, doesn't he?" Lisa volunteered.

Yes, thought Kevin, he looks very sick. There goes the dress rehearsal. But he was determined to rouse his problem baritone.

"Come on, Harley. Time to wake up. Now! Are you hearing me?"

But even as Kevin shook and hollered at the man in the bed, he realized that something was seriously wrong. Something other than too much liquor.

He bent over his star, looking closely at the puffy face, and was almost immediately aware that Gerlach was not breathing.

"Lisa, quick—get to a phone and call 911."

She hesitated, as if waiting for an explanation.

"Come on, girl. This is an emergency. Make that call."

That Harley Gerlach had been drinking was obvious. it wasn't scotch that had given him the tortured face that stared at Kevin. Around his neck was a cord which looked very m like a piano wire. And it was wrapped tightly, cutting deep into flesh. Deep enough to have choked off all breathing. Gia Schicchi was not drunk. He was dead.

CHAPTER 1

The idea for staging an opera on Crooked Lake had come to Kevin Whitman back in the winter when he was putting the finishing touches on the syllabus for his spring course at Madison College on the history of opera. He had decided that his syllabus was on the heavy side. Too much Wagner. Even too much Verdi, although Kevin himself never tired of Verdi. He had begun to consider leavening the course with a comic opera or two when a commercial interrupted the radio program which he had lost interest in at least ten minutes earlier. Irritated by the pitch for a skin lotion guaranteed to turn every woman into Cinderella, he got up from his desk to turn the radio off. But before he got there, the commercial took a musical turn. In the cause of promoting the product, some clever ad agency had borrowed Giacomo Puccini's beautiful aria from his opera *Gianni Schicchi*, 'O mio babbino caro.' Americans in the millions would recognize the tune, even if only a tiny few knew its source. A cliché, yes. But a lovely one.

Kevin decided on the spot that he would add *Gianni Schicchi* to his syllabus. And it was but a few minutes later that an exciting thought struck him: What if he could arrange to stage the opera on Crooked Lake during the summer?

But almost immediately some inner voice spoke up. It reminded him that he hadn't the faintest idea whether such a thing was possible. Where would the opera be presented? What permissions would have to be obtained? How could he assemble a cast? An orchestra? A cast and an orchestra of people who could sight-read, who would not sound like a ragged church choir and a town band? And if that proved to be possible, who would design and construct the set? Make costumes? Conduct the opera? Yes, he thought, his worries multiplying, who would conduct? Me?

It was at that point that this exercise in brainstorming brought Kevin up short. If it could be done at all, he would have to do it, and do it for all practical purposes alone. He knew of no one he could talk into joining him in this harebrained plan. No one on the Madison College faculty. No one among his friends in the city.

Or on Crooked Lake. It was a crazy idea, and he found himself dismissing it as readily as he had first embraced it. Or tried to.

He had an early dinner at the faculty club with a friend from the physics department and was back in his apartment by eight o'clock. And a lonely apartment it was. The ghost of his former wife, Susan, had long ago vacated the place, but no one had taken her place. He had considered a dog, but dogs and big city living did not go well together. Cats were more manageable, but he didn't much care for cats. What he really wanted was a woman, and not just any woman. He wanted Carol Kelleher. Sitting on the couch, listening to a piece of sublime music with him. Padding around the kitchen in slippers and bathrobe, rustling up a breakfast of eggs Benedict. Sharing the big king-sized bed.

But none of this was possible because Carol Kelleher was the sheriff of Cumberland County, too many miles away in remote upstate New York, while he was toiling in the groves of academe, nurturing his students' interest in music, and writing and publishing enough to keep his dean happy. It was not exactly an arrangement conducive to a close long-term relationship. Althoug the spring semester had not yet begun and would not come to a end until nearly five more months had passed, Kevin w impatient for the time to pass more quickly so that he could ret to Crooked Lake for the summer.

This was not the first time that Kevin had been frustra by the problem that jobs and geography created for his relation with Carol. But it was the first time he had considered problem on the same day that he had decided to include Puccin *Gianni Schicchi* in his syllabus. Which had led to the wild idea o staging that opera on the banks of Crooked Lake. He had seen it as a way to enliven the cultural climate up there, only to dismiss the idea as impractical. But now that he was once again regretting the stubborn fact that Carol would always be a long way away from September to May, Kevin revisited the Puccini plan. What if he could bring it off? Might it lead to a visiting appointment at that college on the lake? He was due a sabbatical, which meant that a leave of absence shouldn't be hard to negotiate.

Suddenly, Kevin felt a rush of adrenalin. Yes, he said to himself. None of the problems that had led him to dismiss the idea now looked so daunting. He remembered what an old high school teacher of French used to say: vouloir c'est pouvoir. Where there's a will, there's a way.

Kevin decided to call Carol, and not in her official role. When he had first met her, she was wearing her sheriff's hat, questioning him about his discovery of a dead man on his dock. That had been two summers ago. But what had begun as the investigation of a crime had gradually become something else, something infinitely more satisfying, something which had been renewed the previous summer as they cooperated to solve yet another crime on normally tranquil Crooked Lake. And became lovers.

The phone rang five times in the sheriff's Cumberland apartment before he heard her voice.

"Hello, this is the sheriff."

Her tone suggested that she had been expecting a call in her capacity as the local guardian of law and order.

"Carol, it's Kevin."

"Well, hi down there." She sounded relieved that the call was not about law enforcement. "I was expecting someone else. An annoying problem involving a pair of vicious dogs. But you on't need to hear my tale of woe. To what do I owe the leasure?"

"Just wanted to tell you I love you. But I've got an idea I nt to run past you, so do you have a few minutes?"

"All night if you like. And I love you, too. What's up?"

"I've been thinking," he began and then paused, as if to 1k about what he had been thinking.

"I should hope so," Carol said. "Do you want to tell me .bout it?"

Now she's making fun of me, he thought. Heaven knows what she'll say when I tell her what I'm going to do.

"Look, I've got a plan. A plan for next summer. Are you sitting down?"

"Of course I'm sitting down. Are you all right? Has something happened that I should know about? Why the mystery?"

"Sorry," Kevin answered. "There's no mystery. I just wanted to tell you that I'm thinking about putting on an opera next summer. On Crooked Lake. At Brae Loch College, if they'll let me do it."

There. He'd said it, and it wasn't as hard as he had imagined it would be. Carol, on the other hand, sounded stunned.

"Whoa! You're going to do an opera? Up here? Forgive me for being surprised, but I don't remember you telling me that

5

you're an impresario or whatever it is they call people who do things like that."

"Impresario, no," Kevin said, and then hurried on to explain why he thought his plan might appeal to Carol. "But let's just assume for a minute that it's possible. What if I could enlist the support of the college people, put on a good show, and then use that to sell them on the idea of giving me a visiting appointment for a year. That would mean I'd be on the lake the year around—well, at least for a year."

He didn't have to tell Carol why that would be desirable.

"You'd really do that?" she asked. "Cut your ties down in the city to be up here?"

"I might. But I wouldn't have to resign from Madison. I've got a sabbatical coming. Why not spend it on the lake, sharing my love of music with the students at Brae Loch and sharing my cottage with you. Not now and then, but every day."

But Carol was apparently in the mood to be practical.

"I'd love to have you here. You know that. And you know I can't pack up and move to the city. But—"

Kevin wasn't interested in whatever 'buts' Carol had in mind.

"I haven't got it all figured out," he interrupted, "but wanted to see what you think of the idea. Pretty clever, right?"

"Yes, very clever. And, I would wager, pretty unlike Sure, I'd love to have you around all the time. Like right now, we wouldn't have to be discussing it over the phone. But why you think Brae Loch would be so welcoming? Does it even have music department?"

"Carol, you're not trying to be a wet blanket, are you?"

"Of course not, just trying to be realistic. You took me by surprise, and I suppose my first reaction was that it sounded like one helluva lot of work—if it's even possible."

Kevin knew that Carol was raising the right questions, questions he hadn't given much thought to. Questions he'd have to give a lot of thought to.

"You have put on an opera before, haven't you?" Carol continued, sounding doubtful. "You know, not just taught your students about opera but actually staged one?"

"No, I'm afraid not," he said, somewhat defensively. "That's not my department. But it won't be that much of a stretch."

Determined not to let Carol's doubts dissuade him from pursuing his Puccini plan, Kevin ticked off a list of his credentials, previously unknown to the sheriff.

"You don't get to teach music appreciation like I do if you can't read music, don't have a pretty good ear, can't play an instrument, that kind of thing. So, no, I probably wouldn't be very good at teaching my students to play a piano or a violin or whatever. Or to sing *Aida*. But I do play the piano. Don't laugh, but I'm not bad on wind instruments either. Played oboe and bassoon for awhile. I know that no symphony orchestra would consider offering me a contract, and I wouldn't accept one if it was offered. But I can handle a short opera—provided I can round up a few people with decent voices. Oh, and enough musicians to form a halfway decent orchestra."

Carol was surprised by this oral resumé of Kevin's musical accomplishments. Surprised and impressed. How little I really know about him, she thought. My God, I've been sleeping with him for over a year and I didn't even know he could play a bassoon.

"I'm impressed," she said. And meant it. But she couldn't resist a bit of needling. "Of course I've never heard you sing. That's probably because I've never showered with you."

"I think we can remedy that, don't you? Anyway, I don't have to have a good voice to judge whether others do. And I'm counting on there being a fair number of talented people up there around the lake. It'll just be a matter of rounding them up, rehearsing, and voilà, we've got an opera."

Carol could see that it was pointless to play the hardheaded realist. And maybe, just maybe, Kevin could bring it off. After all, he had been invaluable in helping her to solve the murders which had shocked the region over the last two summers. Besides, if he could parlay his plan into a year's appointment at Brae Loch College, she'd be one happy sheriff.

"Want to tell me what opera you have in mind?"

"I don't think you'd have heard of it," Kevin said, remembering that opera was not her thing.

"Try me."

"Okay, it's Puccini's *Gianni Schicchi*."

"You win. I've never heard of it, much less heard it or seen it. I'm not sure I could even spell it."

7

"It's a man's name, Schicchi—like 'ski key.' He's a smart peasant who outwits the greedy relatives of a recently deceased old man. Fools 'em all and writes a will which gives him most of the estate, him and his lovely daughter."

Carol considered this brief plot sketch.

"So it's sort of a comedy, right?"

"Yes, indeed. I didn't think it would be a good idea to test the waters up there with one of those operatic tragedies. You know, most of the cast dead by the final curtain. I want the audience to leave with a smile on their faces."

"You're probably right," she said, thinking of the tragic deaths which had marred the two previous summers. Deaths which had involved Kevin in the sheriff's ultimately successful search for two killers. "Let's have a summer in which nobody gets killed, offstage or on."

Little did either of them know that this was not to be. Or that solving the murder of an actor playing the part of Gianni Schicchi would turn out to be far more difficult than obtaining the support of Brae Loch College and casting the opera.

CHAPTER 2

It was several weeks later, not long after the beginning of the spring term, that Kevin, armed with Sheriff Carol Kelleher's tentative approval, got around to putting into motion his plan for staging an opera on Crooked Lake. The first order of business was obtaining permission from Brae Loch College to use its facilities. Not once during his summers on Crooked Lake had Kevin even set foot on the campus of the small college. Which meant that he had no idea whether it had an auditorium suitable for putting on an opera. Much less whether the college would embrace his plan if it did have such an auditorium. He would need to be at his diplomatic best to sell the idea to the powers that be at Brae Loch, and he would have to make his pitch in person, not over the phone.

Thus it was on a chilly day in late February that Kevin boarded a flight to the upstate airport serving the Crooked Lake area. He had called Carol and made arrangements to meet her for dinner. He had briefly considered staying at the cottage, but abandoned the idea because of the time it would require to open it and the need to be back in the city for an evening class the following day. It meant that he would have to spend the night in an undistinguished Southport motel, which he did not look forward to. But that wouldn't matter if his visit to the college produced the result he hoped for. The last twenty minutes of the flight took him over familiar snow-covered fields and the dark fingers of the lakes. It was a sight that reinforced his determination to succeed in his mission.

After a brief stop to check in at the motel, Kevin headed up West Lake Road in the rental car, wondering how receptive to his plan Brae Loch's provost would be. I'll know soon enough, he thought, as he first passed his own cottage, made the turn at West Branch, and then drove the last dozen miles to the college.

Brae Loch. Scottish for hill-lake. And there it was, nestled at the foot of a low wooded hill on the shore of Crooked Lake. A modest cluster of buildings, of which the chapel and what looked like an athletic facility stood out. Sidewalks that crisscrossed the quad were filled with students, bundled up against a brisk winter wind, who were obviously going from one class to another. It looked very much like his own Madison College, except that it was smaller and not hemmed in by city streets. Kevin found a parking place behind a dormitory near the lake, and walked back to where he imagined the administrative heart of the college was located. One of the students directed him to an old but still attractive building with the words Menlo Hall chiseled in the stone façade above the entrance.

A businesslike woman at the reception desk consulted the provost's calendar and then called to make sure he was not otherwise occupied. Apparently he wasn't, so she steered him down a hall and past a row of glass cases containing mementos of Brae Loch's history to a door bearing a plaque which read Jason Armitage, Provost.

Now that the critical moment had arrived, Kevin found himself worrying that he had not been more straightforward when he had made the appointment. Concerned that the school's leaders might not be interested in opera, he had spoken vaguely about a plan to raise money for Brae Loch. And the opera, if reasonably well attended, might actually bring in a few thousand dollars. But it would do nothing for the school's presumably small endowment. Kevin feared that his meeting with the provost might be very brief.

The man who greeted him was very tall and very thin. Kevin was reminded of a scarecrow. But the provost's grip was almost painfully strong.

"Professor Whitman, so glad to meet you at last."

At last? The appointment had been made less than a week earlier. But Jason Armitage went on to explain himself, not waiting for Kevin to say anything.

"I was intrigued the minute my secretary mentioned you wanted to see me. You're the man who testified for the prosecution last fall in that case about the dead woman in the ravine. Fascinating case. Not easy to get away from my responsibilities here, but I did get to the courthouse a few times. Indeed I was there when you testified. You're something of a celebrity around these parts."

Whatever Kevin had imagined, it wasn't this. He now realized that he had secured an appointment with the provost not because he could make some money for Brae Loch, but because the provost was interested in meeting 'a celebrity.'

"Hardly a celebrity, I'm afraid," Kevin said, wishing the provost would release the iron grip he had on his hand.

"You're too modest. We haven't had anything like it since I've been here. Sleepy place, Crooked Lake. That's why I watch that *CSI* show, that and the *Law & Order* reruns."

It was becoming obvious that the provost was a crime junkie. For the better part of a quarter hour, they discussed crimes, both real and fictional. Or, more accurately, Jason Armitage held forth on the subject and Kevin muttered an occasional word of agreement. It was not until the provost asked if he might like a cup of coffee that Kevin found an opening to raise the question which had brought him to the Brae Loch campus.

"Ah, that's good," Armitage said of the coffee his secretary had delivered.

"Yes, very good," Kevin seconded the provost, although it was too strong for his taste. "Let me explain why I'm here."

"Money, I think," the provost said. "We're just a little school, as I'm sure you know. Small enrollment, small budget. So what is your interest in us?"

No point in dancing around the issue, Kevin thought, and plunged into his pitch for bringing Puccini to Brae Loch.

"As I told your secretary when I made the appointment, I teach music at Madison College. My specialty is opera. I would very much like to put on an opera here on Crooked Lake. And it seems to me that the logical place to do it is right here at Brae Loch. So my reason for taking your valuable time this afternoon is to ask if it might be possible."

Before Kevin could spell out his plan in any detail, the provost interrupted.

"An opera, you say. I don't know much about opera. Saw *Carmen* many years ago. As I remember it, it was colorful. Some nice tunes. Something about bullfighting, isn't it?"

This wasn't the time for Kevin to explain that *Carmen* was really about an ill-fated affair between a fickle gypsy girl and a soldier who is infatuated with her. At least Armitage had seen an opera and seemed to have liked it. And he hadn't asked what opera had to do with making money for Brae Loch.

"What I'd like to do," Kevin hurried on, "is to stage an opera called *Gianni Schicchi*. It's a comedy and it's short, just one act. I'm confident I can find plenty of local talent, but we would need a place to rehearse and perform. I've been hoping that your

11

college has an auditorium that we could use. We'd be prepared to pay for the privilege, of course, and then recoup the cost by charging a modest price for tickets. I hope I'm not being presumptuous when I say this, but I think it would be a nice feather in your cap—you know, good p.r. for the college."

As soon as he'd said it, Kevin regretted that last bit. But if the provost thought his visitor had gone too far, he didn't say so. To the contrary, he seemed genuinely interested in the idea.

"An opera, right here at Brae Loch College," he said. His tone of voice made it clear that the prospect was intriguing. He rubbed his chin, his mind apparently weighing the pros and cons of Kevin's proposition.

"When would you propose to do this—this opera, whatever its name is?"

"This summer, if it wouldn't interfere with your college's own programs. I figured it might take two months, maybe ten weeks, to hold tryouts, rehearse, and put on three or four performances."

Kevin had no idea how long it would take to get a group of amateurs ready for a production like this. For all he knew, it could take all summer and the result would still be unacceptably ragged. Instead of creating an invitation to join the Brae Loch faculty for a year, what he thought of as his Puccini gig might be a disaster. He could almost hear the jeers and cat calls. He would no longer be a celebrity. He would forever be associated with 'Whitman's folly.'

"I like it, I like it." Jason Armitage got out of his chair and came around the desk, putting a large hand on Kevin's shoulder. "It could give a big boost to Brae Loch's image. No longer just that little school in upstate New York. No, siree. It's the school that brings culture to the Finger Lakes. It does opera."

Kevin was both pleased to hear such a ringing endorsement of his plan and alarmed that the provost was raising the stakes so dramatically.

"Let me ask," he asked, quite tentatively, "if you have an auditorium that would work. We'll need an orchestra pit as well as a stage—not a big one, but one we could put a big bed on, one that could hold a cast of, say, a dozen people."

Kevin was worried that the provost's enthusiasm might not be matched by the college's ability to accommodate the opera.

"We've got two spaces that might do. One's the chapel—it's bigger, has the most seats. Then there's a somewhat smaller auditorium where our dramatic club puts on plays. I'll have one of our people take you around, give you a look at them. As far as I know, and I'm supposed to be the last sign-off on things like this, the theatre will not be in use this summer. Of course, there will be services in the chapel, but I think we could find a way to manage both."

It was at that moment that the provost's brow wrinkled. He removed his hand from Kevin's shoulder.

"You'll be needing a bed, you say? Mind if I ask what for? I don't think the trustees would much care for an opera with sex. Well, I'm sure it would be simulated, but people up here are pretty straight laced. It isn't a sexy comedy, is it?"

"Goodness, no. It's about a guy who cons a bunch of greedy relatives out of their inheritance. No sex at all."

"That's a relief," the provost said, and it was apparent that he meant it. "Sorry I even raised the subject."

It was half an hour later that he walked Kevin to the door, where he turned him over to the care of a student who would show him the facilities. No contract had been signed, but an understanding had been reached as to expenses and other less urgent details.

"Read mysteries?" the provost asked as Kevin was sliding into his coat.

"A few."

"Me too, only I have to confess it's more than a few. Christie's always been my favorite."

Kevin chuckled.

"My provost at Madison seems only to read the ancient Greek tragedies. In the original Greek, if you can believe that. Christie sounds like more fun than Sophocles."

"No contest. I've enjoyed our meeting, Professor Whitman, and I'm looking forward to watching your opera. I'll stay in touch. And you'll let me know how things are shaping up, right?"

"With pleasure."

Jason Armitage waved good-bye as Kevin walked out into a raw, cold February afternoon, never suspecting that he would not be attending a performance of *Gianni Schicchi* the following August.

13

CHAPTER 3

Carol was supportive. Not wildly enthusiastic, but definitely in Kevin's corner. The provost of Brae Loch College was prepared to lend the school's theatre to Kevin for a good part of the summer, guaranteeing that the opera he was planning would have a home during its gestation. The costs, as far as he could calculate them, would be more modest than he had assumed. Now all that remained was the task of assembling a cast and an orchestra that could handle the demands that Puccini had placed upon them. Kevin winced involuntarily as he thought about it. By far the biggest challenge still lay ahead.

He had placed announcements, financed by his own limited savings, in upstate newspapers and radio stations. Those announcements varied a bit from one place to another, but the message was always the same. An opera by Giacomo Puccini was to be presented at Brae Loch College on Crooked Lake in August. Tryouts for the cast and the orchestra would be held in early June. Anyone interested should send a c.v., together with a cover letter, to Professor Kevin Whitman at e-mail or snail mail addresses which followed.

Kevin had blanketed the Finger Lakes area with these announcements, hoping that casting his net widely would generate a musically talented pool of candidates. Of course the prospect of commuting for a considerable distance to rehearse would deter many, but he was counting on the lure of a chance to step out of a humdrum life and appear in a real opera. He had no idea how many would take the bait.

He need not have worried. Within a week after the first announcement went out, he had received over a hundred messages. It was, to be sure, a mixed bag, but there were enough promising ones to buoy Kevin's spirits. At the same time, he realized for the first time the magnitude of the task which confronted him. Carol had been right.

The desk in his study soon contained three piles of messages from would-be members of his fledgling company: those that could be dismissed out of hand, those that definitely merited a tryout, and those that fell somewhere in between. Notifying those that were clearly unacceptable was not particularly time consuming, but he was saddened by the need to dash their misplaced hopes. He dreaded the thought that some of those he had summarily rejected would not quietly accept his decision. He had visions of persistent men and women flooding his in-box with arguments as to why they should be on the Brae Loch stage in August.

But he was both cheered and surprised by the number of applicants who had what sounded like excellent credentials. There were, as he had anticipated, many with extensive church choir experience. More than a few belonged to choral societies. One had once been a member of the Metropolitan Opera chorus. Of instrumentalists there were enough to form a fairly large orchestra, although the violin section would be thin. Some of these people would, of course, prove to have over-stated their skills, but as winter turned to spring and more and more messages came in, Kevin's plan looked better and better to him.

The announcements of the opera circulating around the area said that tryouts would be held in June. But Kevin was anxious to start the process, beginning with the strongest applications. This meant he would have to go up to the cottage, and his school's spring break gave him a window of opportunity to do so. It also meant that he would get to spend some time with Carol.

By the time that Kevin pulled into the driveway behind his cottage on the third of April, he had set up appointments with nine of his operatic wannabes. He had also persuaded Carol to move into the cottage with him for the week.

They had dinner that first night at an old and favorite restaurant, The Cedar Post. She looks absolutely wonderful, he thought, as he watched her studying the menu. He liked her in her uniform, but tonight she was in mufti, and that was even better.

"So, this is the week you start judging talent," she said. "You sounded optimistic. Want to tell me about it?"

"Actually," Kevin began, "I've already judged the talent sitting across the table from me. You're a perfect ten."

"I'll accept the compliment," Carol said, reaching out to take Kevin's hand. "But how about a preview of who's who on your agenda for the week."

"Sure. Nine of them: seven women and two men. That may be my biggest problem. There just aren't enough men. I'm willing to conduct an all-woman orchestra, but I need a bunch of men for the cast."

"Any for the bigger parts?"

"I've got to have a good—and I mean a real good—Schicchi. Plus another man to play his son-in-law to be. They're all important, but those two are really critical. Maybe I'll be lucky, though. The two guys I see this week have both made it fairly clear that they want to be Schicchi. One of them was with the Met chorus for more than a decade. He's my odds on favorite for the title role."

"Sight unseen? Or is it unheard? Maybe he's no longer in the chorus for a reason, like his voice has failed him, or he didn't show up for rehearsals."

"I know. But he's coming in on Wednesday. Anyway, the other guy has an Italian-American name, claims he loves Puccini, knows his big arias by heart. What I'm afraid of is that whoever I don't pick will go off in a mad, refuse to take on another role."

"Sounds like you might need to put on your diplomat's hat," Carol said. "What about the women?"

"I think there may be a good Lauretta in the group. She's the daughter, the one who has that great aria I told you about. But most of the women want to be in the orchestra—a couple of violins, a couple of winds, a cellist. All of them have played in community orchestras."

"By the way, it just occurred to me—aren't you going to need a piano?"

"I will, and the college has let me use one up there for the vocal tryouts. I probably should have one at the cottage, but Susan didn't like the idea and I never pushed her about it."

Carol didn't like to be reminded that Kevin had been married to this Susan woman, and not that many years ago. She found herself wondering where the ex-wife was now. And whether Kevin ever saw her. Carol's decision to spend the week at the cottage, starting that very night, had been a good one.

When Kevin awoke the next morning, Carol was already up and in the kitchen. His first tryout was not until eleven o'clock, but he wanted to see Carol before she left for the day. And have some of the coffee that smelled so good.

"Sorry I can't stay around longer," she announced, as they tackled her breakfast of eggs and toast. "Some of us have jobs waiting for us, you know, not out-of-work tenors."

16

"Unfortunately there aren't any tenors on my schedule," Kevin said, ignoring Carol's stab at early morning humor. "Not sure why, but they're a rare breed. I'll have to make do with baritones this week. Today, though, it's a violinist, name's Mercedes Redman. Teaches over in Ithaca. She looks good on paper. I've never met anyone named Mercedes."

As it turned out, Mercedes Redman was as good as she had looked to be on paper. Indeed, she was little short of brilliant, and Kevin wondered why she was spending her time teaching kids to play the violin when she might well be performing with some symphony orchestra. Before he bade her good-bye, Kevin had not only told her he wanted her for *Gianni Schicchi*, but he also had asked her if she would be willing to serve as his assistant, essentially his alter ego. It had taken no more than five minutes, during which he had laid out a rough timeline for production, for her to accept the assignment. There would be times over the weeks ahead when he would regret the impulse which gave Ms. Redman rather more control over things than he was comfortable with.

If Mercedes Redman was to become a problem for Kevin, there was no hint of it at their first meeting. The foreshadowing of future trouble was rather more obvious, however, in the case of the two baritones. The first to appear for a tryout was a middle-aged man who lived on the east arm of the lake, not more than seventeen miles from Kevin's cottage. He was the man with an Italian-American name, Paolo Rosetti. He arrived at the room that had been commandeered for tryouts precisely at the agreed upon hour, sweeping into the room and greeting Kevin with an elaborate bow and a European-style kiss on both cheeks.

"Ah, Professor Whitman. How do you do. I am Paolo Rosetti, your Gianni Schicchi. This is a wonderful thing you are doing, bringing Puccini to Crooked Lake. All we ever get in these parts is that Andrew Lloyd Webber, or maybe, if we are lucky, a Sondheim show. But real opera? No, never. God bless you."

Kevin stepped back, the better to get a good look at this man who was so effusively showering him with praise. The most striking thing about him was that he was wearing a huge green and gold scarf which appeared to be wrapped several times around his neck. His face was ruddy, whether naturally or from the weather outside was not clear, and was dominated by a pair of the thickest black eyebrows Kevin had ever seen.

"I'm so very pleased to meet you," Kevin said. "And glad you're interested in our plan to do this opera."

Mr. Rosetti rubbed his hands together, as if to warm them, and then proceeded to unwrap the scarf from around his neck. It looked to be more than six feet long.

"Yes, the *Gianni Schicchi*. A wonderful choice. It should be performed more often. What a wonderful rascal, that Schicchi. One of my favorite characters. My voice is just right for him, too. You will see."

Kevin was beginning to feel uneasy. Rosetti was not only trying out; he seemed to be assuming that the role of the eponymous hero was to be his. Well, Kevin thought, we shall have to see about that.

The voluble Rosetti told Kevin he would need to warm his voice up a bit. The cold weather outside, you know. So while Kevin watched and listened, he did a few scales. It was immediately apparent that the man had a big voice. It may not have been a particularly beautiful voice, but it was obvious that he knew how to sing. His resumé had said nothing about voice training, so Kevin asked who his teacher had been.

"Me? Need a teacher? No, no." He threw his arms out wide as if to say 'just me.' "I do it myself, since I was a boy. Always singing."

Eventually Rosetti said he was ready to show off his voice. Kevin hoped the man's choice of an aria would be one he knew, although he was sure Rosetti would say he could do it unaccompanied. Not surprisingly, the choice was from another Puccini opera, *La Boheme*, and for a few anxious moments Kevin feared that someone would interrupt, asking that the volume be turned down. When Rosetti finished, he bowed in Kevin's direction and flashed a broad smile.

"Pretty good, no?"

Kevin wasn't quite sure how to respond. It had not been bad. But it had been invariably loud and occasionally flat. He had no doubt that Rosetti could sing the role of Schicchi, but he feared that it would be a one-dimensional performance. And very probably drown out everyone else onstage.

"You have a very big voice, Mr. Rosetti," he said, hoping it didn't sound like damning with faint praise. He needn't have worried.

"Big, yes," he said, smiling. "This music needs to be heard, even in the very last row. So I do Schicchi, right?"

Yes, Kevin thought, we'll find a place for you in our cast. But Gianni Schicchi? Perhaps. He'd first have to hear the other baritone with an impressive c.v., the one who had sung in the Met chorus. So he assured Mr. Rosetti that he would be in the production without ever quite saying that he would be playing the title role.

They parted company after exchanging a few more words about opera, Rosetti making use of his favorite word, wonderful, several more times. The room seemed unusually empty after his departure.

It was the following afternoon that Rosetti's competition arrived for his tryout. Harley Gerlach had what was easily the most impressive resumé of the many that Kevin had received. He had apparently been a member of the Metropolitan Opera chorus for nearly eleven years, and had on two or three occasions been tapped for small comprimario roles. There was none of Rosetti's bravado about him, yet he gave off an unmistakable air of self-confidence.

"Mr. Whitman, I presume," he said as he entered the room. No doubt he knew very well that this was the way Stanley was alleged to have greeted Livingston. He removed a wool cap, revealing a large mane of white hair, and casually tossed cap and coat onto the piano bench.

"So, it is to be *Gianni Schicchi*," he said. "Good opera. Not Puccini's best, but good. I did the notary role in it once on short notice. This time it will be Schicchi himself, that conniving bastard."

Gerlach laughed. Kevin didn't. It looked as if he had two Schicchis on his hands.

"Delighted you are interested in becoming part of our little company," he said. "You've had a lot of experience in opera, I see. All those years with the Met. Why did you decide to quit?"

"Nothing in particular. I suppose it became boring, same old routine, year after year. All those rehearsals. Besides, the audience doesn't appreciate the chorus. All they ever cared about was the big names—you know, was Pavarotti singing that night? No? Think I'll stay home then."

"That's too bad. But I'm glad you're willing to give it another shot."

19

"Of course. I'm retired, time on my hands. Anyway, it's different, singing the lead. Never did it back in the day when I was at the Met. Now it's my turn."

Kevin tried to pretend he had not heard this. But he could feel a headache coming on.

"Well, this isn't the Met, I'm afraid. I'm doing it because I love opera, want to give the local community a chance to hear one. Cheap tickets, minimal sets, small orchestra—it's really opera on a shoestring."

Gerlach shrugged.

"I know. Figured I might be the only professional in your cast." He paused, as if to give Kevin a chance to feel grateful that he had at least one professional among a bunch of amateurs.

"Let me show you," he said as he moved his coat and cap off the piano bench and took a seat there. "I assume you have a score handy. I'll do one of Schicchi's numbers."

Kevin had, of course, acquired copies of the score. He retrieved one and watched as Gerlach leafed through it and found the part he wanted to sing. He clearly intended to be his own accompanist.

What followed solved Kevin's casting problem. Schicchi's music was not beautiful, nor was it supposed to be. But Gerlach sang it with feeling, his voice under control from the opening bar. Kevin could almost see the man onstage, setting those greedy relatives up for their disinheritance. Paolo Rosetti would have to take on another role. Gerlach was going to be Kevin's Gianni Schicchi.

They spent half an hour chatting about opera, Gerlach holding forth on his favorite moments onstage and backstage at the Met, Kevin asking the questions which would give the ex-chorister a chance to show off his knowledge. When he finally left, Gerlach had been told that he would indeed be the title character in Crooked Lake's production of *Gianni Schicchi*. He had also left Kevin with two worries. One was how he would break the news to Rosetti. The other was how to cope with Gerlach's sense that he was a giant among pygmies. Both problems would require a great deal of tact and diplomacy. Kevin hoped he would be up to the task.

CHAPTER 4

"C'mon, time to get up!"

The peremptory voice came from somewhere off to Kevin's right. He rolled over and half opened his eyes. It was Carol, bending over the bed, a smile on her face.

"You said something about meeting somebody up at the college," she said. "You won't make it if you don't get started."

"What time is it?" he asked in a sleepy voice.

"Almost eight."

Kevin groaned and sank back under the covers.

"It'll be your funeral, not mine," Carol said over her shoulder, as she went back to the kitchen.

Reluctantly he got up, groping under the bed for his slippers. It was the morning of his second day back at the lake cottage for the summer. May 24th, if he had his dates straight. Why on earth had he agreed to meet this man from Rochester at nine a.m.? Ten or even eleven would have done just as well. But it was too late for that now. If he wanted to meet the man who might be the opera's love interest, he'd have to get moving.

Kevin had spent much of the previous evening discussing with Carol the progress he had been making in assembling a cast and orchestra for the Brae Loch production of Puccini's opera. He was pleased to report that he had a small but quite decent group of musicians lined up to play the opera's challenging score. Nineteen in all. One more violinist would be nice, but it could have been much worse. And every role had been cast except for Rinuccio, the young man who wants to marry Schicchi's daughter, and one of those hard to find tenors.

It had been his original intention to hold tryouts in June, but it had soon become apparent that he would have to move faster. So he had squeezed in dozens of sessions with area hopefuls on weekends when he could get away from the city. The result was that everything was now in order except for that one elusive tenor. And the man from Rochester looked promising. He had only heard about the opera a few days earlier, but he had hastened to contact Kevin and present his resumé orally over the phone. Today they would meet.

"Are you sure you're awake enough so I can leave and not worry that you'll miss your appointment?" Carol asked as she set a cup of coffee and a bagel in front of him.

"I'm awake," he answered. "Tired but awake."

"Good. I'm not sure I like this role of 'she who must be obeyed.' But I don't want it said that the Crooked Lake opera didn't get off the ground because the sheriff didn't get the maestro out of bed."

Kevin leaned across the breakfast table and gave her a kiss. He was looking forward to playing house with Carol. This summer for sure. All of next year if his plan came to fruition.

The sheriff left shortly for her office in Cumberland. Kevin pulled out of the drive at 8:45, which meant he would have to drive faster than the posted speed limit if he was to make his appointment on time. He hoped that one of Carol's officers would not be cruising the nearby roads, ready to pull him over and enjoy the irony of ticketing the boss's lover.

He made it to campus late by about eight minutes. Sean Carpenter was waiting for him on the steps of Wayne Hall, where they had agreed to meet.

"Sorry to keep you waiting," Kevin said as they shook hands.

"No problem. I'm just enjoying the morning, watching the kids. Must be final exam week—they mostly look tired and worried."

"I wouldn't know. Semester's over at my school, thank goodness. Let's go on in and have a talk about Puccini."

They did talk, and Carpenter did sing, a very impressive rendition of Rodolfo's signature aria from *La Boheme*.

"The role's yours if you can manage the commute from Rochester," Kevin said when the tenor had finished.

"No problem. Like I said, I've always wanted to do something like this. I used to joke that in another incarnation I'd be a world-famous tenor. And what did I become in this life? An accountant. That's right, an accountant, for God's sake. No, I'd come down from Rochester every night if I had to. It's not a bad drive. I just hope I'll have an attractive Lauretta. Do you know who's singing her part?"

"I do. She's a college student, getting her degree in music. Her name is Heather. Heather Merriman. Bright young woman. And, yes, she's attractive. She lives on the lake, usually spends her summers waiting tables at an area restaurant. Tells me she's been liberated, that her days as a waitress are over. I think you'll like her."

"Do me a favor, will you? Don't tell her I'm old enough to be her father. She'll find out soon enough."

This last remark stuck in Kevin's mind long after Sean Carpenter had left to go back to Rochester. The possibility that members of his little company might strike up relationships hadn't occurred to him. A summer romance? He considered his impressions of the people with whom he would be working. It was a decidedly varied group in every sense of the word. Some were young, and some were well on their way to senior citizen status. Some were extroverted, while several were almost painfully quiet. There were gifted musicians, and then there were those of lesser talent whose accomplishments were the result of dogged determination. Four of the troupe lived on the lake, and one hailed from Southport. But others would travel farther to make rehearsals, in some cases much farther.

As Kevin headed back to his car, he spotted Jason Armitage, coming toward him.

"Well, well, it's our impresario," the provost called out. Kevin hadn't liked the word when Carol had used it. He liked it even less coming from the man who was making all of this possible.

"Hello, Mr. Armitage."

"How's everything going? Gathering speed, I should think. Are my people being helpful?"

The provost was simply being friendly, but Kevin decided it was time to confront the man with the facts of life in putting on an opera.

"I don't have it with me, sir, but I need to speak with you about our schedule. We're just about ready to begin, and that will mean orchestra rehearsals—quite a few of them. And I'm going to have to spend a lot of time with the cast, especially when we have ensemble scenes. There are a lot of those, and they can be tricky. Would it be possible for me to come by, say this afternoon, with a list of the times when we're going to need the use of the auditorium and the stage?"

23

"Of course, you know I'm at your disposal. Why don't you speak to my secretary. She'll know what I've got on this afternoon. If we can't do it today, we'll do it soon. Okay? And do keep me posted on how it's shaping up. Can't wait to see it."

The provost went on his way, leaving Kevin to ponder the large gulf that lay between his needs and the appreciation of those needs by Brae Loch's leader.

By the time he reached his cottage, Kevin was feeling good about the way in which things were shaping up. His little company was considerably more talented than he had expected. There was every reason to think that come August they would be able to mount a respectable production of Puccini's comedy. Kevin was whistling Lauretta's aria as he climbed out of the car.

He stopped in mid phrase when he heard the phone ringing. Carol? He was anticipating the pleasure of sharing the good news with her about the morning's tryout when another woman's voice greeted him.

"Mr. Whitman?"

"Yes, that's me. What can I do for you?"

"What you can do for me is get rid of that Harley Gerlach."

For a moment Kevin was almost literally speechless. He started to ask the caller to repeat what she had said, but there was really no need to do that. Her message had come through, loud and clear.

"I'm sorry, but who is this?"

"Janet Myers. I'm one of the people in your opera. I sing the old woman, remember?"

He remembered. A woman of middle age who appeared to have had a recent face-lift. Good voice, strong personality. And that strong personality was on display as she explained the reason for her call.

"I had no idea you were giving Harley a part in the opera. I just heard it last evening from a friend. I tried you earlier, but you must have been out. Anyway, he's got to go. I won't be on the same stage with the man. It's him or me."

The Myers woman sounded as if she meant it. An ultimatum from a prima donna.

"I'm not sure I understand," Kevin began. And he didn't understand. Why on earth would this woman be demanding that he

24

sack his Gianni Schicchi? Before the troupe had even assembled, been introduced to each other, had a rehearsal.

"You don't need to know. It's just that I won't go anywhere near that man. He's a monster. If you don't get rid of him, you'll see. He'll ruin your opera. He ruins everything he touches."

"Ms. Myers, I'm sorry that there's some kind of a problem between you and Mr. Gerlach. But try to understand. It's taken me weeks to select a cast, and it seems to me that all of you are just right for your parts. You'll make a wonderful Zita. And Mr. Gerlach is a good choice for Schicchi. He's had a lot of experience, sang in the Met chorus, already seems to know his part. I don't see how I can suddenly yank him out of the key role in the opera. What could I possibly tell him?"

"No, you don't understand. How could you? But it's different with me. I was married to that man. For six long and terrible years. Impossible years. You want to know about bitter divorces? Ours belongs in *The Guinness Book of Records*. The man is a monster."

The situation was now much clearer. Myers had twice referred to Gerlach as a monster. But it sounded like many another divorce to Kevin: two incompatible people who would forever pick scabs on old wounds. Must he question all members of his company about their private lives to avoid unpleasantness on the set? Damn. His bad luck that two members out of a small company of thirty would know each other—and hate each other.

For the next fifteen minutes, Kevin reasoned with Myers, then pleaded with her. In the end, she reluctantly agreed to stay in the company, even if he had to stick with Gerlach. But when he hung up the phone, he was far from certain that she would stay the course. He doubted that he had heard the last of the Gerlach-Myers troubles.

Oh, well, he said to himself as he turned his attention to lunch, if that's the only problem we have, we'll make it. Unfortunately, Janet Myers' dislike of Harley Gerlach was not to be the only problem to plague the production of Puccini's *Gianni Schicchi.*

CHAPTER 5

It was the 30th of May when Kevin first met with the entire cast and orchestra of the Brae Loch production of *Gianni Schicchi.* Actually, it was not the entire cast. Two members of the orchestra, a clarinetist and a trumpet player, were absent, the former after a long and somewhat rambling apology to Kevin, the latter without explanation. But every cast member, from Harley Gerlach's Gianni Schicchi to a meek little man who had the opera's smallest part, was present. After a brief welcome and a few words about his expectations, Kevin handed out a rehearsal schedule and then turned to the task of introducing everybody.

It went quite well for awhile, with each member of the company telling the others his or her name, something of his background, and why he wanted to participate in the opera. Kevin tried not to pay attention to Paolo Rosetti, who stood in the back of the room, glowering throughout the introductions. He hoped Paolo would not spoil the day by saying something unpleasant about the man whom Kevin had selected to sing the title role. But it wasn't Rosetti who first offered an unpleasant word. It was Arthur Conklin, a cellist, who had been one of the first people Kevin had recruited. That had been back in April, and his recollection of the man was limited to the impression that he made beautiful music with his cello.

"It looks like what we're doing is introducing ourselves, so you can call me Arthur. I'm Arthur Conklin, and I run a chain of nurseries in the area. But that's irrelevant. I'm here because I play cello in my spare time, part of a string quartet. Our violist is here, too—Sandy Temple over there."

Conklin pointed to Temple, who waved at the assembled company.

"I'm grateful to Mr. Whitman for organizing our little treat for the Finger Lakes community. It should be a lot of fun— hard work, but fun. I don't know most of you, but I can tell you that we may have a problem. Forgive the expression, but there's a nigger in the woodpile, right here in this room."

There was a collective gasp from most members of the troupe, followed by a deathly silence. Kevin was in shock. He had to say something, but wasn't quite sure what. Conklin beat him to it.

"I suppose I owe you all an apology. I should never have said that. I'm not that kind of person, as you'll see."

Kevin half expected him to say something about some of his best friends being black, but he didn't. It had probably just been an off-the-cuff remark, the casual use of an old expression that was both dated and offensive. But it also had been meant to convey the message that Conklin detested some member of the company, and that was almost as troubling as the racial slur. Was this little company going to be riven by interpersonal quarrels? First Janet Myers, now Arthur Conklin. Myers had apparently had a very bad relationship with Harley Gerlach. Now Conklin. Who was it that he disliked? Even hated? Who would have guessed that a company of only thirty members, recruited from a four-county area, would turn out to include people who harbored deep-seated grudges against each other.

"I think we all accept your apology, Mr. Conklin," Kevin said, not being sure that everyone present would agree. "Perhaps we can go on now."

He turned first to Mercedes Redman, who was sitting next to Conklin. Happily, neither Redman nor anyone else added to the unpleasantness. Even Mr. Rosetti chose not to use the meeting to pursue his complaint against Kevin's choice of Gerlach to play Gianni Schicchi. But he touched on his grievance indirectly by emphasizing that this was not just any opera, but an Italian opera, and that Italian artists like himself would have a feel for it in their bones. The implication was that those without an Italian background would have no such feeling.

There followed a discussion that touched on everything from scheduling conflicts to Kevin's decision to do the opera in English. Rosetti, not surprisingly, was the most vocal of the advocates for presenting it in the original Italian. But Kevin was adamant that it should be sung in English. Moreover, he had already acquired copies of the score using the English translation. It was the fact that they were hungry rather than that they had settled all issues to everyone's satisfaction that brought the discussion to a close at 1:45.

Kevin watched as they collected their music and their schedules and drifted out of Wayne Hall singly and in small groups. He would need to get a better feel for the animosities that obviously existed in his company, and then work to make sure that they did not affect the production. But except for the fact that Rosetti and Myers were studiously avoiding Gerlach as they left, he learned nothing more that day about bad blood between members of his cast and orchestra. He did notice his Rinuccio, Sean Carpenter, hurrying to catch up with Heather Merriman, and doubted that it had anything to do with practicing their duet. Only Mercedes Redman remained.

"How do you think it went?" he asked her.

"All in all, not bad, except for that awful cellist. But they think it's going to be easy. And it isn't. We've got to arrange more rehearsals. I have no idea how good my orchestra is. You say they're pretty good. I hope so, but they've never played together. It's one thing to read music and produce nice sounds in your living room, but putting all the parts together is another story."

Kevin looked at the woman he had decided would be his assistant. She had just told him that she needed more rehearsals for her orchestra. *Her* orchestra?

"Let me tell you what I think we should do," Redman continued. "Why don't you concentrate on the singers and let me handle the orchestra? You know, at first, before we try to put it all together. There's a lot to do between now and August, and we'll make better progress if we divide up the labor. If you give me a roster of the players with their cells and home phone numbers, I'll get started."

What have I gotten myself in for, Kevin was thinking, as he listened to his assistant maneuvering to make him her assistant. He remembered that she had had a masterful tryout, and her resumé was excellent. But should he entrust her with whipping this amateur orchestra into shape?

"Well, I suppose—" Kevin started, only to be interrupted by Redman.

"Good. I'll be adding some rehearsal time. Don't worry, I'll tell the provost, whatever his name is, to pencil in some additional hours for the auditorium."

———

Dinner over, Kevin and Carol moved to the living room with their coffee. And their tales of the day's highlights and lowlights.

"You don't want to hear any more about my day," Carol announced. "Not one to make you feel good about your fellow man. But that's old news. I want to hear about the opera. You up and running at last?"

Kevin considered the question.

"Not sure whether we're running yet. But I guess we're underway. Funny thing, though. I figured the toughest part of this would be recruiting a bunch of reasonably talented people who would love the idea of doing an opera without pay. Doing it because they love to make music. Turns out that was no problem at all. But I've learned that you can love music and dislike the musician."

Kevin mentioned a few of what looked to be prickly personal relationships within the company, and then brought up the case of Mercedes Redman.

"Sounds to me like she staged a coup d'état," Carol said. "What's she like, aside from being hard to say 'no' to?"

"She's really a good violinist," he said.

"That's not what I mean. Young, old, attractive, plain? How about a three dimensional portrait?"

It dawned on Kevin that Carol might be sizing up what she imagined to be the competition.

"Oh, that. Well, she didn't list it on her resumé, but I'd guess that she's somewhere around 50. Maybe a few years older than that. Good looking in a way, but nothing flashy. Husky voice, sort of like Lauren Bacall used to have. Now that I think of it, she reminds me a bit of Bacall."

Could Carol really be worried about Mercedes Redman? He hadn't seen her as other than a good musician who was more than a bit pushy.

"Is she married?"

"Good grief, Carol, why all of the questions? I don't know whether she's married. Or has kids. For all I know she's a lesbian. What matters is that she's a music teacher who thinks she can help make *Gianni Schicchi* work. My guess is that she can. She's eager to try, and I think I'll let her."

"I'd be careful, if I were you," Carol said. "This is one of those cases where I'm not sure two heads are better than one."

"Well, if there's to be a second head, I'd rather it be yours. But I can't think of anything you can do that needs doing. Of course, if you could play the violin I'd put you in the orchestra in a second."

"But I can play the violin," Carol said. "You haven't been paying attention."

"You can? That's terrific. Why didn't you tell me?"

"But I did. Last summer when you'd sort of taken over the search for Sandra Rackley's killer. Remember? I reminded you that I was the sheriff, and that I wasn't sure I was happy playing second fiddle in my own investigation."

Kevin almost spilled his coffee.

"That's awful, Carol, really, really bad. You had me thinking you really are a violinist."

"You need to work on your sense of humor," she said, feeling just a bit smug and very happy to be sharing Kevin's couch with him. And his bed.

CHAPTER 6

Three weeks into June, and rehearsals for *Gianni Schicchi* were well underway. Unfortunately, Kevin had been seeing less of Carol than he had expected to or wanted to. Part of the problem was that there had been some kind of powwow of state sheriffs that took Carol away for the better part of one week. The principal thief of his time, however, was the rehearsal schedule, now heavier, thanks to Mercedes Redman. It kept him busy four nights out of the week, plus parts of either Saturday or Sunday. Night rehearsals were necessary because most members of the company had job responsibilities. It had quickly become apparent to Kevin that on those nights he could not count on being home before ten or even eleven and, to Carol, that there wasn't much point in staying over at the cottage when Kevin would be so late.

The result was that it was on a Friday evening in late June that the impresario and the sheriff had their first real opportunity since rehearsals had begun to sit down and talk about things.

"Are you as tired as you look?" Carol asked. She sounded genuinely worried.

Kevin smiled, but did not choose to pretend that he wasn't tired.

"Didn't know it was that obvious," he said. "I had no idea it was going to be this demanding. You know, the opera."

"If I were one of those people who like to say I told you so, I'd say I told you so. But somehow I don't think you're going to chuck the whole thing. You aren't, are you?"

"No way. If anything, I'm more psyched now than I was back when I first thought about it. But I'm going to have to lean on some of the others a bit more. Like Mercedes. She can handle the orchestra. Maybe my Schicchi, that guy who sang at the Met— maybe he can do some tutoring of the cast. That way I wouldn't have to be up at Brae Loch every night."

"I wouldn't complain," Carol said, moving closer to him on the couch.

"Me either. You know, it's kinda funny. Doing the opera was supposed to get me a visiting appointment at Brae Loch so I could see more of you. And look what's happened—I've seen you all of three times in the last ten days."

Carol leaned over and kissed him.

"That's partly my fault," she said. "Anyway, it sounds as if you've got a plan to lighten the load. Are the Mercedes woman and that other guy up to it?"

"Oh, she's up to it all right. She's a helluva lot better than I am, to be honest about it. I think she'll be relieved if I stop pretending that I'm needed at orchestra rehearsals. I'm not so sure about Gerlach—that's his name, Harley Gerlach. He's certainly capable of helping some of the others. But I worry about the idea of turning the vocal rehearsals over to him."

"Why's that?"

"You'd have to meet him, watch him. And I mean watch him interacting with other people. Or just watch the faces of other people when he's around. He's got an ego problem. Thinks he's God's gift to the music world. And he makes sure everyone knows it."

"Are you regretting you gave him the juiciest role in the opera?"

"No, it's not that. He's good, really good. In fact, I can't understand why he's no longer with the Met chorus. My guess is that something happened, something he has no intention of telling me about. What he did tell me was that what had been fun was now simply boring. Could be, but I have my doubts. Anyway, it doesn't matter, just so long as he stays on the wagon and doesn't alienate the rest of the cast."

"Stay on the wagon? You mean he's got a drinking prob-lem?"

Kevin sighed.

"You up to hearing about my troubles with Harley Ger-lach?" he asked. "If you are, why don't I freshen your drink. It'll help."

He disappeared into the kitchen, remembering all too well several moments of unpleasantness that had marred rehearsals.

———

The first of those moments had occurred the very first night that Kevin had worked with the cast. They were supposed to have gotten underway at seven, but Gerlach didn't arrive until nearly a half an hour later. Kevin was discussing with the greedy relatives in the cast how he wanted them to approach the search for the will when Gerlach came down the aisle from the back of the auditorium.

"I don't hear any singing," he said in a loud voice.

"We were waiting for you. And you're late." It was Paolo Rosetti who had said what was on all of their minds.

"Late?" Gerlach then repeated himself. "Late? I don't make my first entrance until you've all been onstage for a good fifteen minutes or more. You should know that."

As he heaved himself up onto the stage he stumbled, and one of the cast members stepped forward to give him a hand.

"Leave me alone. I'm all right." It wasn't that he had rejected the offer of assistance which shocked the others, it was the decidedly unpleasant tone in which he had done it.

He brushed off what was presumably stage-floor dust and turned to Kevin.

"I'm here, so we can begin. You going to block out our positions? We can't be just anywhere on the stage, you know."

The words were slurred, and it was immediately apparent that Harley Gerlach had been drinking. Drinking heavily.

"We'll get to that in due course," Kevin said, pretending not to notice that the man who was to sing the title role was very probably drunk.

Rosetti wasn't so diplomatic.

"What's going on here? We drink after the show. Not before. You need to show Professor Whitman some respect. Professor Whitman and Puccini."

"Just who do you think you are to judge me?" Gerlach leaned forward to get a better look at the man who had criticized him.

"I'm Paolo Rosetti, that's who I am."

Kevin waved his score and moved to cut off this unpleasantness between cast members. It wasn't easy. Rosetti was still nursing a grudge that he hadn't been given the lead; Gerlach was simply being an in-your-face drunk.

The entire cast had become aware of the tension between the two men well before that evening's little confrontation. Rosetti had made clear in conversations with his fellow cast members his belief that he should be the opera's Gianni Schicchi. And Gerlach had made it clear that he thought Rosetti was a fool and that he did not suffer fools gladly.

Gerlach's drinking problem had only made already difficult matters worse, Kevin told Carol, recalling one particular
episode.

It had occurred the previous Tuesday, when Kevin had
been working with the opera's young lovers. Heather Merriman,
who had the opera's best-known number, sang it in her naturally
beautiful voice. But she was somewhat tentative, not surprising in
view of the fact that she was by far the youngest and least
experienced member of the cast.

Kevin had complimented her and then started to make a
suggestion when Gerlach, who had been watching and listening
from the front row of the auditorium, interrupted.

"My dear Lauretta," he said, referring to Merriman by her
character's name, "what you're singing isn't just a pretty tune. It's
an appeal to me, your father, Schicchi. But if you think your aria
impressed me, it didn't. What it made me want to do is walk off
the stage and get myself another scotch."

"I think you've already had enough scotch, Gerlach, so
why don't you shut up and leave her alone."

It was Sean Carpenter, the opera's Rinuccio, who had
come to the young woman's defense.

"Well, well, if it isn't Sir Lancelot to the rescue," Gerlach
said, his voice dripping with sarcasm.

"You're damned right. If anyone is going to offer advice
to Heather, it's the professor."

Gerlach got up from his seat in the auditorium and came
up onto the stage, elbowing a couple of other cast members aside.
Kevin tried to intercept him, to no avail.

"You don't know beans about this opera," he said in a
boozy voice, his face only inches away from Carpenter's. "You've
just got a thing for the kid. How gallant."

Every member of the company knew by this time that
Carpenter was more than professionally interested in the woman,
aware that he might like to turn his onstage relationship with her
into an offstage affair. One or two had been overheard expressing
their disapproval of what looked like Carpenter's interest in a
woman no more than half his age.

It was equally obvious that Merriman did not reciprocate
his interest in her. Realizing this, several members of the cast had

taken it upon themselves to be protective of her. But Gerlach's stinging critique of her singing had hurt, and Carpenter's support only embarrassed her. Heather began to cry.

"Don't. Please don't," she said, her words presumably intended for Carpenter, as she turned to Kevin for help.

Eventually things settled down, but the episode had left a bad taste in everyone's mouth. Gerlach made no effort to hide the nips he took from a flask in his jacket pocket, and Kevin ultimately decided to bring the rehearsal to an early end.

———

The third problem which Kevin reported on to Carol did not lead to harsh words between cast members. But it did not bode well for the production of *Gianni Schicchi*. It occurred one night when Kevin, who had been at the piano, turned the accompaniment over to Redman and briefly went to the back of the auditorium to get a better sense of how voices were carrying.

Harley Gerlach was dictating the opera's false will to the notary onstage, and his former wife was out in the auditorium, talking to the cellist who had made the offensive racial remark at the first meeting of the company.

Kevin started to ask them to tone it down when he realized that they were discussing Gerlach. And it was obvious that they shared the view that the company's Gianni Schicchi was, to put it charitably, a thoroughly despicable man.

"I somehow assumed that Harley was your 'nigger in the woodpile,'" Janet Myers said. "But how did you know I used to be married to him?"

"I can't remember when or where I heard, but sooner or later victims of the same person become aware of each other. And what he'd done to our lives. We should create a support group, don't you think?"

The orchestra wasn't rehearsing that evening, but Conklin had come to Brae Loch anyway. What he was saying to Myers made it clear that his reason for being there was that he wanted to study Gerlach, this man who had destroyed his marriage.

"I almost quit when I learned that Harley was in the cast," Myers said.

"Can't say I blame you," Conklin said, "but it was different for me. I knew Gerlach lived in the area, and like you, I didn't want anything to do with him. Then when I heard about the Brae

Loch opera, I figured he'd be in it. And all of a sudden I had to be here, too. Not quite sure why. The fascination of evil, I guess."

"Does he know you? I mean did you ever meet?"

"No, never. But I knew the name. It's not all that common. Helen eventually told me herself that the other man was Gerlach. She told me before she died—I think she felt she had to make one of those deathbed confessions. Told me all about him, about his singing at the Met—she'd actually seen him there, probably had heard some inflated story about how big he was in the opera world."

"But does he know who you are—that you're here, playing all the while he sings his miserable little heart out?"

"Not sure. But, yes, probably. After all, my wife's name was Conklin, and we're a small company. Anyway, he's seen us talking, and I doubt that he thinks we're discussing Puccini."

"So what are you going to do?" Myers asked.

"Do?" Arthur Conklin looked as if he didn't know what she meant.

"Yes. You know, pretend you don't know him. Or maybe confront him."

"No idea. Right now I'm just trying to figure out what makes him tick. Just watching him playing the 'big I am.' For all I know, he'll never say anything, just act as if we're fellow musicians who have a chance to be part of an amateur opera production."

"I wouldn't count on it," Janet Myers said as she stood up and headed back to the stage for an ensemble scene which followed.

———

"Has all of this taken away your appetite?" Kevin asked.

"Not in the least," Carol answered. "Just because your man Gerlach is doing his best to put everyone on edge doesn't mean I'm not ready for one of your dinner surprises. What's it going to be, by the way?"

"Not much of a surprise. Would you believe hamburgers? Assuming, that is, my fire isn't just ashes by now."

He got up and headed for the deck and his old grill, Carol right behind him.

It was a beautiful evening, the hill across the lake bathed in a golden glow from the setting sun. Carol wrapped her arms around him from behind, and they watched the light slowly fade for several minutes before Kevin announced that he'd better be starting the burgers.

"There are too many Gerlachs in this world," she said. "I used to see them in my law practice, and I've run into a few here on Crooked Lake. Remember Britingham?"

"How could I forget him," Kevin said. After all, his relationship with the sheriff had begun the morning he found him dead on his dock.

"Annoying as he is, though, Gerlach can't be as bad as Britingham. Anyway, he's got a great voice. You said it yourself. By the time the curtain falls on the last performance of your opera, I bet you'll be singing his praises. He may turn into your ticket to a sabbatical at Brae Loch. Then you'd forgive him for everything, wouldn't you?"

"That I would," Kevin said. As he put the burgers on the grill, he had no idea that he would never have a chance to forgive Harley Gerlach, much less sing his praises.

CHAPTER 7

"I've got a bed outside in the truck," Andy Rogers said. "They told me to bring it over to the college. Where's it supposed to go?"

The woman at the front desk in Menlo Hall was obviously surprised by the question.

"A bed? I don't know anything about a bed. Are you sure it's to be delivered at Brae Loch?"

"That's what Joe told me when we loaded it onto the truck. Here, let me show you the invoice."

Phyllis Melton reached across her desk and took the paper from Rogers. She studied it silently for a minute, her expression gradually turning into a scowl.

"The name here is Whitman, and that means it's for that opera they're doing." Her tone of voice suggested that she wasn't particularly happy with Whitman and his opera.

"I'll be glad when they're gone, all of them," she said, making it clear that she was indeed unhappy with Brae Loch's involvement in the production of an opera. "Always coming in here with questions—where's so and so, who's got a key to some room, have we got a saw—need it for work on the set. And on and on it goes. Anyway, the bed must be going over to the auditorium. We've got a student assistant who can show you where to put it."

Ms. Melton turned from her desk and called out in the general direction of the mail room off to her right.

"Chris, are you there?"

No one answered her, so she raised her voice and tried again.

"Christopher Ellis, we need you out front. Man here needs to take a bed down to the auditorium."

It took a minute, but a lanky young man with a mop of curly blond hair soon made an appearance.

"See if you can help this young man deliver a bed. It's going to the auditorium. He may need another strong back."

"Probably won't be necessary," Rogers said. "Joe's waiting for me out in the truck."

The two men disappeared out the front door, Ms. Melton watching them go.

It didn't take long for the bed to be set up on the stage where it was to serve as the principal piece of furniture on the spare set for Puccini's opera. Chris looked at his watch and decided to take a walk down to the waterfront. He had finished the task of sticking the day's mail in the pigeon holes reserved for Brae Loch's faculty, and Ms. Melton would have no idea how long it had taken to unload the bed.

Chris cut around the chapel and took the path that led to the boathouse where the school's sailing club stored its boats. The beach stretched out for perhaps sixty yards to the north of the boathouse and gave way there to a pair of docks and a swimming area, cordoned off by ropes held up by bright red buoys. The area was deserted except for a woman in a two-piece bathing suit who was lying on the bank above the beach.

She appeared to be asleep. The blue and gold suit concealed little of what Chris thought was a nice body. He wondered if he had seen her around campus, perhaps in one of his classes. If only she would turn over.

As if she had heard his thought, she opened her eyes and pushed herself up onto an elbow.

"Hi. Mind telling me what time it is?"

Slightly embarrassed to have been caught staring at her, Chris produced a sheepish smile and informed her that it was now close to noon. The last classes of the morning would be getting out in a few minutes.

It was a small college, and registration for summer classes was modest even by Brae Loch standards. She looked like a student, but Chris was sure he had never seen her before. How could he not have noticed her?

"Do you have to change for class?" he asked.

"No, no. Nothing like that." She favored him with a pleasant smile and rolled over on her back.

"Mind if I sit for a minute?" he asked, surprising himself by doing so.

"No, not at all. I've got another five minutes, maybe ten. What's you name?"

"Chris. Chris Ellis. I'm working for the provost. And taking classes, of course. Business. What's your field?"

She laughed.

"I'm not a student here. Actually I go to school over in Buffalo."

Chris was puzzled and said so.

"You probably know that they're putting on an opera," she said. "Well, I'm in it."

"You sing?" Chris made it sound as if he didn't know that young college-age girls could sing.

"Yes, I do. At least I'm learning to. It's a great part. And by the way, my name is Heather."

Chris had barely been aware that an opera was to be performed at Brae Loch in a couple of weeks. And here he was having a conversation with a member of that opera's cast, a beautiful girl who didn't look at all like someone who would be into that kind of high-brow stuff.

"I just helped deliver a big bed to the auditorium," he said. "They told me it had something to do with your opera. Want to tell me about it?"

Heather laughed good-naturedly.

"Sure. You see, this old man has just died and his greedy relatives all want to find his will, find out what he left them. Unfortunately, he left everything to the church. But there's this guy—he's my father in the story—he gets an idea. Why not climb into the bed, pretend he's the old man, still alive, and dictate a new will. Everybody's excited, thinking they're going to make out like bandits. Daddy's got other ideas, though. He leaves everything to himself, which makes it possible for him to help me marry my sweetheart. So you see, without that bed, none of it would have worked."

"Sounds sort of improbable to me," Chris said when she finished her capsule summary of the plot of *Gianni Schicchi*.

"It is. You have to suspend disbelief."

"What's that mean?"

"I guess it's what makes opera opera. It isn't realistic. But this one isn't as outrageous as most."

"Well, I guess I'm glad I got to help with the bed."

Heather broke into laughter again.

"And we're all going to be grateful," she said. "That cot we've been using is a disaster—much too small. No way anybody could hide in it."

It was at that moment that a man came hurrying down the bank from the direction of the campus. Neither Chris nor Heather had seen him.

"Lauretta! Where have you been?"

The man who approached looked agitated.

"Hi, Sean. I thought we said 12:30."

Chris Ellis tried to follow this exchange, a puzzled expression on his face.

"We did, but no one had seen you, so I started to worry. What are you doing here?"

By here, it was obvious that he meant on the beach. In a bathing suit. And talking to a stranger.

"It's called rest and relaxation. This, by the way, is Chris Ellis. He's the one who got us the new bed. Have you seen it? Chris, this is Sean Carpenter, the man I'm supposed to marry in the opera."

Chris was still puzzled.

"I'm sorry, but you called her Lauretta, didn't you?" he said to Carpenter.

It was Heather who answered his question.

"Oh, that," she said. "Sean thinks we should stay in character. Thinks it helps us get inside our parts. He's Rinuccio. I'm Lauretta."

Carpenter shook his head.

"You ought to try harder," he told her. "It really works. Anyway, we ought to get moving. Why don't you run along and change. I'll wait here for you."

It was clear that Heather's onstage partner had taken charge, that she had been told to get dressed, that Chris had been told to get lost. It was the end of what had been a very pleasant interlude in the day of the Brae Loch business major.

CHAPTER 8

The bed. It was the object of everyone's attention, the subject of everyone's conversation. The cast and the orchestra were arriving for what would be one of the first attempts by the entire company to rehearse together. The small cot that had served as a stand-in for a proper bed had been relegated to the wings, and the king-sized four-poster which had been donated by Mueller's Furniture Store in Yates Center now occupied center stage. Moreover, the provost had persuaded his wife to let the college borrow some of their bedding, so the bed now sported a large colorful spread and a couple of matching pillows.

Two or three members of the company wanted to test the big bed, and it wasn't long before a small queue had formed for a chance to crawl under the covers and play at being Schicchi. It was as if they all had come to the realization that opening night was just around the corner, and the thought had made them momentarily giddy. Mercedes Redman was growing impatient with this particular form of tomfoolery, but not everyone had arrived and she knew she would have to put up with it for awhile longer.

Puccini's Zita, otherwise known as Janet Myers, was taking her turn under the covers when her ex-husband made a belated entrance via the back of the auditorium.

"So here we are, we happy band of mischief makers," he announced as he marched down the aisle. And then he noticed the bed.

"My bed! At last, my bed! Who's responsible for this miracle?"

"It's courtesy of the local furniture store," Kevin spoke up. "Delivered this morning. Makes us look professional, don't you think?"

"Still a sow's ear, silk purse problem, but it's an improvement," Gerlach said as he climbed onto the stage. He went straight to the bed and proceeded to throw himself down on it.

The howl that ensued could have been heard in Menlo Hall. Harley Gerlach knew immediately that he had landed on something other than the mattress. Janet Mycrs knew just as immediately that a heavy weight had fallen on her. There was a violent thrashing about as Gerlach scrambled off the bed and Myers extricated herself from the bulky spread.

Two surprised and angry members of the cast stared at each other from opposite sides of the bed, momentarily speechless. It was Myers who found her voice first.

"You miserable cretin," she hollered at him. "If I've got a broken rib, I'll sue you from here to Sunday."

Kevin hastened to the scene unfolding before him, instantly worried that his Zita might have been hurt and anxious that this most unfortunate chance encounter on the newly arrived stage bed might derail the whole production of the Puccini opera.

"Not to worry, Professor," Gerlach said, recovering his composure. "She'll be just fine. If I'd known she was hiding under the covers, I wouldn't have gone near the bed. In fact, what the hell was she doing there? That woman has no business being in my bed. Ever."

"It's not your bed. This is an opera, damn it, and it's just a stupid prop."

Janet Myers turned on her heel and stormed offstage. Gerlach watched her go, then burst out laughing. No one else found the situation funny. Mercedes Redman was in shock. Kevin Whitman was fighting off panic.

————

It had taken Kevin the better part of fifteen minutes to calm Janet Myers down. It had taken even longer for the company to get in the mood to rehearse *Gianni Schicchi*. Mercedes Redman had taken a long walk, after which she returned to the auditorium, still wondering what she had gotten herself into but more determined than ever not to let the troublemakers win. And there was no shortage of troublemakers. Gerlach was the worst, with his ex-wife currently running a close second. But although Mercedes had worked primarily with the orchestra, she had already seen enough of Paolo Rosetti and Sean Carpenter to realize that it might not take much to set off one or the other or both. And then there was Arthur Conklin, he of the 'nigger in the woodpile' remark. Who knew what—or who—might prompt him to say or do something that would place the production in jeopardy.

43

And none of these potential problems had anything to do with such basic issues as keeping the singers and the orchestra on the same page or covering up for a member of the cast who suddenly forgot his lines or—heaven forbid—came down with an eleventh-hour case of laryngitis. Kevin's worries were such that he had shifted more and more of the musical preparation to Redman. He found himself struggling with matters he had counted on the university people to handle, even including the printing and selling of tickets. On more than one occasion he had been reminded that the provost had consented to all of this because he viewed Kevin as a local celebrity, not because he loved opera or thought the college might benefit significantly from venturing into the realm of high culture.

When the evening's rehearsal finally began, Kevin took up the baton for the first time so that Mercedes could assume her place in the orchestra's string section. It took only about three minutes for him to realize that Carol had been right. He was a teacher of opera, not a conductor. Oh, he could follow the score and wave his arms in time with the music, but he knew that his effort deserved at best a weak C. Maybe even a D.

Happily, his plan for the evening did not call for rehearsing the entire opera. They were concentrating on the part where Schicchi, pretending to be the old man, dictates the will and the relatives react to the shocking realization that he is leaving everything valuable to himself. The plot called for the dispossessed relatives to turn on Schicchi in anger, calling him a robber and a scoundrel. And it was clear from the look on some of their faces that that was exactly what they thought of the man playing Schicchi. To Kevin's great relief, however, his players stayed in character. No more unpleasant words were exchanged, at least not within his hearing. He had no idea, of course, what was said outside the auditorium, as members of the company headed home after the rehearsal.

———

It was after ten when Kevin arrived home, kicked his shoes off, and opened a bottle of beer. He was almost too tired to eat. Instead, he took his beer out onto the deck to take a look at the moon which had risen above the hill on the other side of the lake. It was a cloudless night, and a white ribbon of light from the moon's reflection stretched across the dark water from the far shore all the way to his own dock. A beautiful sight. He wished Carol were there to enjoy it with him.

Two more rehearsals lay ahead, the second being the dress rehearsal which would bring to an end preparations for the opening of *Gianni Schicchi's* brief run at Brae Loch College. Of course the label 'dress rehearsal' didn't quite fit this production, inasmuch as there would be no costumes. The decision to present the opera in contemporary everyday clothes had been dictated by the need to keep expenses to a minimum. Few in the audience would know or care that Puccini had set his opera in Florence at the end of the 13th century. The story is, after all, timeless. Greed, it would seem, is forever with us. And all ages and eras have known imposters and con artists.

It had been an exhausting experience, and Kevin was glad that it was coming to an end. Now if only he could send several hundred, perhaps even a thousand, locals and summer residents home happy, it would have been worth it. Particularly if Jason Armitage, the crime junkie who also served as Brae Loch's provost, could be persuaded to offer Kevin an appointment as a visiting professor of music.

CHAPTER 9

Tuesday afternoon. 5:20, give or take a few minutes. Dress rehearsal was scheduled to begin in just over two hours. Kevin would have preferred to have been at the cottage, enjoying an early dinner. But he was anxious, worried that something would go wrong, something that would signal that his little company needed another week or more to get ready for the unveiling of Puccini's opera. So instead of having dinner, he was wandering around the Brae Loch campus, stoking his anxiety. There was really nothing he needed to do, nothing he could do at this late date but raise his baton and start the music.

It was as he was climbing the front steps of Wayne Hall that he heard Lisa Tompkins call out his name in a voice much louder than seemed possible in view of her diminutive size. And it was less than a minute later, in response to her appeal for his help, that he discovered Harley Gerlach, dead, in the big bed on the stage of the auditorium.

That Gerlach was indeed dead was not in doubt, which made the call he had asked Lisa to make to 911 superfluous. A call to the sheriff was another matter.

Fortunately, Carol was in her office.

"Carol, you've got to get down here to the college right away. And I mean immediately. We just found one of the members of the cast, dead. Dead, and obviously not of natural causes. It's Gerlach, and he's been strangled to death with what looks like a piano wire."

He fully expected her to say something like 'not again,' reflecting the fact that this would be the third murder on Crooked Lake in just three years. But whatever Carol may have thought about such an improbable development, she didn't mention it, focusing instead on the problem at hand.

"No question about him being dead? And strangled?"

"No, he's dead all right. The wire's still around his neck."

"Okay, now listen to me. I'll get my men over there as fast as I can. And I'll be right behind them. I want you to keep people away from the body. Do whatever you have to do—tell them it's an order from the sheriff. Just where is he anyway?"

"He's in that bed on the auditorium stage."

"Anybody else around?"

"Yes, the woman who found him, a member of the orchestra. The rescue squad should be here soon. And my people will be coming in for the dress rehearsal. It's scheduled for 7:30."

"That's not good," Carol said, obviously worried about all these people messing up the crime scene. "You've really got to assert your authority. Nobody, not even the paramedics, are to get near the body. Or the bed. Keep everybody off the stage if you can until we get there. Why don't you call campus security, get some help until my guys arrive."

Kevin could hear Carol catch her breath on the other end of the line.

"Kevin, I'm sorry. Really sorry. You don't deserve this. But I've got to get busy, get the word out to my team. Now. And get myself over to the college. Be tough, okay?"

Kevin would try to be tough. He wasn't keen on asking campus security for help, but he knew he would have to tell the provost what had happened. And he'd have to do it immediately. Much as Jason Armitage was a self-confessed crime junkie, he would not be pleased with this turn of events. Any public relations benefit that might have accrued to Brae Loch College would be eclipsed by the negative publicity generated by a murder on campus.

In any event, there would now be no performances of the Puccini opera at Brae Loch this summer. Kevin could imagine that Paolo Rosetti might offer his services as a replacement Gianni Schicchi, but who then would assume Rosetti's part, and the part of whoever stepped into that role. But Kevin knew that all of this was mere idle speculation. It may have been an old theatre tradition that the show must go on, but that tradition was irrelevant in this situation, in this place, at this time. No, twenty-nine singers and instrumentalists would go home without adding an appearance in an opera on Crooked Lake to their modest resumés. And one of those twenty-nine might be a murderer.

It was way too soon to be thinking about the odds on who among the company's members would turn out to be Gerlach's killer. The guilty party might be someone uninvolved in the production of the opera. After all, Brae Loch's students, faculty, and staff all had access to the auditorium in Wayne Hall. Even the provost could have done it. Hypothetically, of course.

Kevin shook off these thoughts, left an urgent message for Jason Armitage, and took Lisa Tompkins aside to tell her what she must not do. He then turned his attention to the delicate matter of how he was going to keep the paramedics from doing what they had been summoned to the college to do.

Happily for Kevin, Officer Barrett of the Cumberland County Sheriff's Department arrived before the paramedics, followed within three minutes by Deputy Sheriff Bridges. Kevin had known from the moment he realized that Harley Gerlach was dead that he would be much involved in the investigation of who had killed him and why. After all, he had been a front-row observer of the frictions that had beset the company from the moment it first assembled back in late May. He had been witness to the hostility which Gerlach stirred up in others, and while he could not imagine anyone hating the man enough to kill him, he was aware that while he had initially been shocked by his death, he had not really been surprised. But for now, however, he was glad to step aside and let the professionals take charge.

———

When Lisa Tompkins discovered Gerlach in the big bed, she was the only person in Wayne Hall. When the sheriff arrived, it was one of the busier places on the Brae Loch campus. Some of the opera company had trickled in and were sitting in the first few rows of the auditorium, thinking their thoughts and talking quietly among themselves. The paramedic team was on the stage, behind the drawn curtain, its life-saving mission thwarted by Gerlach's death and not quite sure what to do next. The provost and several members of the college administration were over on one side of the auditorium, engaged in conservation with Deputy Sheriff Bridges and conspicuously anxious to have the body of the opera's deceased star removed from the premises as quickly as possible. Bridges' colleagues were scattered around the building, urging the restless to be patient and making sure that no one left until the sheriff granted permission.

Kevin had stepped outside for a much-needed breath of fresh air, having assured the officer on duty that no, he wasn't leaving, and that yes, the sheriff would approve of this violation of her instructions. She pulled into a No Parking zone already occupied by four other official cars. A small but growing crowd of students had gathered nearby, and a few of them tried to get the sheriff's attention as she stepped out of her car.

"What's going on in there?" one of the students asked.

"Not sure," she said as she hurried up the steps to where Kevin was standing. "You'll hear about it soon enough."

In other circumstances, Carol would have run into Kevin's arms. But not with all those students behind her. Or with a recently murdered man waiting somewhere just beyond the heavy doors that were the entrance to Brae Loch's auditorium.

"I can't believe this," she said.

"Neither can I," Kevin agreed. "Thank God you're here. It's not bad now, but there are a lot of people in there who are going to get frustrated just sitting around. I can see it coming."

"Well, they'll just have to get used to frustration," Carol said. "Let's get inside."

She surveyed the scene from the back of the auditorium. It confirmed her fear that this was going to be a long evening.

"I'm afraid I'm going to have to talk to the members of your company. All of them. And one at a time. I need to know where they were this afternoon. Whether any of them could have been here, killing your man Gerlach."

"You don't think somebody's going to confess, do you?"

"Highly unlikely, but I can't just tell them to go home, have a nice evening. Not when one of them might well have been the strangler."

"It's really a mess, isn't it?"

"I take it the body is onstage, behind that curtain. One of my men had better be there with it. Let's go."

Sheriff Kelleher was in her take-charge mode as she strode down the aisle. When they reached the front of the auditorium, she stopped and addressed the members of Kevin's small company.

"All of you people are here for the opera production, right?"

Heads nodded and several members of the company mumbled what sounded like 'yes.'

"Okay. I'm the sheriff, and I'm going to want to talk with each of you, just as soon as I take a look at the situation backstage. So just stay in your seats, make yourselves comfortable. I'll be back in a few minutes."

"I have to be getting home, Sheriff. How long before we can go?" It was a man at the end of the front row.

"I've no idea. According to Professor Whitman, you all came here for a dress rehearsal, so I assume you planned to spend the evening. It looks like you'll be doing just that, minus the rehearsal."

There was some predictable grumbling, but no one challenged the sheriff. She and Kevin went up the steps to the stage.

"Am I glad to see you," Officer Barrett said as Carol pushed her way through the curtain. The members of the paramedic team looked as if they agreed.

"I assume no one's touched the body." It was more a statement than a question.

"Not since I arrived," Barrett said. "These guys figure they're not needed. They'd like to go."

"Yes, I'm sure they do, and I think that should be possible," Carol said, turning to the man who appeared to be the head of the rescue squad. "Sorry you had to wait. There's just one thing I'd like you to do. You are trained to recognize rigor mortis when you see it, is that right?"

"Yes, ma'am."

"That's good, because the coroner isn't here yet. Let's take a look at our victim."

Carol carefully pulled the spread down, revealing Gerlach's face and upper torso. The appearance of the face made it clear that he had been strangled. The presence of the wire that had choked off his life removed any doubt.

"Now," Carol said to the paramedic, "tell me whether you see signs of rigor and how far it's progressed. But be careful. Don't touch the body any more than you have to."

She was reasonably confident that she could have made the determination herself, but it would be better if someone trained to spot rigor mortis could do it. She knew that it typically started in the face and gradually moved downward to the larger muscles. What was important in this case was what it could tell her about the time of death.

"I'm no expert," the paramedic said, "but it looks like the process has begun but not progressed too far. He's been dead, oh, probably four hours, maybe five at the most."

Carol looked at her watch, which told her it was now just minutes before seven. Gerlach had been dead since mid-afternoon, possibly as early as two. Which information would help her a bit when she questioned the members of the opera company. She turned to Kevin.

"You found him at five something?"

"That's about right," he replied.

"Okay, so by then he'd been dead two or three hours. His killer could have done the deed, had plenty of time to go home, then come back in time for the rehearsal. Or maybe he never left the college after strangling Gerlach. I'll be interested to see what they say when I ask them to account for their afternoons."

"I'm not sure some of them could have killed him and then gone home before rehearsal. Too long a drive, like for a guy who lives in Rochester. Even for people from around Ithaca. I'd bet whoever killed Gerlach stayed right here. The interesting question is whether anyone saw him. Or her."

And, Kevin was thinking, what had Gerlach been doing on campus hours before the dress rehearsal. Even more importantly, how his killer would have known he'd be there.

"Putting on your sleuth's hat, are you?" Carol asked.

"Just trying to figure out how it happened that somebody managed to hang a 'show cancelled' sign on *Gianni Schicchi* only hours before the dress rehearsal."

"I really am sorry this is happening to you," Carol said, and she said it with feeling. "But right now I'd better start asking questions of those musicians out in the auditorium. Why don't you get busy smoothing ruffled feathers with the Brae Loch people."

The sheriff thanked the paramedics for their help and their patience and headed out to the auditorium to begin her investigation of Harley Gerlach's murder.

CHAPTER 10

When Carol reemerged from behind the curtain in the Brae Loch auditorium, the murmur of voices in the front rows quickly ceased. People straightened up in their seats, some of them clutching their instruments, others starting to get up as if the sheriff's appearance signaled that they might now be free to go.

It was not to be.

"Sorry to keep you waiting, but there were a couple of things I had to take care of first," Carol said in a conversational tone of voice. "Give me one more minute while I speak to the provost over there."

The restless members of the small opera company settled back in their seats while Carol and Kevin walked over to join Deputy Sheriff Bridges in conversation with Jason Armitage.

Introductions over, Carol proceeded to make clear to the provost what was going to happen to heretofore quiet little Brae Loch College.

"Sorry we have to inconvenience you, but this building is going to have to be off limits to everyone except the police. We've got a crime scene here, and it's going to include the whole stage, the wings, and that small rehearsal room Professor Whitman's people have been using. Maybe it should be even larger. In any event, you're going to have to lock the building down and let me have the keys. I regret this as much as you do, but I'm sure you understand the problem."

The provost could not be expected to be happy with the sheriff's edict, but Kevin thought he caught just a momentary gleam in Armitage's eye. Probably picturing one of those yellow crime-scene ribbons backstage, imagining the Brae Loch auditorium as a real life version of some back alley in *Law & Order*. For a brief moment the provost's love of the drama of crime and law enforcement might almost have outweighed his professional concern for the college, but the unpleasant reality of the situation quickly reasserted itself.

"How long do you expect this to last?" Armitage asked.

"I really can't say," Carol answered truthfully. "A man has been murdered, and a lot of people could have done it, most of them right over there in the front rows. I hate to think of the possibility that he was killed by somebody from the college community."

"You can't possibly think—" Armitage began.

"Oh, but I can," Carol interrupted. "Highly unlikely, so let's not start imagining the worst. Officer Bridges and I are going to start asking some questions of those restless members of the opera company. All of them. I'd guess it'd take about two hours, maybe three. By that time the coroner will have come and done his job and the body will be gone. What I'd suggest is that you go outside and see what you can do to disperse that crowd of students. They'll know this isn't something routine—too many police cars. No need to alarm the student body, though. This isn't one of those horrible campus shootings everyone knows about. You'll think of something sensible, I'm sure."

The provost didn't look as if he would be able to think of something sensible to say. And he was clearly not pleased with the thought that the sheriff and her men might still be on campus for another three hours. And after that for how many days?

Before fading into the role of fifth wheel in the sheriff's investigation of Harley Gerlach's death, Kevin slipped her a hastily scribbled note containing three names, those of Myers, Conklin, and Rosetti.

"You ought to talk to these people yourself," he whispered. "From what I've seen and heard, they're the ones who've seemed most hostile to Gerlach."

"Okay, but let's not make it too obvious that anybody in your troupe is a prime suspect. How do I recognize them?"

Kevin did his best to describe these three members of the company without appearing to do so, no easy feat in view of the fact that most of the restless occupants of the front rows in the auditorium were watching them. He hoped he had been successful.

"You've been very patient," Carol said as she walked over to face the company, knowing full well that they had not been patient. "Now this is what we're going to do. Officer Bridges and I are going to talk briefly with each of you, one at a time. We need to know what, if anything, you may have heard or seen that can help us determine just what happened here this afternoon. We'll also need some personal information, like where you live and how we can reach you. It seems likely that we'll want to be in touch with you again, and sooner rather than later."

Carol paused, aware that what she would say next would not please these people.

"One more thing. We're investigating a very serious crime. It's called murder. Which means that anyone we need to talk with, anyone who might help us, be nearby. What I'm saying is that I don't want any of you to leave the area. Not until I say so. I'm sorry if this may interfere with your plans, but I'm sure you understand why it's important."

"Are you saying that you suspect one of us having killed Gerlach?" The question was asked by the large and somewhat florid man Kevin had identified as Paolo Rosetti.

Carol had been careful not to say that, but it was not surprising that Rosetti and almost certainly others had inferred as much.

"No I'm not. I have no idea who might have killed Mr. Gerlach. But we have to start somewhere, and the logical place to start is with people here at Brae Loch College. That does include all of you. It also includes faculty, students, anyone who had reason to be on campus this afternoon. Like I said, I want you to stay around because I may need to ask more questions."

There was a lot of grumbling in the front rows, but Carol ignored it and told her deputy sheriff to start with a man who was hugging what looked like a trumpet case. She then beckoned to the woman Kevin had identified as Janet Myers and escorted her to a corner of the auditorium.

―――

"It'll take me awhile to get to know all of you," she began. "So let's see, you are . . .?"

"I'm Janet Myers, and let me save you some time. I'm Harley Gerlach's ex-wife, as you'd have discovered soon enough in any event. We divorced quite some time ago, and it was more than just a matter of incompatibility. He was an incorrigible womanizer. But did I kill him? No, I did not."

Carol had known that Myers had been married to Gerlach. Kevin had told her so in one of their conversations about how the production of *Gianni Schicchi* was going. But she was surprised that Myers had unburdened herself of this information so quickly.

"So you and Mr. Gerlach had what sounds like an unpleasant divorce. But you both chose to stay in this area. Not exactly neighbors, but not all that far apart. Want to tell me whether your paths have crossed since the divorce?"

"You don't understand," the Myers woman said. "When we were married we lived down in the city. It wasn't until later that I moved to Southport."

"And why Southport?"

"An old college friend lived there. I guess I needed some comforting, so I sort of invited myself to spend a week with her. One thing led to another. I met a friend of hers, Charles Myers, and we hit it off. Got married a few months later. Believe me, it's been the difference between night and day, Harley and Chuck."

"And how does it happen that Gerlach also lives in this area? Did he follow you upstate? Couldn't bring himself to accept the divorce or something like that?"

"I didn't have any idea that he had moved to Crooked Lake. I never told him I'd moved up here, although I suppose he could have learned it from a mutual acquaintance in the city. I didn't know he was in the area until one day last summer. They had an arts and crafts show in the town square down in Southport. In one of the booths I saw some watercolors which looked like his style. And they were his—his signature was on them. I was surprised. No, better to say I was shocked."

"So Mr. Gerlach was both a singer and an artist."

"Yes, and to be perfectly frank, he was pretty good at both. Too bad he wasn't as nice a human being. After I discovered that he lived in the area, I made some inquiries and learned that he had moved here about two years ago. Bought a house up on the bluff down near the fork in the lake. It became a studio for his painting."

"Seems strange, his resettling in the same area you'd moved to. I'm not one who believes in coincidences. Especially when the place you both ended up is practically no man's land where most people are concerned. Did he make any effort to contact you before this opera business?"

"Never. I'm not sure he even knew I lived in Southport. Until we both found ourselves in the cast of Whitman's opera, that is."

Carol studied Janet Myers, expecting to see what—a hint that the woman was not being entirely honest with her? That it hadn't been a rare coincidence that had brought them both to Crooked Lake? That they had had some kind of relationship since the divorce?

"I understand that Mr. Gerlach had a career with the Metropolitan Opera," she said, not offering an explanation of how she had acquired this information about Gerlach's life. "If you knew he was living in this area, you must have figured that he'd be interested in the opera here at Brae Loch. That there was a good chance that he'd be in the cast. Did that give you pause? About trying out for the opera?"

"Look, I'm a pretty fair musician myself, and I liked the idea of doing something with my voice besides singing in the church choir on Sundays. The news about the opera was intriguing. I tried out, Whitman liked my voice, and he put me in the cast. When I realized that Harley was going to be in it, too, I asked the professor to get rid of him. I told him it was him or me, but I guess that was asking too much. Anyway, I stuck it out."

Janet Myers suddenly burst into laughter.

"Quite a joke, isn't it? Now there won't be any opera. Not for Harley, not for me."

Carol had not had time to give much thought to the matter of whether Gerlach's death would cancel Kevin's production of *Gianni Schicchi*.

"I have no idea whether the opera will be cancelled," she said. "Professor Whitman has invested a lot of his time and energy in it. The college has a stake in it, too. Maybe it can be salvaged."

"No offense, Sheriff," Myers said, "but you can't imagine how hard it would be to shuffle parts, especially when the lead character is gone. There aren't any understudies hanging around on Crooked Lake. No, take my word for it; there will be no opera at Brae Loch this summer."

It was time to change the subject, to find out what Janet Myers had been doing during the time when her ex-husband was being strangled to death.

"I need to talk to you about what you were doing today," Carol said. "I'll be asking everyone the same thing. I'm hoping that maybe somebody will be able to help me figure out what happened—you know, how Mr. Gerlach met his death. So why don't you tell me about your day."

"Not much to tell, Sheriff. Chuck and I had a lazy morning, we had lunch around—oh, I'd guess one o'clock—and then he went off to the office. I think he was going to catch up on some paperwork."

"And you?"

"I took a drive."

"A drive? Want to tell me about it?"

"There's nothing to tell. I was uptight. You know, butter-flies about the dress rehearsal I suppose. I wasn't going anywhere, just driving around—thinking about my part, going over my lines."

"And where did you go?"

"Nowhere in particular. You know, the back roads around here. They're pretty quiet, making it easy to get away from whatever's bothering you."

"And was something bothering you?"

Myers' face reflected the fact that she wasn't happy with this line of questioning.

"No, it's like I said, I just needed to think about the opera."

"Okay. How long were you out driving around?"

"I can't be sure. Maybe an hour and a half, maybe two hours. I like that road up top of the bluff, and—look, I wasn't really thinking about the time."

"While you were driving around, did you go to the college?"

"No, not until this evening when I came over for the dress rehearsal. But by then I'd been back home, cooked dinner, said good-bye to Chuck."

Carol had tried to contain her mounting frustration with this recital of Janet Myers' afternoon. She knew what the answer to her next question was going to be.

"Did you see anyone during your drive? I mean people you know, friends, members of the opera company?"

What she meant, of course, was whether anyone had seen her and would be in a position to vouch for where she was and when.

"No, I'm afraid not."

When Harley Gerlach's ex-wife departed from the auditorium, Carol had learned two things. One was that the Myers woman had no alibi for the time period when Gerlach had been strangled. The other was that it was going to be a very long evening.

CHAPTER 11

Carol looked at her watch for probably the tenth time that evening. It was 11:20. It had been a long day.

She looked around the auditorium. It was now nearly vacant. Sam Bridges had just concluded the last of his discussions with members of the company and was leafing through his notes, waiting for the sheriff to call it a night. Kevin Whitman was sitting down in the front row, talking with an unfamiliar young man. The man was presumably one of the provost's staff, somebody who had been asked to stick around to represent the college until the sheriff had concluded her interviews. Kevin had spent much of the evening trying to keep the lid on the discontent of the dwindling numbers of his small company. But now they had all gone, as had everybody else, including the late Harley Gerlach, and Kevin, too, was ready to go home.

"Come on, Sam, let's get out of here," Carol called out as she got up and walked down to where Kevin was sitting. It was much too late for her to be going back to the cottage with him, but she needed to have a word with him before she left.

She thanked the Brae Loch staffer for his patience and the college's help, and turned to Kevin.

"My God, what a night. I'll bet you're exhausted, physically and emotionally." She said it quietly but with feeling. "We've got to get together tomorrow, okay? I need to sit down with Sam, go over his notes with him, then spend some time with you. I've found out a few things that might be interesting. Hope Sam has as well. But it's important that you and I discuss what we've learned from these people. You'll know better than I will what to make of what they've told us. Whether it rings true or not. At least I hope you will."

"Of course. Anytime you're ready." Carol thought he sounded numb, as well he might be.

"I can't be sure how long it'll take for Sam to fill me in, but I'll give you a call as soon as I'm ready to leave the office."

Carol reached out and touched his arm.

"I really am sorry this happened, Kevin."

"I know. We'll talk about it tomorrow. Let's get some sleep."

By 11:30 the auditorium in Wayne Hall on the Brae Loch College campus was empty and dark.

———

"Ready?" It was Carol, calling from Cumberland, and Kevin, anticipating the call, had just started a second pot of coffee.

"I've been ready since the middle of the night. Spent most of it trying to figure out who might have killed Gerlach. I'm no further ahead than I was when I left the college last night."

"Neither am I. But I'm on my way. Looks like I could be staying over the lunch hour. Have anything in the frig for a hungry girl?"

"Always."

It was at best a thirty-minute drive from Cumberland to Blue Water Point, and Carol would usually have treated it as a welcome break, a time to enjoy a beautiful August day. But today her mind was reviewing the results of what she and Sam had learned—or not learned—the previous evening.

Sam had interviewed most of the company, and with two exceptions had learned nothing which would seem to have any bearing on Gerlach's murder. And neither of those exceptions looked to be particularly dramatic. She herself had spoken with only ten of Kevin's troupe, and three of the ten had taken most of her time. That was more because Kevin had singled them out for special attention than because they had told her anything that seemed to have a bearing on the case.

Before she reached West Lake Road, Carol decided to add a few minutes to her trip and swing by the college to make sure that Wayne Hall had indeed been secured. It had been, and Officer Barrett was busy asserting his authority. He was talking with some students when she pulled into a reserved parking space in front of the building. A brief conversation with her colleague made it clear that the Brae Loch people were cooperating, but that the provost himself had come around three times to 'see what was happening.' Of course nothing was happening, and Barrett looked bored.

It was close to one o'clock when Carol pulled in beside Kevin's Camry.

"How'd you sleep?" she asked as she disengaged from their first hug in two days.

"Not so good. I still can't believe that twenty-four hours ago I was worrying about the dress rehearsal, afraid we'd sound pretty ragged."

"I'd be willing to bet there's someone else who didn't sleep that well either. What are we going to call him, the Puccini strangler?"

"Him or maybe her. I don't know. Maybe he slept just fine, having put Gerlach out of his misery. Let's have some lunch."

Having finished a pedestrian lunch of tuna fish sandwiches, coffee and an apple, Kevin and Carol settled down on the deck to go over the results of the interviews. It was only with some difficulty that they managed not to be lured into the water by the warm afternoon sun and the light waves that were quietly lapping on the shore by Kevin's dock. But there was a murder to be solved—a murder which had brought to an abrupt end any thought that Crooked Lake would be the setting for an opera production this summer. And neither the sheriff nor the professor had any idea who had snuffed out Harley Gerlach's life the previous day.

"Learn anything at all last night?" Kevin asked. He didn't sound as if the answer would be yes.

"I suppose you could say so, but damned if I know whether it's the truth or simply what some of your people want me to believe is the truth."

"Well, let's hear it. Anyone tell you he was in or around Wayne Hall at any time during the afternoon?"

"Just one. And it's a she. A young woman named Heather Merriman told Bridges that she was on the campus much of the afternoon. Said she often spent the afternoon there. Since the rehearsals began, that is. Sunbathing, I guess. Claims she needed to get away from an annoying brother over at her family's cottage. And occasionally to go over stuff about her role with a guy who plays her sweetheart in the opera."

"Yeah, that figures," Kevin said. "I'm not so sure she needed to go over what you call 'stuff,' but this guy—his name's Sean Carpenter—looked like he's interested in her for more than her voice. He tried to act as if he was simply being paternal, protecting her from the bad guys like Gerlach. But I think he had the hots for her. She's attractive, and he struck me as one of those men who have a thing for pretty girls. Even if they're young enough to be his daughter."

"Anyway, Merriman was there. She wasn't sure for how long, but it was from some time after lunch until around four. She told Sam she didn't see anyone, but that may have been because she was down on the beach, not up in the auditorium. But she did hear someone. Gerlach."

"No kidding?"

"She said she had to use the bathroom, so she went back up to Wayne Hall where she knew there was one. She heard Gerlach singing in that little practice room off the stage."

"She heard him but didn't see him?"

"Right. Apparently the door was closed, and there was some sort of informal rule among the cast that you didn't bother someone when they were exercising the vocal cords."

"When was this?"

"She wasn't sure. Probably sometime between two and three."

"How did she know it was Gerlach?" Kevin asked.

"The way she told it to Sam is that what he was singing was from Gianni Schicchi's role. Of course Sam had never heard of Gianni Schicchi, so he had to get her to spell it out for him. Anyway, she was sure it was Gerlach practicing his part. Which doesn't help us very much, does it? We know he was there. Probably warmed up his voice, then went out onto the stage and crawled into that bed—where our murderer found him and strangled him."

"What about Carpenter, the guy who's acted interested in Merriman? Did he show up during the afternoon?"

"Not yesterday. At least she didn't mention him. Do you think maybe he did and she decided not to mention it?"

"I don't really know her very well—or him, for that matter," Kevin admitted. "But I'd be surprised if she'd be covering for him. If anything, she seemed to find his attention uncomfortable."

Carol reached over and picked up her small pile of notes on the interviews.

"Who'd you like to hear about next?" she asked.

"How about the people I wanted you to interview? The ones who've said things that make it clear they didn't like Gerlach. That would be his former wife, the man who wanted his part—that's Rosetti, and Conklin, the guy whose wife Gerlach had apparently had an affair with. It'll probably turn out that none of them had a damn thing to do with his death, but it gives us a place to start."

Carol shuffled the papers containing Bridges' interview comments and her own until she came to one headed Janet Myers. After a few lines devoted to her failed marriage to Gerlach and her move to Crooked Lake, it came to an abrupt end with the words "spent the afternoon driving aimlessly around—saw no one—was seen by no one."

"That's it?" Kevin asked after quickly scanning Carol's notes.

"I'm afraid so. She says she never went near the campus, but she doesn't seem to have anyone who can back her up."

"It's too late now, but I think Brae Loch made a mistake in not creating some kind of temporary parking permit system for the opera company. It probably wouldn't have done any good, but as it is, my people were simply driving in and out, parking wherever they found a place. I'd guess that unless any of them had an unusual car, say a Rolls or a Bentley or maybe a fire engine-red Porsche, nobody would have known they were there."

"I'll have one of my men talk to Brae Loch security or whatever they're called, see if anyone remembers somebody poking around Wayne Hall. Funny, isn't it? Seems like there's a news story every month or so about a crime on some college campus. But it doesn't make much difference. These places are always wide open, students, visitors, who knows, all wandering about. It'd be pretty hard to recognize a guy bent on mayhem, much less stop him."

"Or her," Kevin added, thinking of Janet Myers.

Carol picked up her papers and pulled out the ones with notes on her conversations with Conklin and Rosetti, the other two members of the company Kevin had said she should interview herself.

"I didn't make much headway with your other prime suspects," she said, and started to walk him through her interviews with them.

Kevin interrupted her.

"Let's not call anyone a prime suspect," he said. "It's too soon. I don't want to get fixated on someone just because I know there'd been tension between him, or her, and Gerlach. Truth is, most of the cast probably hated his guts. He sure gave a lot of my people reason to dislike him. You take Carpenter, that guy who's got a thing for Merriman. He didn't like the way Gerlach treated her, made it obvious. Or Redman—she's the one who's been putting the orchestra through its paces. She doesn't say much, but I think Gerlach annoyed her. You could see it on her face whenever he tried to upstage the other members of the cast. And that was most of the time."

It was Carol's turn to interrupt.

"Okay, he was a pain in the ass, so any one of them could have strangled him. But you asked me to talk with three people who apparently had issues with him before rehearsals ever started. Let me tell you what they told me. It isn't much."

She began with Conklin.

"He came right out and told me that Gerlach had had an affair with his wife. Happened a little over a year ago. It seems it started when Gerlach attended a program featuring a string quartet that Conklin plays in. Helen—that's the wife's name—was there, and apparently that was the beginning of a relationship with Gerlach. It lasted right up to the time that she died. She fell down the stairs in their house, suffered a head injury, never recovered. Anyway, Conklin was up front about all this. Guess he figured I'd hear about it one way or another, so why not just tell me himself."

"What did he say about yesterday afternoon? I don't suppose he confessed to lurking around the auditorium."

"I'm afraid not. Says he didn't arrive on campus until around 6:30, shortly before the scheduled dress rehearsal. By that time Gerlach's death was common knowledge."

"What did he do before that?"

"Spent some time on the computer at the house. Business, he said. Made the rounds of his nurseries."

"So he has an alibi," Kevin said.

"At the nurseries, I suppose, but there's no one else at the house in Geneva, not since the wife died. I decided it was a bit premature to quiz him about neighbors seeing him leave, but he volunteered that he waved good-bye to someone who was mowing a lawn next door."

"Sounds like he figures you might suspect him."

"No question. He said as much, then dismissed the idea as ridiculous."

"That leaves Rosetti, our Schicchi wannabe."

"Right. He's a character, isn't he? Not that big, but he seems like he's several times life size. Sucks the air right out of the room. Tell you what. Let me fill you in on Rosetti—it won't take long. Then let's take a swim before I plow through the rest of this file."

"Love to, if you feel you can take the time."

"This is one of those days when I feel I have to take the time. But let's do Rosetti first. He's another one without what you might call an ironclad alibi. Says he spent the afternoon fishing."

"Fishing? In the afternoon? Everybody I know who does much fishing says they do it in the early morning."

"Well, Mr. Rosetti seems to be an exception. According to him, he took his boat out after lunch, spent the next several hours on the lake."

"Catch anything?"

"The way he tells it, no. A few bites, but that's all."

"And he spent most of the afternoon just sitting in his boat? Sounds awfully boring to me," Kevin said, reflecting his own lack of interest in fishing. "Wonder what he was thinking about all that time."

"He says he was becoming anxious about the opera—about his role. Needed to have some quiet time to go over it in his mind."

"I don't suppose he volunteered any information about chitchat with fellow fishermen."

"Afraid not. He didn't say anything about neighbors seeing him take off or return either."

"Where's he live?"

"South of Yates Center on the other side of the lake. According to Sam's and my notes, he probably lives about as close to Brae Loch as anyone in your company."

Kevin shook his head. It didn't sound as if Carol had learned anything which ruled out anybody as Gerlach's murderer. They set aside the pile of interview notes, went back into the cottage to put on their bathing suits, and headed for the water.

CHAPTER 12

While Kevin and the sheriff were reviewing the information gleaned from the other interviews with members of the opera company, the provost of Brae Loch College was engaged in a serious discussion with Deputy Sheriff Bridges back on campus. From Jason Armitage's point of view, their discussion was not going well.

"I don't think you understand," he said. "It hasn't been 24 hours since that man was murdered, and already I have had two phone calls from anxious parents. One of them announced that she was withdrawing her daughter from the school, and the other sounded as if he might do the same thing. For all I know, my secretary has fielded half a dozen more such calls from parents while I've been down here talking with you."

"Well, why don't you just ask these parents to bear with you for awhile. The sheriff is as interested in the college getting back to normal as you are, but we can't afford to overlook something that could let whoever killed Mr. Gerlach get away with it. Anyway, there's no reason to think this has anything to do with the college. I'm sure there's not a killer loose on campus, and you can reassure the kids and their families that there's no reason to worry."

Sam had no idea who had strangled Harley Gerlach, and for all he knew his casual dismissal of the idea that it had been someone from the college might turn out to be dead wrong. But he'd been trying without success to put the provost at ease for almost a quarter of an hour, and he was prepared to say almost anything if it would persuade the man to go back to his office and let him rejoin Officer Barrett to finish their task of scouring the crime scene for evidence.

"What are you looking for that is taking so long to find?" Armitage asked.

"No way of knowing until we find it," Sam said, trying to sound as if he'd had lots of experience with difficult crime scenes.

"Things like fingerprints?"

"Yes, of course, but that's only a part of it. And let me tell you, there are fingerprints all over back there—the bed, the other furniture, the piano, the piano bench, music stands, the door knobs and door frames, the pulleys that open and close the curtain. Not to mention the fixtures in the bathroom, the vending machine, the tables and chairs in those other little rooms, whatever they're for. Wall to wall prints. It'll be a nightmare trying to sort them out."

The provost listened to this catalog of surfaces which appeared to be covered with fingerprints and experienced a growing feeling of guilt. It wasn't his fault, of course, but it was clear that the custodian who was responsible for Wayne Hall had not done any dusting and polishing there for several days.

"I'll have to look into it," he said. "Our people should have cleaned here this week, but it sounds as if they didn't."

"I wouldn't worry about it," Sam said. "Unless it was cleaned late yesterday morning or midday, it wouldn't have helped us much. Anyway, like I said, we're looking for more than fingerprints."

And they hadn't found much of anything that looked as if it could shed light on the mystery of Harley Gerlach's death. The waste container in the bathroom contained most of what might or might not prove to be important evidence, and Sam was inclined to doubt that it was important. With the possible exception of the note. There were quite a few wadded up paper towels, a used maxi-pad wrapped up in toilet paper, a gum wrapper, a tiny battery from a hearing aid, and, perhaps most significantly, a crumpled piece of paper on which had been scrawled an unfinished note. The note contained no name, so it provided no information as to who had been writing it or for whom it was intended. It consisted of but six words:

How about Tuesday noon? We could

It was now Wednesday afternoon, so whoever had started to write the note was talking about the previous day, the day when Gerlach had been killed. Or was he? Maybe the reference was to some earlier Tuesday. But no, the custodial staff may have been lax, but it was doubtful that they had failed to clean in Wayne Hall in over a week.

Sam shook his head. What did he know? For all he knew, Brae Loch College was having problems with its staff. They might be on strike. He immediately rejected that thought. It was highly unlikely that they were even organized, more likely that they would be fired if they walked off the job.

He turned his attention to the other things in the waste container. It shouldn't be hard to find out if anyone in the opera company wore a hearing aid. Or chewed gum. And then there was the maxi-pad.

The provost had finally left to do whatever it was that provosts had to do, and Barrett had just stopped pounding out a poor rendition of chopsticks and was coming out of the piano room in the wing adjacent to the stage.

"Do you have a piano in your house?" he asked.

"No, why?"

"Or do you know anything about pianos?" Barrett obviously did not.

"Is something wrong with the piano?"

"I don't know. But it looks like they were going to do something to the one back there. There's a coil of piano wire on the floor over in the corner—at least that's what the label says it is. And there's some other stuff in there, probably things a piano tuner or repairman needs."

"Yeah, I noticed that. I know as much about pianos as you do, and I doubt if the sheriff knows much more. She can ask her friend Whitman about it. No big deal. It probably needed work and they just hadn't gotten around to doing it."

"I was just thinking about the guy that got killed. They said it was done with piano wire, and it seemed kinda strange that a coil of wire was handy, just lying around backstage here."

"It'll be easy to check that out. Why don't you stay here while I go up to the head shed and see what's up with the piano."

It took a little over half an hour for the deputy sheriff to find out why the murder weapon had been so conveniently located only a few yards from the bed where Harley Gerlach was strangled. The provost knew nothing about the piano wire, but his secretary put Sam in touch with the chairman of the school's small music department, who gave voice to what was apparently long-standing frustration over the condition of the piano in Wayne Hall.

"Don't get me started," was the way that Valerie Cubbins, the department chairman, responded to Sam's question. "That piano needs lots of work. I'm surprised that the opera people didn't complain about it. We had someone scheduled back in June, but you know how it is. One thing after another. He had an emergency appendicitis that set him back a few weeks, then it was cancelled appointments. Several of them. Promises, promises. I talked to him just the other day and he says he'll be here before Labor Day for sure. I'm not holding my breath."

"So the piano wire's been around for quite awhile?"

"Right. We ordered it back when we expected the work to be done in June. Why are you interested in the piano wire?"

Sam was surprised that she had not heard about its use as a garrote.

"I'm sorry. I didn't realize that you didn't know about the death of one of the opera people. It happened yesterday. He was strangled, and it was done with a length of that piano wire."

"Oh, my god, that's terrible," Cubbins said, sounding as if she meant it. "The word was out that somebody'd been killed, but I hadn't heard anything about strangulation. At Brae Loch! That's terrible."

Professor Cubbins made it sound as if a death by strangulation was especially terrible because it had occurred at her school. As Sam left to rejoin Officer Barrett back in Wayne Hall, he found himself wondering if the chairman of the music department might be sharing the provost's worry that this news might lead to enrollment problems for Brae Loch.

CHAPTER 13

His name was Francis Farris, but everyone who knew him called him Jeff. And he was Jeff because he reminded them of the Jimmy Stewart character L.B. Jeffries in Hitchcock's famous film *Rear Window*. Wheelchair bound since youth, his principal pleasure in life, much like Jeffries', came from observing his surroundings through a powerful telescope. He enjoyed observing the birds which frequented the area, but his favorite pastime was people watching, and the favorite people to watch were Harley Gerlach and the women who went into and out of his house.

On this particular morning, Jeff turned his telescope until it faced Gerlach's house nearly a hundred yards down the hillside from the small second-story balcony on which he was sitting. He adjusted the scope until it gave him a clear and close-up view of the back porch of his neighbor's home. The porch held a small stack of wood on one side and a fancy outdoor grill across from it beside a flight of steps which provided access to a detached garage and an expanse of yard dominated by several flowering shrubs the names of which Jeff did not know. Otherwise the porch was empty, which was not surprising inasmuch as the front porch on the other side of the house had a spectacular view of Crooked Lake. That was where Gerlach and his company would be sitting on pleasant evenings of the kind that the area had been enjoying for much of the month of August.

Jeff, like Gerlach, had a good view of the lake. Their homes occupied what was arguably the premier real estate on the lake. For decades the hill which bisected the lake, giving it its distinctive Y-shape, had had almost no homes or cottages other than those which crowded the shoreline. Except for a few small farms along its crest, the hill, or bluff as the locals called it, had remained a forested area, and most lake residents preferred it that way. But then some developer had moved in, cut down the trees on the sloping hillside at the end of the bluff, and erected a handful of large and widely spaced houses, each overlooking the lake from a vantage point high above the water. The owners of these mansions may not have had easy access to the water, but they shared a glorious vista, stretching south from their decks and porches toward Southport at the end of the lake.

Jeff Farris was not bothered by the fact that he couldn't easily use the lake for swimming and boating. What mattered to him was his telescope, and what better place was there for observing the world around him through that telescope than his balcony, so high above the lake. And above Harley Gerlach's house.

It was Wednesday afternoon, the day after Gerlach's murder, and Jeff was unaware that his neighbor had met his death by strangulation at Brae Loch College. But Gerlach almost never closed his garage doors, so Jeff was aware that his car was not in its accustomed place in his garage. Nor had it been there since early that morning. In fact, Jeff was fairly certain that the car had not been in the garage or on the blacktop apron in front of the garage since sometime before noon the previous day.

It wouldn't have been the first time that Gerlach had been away over night, but Jeff's interest in the missing car on this particular afternoon was stimulated by the fact that his neighbor had had two visitors within the last twenty-four hours. The first had arrived the previous afternoon, shortly after 1:30. It was a woman, and she arrived in a recent model black BMW bearing a New York license plate. He had recorded the number on the plate in a spiral notebook he kept for such purposes. The telescope had given him a good look at the woman. She appeared to be in her early fifties, although Jeff had to acknowledge that he was not very good at judging age. While she was not beautiful by any means, she was not unattractive. Her hair was showing some signs of grey, but she wore it in a becoming mannish fashion. A pair of designer jeans and a stylish white blouse added to the impression the BMW had made on Jeff: She was a woman of class and probably of means. He had a pretty good mental file of the women who had been visiting Gerlach, and he was quite sure he had never seen this one before.

He had watched her as she stood beside her car looking the house over. She made no effort to try the porch door, and eventually walked around the house, disappearing from Jeff's line of vision. After a few minutes, she reappeared. After considering the house for a moment, she finally tried the door. Finding it locked, she returned to her car and sat there for awhile, as if deciding what to do next. It was the better part of fifteen minutes after arriving that the woman started the engine, turned around in the driveway, and headed back toward the upper bluff road.

Jeff had not given a great deal of thought to the woman after she left, not, that is, until a second visitor arrived. That visitor had driven up that very morning, just before noon. This time it was a man, and it was a Cumberland County Sheriff's Department car that he stepped out of. Unlike the previous day's visitor, the officer went directly to the back door. He obviously had a key, because the door opened and he disappeared into the house.

Jeff's interest in his neighbor had been partly simply curiosity, that of someone whose handicap had turned him into something of a voyeur. But it also had something to do with the fact that most of Gerlach's visitors were women. His notebook included two that he had come to think of as regulars, plus a third who had been a regular about a year ago before she suddenly dropped out of sight. There had been two others, including one who was somewhat younger than the rest, but he had seen each of them only once. And then there had been the visitor the previous afternoon.

He had assumed, almost from the first, that these women were having affairs with Harley Gerlach, and he had marveled at the man's ability to juggle so many. Now, he thought, as he stared through his telescope at the open back porch door, perhaps Gerlach's juggling act had finally caught up with him. There might, of course, be other reasons why an officer of the law was paying him a visit. An officer who had a key to the house and had let himself in. But Jeff had a fertile imagination, and he had spent so much time spying on his neighbor and the women who came and went with such frequency, that he had created an imagined life for Gerlach that could not be dislodged by more mundane explanations for the presence of an officer of the law.

What, Jeff wondered, was the officer doing? Why had he not knocked? He hadn't behaved as officers of the law typically did on the TV shows Jeff watched. He had just marched straight into the house, letting himself in with a key which he must have gotten from the owner. So he had known that Gerlach was not at home. Perhaps there was some problem and Gerlach had needed help. Perhaps he had been in a car accident. But if that was the case, what was it that Gerlach or the police needed that was at the house?

Jeff Farris might have spent the rest of that day and perhaps several others speculating on this mystery unfolding some
hundred yards down the hill from where he sat in his wheelchair.
But he was destined to have his questions—or at least some of
them—answered much sooner. When the officer emerged from the
house, his eye caught a flash of bright light somewhere above him
on the hillside. The flash of light was due to the fact that the
telescope was so positioned that it reflected the sun's rays. The
officer, whose name was Jack Grieves and who was a member of
Sheriff Carol Kelleher's modest law enforcement staff, guessed
what it was that had temporarily blinded him, and determined to
pay a visit to the owner of the house further up the hill.

———

"Hello." Officer Grieves announced himself when the
door opened. "I'm from the sheriff's department, and I wonder if I
might ask you a few questions."

Farris acted surprised to see an officer of the law on his
doorstep, even though he had watched the man climb the hill with
the obvious intention of talking to him.

"Questions? Why, of course, but is something wrong?"

"Not where you're concerned, Mr.—I'm sorry, but I don't
know your name."

"Farris. Francis Farris. Come on in."

Jeff spun his chair around and led Grieves into the living
room, which was sparsely furnished and didn't look as if it was
much used.

"I couldn't help but notice," Grieves began, "that you
seem to have a telescope on that upstairs balcony of yours. Am I
right, there is a telescope up there?"

As he said it, it occurred to him that Farris would have a
problem making the trip up and down stairs. Perhaps he was not
the person who used the telescope, which prompted a second
question.

"You don't live here alone, do you?"

"Well now, that's two questions, isn't it? Answers are yes
and sometimes. I do have a telescope on the balcony. Great for
bird watching. It's a great hobby, especially when you spend your
time in a chair like I do. And I'm alone most of the time. I own
this place jointly with my brother, but he lives down in St. Thomas

most of the time, probably spends three months a year up here, something like that."

Farris smiled.

"I bet you thought I couldn't get myself up to the balcony, didn't you? Take a look back here," he said, wheeling his chair around a corner and beckoning Grieves to follow him. He pointed with obvious pride at an elevator in an adjacent room.

"This used to be a dining room, but I take my meals in the kitchen. I call this my launching pad. It whisks me up to my telescope any time I feel the urge to look around for orioles or whatever birds are in season."

Farris was clearly pleased with himself and with his hobby.

"Looks like a neat arrangement," Grieves said. "I was wondering if you ever do more than look for birds through that telescope of yours."

"Let me guess," Farris said. "You're interested in whether I might take a look at Mr. Gerlach's house from time to time. Is that it?"

"Yes, it is. You may not have heard, but your neighbor is dead. We're pretty sure he was murdered. Just yesterday, over at Brae Loch College. So I'm naturally interested in whether you might have seen anything recently that could help us in our investigation."

The news that Harley Gerlach had been killed came as a real shock to Jeff Farris. And it created a small moral dilemma for him. Should he, as a matter of civic duty, share information about Gerlach's habits with the officer? Or should he stay mum rather than divulge his not very admirable voyeuristic habit? He made a spur of the moment decision to try to have it both ways.

"No, it's like I said, Officer. I'm a bird watcher. That's why I keep the feeders full, all year round, and those little bottles of sugar water that attract the hummingbirds. But some things you can't help noticing. Like yesterday. Some woman came to see Mr. Gerlach. I just happened to get a glimpse of her when I was setting up my telescope. Other than that, I'm afraid I can't help you."

Grieves was obviously much more interested in the woman than the hummingbirds, and said so.

"Tell me about the woman. Do you remember when you saw her? What she looked like? What kind of car she was driving? How long she stayed?"

Of course Jeff knew the answers to all of these questions, but he chose to be vague.

"I wasn't really paying attention," he lied while trying to sound as if he regretted not being able to be of more help. "It was sometime after my lunch. I don't think she stuck around very long, but I didn't see her leave."

"The car? Did you recognize the make?"

"Sorry. It's quite a distance down to Mr. Gerlach's place, you know. It was a dark car, maybe blue or even black."

"So you didn't get a good look at the woman?"

"I really wish I could help, but the answer is no. I think she was wearing slacks, not a dress. Do you think this matters? Like maybe she had something to do with Mr. Gerlach's death?"

Frustrated in his quest for useful information, Grieves eventually suggested that they go up to the balcony so that he could take a look at the telescope. He let Farris show him how to adjust it, and after training it on a couple of the feeders he turned it so that it brought Harley Gerlach's house into view. It appeared to be only a very few yards away, everything clearly defined in the bright afternoon sun.

If only Mr. Farris had been paying attention to what was going on at the Gerlach house, he would have been able to provide precise answers to all of his questions. Officer Grieves was not happy about the report he would be making to the sheriff. Not only had he found nothing in Gerlach's house which told him anything about the victim's plans for the day he was murdered, but he also had been unable to obtain a good description of a woman who had paid a visit to Gerlach's house that day.

CHAPTER 14

Kevin pulled into the Brae Loch campus and found a parking spot not far from Menlo Hall. He dreaded the meeting with the provost, but told himself for at least the third time that morning that it was better to have it done with than to leave it hanging over his head.

Mrs. Melton welcomed him with what seemed like more enthusiasm than she had displayed on recent visits. Probably glad finally to have the opera people off the campus and out of her hair, he thought. She had managed to appear constantly harassed since they first met, and the added burden of dealing with the demands of Kevin and his company might well have rankled.

"Good morning," he said cheerily. "I have an appointment with Mr. Armitage, as I'm sure you know."

"Yes you do, and I cleared his calendar so he'd be ready for you. I'll let him know you're here."

She vanished into the inner sanctum, where she stayed longer than Kevin thought necessary to announce his arrival.

When she returned, she was wearing a broad smile. She waved him on in for his meeting with Armitage.

"Ah, good morning," the provost said, rising from his chair and extending his hand. "But then I suppose it's not really appropriate to call it a good morning, is it? Everything was going so well—at least I assume it was. And then this terrible business. How are you holding up?"

"I'm okay," Kevin replied. "Happy? No. But we'll pick up the pieces and go on."

"Go on? Are you thinking of going ahead with the production? I thought it wouldn't be possible. Not when you lost your leading man."

"That's not what I meant. You're right; it won't be possible to do the opera now. I knew that the minute we found Mr. Gerlach. If we were a professional opera company, we'd have a cover, someone ready to step in at a moment's notice. Not on Crooked Lake. No, it'd be way too complicated, not to mention the problem of rescheduling dates for the performances, dealing with ticket problems, things like that. It would be a nightmare, for me and for you. I'm afraid there won't be any *Gianni Schicchi* up here this summer."

The provost looked relieved that Professor Whitman's misadventure had come to an end.

"I'm sure you're terribly disappointed. So am I. It would have been a big event for us."

"I thought so, too, but I guess it just wasn't to be. I hope you don't lose any students because of this. Somebody said that some of your parents are worried. I can empathize. After 9/11, we had some anxious moments at Madison College—parents afraid that their sons and daughters could be vulnerable to terrorism down there. But we came through it okay. I'll bet you do, too. I can't imagine any crime wave on Crooked Lake, much less at Brae Loch."

"I hope you're right. There've been phone calls, questions. My response is to tell them it isn't about the college; it's about somebody we leased our auditorium to. Sorry to shift the blame to you, but we needed a scapegoat. Besides, it's true."

Armitage chuckled when he referred to Kevin as his scapegoat, then abruptly stopped when he saw that Kevin didn't find it particularly funny.

"Look, Professor Whitman, I really am sorry about what happened. No point in us spending our time exchanging regrets. Let's talk about money."

This was the reason Kevin had made the trip to the college, and this was the subject he dreaded. They had both assumed that the costs of the opera production would be largely borne by the college, and that those costs would be recouped by the sale of tickets to the two performances. Now there would be no performances, which left Kevin hoping that the college would simply assume responsibility for the costs and doubting very much that it would do so.

"Yes, there is the matter of money," he said. "I think we've been pretty frugal. It's been a bare-bones production. It's mostly about our use of your auditorium, and I was hoping that we might get a pass on that. What it leaves is mostly the printing of programs and tickets."

"We appreciate your frugality, but we run on a shoestring here at Brae Loch. I had my people come up with some figures, and it looks like we're talking about $2,800. Something like that. I had them shave the total a bit. We know the cancellation isn't your fault. I know this is awkward."

The provost paused, waiting for Kevin to say something. Kevin knew that the dollar figure he'd been given was ridiculously modest, that Armitage could have rented the auditorium for ten weeks for a much larger fee. But Kevin also knew all too well the state of his own finances. He could write the college the check, of course. But he wasn't happy with the way his great idea about bringing culture to Crooked Lake and creating an opportunity for a visiting appointment at Brae Loch College had worked out. No opera, no visiting appointment. And at a cost of $2,800.

"What you suggest is reasonable," he told the provost. Reasonable, he thought, but not what I wanted to hear. Oh well, at least the provost had temporarily abandoned his fascination with crime and had not once seemed morbidly curious about Harley Gerlach's death and the search for his killer.

CHAPTER 15

When Kevin walked into the cottage after his discouraging meeting with the provost at Brae Loch, the phone was ringing. He hoped it was Carol, whom he had not heard from since the day after Gerlach's death. It wasn't.

"Professor Whitman? It's Mercedes Redman."

"Hi. Calling to commiserate over the demise of *Gianni Schicchi*?"

"No, and then maybe yes. Do you have any time in your schedule to talk with me? Or perhaps I should say to let me talk to you? Even this afternoon?"

Kevin's 'second in command' over the course of rehearsals for the opera that never made it to opening night was the last person he might have expected to call. She had been, in his opinion, all business, and not someone likely to be broken up either by Gerlach's murder or the eleventh-hour collapse of Crooked Lake's abbreviated opera season. But Kevin had not really known her well, and he may have been mistaken.

They agreed on four o'clock, which would give her plenty of time to make the drive from Ithaca. It also gave Kevin time to straighten up the cottage and prepare a pitcher of iced tea. He gave a minute of thought to what music he might have playing on the Bose when she arrived, but decided against it. After all, he wasn't seeking to impress the woman.

Mercedes drove up in a very old car that Kevin was unable to recognize. A Studebaker? He wondered if she had trouble getting it serviced. As she climbed out of the driver's seat, she favored him with what could at best be described as a tentative smile. It looked as if whatever she wanted to talk about might be unpleasant.

"Thanks for seeing me. I know you must be busy, what with having to pick up the pieces after Harley's death. Any news on that front?"

"Not yet," Kevin said. He had been involved in two of the sheriff's investigations of other than natural deaths, and he was well aware that it would almost certainly take some time before this case could be closed. If it could be closed. For some reason he could not explain, he had begun to have doubts about solving this one.

Mercedes Redman had not been inside the cottage since her tryout back in the spring. Nor had they been particularly close over the course of the summer, this in spite of the fact that she had been his de facto partner in whipping the little opera company into shape. As they walked through the cottage, Kevin found himself observing her, trying to figure out just who she really was. Other than a very good violinist.

She accepted his offer of tea, and they took seats on the deck where they had a good view of the late afternoon sunlight on the bluff.

Kevin felt no need to press her for an explanation of her unexpected visit to his cottage. She would tell him why she had come in her own good time. They chatted for a few minutes, touching on the view, how sorry she was that they wouldn't be staging the opera, her pleasure in the progress one of her better students was making, and her regret that she probably wouldn't be seeing more of Heather Merriman, of whom she had become quite fond.

"But it's Harley I want to tell you about," she said finally. "You know that I found him difficult. Actually, I thought he was a pain in the ass. Critical of everyone, always trying to upstage his colleagues. And unreliable, what with his drinking. But I thought you ought to know that I'd gotten to know a different Harley over the last few weeks. I didn't say anything about this when the deputy sheriff questioned me the other night over at Brae Loch. In fact I lied to him about how well I knew Harley. And I've been worrying about it, because I'm sure it will come out one of these days and then I'll be in trouble. So I thought it would be a good idea to talk with you and see what you think I should do."

Kevin had no idea where this was going, but he assured her that he would listen with an open mind. He hoped that he was not about to be put in some kind of compromising position by Mercedes Redman.

"I think I should begin at the beginning," she began. "About three weeks ago, Harley stopped to have a few words with me after rehearsal one night. He didn't sound drunk, and for a change he was pleasant. He said something about what a good job he thought I was doing. I'd been given lemons, he told me, and had been smart enough to make lemonade. I wasn't sure the cliché was really a compliment, but I decided to go along. Well, we chatted for a minute or two and then he asked if I would join him for a cup of coffee. To say I was surprised would be a very big understatement. Anyway, I declined—politely, I think—and figured that was the end of it."

"But it wasn't the end of it, is that what you're telling me?" Kevin asked.

"Right. In fact he made the same offer after the next rehearsal. This time I didn't have an urgent need to get home, and I didn't want to appear needlessly rude. So I agreed. We stopped off at a place in Southport that was still open. We talked about a lot of things, and to my surprise he turned out to be a good listener. The conversation never got personal, if you know what I mean. But he asked about my life as a teacher of violin, where I'd gotten my music education, how I liked living here in the Finger Lakes, that kind of thing. He didn't tell me much about himself other than saying how important opera was to him. Opera and painting. Did you know he was a painter?"

"I only heard about it after his death. The sheriff mentioned that somebody she was talking to had seen some of his work."

"Well, as I was saying, we talked. Just talked, for maybe 45 minutes. Then I said good night and took off. Fini. Or so I thought. It was early the next week when Harley suggested coffee again. It was the same routine—same place, same kind of conversation. And again, nothing really personal. He never even asked me if I was married or had kids. I chose to reciprocate and not ask him about family. By the time I left him that night I knew almost nothing about his personal life, but quite a bit about his interests. And I knew I'd been too quick to judge him. Of course I couldn't forget how obnoxious he'd been on the stage, but there was obviously another side to the man. A real Jekyll and Hyde."

"I suppose there are two sides, maybe more, to all of us. But I wouldn't have guessed it about Gerlach."

"Neither would I. Anyway, my story doesn't end there, and it's what I'm going to tell you now that has me worried. The sheriff isn't going to be happy with me. I'm sure she's going to suspect that there's more to my relationship with our Gianni Schicchi than there is. And I can't say as I'd blame her."

Kevin listened with a sad feeling that he knew what was coming next. No, he thought, not Redman, too.

"I met him after rehearsal one more time. It was only a few days before he was killed. This time it wasn't coffee. No, come to think of it, it was. But it wasn't in Southport; it was at his house up on the hill above the lake. He said he thought I might be interested in seeing his art. And some opera memorabilia. It sounded okay, just an extension of the conversation we'd been having, a chance to see some of the things we'd been talking about."

Mercedes paused, taking her eyes off the sunlit bluff across the lake and looking at Kevin.

"I know what you're thinking, and it's what the sheriff will be thinking, too. But nothing happened. He was a perfect gentleman. Never even hinted that we might do anything but talk and admire the house. And it's a fascinating place. Full of some really good prints and his own watercolors. Not to mention some neat posters from his days at the Metropolitan. And photographs. He's a photographer, too, and a good one. It sounds funny, my saying so, but I had a really good time that evening."

Kevin was both relieved and worried when Mercedes came to the end of her story. She had not, if he were to believe her, become another of Gerlach's conquests. Yet he did not know and probably would never know whether her story was true. The only person who might have told a different story about that evening at the house on the bluff was now dead. Kevin also knew that he would have to pass this information on to Carol. Mercedes would not have confided in him if she hadn't expected him to tell the sheriff what he had heard. And do so in a way that would be supportive of her story.

Mercedes was changing the subject, but Kevin hardly heard her. He was feeling uncomfortable about what he would have to do, what Redman wanted him to do. And why had she shared this tale of a non-affair with Harley Gerlach anyway? No one need ever have known.

CHAPTER 16

Mercedes Redman had taken her leave, and Kevin was about to give Carol a call to see if they might get together for dinner when he heard someone knocking at the back door. He cursed quietly under his breath.

The man at the door was Paolo Rosetti.

"Paolo!" he said, his voice registering the surprise he felt at the sight of the man who had wanted the part that went to Harley Gerlach. "How are you? Forgive me if I sound surprised, but I am. Surprised, that is."

"I should have called first," Rosetti said, "but I was on my way back from Southport, and it's better to talk with you in person than on the phone, yes? Is this a good time? I mean, you don't have company, do you?"

"No, no. It's okay. Come on in."

Kevin was not in the mood to talk with Rosetti, and he was almost instantly worried that it would be hard to get rid of him.

"I'm sorry," he said, "but I was just about to make an important phone call. Why don't you make yourself comfortable. Deck or living room, it's up to you. Let me make that call, and I'll be with you in a moment."

He watched Rosetti take a seat on the deck and then went into his study and dialed the sheriff's office.

She sounded harassed, and he was afraid that she would beg off dinner. But whether it was because she had really missed his company or because she needed to discuss some development in the Gerlach case, she agreed to meet him. There wasn't time to whip up a decent meal, especially with Rosetti making himself comfortable on the deck, so they decided on The Cedar Post at seven.

"Can I get you a beer?" Kevin asked his visitor. He'd have preferred not to make the offer, but common courtesy prevailed. And Rosetti, of course, said yes.

"Well, now, what brings you here today?" he asked after handing Rosetti his beer.

"The opera, Professor. The opera. I haven't heard from you about our plans. I'm sure it's been taking you some time to make the necessary arrangements with the college. But I have to know when we're doing it, when we'll be getting back to rehearsals. It won't be too hard, but it'll take a bit of work, don't you think?"

Kevin stared at the man. Had he lost his mind? Could he really believe that the opera would go on as planned if a few days late?

He started to say what had to be said to disabuse Rosetti of the idea that the 'Brae Loch Opera Company' still had a future. But Paolo was just getting warmed up.

"I know just how we do it. Do you want to hear my plan?"

"But Paolo, we—"

Rosetti plunged ahead, ignoring whatever it was that Kevin wanted to say.

"I'll be your Schicchi. You know I can do the role. I know it by heart. Mr. Goldman takes over my role as Simone, and we're all set. Right?"

Even though he knew that none of this was going to happen, period, Kevin found himself poking holes in Rosetti's idea.

"So Goldman takes your part. Then who takes Goldman's part? Who sings Betto? And if someone else does Betto, who will sing his part? You know, Paolo, we don't have enough people."

"No problem. We double up. Somebody sings two roles. Who's to know? They're small parts, easy to learn. What matters is Schicchi, and here I am."

Kevin felt a headache coming on. Paolo Rosetti was looking at Harley Gerlach's death as his golden opportunity. He was going to get the leading role he thought he should have had from the beginning of the casting process. Everything else was incidental. All Kevin had to do was shuffle roles, tell the provost to change the dates, and hope that there was no one in the audience who would know that what he was doing was not exactly what Puccini had had in mind.

"I wish it were that simple, Paolo. I really do. I had high hopes for this production. You know that. And we've worked hard at it. You and everyone else. But we can't just dismiss the murder of our leading man as an inconvenience to be overcome, can we? I mean, things have changed. For the college, for all of us. There's a criminal investigation going on, and it takes precedence over the opera. They're trying to find out what happened to Harley, and here we are arguing that the show must go on."

"Please, Professor, I feel badly for Mr. Gerlach, just like you do. It was a terrible thing, him getting killed like that. Why not turn our opera into a kind of memorial to Mr. Gerlach?"

It was apparent that the idea had just occurred to Rosetti. He was visibly excited.

"That's what we'll do! It'll be a memorial service. An opera as a memorial service! What a great idea. The programs can even be dedicated to him. To Harley Gerlach, in Memoriam— that's what they'll say."

Kevin listened in disbelief. Paolo Rosetti, who would have no interest in drawing attention away from his own performance as Gianni Schicchi, was proposing to pay tribute to the man who had been scheduled to sing that role.

"That's a very thoughtful gesture, Paolo, but we just can't do it. I've already notified the college that the opera has been cancelled. The provost would probably have cancelled it anyway. I just saved him the unpleasant duty of telling me that there wouldn't be any opera at Brae Loch this summer."

But Rosetti wasn't about to give up so easily.

"Professor," he began, using the title Kevin had tried so hard to persuade the company not to use. "It isn't too late. Think of all the hours we've spent on it. *Gianni Schicchi* would be the biggest thing to happen to Crooked Lake since the flood of 1972. If you like, I can go with you and explain to the people at the college that we have to do it. I'm sure they'd understand."

This was a conversation—an argument, really—that had to come to an end. There would be no opera, and if Rosetti was determined to be in a funk about it, that was his problem.

"I suppose we could kick this around for the rest of the afternoon," Kevin said, "but the decision has been made. I know you're disappointed. So am I. But it's over. So let's try to forget it, and in the meanwhile hope that the sheriff nails whoever killed Harley—and put an end to the opera by doing so."

Kevin quickly changed the subject before Rosetti could think of some other way to keep his dream alive.

"We all need a break. The sheriff says you took time off the other afternoon to go fishing. Not a bad idea. Maybe we all should go fishing. Put the opera business behind us."

He had not even thought of it as a way to test Rosetti's claim that he had spent the afternoon of Gerlach's murder fishing. It was just something that had come to mind as he tried to bring the discussion of *Gianni Schicchi* to an end. But Paolo didn't say a word, and the shadow that came over his face made it clearer than words that he was not about to discuss fishing.

Two minutes later he was gone. There was still a chill in the air.

    ————

It was 7:30 and Carol was toying with her salad as she recounted what she and her staff had been doing.

"It's been mostly about checking up on what your people were up to that afternoon. Most of their stories sounded straightforward. But I couldn't just take them at their word. It's not easy. You don't want to start asking family and neighbors whether so and so was where he says he was. That gives the impression that you think they're lying, or shading the truth, when we have no reason to believe that they are. Anyway, it's delicate work. Takes diplomacy."

"So have you learned anything? Anybody give you a phony story?"

"I can't be sure, but I don't think so. One of the members of the orchestra—name's June Neary—said she'd remembered doing something she hadn't mentioned to Bridges. But it doesn't sound important. So no, things look pretty much as they did when we left Brae Loch the night of the murder."

"Then I guess I'm the one who's got news. I've had two interesting conversations that I think you'll want to hear about. Especially one with Mercedes Redman. It doesn't have anything to do with what she was doing or where on Tuesday afternoon. But it's important. At least I think it is."

"Redman? Your second in command?"

"Right. She drove over from Ithaca to see me today. I was surprised to hear from her, but she made it sound as if she had to talk with me, and not over the phone. To make a long story short, she told me that she had been into some kind of relationship with Gerlach and that she hadn't told you about it."

"No she didn't," Carol said, sounding as if this might indeed be important news.

"Without ever saying so, she seemed to want me to be the one to tell you about it. You know, she was confiding in me as a colleague, which I guess was easier than confessing to you that she had lied about how well she knew Gerlach."

Carol shook her head.

"Another notch in Gerlach's belt, is it? First Myers, then Mrs. Conklin, now Redman. I hope we don't find he'd also been bedding that young Merriman girl."

"It's not like that," Kevin said. "At least that's not what Mercedes told me. The way she tells it, they just talked, drank coffee, got to know each other better. Oh, and he invited her up to his house to see his etchings. Sorry. All kidding aside, she said he seemed like a nice guy, not at all the boor and the drunk he was at rehearsals. She was very complimentary of his talents, not just as a musician, but as a painter and photographer, too. Her picture of him doesn't match mine, but I don't think she's someone who'd be easily fooled. Unless, that is, she's still lying. That they really were having an affair."

"I wouldn't discount that possibility," Carol said. "But why would she unburden herself to you like that?"

"Probably because she figured that someone knew and that somehow the fact that she had spent time with him would come out. It's called preemption."

"But what does this relationship—whether it's romantic or platonic—have to do with Gerlach's death?"

"Who knows. I guess that's for you to find out. Or us. After all, I created the situation where Gerlach and these other people in his life all came together, so I ought to be involved in trying to untangle things. Agreed?"

"I don't think it would matter if I didn't agree, Kevin. You couldn't stay out of this investigation even if you wanted to, and you don't want to. Besides, you know these people better than I do. I'll welcome your help."

Kevin reached across the table and took Carol's hand.

"Now that that's settled, let me tell you about my other visit from a member of the *Gianni Schicchi* cast. It was Rosetti, and he dropped by not long after Mercedes had left. It was a busy day at the cottage. Anyway, he came to argue the case for going ahead with the opera. The way he saw it, it would be no big problem. He'd take over Gerlach's role, we'd shuffle a couple of parts, and voilà, the show would go on. And believe me, he was tenacious. I had to tell him that I'd already made my decision and notified the college. He was not in a good mood when he left."

"Sounds like a lot of chutzpa to me," Carol said. "Did he really think he could step into another role in the opera at the last minute, just like that?"

"Rosetti doesn't lack for self-confidence. And the truth of the matter is, I think he could have done it. I'd bet he knows the part, and he'd told me from the beginning that he should have been my Gianni Schicchi. If he's a suspect in Gerlach's murder, it'd probably be because eliminating Harley would let him take over the lead and be the star of the production."

"That doesn't sound like a very realistic motive," Carol said. "More like the plot of an old Hollywood movie or Broadway musical—the leading lady can't go on and the understudy gets her big chance and becomes an overnight star."

"I know, but you don't really know Paolo."

Nor do I, Kevin said to himself. In fact, I don't really know any of the people I recruited for my opera.

CHAPTER 17

The last thing they had discussed over dinner at The Cedar Post the night before had been Officer Grieves report on his trip to Gerlach's house on the bluff and his conversation with the neighbor with the telescope. Grieves had only been looking for evidence of Gerlach's plans for the day he was killed, and Carol had decided that a more thorough search of the house was in order. She hadn't been sure just what she would be looking for, but there might be something that would shed more light on why somebody wanted him dead. While she was at it, she'd pay Mr. Farris, the voyeuristic neighbor, a visit. And she'd take Kevin with her. Given his greater familiarity with Gerlach, he might spot something the importance of which would escape her.

Carol was to have picked Kevin up at nine, but as it turned out, they had to postpone the trip for a few hours. The reason was that Doc Crawford, Cumberland County's medical examiner, called Carol—got her out of bed at an early hour in fact—to tell her that he'd completed the autopsy on Gerlach. Her initial reaction was to defer a meeting with him until afternoon. After all, it had been clear that Gerlach had been strangled to death, and the time of death was not in much doubt. But the medical examiner had been insistent that they get together right away, so she called Kevin and rescheduled their trip to the bluff for after lunch.

Doc Crawford confirmed what she had assumed: strangulation was indeed the cause of Gerlach's death. This laid to rest the possibility that it was something else that had done him in, with the piano wire, a red herring, wrapped around his neck only after he was dead. And he had died, as the paramedic had suggested, sometime after two o'clock in the afternoon of the scheduled dress rehearsal.

The reason Crawford had wanted to see the sheriff earlier than later that day had more to do with his own schedule than with any surprise findings from the autopsy. But he did want her to know what Gerlach had had for lunch on the day he died, just in case that information might tell her where he had eaten. She doubted that it was important, but made a note of the fact that it had been spaghetti and meatballs. Moreover, he had washed it down with lots of alcohol, enough in fact that he would have been drunk or close to it when he crawled into the bed on the stage of Wayne Hall.

When Carol picked Kevin up at the cottage for the trip over to Gerlach's place on the bluff, she was no longer thinking about the autopsy report. It had told her nothing she didn't already know, except that he apparently liked Italian food. Paolo Rosetti would have been pleased with his rival's choice for his final meal.

———

It was a grey day, but the rain which had been forecast had not yet started to fall. The drive along the crest of the bluff was pleasant in spite of the overcast skies, and they talked more about their love of the lake and its lightly used back roads than they did about the case they were investigating.

The garage and the parking apron behind the house were empty. Carol preceded Kevin up the back porch steps, being careful not to look too interested in the house which sat about one hundred yards further up the hill. She assumed that Mr. Farris was observing them, or would be shortly when he realized that a police car had pulled into the drive. She would deal with Farris later.

Neither Carol nor Kevin had given a great deal of thought to just what it was that they expected, but the sight that greeted them when they entered the house was impressive by any standard. The mudroom through which they entered led into a modern kitchen, complete with a central island and a long breakfast bar with three stools. Beyond the bar, and in full view from the kitchen, was a spacious living room, the walls of which were covered almost to the ceiling with paintings and photographs. This gallery ran all the way around the room except for a fieldstone fireplace and a wall-length picture window through which they could see the lake far below.

They spent the next few minutes orienting themselves. A room which had obviously been Gerlach's study and music room contained a grand piano, an oversized teak desk, and a comfortable-looking leather chair which appeared almost large enough to seat two people. Unlike the living room, its walls were decorated with posters and artfully framed playbills, all attesting to Gerlach's background and interest in opera. Next to the big chair stood a floor-to-ceiling bookcase. Kevin studied the titles of the books and concluded that with but a few exceptions they all were about music and primarily about opera.

While Kevin was admiring Gerlach's library, Carol disappeared into his bedroom. It, too, had a large picture window overlooking the lake, and the art on the walls, like that which had greeted them in the living room, consisted mostly of vivid watercolor paintings. Each of them carried the artist's name, printed in bold letters in the lower right-hand corner. The name, of course, was that of Harley Gerlach. While the subject matter of these paintings varied somewhat, the majority were landscape scenes with lots of blue water and seasonal foliage that ranged from the bright greens of late spring to the fiery reds and golds of autumn. His range may have been narrow, but he really had talent, Carol thought.

But what interested her most about the room was the fact that it looked much larger than it was. And the reason for this illusion was that the ceiling was mirrored from wall to wall. The result was that the number of Gerlach's paintings on the walls appeared to have doubled. More importantly, and this must have been Gerlach's purpose, the occupant of the room's four-poster bed would have a strikingly dramatic view of himself—and of his partner, if he were sharing the bed. Carol had heard enough about Gerlach to assume that he had frequently shared the bed. She wondered if any members of the Brae Loch opera company had been among those he had entertained beneath that mirrored ceiling.

Ten minutes and six rooms later, Carol and Kevin found themselves back in the living room, exchanging impressions of the late Harley Gerlach's house. They had made no attempt to search for anything, and were not even sure what they might be searching for. But the time had come to do more than admire the view, the art, and the other furnishings.

"How do you want to do this?" Kevin asked.

"I suppose we need to go through his effects, anything that might give us a clue as to his extracurricular activities. Who, when, where—that sort of thing. But first, I'm going to tackle the kitchen. Doc Crawford says the autopsy showed that he'd just eaten a lunch of spaghetti and meatballs. I'd like to find out if he had lunch here or if he ate out. Shouldn't be hard to get an answer to that question. Why don't you start with the study."

"Okay. Just let me take a look at these pictures first."

Kevin was peering at a row of photographs that, unlike most of the others in the living room, were of people rather than landscapes.

"Guess I was wrong about that," he said, straightening up. "I thought some of my opera people might have had their pictures taken with Harley, but if they did, those pictures aren't here. I'll check out his darkroom before we leave."

Carol went into the kitchen to look for evidence that Gerlach had had a lunch of spaghetti and meatballs on Tuesday. Kevin went into the study to look for—what? He hoped he'd recognize whatever it was if he found it.

He was still rummaging through the desk drawers when Carol reappeared.

"I'm ninety-nine per cent certain that he ate his lunch out someplace. The breakfast dishes are still in the sink, and there's no sign of anything that looks like spaghetti or meatballs anywhere—on the counters, in the wastebasket, in the fridge. Which means we're going to have to draw up a list of places in the area of the lake that serve lunch on Tuesday, find out if any of them served what he had for lunch, and see if their staff can remember him being there."

"Why is it so important?"

"Probably isn't. But it's just possible that we can recreate his schedule for Tuesday if we know where he ate and how long he was there. Maybe identify people who saw him."

She came over to the desk and looked down at the pile of files Kevin had pulled out of the drawers.

"Find anything yet?"

"Come on, Carol. I've only been at this for five minutes. Here, why don't you start on the files. I want to go through the bookcase. You want to know where he was for lunch on Tuesday, and I want to see if there's anything that can tell us what he's been up to over the last few months, even years. And with who."

"With whom, Kevin. Whom. You're the teacher, remember."

Kevin gave her a wry smile and handed her a batch of files.

For nearly a quarter of an hour, Kevin perused the shelves of the big bookcase, intrigued by the impressive collection of volumes in the field he had shared with Gerlach. He was briefly considering borrowing a couple of the books when he came upon

91

what looked like a scrapbook, wedged between a pair of treatises on baroque opera.

It was a scrapbook, and it contained photos, neatly mounted and labeled. The photos were all of women, most of them with Harley beside them. Some had been taken elsewhere, in places and at dates not identified in the labels. In fact none of the pictures bore dates. But four of them were relatively recent because they had been taken in the house on the bluff, the house Gerlach had lived in for only a few years, the house Carol and he were searching at that very moment.

There were only thirteen photos in the scrapbook, one to a page, which left most of the album empty, still waiting for the women who would grace its pages. Kevin quickly skimmed through the album. The last picture was of a woman he knew. It was Mercedes Redman. She was seated on the couch in the living room, her hands folded in her lap, smiling at the camera. She was wearing a pant suit which Kevin had seen her in on several occasions over the summer. She looked at ease, her smile a natural one. Beneath the picture was a single word, written in black ink and bold letters: Mercedes.

"Carol," he said as he walked over to the desk. "Look at this."

She quickly skimmed the pages of the album.

"Gerlach's harem, right?"

"That's what it looks like. But I can't be sure. The only one I recognize is Redman."

"Redman and Myers. Look here at the first page. Isn't that Gerlach's ex-wife?"

Kevin studied the picture of a brunette, probably in her thirties, standing next to a fireplace, her arm draped across the mantle. The setting was not one he recognized, but the woman, on closer examination, did look vaguely familiar.

"You think that's Myers?"

"I do," Carol said. "She's older now, of course, wears her hair differently, but I'm pretty sure she's the ex-wife, the one who's living in Southport and was a member of your cast."

"It makes sense, I suppose. If this is an album of Gerlach's conquests, she'd be in it. Unless it's just his extramarital conquests. But why are we assuming these are the women he's had affairs with? There might be another explanation for the scrapbook. When Redman told me about seeing Gerlach, she made it very clear that there was no affair. If we're to believe her, they never went to bed together."

"Why should we believe her? It looks to me as if Gerlach's scrapbook tells a different story. It's a case of she said, he said. Anyway, I can't see why he'd create a scrapbook like this unless it was to keep a record of the women he'd seduced. It's too selective, too chronological. Here's Myers, the first of thirteen, which she might well have been. And Redman's the last, and that sounds right because they only met this summer. I'll make you a bet that back there on page two or three is the woman Gerlach was involved with when he was married to Myers. The cause of their divorce."

It does make sense, Kevin thought. And if Carol is right, then there's another woman in the album we should be thinking about.

"I think I told you about the conversation I overheard one evening at rehearsal. Between Myers and Conklin. Conklin made it clear that it was Gerlach who had destroyed his marriage by taking up with his wife. And her name is Helen. Or was Helen. She apparently died not that long ago—confessed to her affair with Gerlach before she died."

Kevin turned to page ten of the album and pointed to the picture of a slender blonde who was posed in almost exactly the same place as Mercedes Redman was for her picture. Beneath the photo was the woman's given name: Helen.

———

A little over an hour later, Carol and Kevin had completed their search of the house. It had turned up nothing more of interest—nothing in the study, nothing in the master bedroom, nothing in the darkroom. Except for the breakfast dishes in the kitchen sink, the house was in immaculate condition, much as if it were ready for a real estate agent's walk through with a prospective buyer.

Carol had been struck by the absence of a computer. It appeared that Gerlach had been something of a Luddite, unwilling to adapt to technological change. While there were a few CDs in a cabinet in the living room, most of his record collection was on an earlier generation of LPs. And there was a turntable to play them on. But the absence of a computer simplified their search for clues of the life Gerlach had led. There would be no undeleted e-mail correspondence, no electronic evidence of whom he talked to, what was on his mind, what he had been doing.

"I'm going up the hill to talk with Francis Farris," Carol announced. "Grieves thinks he knows more about what Gerlach has been doing than he lets on. I think I should see him alone. He'd only wonder about you being with me, and I don't want to have to explain. So why don't you stay here, give me a chance to question him."

If Kevin was disappointed that Carol wanted to see Farris by herself, he didn't show it.

"No problem," he assured her. "I'd like to look over Harley's books. It's a collection to die for."

So Kevin selected a book he hadn't heard of on the contribution to opera of Hector Berlioz and took a seat in the huge chair in the study. Carol set off from Gerlach's house to talk with Francis 'Jeff' Farris, who at that moment was on his balcony watching her through his telescope as she climbed the hill.

CHAPTER 18

"Mr. Farris?" the sheriff called through the screen door. She had knocked several times, but no one had answered or appeared at the door. She knew he was at home, having seen him on the balcony as she walked up the path from Gerlach's. Grieves had told her about the elevator, so she knew that coming down from the upper floor would not pose a problem. What was Farris doing? Was he trying to avoid her? He had surely seen her, much as she had seen him. Perhaps he had decided that he didn't want to talk to an officer of the law. But why would he be reluctant to talk with her?

Carol decided that she should be a bit bolder. She pushed the screen door open and walked into the house, calling out his name again as she did so. It was then that she heard a humming sound from somewhere ahead of her in the house. The elevator, she thought, and momentarily she heard the clang of its door opening. A few seconds later, Jeff Farris wheeled himself around the corner into the kitchen.

"Did I keep you waiting?" he asked.

"No," Carol said, choosing to be pleasant. "I just thought maybe something was wrong."

"No, no. I just don't get around that fast."

Farris did not elaborate, and Carol wasn't interested in having a discussion about it.

"I'm Sheriff Kelleher," she said, "and you're Francis Farris. My colleague spoke to you the other day, and I thought it would be a good idea to come around and introduce myself. I think Officer Grieves told you why we are here. Your neighbor, Harley Gerlach, died on Tuesday. It happened over at Brae Loch College where he was rehearsing for a program they were putting on. Unfortunately, he didn't die from natural causes and it wasn't an accident. Somebody killed him, and we're trying to find the person who did it."

"You surely can't think it was me," Farris protested. No expression of shock over the loss of a neighbor, just a protestation of innocence.

"No, Mr. Farris, I'm sure it wasn't you who killed him. But we need information, and he doesn't seem to have any family or relatives upstate. So I'm asking around, trying to find out who knew him, who can tell us something about the people in his life. You seem to be his closest neighbor, so I thought maybe you could help us."

"I wish I could, but I'm afraid we haven't seen much of each other. I've never been in his house, and he's never been in mine. Not very neighborly, I'll admit. But I don't get around very well, and—well, it just didn't work out."

"I understand. But I'm sure you can see his place very clearly from up here. I wonder if you can tell me anything about the people who've visited him, let's say recently, this summer."

"I suppose your colleague told you about my telescope. But I'm not nosy. Like I told the officer, I use the scope for birding. Wonderful habit. You should give it a try."

"I might do that if I can find the time," Carol said. "Look, I'm not being critical of you. But I can't believe you haven't observed Mr. Gerlach's house, people coming and going. I know I would have. It's the natural thing to do."

Carol decided that she didn't want to dance around the issue of Mr. Farris's respect for his neighbor's privacy.

"Let me put it this way. I'm investigating a murder. I need all the information I can get, and I think you're in a position to give me information. I can't believe you haven't seen things down there at the Gerlach house. I want you to tell me about them. I don't want you to try to decide what's important and what isn't. I'll make that decision. So let's go up to your balcony, and then you can tell me what you've seen—make that whom you've seen—and when."

Carol walked quickly over to the elevator, leaving Farris to follow.

"Nice view, just like I thought it would be," she said as they reached the balcony. She didn't need to wait for Farris to train the telescope on Gerlach's place. It was already pointing directly at it, and the grill on the back porch she saw as she looked through the scope was so close it looked as if she could reach out and touch it.

"Perfect. You could see whether Mr. Gerlach needed a shave, couldn't you? Or whether a female visitor was wearing a ring? Right?"

"I guess so," was the weak reply.

"Now, when was the last time you observed someone coming to visit Mr. Gerlach?"

"It was Tuesday," he said, having made the decision to cooperate with the sheriff.

"And what can you tell me about this visitor?"

Grieves had already told the sheriff that it had been a woman and that she had been driving a dark car. Carol was confident that Farris could flesh out this unsatisfactorily vague description.

"It was a woman, middle aged, well dressed."

"What do you mean by middle aged? Forties? Fifties? Sixties?"

"Well, I've got a sister who's in her early fifties. I'd say this woman was around that age, maybe 55 at the most. That's a guess, you know."

"Okay. And you say well dressed. What was she wearing?"

"Jeans and a white blouse. They looked like good quality clothes. In fact, she looked like someone who had an eye for fashion, you know, one of those women who always dresses smart."

"Hair?"

"Graying just a bit. But neat. And cut fairly short."

"Did you notice anything else about her?"

"Only what she drove up in. It was a black BMW. Here, I've got the license number written down."

Farris turned around until he could reach a small rustic Adirondack table next to the railing. He pushed aside a bird guide and picked up a small spiral notebook.

"Here it is," he said, and read off the number he'd seen on the New York license plate.

"Let me have a look at that," Carol said, as she took the notebook out of Farris's hands.

"Hey, you can't do that, it's private." Farris had only reluctantly agreed to cooperate with the sheriff, and he was now making clear his opinion that she had gone too far.

"Oh, I think I can, Mr. Farris. You surely don't want me to charge you with obstruction of justice. As far as I know, you haven't done anything illegal, but that could all change if you don't cooperate with my investigation of Mr. Gerlach's death. Do you understand?"

A very unhappy Francis Farris nodded that he did.

"You seem to have a lot of potentially useful information in this notebook," Carol said as she leafed through it. "You should be pleased to be able to help us law enforcement types."

Farris lapsed into a sullen silence while the sheriff studied the notebook.

"Now this is interesting," Carol announced. "The last entry before the one about the lady in the BMW was made on August 10th. You say Gerlach and a woman drove up—two separate cars—around 8:30 in the evening. That the woman was driving an old Studebaker. That they went into the house and stayed there for about an hour, when the woman left by herself. There's not much here about the woman. Do you want to add to what you wrote that night?"

"As I remember, the light wasn't so good. She was kinda short, and she wasn't dressed upscale like the one this Tuesday. I guess you'd say she was pretty average."

"Less attractive than Mr. Gerlach's other visitors?"

Farris looked puzzled, as if the question was one he hadn't considered before.

"I'm not sure. None of the women I've seen down there are what you'd call lookers. Too old, for one thing."

The neighborhood voyeur seemed to be of the school that thought middle-aged men should be looking for young trophy wives. Carol chose not to comment.

She briefly studied the entries on the other women who had visited Gerlach since Farris had taken to spying on his neighbor. There were only four in all, which probably meant either that the telescope was a relatively new toy or that Gerlach's sex life on Crooked Lake had had its fallow periods.

Of the other women mentioned in the notebook, only one had made an appearance in Gerlach's driveway in the last five months. The others, each of whom had been a visitor on several occasions, had, for whatever reason, disappeared from his life some time ago and well before the ill-fated attempt to stage *Gianni Schicchi*. It was possible, but not very likely, that one of them had borne a grudge against Gerlach that led ultimately to his death by strangulation at Brae Loch College just a few days earlier. Carol knew, however, that she would have to track down and question all of the women Farris had briefly described in his notebook.

After thanking him for his help and assuring him that she would be in touch again soon, Carol headed back down the path to where Kevin would be waiting, pondering what she had learned. It would be no easy task to locate some of the women who had been visiting Gerlach. All she had to go on were Farris's sketchy and possibly unreliable notes on their appearance and the cars they were driving. But one car held out more promise as a lead, even if Farris had not recorded the number on its license plate. He had, however, identified it as a Studebaker. Not many of them around, Carol thought. I'll put Bridges on it tomorrow.

CHAPTER 19

Identifying the owner of the Studebaker turned out to be even easier than Carol had expected. And it was Kevin who supplied her name. They had been discussing Farris's report on their way back to the cottage, and when she mentioned that Gerlach's visitor of August 10th had been driving a Studebaker, Kevin interrupted her.

"That's got to be Mercedes Redman," he said. "She told me she'd been over to his place, and she drives a Studebaker. An old one that needs a wash. Unless he was specializing in women who drive Studebakers, she's the one you'll want to talk to."

"Good. I've got to start somewhere, so I guess I'll call her and take a trip over to Ithaca. And then there's the Myers woman. She told me she was driving around, nowhere in particular, the afternoon Gerlach was killed, and Farris says some woman dropped by that same day. Can't imagine why his former wife would be that woman, but maybe she had her reasons. Do you know what kind of car she drives?"

"Pretty sure it's a BMW," Kevin said.

"Which means we're still batting a thousand," Carol said. "Farris identified the car he saw as a BMW, so odds are it was Myers. Only she wasn't just driving idly around our back roads, like she said; she was going to see her ex. That makes two of your company I've got to talk with. Pronto."

"What about Mrs. Conklin?"

"I won't be seeing her. She's dead, or so her widower told me."

"That's not what I mean," Kevin said. "I was wondering whether your man Farris remembers seeing her at Gerlach's. We know she was part of his harem. His photo album tells us that."

"There's a good chance he did, but it would have been many months ago and there aren't any names in his notebook. We're going to have to dig a bit and come up with more information about her—when she died, and so on. Along with a picture. Tell you what, why don't you go over to Geneva, see what

100

you can find in the local paper's files. No reason you can't make time for it, is there?"

"No, none at all." Kevin was well aware that there were aspects of the sheriff's investigation into Harley Gerlach's death which he would have to stay out of. Looking into Arthur Conklin's marriage was not one of them, as long as it did not entail questioning Conklin himself. Kevin could once more assume the role of private detective, a role he thought he had played so well the previous summer when they were tracking down the killer of that woman from Chicago. Had he forgotten her name already? No, he remembered, it was Rackley. Sandra Rackley. Now, more than a year later, a murderer had struck again on Crooked Lake.

Carol dropped Kevin off at his cottage and set off for Cumberland, hoping that Bridges and the other officers who had been working on the case would have made progress in identifying the author of the note fragment found in Wayne Hall's bathroom wastebasket.

It's too late in the day, Kevin decided, to go over to Geneva and hunt through the local paper's files for Helen Conklin's obituary. He'd do that tomorrow. Right now, he thought, I'll take a swim.

His favorite form of exercise was swimming. It had been an important factor in the decision some years back to buy the lake cottage. Susan hadn't enjoyed it nearly as much as he did, but she was no longer a part of his life. Carol loved swimming and was good at it, even though she rarely had time to join him in the water.

It turned out to be just as well that he hadn't tried to fit the Geneva trip into what was left of the afternoon.

He had changed and was standing at the end of his dock, watching several gulls that were wheeling about above the water some thirty or more yards offshore. Kevin had always assumed that the gulls he saw on Crooked Lake were refugees from their saltwater habitat well to the east and south. He was wondering whether they migrated or otherwise changed their fishing grounds during the winter when the lake could freeze over. It was while he was entertaining these thoughts that he spotted a boat coming his way. It was moving slowly, and it appeared that someone was swimming alongside of it. Whoever it was, they were heading almost directly for his dock.

It was not until they were within fifteen feet of the dock that he thought he recognized the swimmer.

"Miss Merriman?" he called out.

The woman in the water stopped swimming and looked up at the dock and the man who was standing there.

"Professor Whitman?" She was obviously surprised to find herself face to face with the director of the ill-fated Brae Loch opera project.

"That's right," he said as she reached the dock and the rower of the boat pulled it alongside. "What are you doing here?"

Heather Merriman backpedaled a few feet.

"I'm sorry," she said, and she sounded as if she was embarrassed. "I had no idea you lived here. I didn't mean to bother you."

"Hey, no problem. You aren't bothering me. Quite the contrary, I'm glad to see you. Didn't expect to see you arriving quite like this, though."

"Oh, I was just taking my annual swim across the lake," she said, her voice betraying her nervousness. "Only I didn't know I'd end up at your cottage."

"Here," Kevin said, extending his hand. "Why don't you come up on the dock. You must be exhausted."

Heather let him pull her up out of the water.

"Jimmy, let me have my towel." The boy in the boat tossed her a large brightly colored beach towel, which she quickly wrapped around herself as if she were concerned that the professor would see her in her bathing suit.

"No, I'm not exhausted," she said, her face sporting a smile for the first time. "I do this every year. It isn't that far or that hard."

Kevin had often thought about swimming across the lake. It seemed to be a rite of passage for many of the young people who lived or summered on the lake, and he didn't think of himself as too old to do it. But in spite of the fact that he enjoyed swimming, he had never gotten around to tackle the cross-lake swim.

"How far do you think it is?" he asked her.

"I'm not sure. Half a mile, probably more, but nowhere near a mile. My dad used to worry about me doing it, but it's really safe if you have a boat along with you. I've been doing it since I was eleven."

Heather Merriman was now several years past eleven. In fact she was past high school and in college, an attractive young woman with a good summer tan and a promising soprano voice who was to have been one of the stars of the opera that was supposed to be having its premiere at Brae Loch College the very next night.

"Well, good for you," Kevin said.

"I mustn't forget my manners," she said, turning to the boat. "This is my brother, Jimmy. He doesn't like to come along with me, but he's a good sport. Aren't you, Jimmy?"

The boy in the rowboat had a family resemblance to Heather, but was several years younger. He mumbled something by way of acknowledging that he was indeed Jimmy Merriman and that he was willing, however reluctantly, to accompany his older sister when she swam across the lake.

"I really can't keep you, Professor Whitman. We'd better start back." Heather started to unwrap the towel.

"What's the hurry? Won't you stay, have a Coke or some iced tea with me? We haven't talked since the opera was cancelled. Or even very much back when we were rehearsing. I'd enjoy hearing what you've been thinking about it, what your plans are."

"You really wouldn't mind?" Miss Merriman suddenly sounded as if she would welcome the opportunity to talk with the man who had given her the chance to sing Lauretta's great aria in *Gianni Schicchi*.

"Absolutely not. Jimmy can stay, too, if he likes. Otherwise, I'll be happy to drive you home. I assume you must live pretty much straight across from here."

"I do, and I think you can see it from here. It's that white one with a second-floor deck," she said, pointing toward the far shore. "What a coincidence, you living almost directly across from my parents' place."

Kevin thought that the cottages on the other side of the lake all looked pretty much alike from this distance, but he agreed that he could see the Merriman place.

"Are you willing to stay awhile?" he asked, now interested in hearing how members of his company were taking the unexpected cancellation of the opera. The only ones he had heard from were Redman and Rosetti, and the former had been preoccupied with telling him about her relationship with Gerlach

103

while the Schicchi wannabe had been interested only in promoting his own star turn.

"Sure. Jimmy won't care."

Nor did he. In fact he seemed relieved to be given permission to take off and to do so at a faster pace than would have been necessary had his sister been swimming beside the boat.

Kevin produced two Cokes and he and Heather settled into chairs at the end of the dock. He realized that he hadn't really talked with her since their interview back in the spring. Or given much thought to how young she was. Sitting beside him on the dock, she looked very much like his students back in the city. Barely out of her teens, if that. Unquestionably the youngest member of the opera company, most of whom were at least twice her age. He wondered if she would really pursue a career in music. She had talent, and he hoped she would.

"It's a shame that we aren't going to have a chance to stage the opera, isn't it? I was particularly looking forward to the audience cheering your big aria."

"It's nice of you to say that. Tell you the truth, I was scared. I haven't done anything like that, ever. There was a high school musical several years ago, but it was just a lightweight thing, nothing like opera."

"You'd have been just fine. You've got a beautiful voice, and I'm sure you'll have other chances to impress people with it."

Heather blushed through her tan.

"Does anybody know what happened to Mr. Gerlach?" she asked.

"If you mean does anybody know who killed him, I'm afraid the answer is no. They solve these cases in an hour on TV, but in real life it takes weeks. Sometimes months."

Kevin knew this from firsthand experience, but was not about to discuss his own recently acquired role in solving crimes with Heather Merriman.

"I feel kind of bad," Heather said. "I didn't much like Mr. Gerlach, and now he's dead. Maybe I should have tried harder to understand him. He was really good. I mean he knew a lot about opera. If I'd paid more attention, he could have taught me things."

"Perhaps. But let's face it; he wasn't a very nice man. It was terrible, his being killed like that, but you don't have to feel guilty that you didn't like him. I don't think anyone else in our company liked him either."

Heather considered this while she adjusted a strap on her bathing suit.

"Professor Whitman, would you mind if I asked you a personal question?"

This sudden shift in the conversation caught Kevin off-guard. What was this going to be about? He was suddenly nervous.

"Well, of course not," he replied, not entirely sure that he wanted to hear her question. "But please, don't call me professor. It's much too formal."

"I know I should talk about this with my parents, but they aren't comfortable discussing things with me."

Kevin suspected that it was Heather who wasn't comfortable talking about things with her parents. He realized that he was in the habit of steering his students back at Madison College to counselors, but there were no counselors near at hand on Crooked Lake.

"It's about Mr. Carpenter," she continued. "He's very nice. And he's been a lot of help. You know, working with me on the music and the stage business. He's like a teacher—well, I guess you could say he is a teacher, and he's helped my confidence a whole lot."

She paused, obviously trying to decide what to say next, because what she had said about Sean Carpenter's mentoring role didn't suggest that she might have a question. Kevin chose to say nothing, to let her go on in her own way when she was ready.

"I've liked him as a teacher. And appreciated what he's done for me," she continued, "but something isn't quite right."

She paused again, then started over.

"Like I've said, he's a good man. Wouldn't you agree?"

"He was a good Rinuccio in our opera, that I know," Kevin answered, finessing her question. "But I'm afraid I didn't really know him well."

"No, I suppose not. The problem is that he seems to be interested in me," Heather said, finally getting to her point. "Not just interested in my role as Lauretta. We were supposed to be getting married in the opera, but that was just in the plot. He's interested in me as—what should I say?—as a person. Romantically. I think he believes he's in love with me."

Kevin wasn't surprised by this. He'd wondered about Carpenter ever since the initial interview, when the man had expressed an interest in who would be his partner onstage and asked that she not be told that he was twice her age.

"I don't know what I should do," Heather said. "He's old enough to be my father. I'm not interested in him—not in the way that he'd like me to be. In fact he bothers me. No, that isn't how I should put it. But he doesn't leave me alone. He's always hanging around. During rehearsals, he was always trying to protect me from Mr. Gerlach. It was almost embarrassing. Actually, it was embarrassing."

"Then you must almost be relieved that it's over. The opera, I mean."

"But it isn't, Professor Whitman," she said, ignoring his plea to forego the title. "He still won't leave me alone. He's called three times since that horrible day when Mr. Gerlach was killed. He wants to come down to the lake and see me. Just yesterday he suggested that he could pick me up and take me up to Rochester, show me around, have dinner at a nice restaurant. I'm afraid he's got an idea we could spend the night in his place up there."

"That doesn't seem likely, because I'm pretty sure he's married."

"He is? Oh, my God, it's even worse."

Heather Merriman sounded like a very troubled woman.

"You said you had a question for me," Kevin said. "I assume that what you want to know is what you should do about Sean Carpenter. Believe me, I'm no expert in matters like this, but it seems to me that you should be frank with him, brutally frank if you have to. Tell him that you have to get on with your life, and that you aren't interested in seeing him. Thanks for his friendship at Brae Loch, but now you're going back to being a music major in college and doing the other things that twenty-year-olds do."

"That sounds so cruel."

"You may have to be cruel. The alternative is to have to contend with his unwelcome presence in your life for heaven knows how long. I'm sure if you're tough, he'll get the message and back off."

Heather tugged at the errant strap of her bathing suit for a moment and then posed another question.

"Okay, I say 'no' to Sean, but what about Mercedes Redman?"

Mercedes Redman? What was Heather's problem with Redman?

"I'm afraid I don't follow you."

"And I'm not sure myself. But it's funny. She and I didn't talk much over the summer—just the occasional bit about something in the score. But as we were getting to the end of rehearsals, she began to seek me out—you know, find an excuse to talk with me. And mostly she didn't talk about the opera. She sounded interested in me, my career plans, what I did with my spare time, and so on. Which was fine, I guess. But it began to get personal. She wanted to know if I was dating anybody, and what we did. It just wasn't the kind of conversation you have with somebody you hardly know."

"What do you make of this?" Kevin asked. He had a hunch what was on Heather's mind.

"I don't really know. I'm probably imagining things. But it hasn't stopped with Mr. Gerlach's death. She called me yesterday and tried to talk me into transferring to a university over in Ithaca. That's where she lives. She said she could help me better if we were closer. She even offered to let me share her house— said she had a spare room. She talked about our mutual love of music, but there was something weird about it."

By this time, Kevin knew what was on Heather's mind. He, too, felt awkward talking about it, but there was no use in pretending that he didn't understand.

"So I gather that you think she's been coming on to you. That she might be interested in a lesbian relationship. Is that it?"

"I guess so. I wish you could tell me that you know she's not a lesbian, that I'm making all of this up."

"I have no idea about Ms. Redman's lifestyle, Heather. We have never discussed anything except opera, especially Puccini's *Gianni Schicchi*." This was a lie, of course, inasmuch as they had had a rather detailed conversation about her relationship with Harley Gerlach only two days earlier. But he didn't want to be drawn into a discussion with Heather about Mercedes Redman, a discussion in which neither of them had any real idea of who she was other than a teacher of violin who had done a very creditable job of whipping the Brae Loch orchestra into shape.

"Maybe I'm wrong. I hope so."

"My advice is pretty much what it is for Carpenter. If you're uncomfortable with Mercedes, I'd politely tell her you're happy in school where you are and find ways to be busy when she suggests getting together. She'll get the message."

Kevin doubted that Heather had derived much comfort from his advice, but she thanked him and let him drive her home. The conversation shifted to other things, but on his trip back to the cottage Kevin found himself worrying about her and about what he had learned about two of the other members of the company he had assembled for the stillborn production of *Gianni Schicchi*.

CHAPTER 20

Sam Bridges' report was not what Carol wanted to hear. She had left to him the task of figuring out who had written the unfinished note found in the backstage bathroom of Wayne Hall. The note had made a cryptic reference to something happening on Tuesday, but did not say what that something was. Nor did it say for whom the note was intended. It did not even specify which Tuesday it referred to, although Sam had assured the sheriff that it had to be the day on which Gerlach had been murdered.

Carol read the note again, as if repeated readings would make its meaning clearer.

How about Tuesday noon? We could

Carol remained doubtful that it was important. But in view of the fact that no one but members of Kevin's opera company had been using Wayne Hall, and that one of the members of that company had been murdered there on Tuesday, she knew that she would have to make every effort to find out whoever it was that had written the note. Or started to write it.

Who were 'we'? What could 'we' do? Kill Harley Gerlach? Highly improbable. It was much more likely that the note had to do with the opera, such as practicing a passage that wasn't going that well.

But Sam's report had been unhelpful. All he had had to work with were the cards on which members of the opera company had written their names, addresses, phone numbers, and e-mails. Carol had congratulated herself on having the cast and orchestra members write this information down themselves when she and Sam had interviewed them. It held out the possibility that the handwriting on the note would look like that on one of the cards she had collected. But according to Sam, there was no match.

"Nothing close?" Carol asked, her disappointment showing.

"Depends on what you mean by close. There's only one that looks remotely possible to me. Her name's Rachel Berman. Here, take a look for yourself. I don't think she wrote the note."

Carol placed the Berman woman's card and the note side by side on her desk and studied them carefully for the better part of a minute.

"No, I see what you mean. They don't look very much alike to me either. And you say that's the closest there is to a match?"

"Definitely. You can look 'em over yourself, but I'd be surprised if you don't agree with me."

She saw no good reason to spend time doing what she'd asked Sam to do. This was the sort of task where his judgment was pretty certain to be reliable. Maybe better than hers.

"I wondered why the note didn't match up with any of their handwriting," Sam said, "and I think I know why. If, that is, one of them wrote the note. Just look at the paper the note was written on."

The small piece of paper, crumpled when it had been fished out of the wastebasket, had now been flattened and smoothed out. It had several dents where the letters were. In two places the dents were actually small holes in the paper.

"Why would those little dents be there? Do you see how they go in, not out? Tell you what I think. If you write on a piece of paper that's lying flat on a desk or another hard surface, there won't be any dents. But if you write on a piece of paper that's resting on a soft surface, one that gives as you write, your pen pushes the paper down. Sometimes the pen point will actually break the paper. Here, let me show you."

Sam took a piece of paper from a pad on the desk and asked Carol to stand up.

"What I'm going to do is write a note, using your shoulder as my desk."

He placed the paper on the padded shoulder of Carol's jacket and wrote a few words.

"Okay, now look what we've got. The paper gave a bit when I pressed down, leaving those dents. I was careful not to press down too hard, but I still broke through the paper here. And writing the note was awkward, me standing up like that. So it doesn't look very much like my handwriting, does it?"

Carol was thoroughly familiar with her deputy's handwriting, and what she was looking at bore little resemblance to it.

"What I think," Sam continued, "is that whoever started to write the note didn't have a hard surface close by, wasn't planning on writing a long note anyway, and simply rested the paper on whatever was at hand. And it was a soft surface, the angle was awkward, and the result was a note that doesn't resemble what he wrote on the card. Remember, we had a clipboard for them to use, and they were sitting down when they wrote."

Sam Bridges was no handwriting expert, and his explanation for their problem was of doubtful scientific value. But Carol was impressed. Unfortunately, they were no closer to identifying the person who had written the note. Or started to.

"Why do you suppose he stopped in mid-sentence?" Sam asked.

"He or maybe she, Sam. I don't know, but I'd guess that whoever wrote it wasn't with the person he was writing it for. Why write a note when you can simply talk to someone? But then the other person walks in, there's no need to finish the note to him, so you wad it up, toss it out, and simply tell the other person what you were saying in the note."

"You think that's what happened?"

"It makes sense to me. Of course he could have changed his mind and decided not to write the note at all—not to do whatever it was he was going to do on Tuesday. But I'd bet on the other scenario."

They spent a few more minutes speculating about the note fragment before Sam brought up the matter of fingerprints.

"I tried to get prints, but I'm afraid we were careless when we were going through that wastebasket."

"It happens," Carol said, knowing that Sam was too experienced to be careless about such things. "But we aren't about to go around taking prints of all of the people in the opera company anyway. The handwriting was the more logical place to start—it just didn't work out. If we solve this one, it's going to be other things, not that damned note, that break the case."

Carol hoped that she was right about the note.

———

Later that afternoon when she was leaving the office, she ran into Officer Grieves in the parking lot.

"Another long day," she said. "How are you doing?"

It was not a question to be answered, just a matter of being friendly to one of her junior officers. But as she said it, she remembered that Grieves was supposed to be looking for Harley Gerlach's car. She decided that she was genuinely interested in how he was doing.

"What can you tell me about the car?" she asked.

Grieves looked at her with a blank expression.

"The car?"

"Yes. Gerlach's car. Have you found it?"

"Was I supposed to be looking for it?"

Carol would have to bring a halt to this aimless game of verbal ping-pong.

"Come on, Jack. We know Gerlach's car is over at the Brae Loch campus. We can't just leave it there. You were going to find it, remember?"

Jack Grieves was beginning to look uncomfortable.

"I'm sorry, Carol, but no, I don't remember. I'll be glad to go get it, but I'm sure you never gave me that assignment."

Now it was Carol's turn to be uncomfortable. Was it possible that she had been so preoccupied with other things, including other issues of the Gerlach case, that she had only intended to give this assignment to Grieves? Or had she asked someone else to take care of the car? In any event, there was no point in criticizing her colleague for failing to do something she might never have told him to do.

"Never mind. Maybe I gave the assignment to one of the other men. We'll sort it out at squad meeting on Monday. It's hardly an urgent matter. I just don't want to have it towed. The college people wouldn't know it belonged to Gerlach."

"You had me worried there for a minute," Grieves said. "I like to think I know what I'm doing. Well, most of the time anyway."

"I never doubted it, Jack. Have a good weekend."

When Carol set off for home, her mind turned away from the frustratingly incomplete note in the Wayne Hall wastebasket and the failed communication about Gerlach's car. She thought instead about what she hoped would be promising visits to Janet Myers and Mercedes Redman.

CHAPTER 21

It was going on six o'clock that same evening, and two old friends were having a beer and a conversation at a pub called Beer and Burgers in Yates Center. One of the men was Ben Robertson, the owner of a small boatyard on the east arm of Crooked Lake known as Ben's Marina. The other was Bill Parsons, the senior member of the Cumberland County Sheriff's Department. Parsons typically spent his days motoring around the lake in a patrol boat, looking for people who were in violation of one or more of the rules governing boating and fishing. His day had been uneventful, but he was tired and welcomed an opportunity to relax a bit with Robertson.

"Ever feel bored doing your thing?" the marina owner asked.

"Oh, yes. There are days when it's the same old, same old. This was one of them. For a change, everybody was behaving. No crazies out there in their personal watercraft, no one fishing without a license. Not even anybody who'd run out of gas in the middle of the lake. It was one of the easier days. But that's okay. Who knows, tomorrow could bring some kind of accident, and I'd rather be bored than have to rescue somebody."

"Ever calculate how much gas you use up in a day?" Robertson was enjoying talking with his friend about his job.

"Yeah. We've got a log where we keep track of how many miles we cover, how much gas we buy. And how much it costs. Prices are on the rise, Ben. I'm sure you know it as well as I do. Bet you hear plenty of griping from your customers. But I haven't seen any drop-off in boat traffic. Not yet. "

"Guy was talking about oil last night on TV. Said the price of oil could set a record by Labor Day. He said something about the Feds taking some kind of action to help us. Of course he was thinking about cars and trucks, not boats. But I'm worried about a drop-off in business."

"Well, good luck," Parsons said. "From where I sit, it wouldn't hurt to cut down on the boat traffic."

"I know, Bill, but it's my bread and butter." The owner of the marina gave his friend a wry smile. "Anyway, business at my place hasn't started to tail off. We even had a bit of a brouhaha the other day—people lined up, couldn't get to the pump."

"What happened, you selling it at discount?"

"No, some stupid guy had tied his boat up at the end of the pump dock. Blocked access. None of my people realized it until a couple of boaters began hollering for service. I went down to the dock myself, and they were right. This little aluminum fishing boat had been parked right where customers had to pull in to get gas. No one had a clue where the owner of the boat had gone."

Parsons chuckled.

"If that's the worst you have to contend with, you're in better shape than I am."

"I know, but it was a nuisance. We had to untie the boat and pull it up on the beach over where it was out of the way. No idea how long it was there. I never saw anybody come to pick it up, but it was gone when I called it quits for the day."

"So you never did see the guy you wanted to take out your anger on. Right?"

"It wasn't like that. I wasn't angry, just frustrated. And to be perfectly honest about it, I was just a little bit curious. You'd have been curious, too, if someone you didn't know had just pulled in and left his boat tied up to your dock. Even if it wasn't anything exciting, which it wasn't. Just an old Larson with a not very powerful Mercury outboard."

"Ever get the guy's name?"

"No, and once he'd picked the boat up, it didn't matter. I was glad to get rid of it, no questions asked."

Robertson and Parsons had another beer, after which they went their separate ways. It is doubtful if they would ever have discussed the old Larson fishing boat again if Sheriff Kelleher had not overheard her colleague telling Officer Barrett about it in the squad room the following morning.

———

"When did this happen?" she asked.

"Sometime recently, I suppose. Why, is it important?"

"Probably not. But I'm interested in anything out of the ordinary happening close to the college on the day that guy got

114

murdered there. And Ben's marina is pretty close. What would you say, a mile?"

Parsons thought about it a moment.

"It's got to be less than that. Maybe three-quarters of a mile at most."

"Close enough," Carol said. "I think I'll go down and talk to Robertson. Maybe he'll remember the day, give me more details about the boat."

"I'm sorry, Carol." Parsons started to apologize. "It never occurred to me that it could have anything to do with the trouble at Brae Loch."

"Odds are it doesn't. No need to apologize. You haven't been on the Brae Loch case."

Parsons and Barrett went their separate ways, and Carol, after ten minutes spent on paperwork left over from the previous day, took off for Ben's Marina.

"Morning, Sheriff," the owner greeted her as she entered his tiny office. "What brings you down here today?"

"I could tell you that it's always a pleasure to see you, Ben," she said, "but the truth is I need to ask you about something Bill Parsons told me this morning. He says you had some trouble recently with some guy who parked his boat so your customers couldn't get to the gas pump."

Robertson was surprised that the sheriff had paid him a visit the very next day to talk about something so trivial, and he said so.

"Oh, that. It wasn't a big deal. More of a puzzle where the guy went to, leaving his boat for all that time."

"What I want to know," Carol said, "is when this happened. Do you remember what day it was?"

"Sure. It was Tuesday. Why? Do you think you know who it was?"

"No, but I am interested in the date. Tuesday, that was the day when a man was killed over at the college. You know about that?"

"Of course. Everybody's talking about it. You don't think the guy who did it is the same guy who left his boat here at the marina, do you?"

It was a logical question, and Carol knew that she wouldn't be talking to Ben Robertson if the thought had not occurred to her. But it had been only a fleeting thought, not part of any serious attempt to consider the issue of who might be Harley Gerlach's killer.

"It's extremely unlikely," she said. "But I don't have the luxury of dismissing something out of hand just because it's unlikely. As of now, we don't have any solid leads. So, yes, I'm interested in finding out who parked his boat at your pump dock on Tuesday."

"Wish I could help you, but I never saw him and neither did Joel. He was helping me that day, but he'd gone on an errand, picking up some bait."

"Do you remember ever seeing the boat before?"

"Can't say. Boats like that are a dime a dozen, nothing distinctive about 'em. And if you're interested in the registration number, I'm sorry but I can't help you. We expected whoever had left it to come back right away, so we just pulled it up on the beach and ignored it."

"You don't need to feel sorry, Ben. You had no reason to know I'd be interested. And like I said, it probably isn't important."

But Carol couldn't let it go.

"One more question. Was there anything in the boat, anything that might give us some sense of who the guy is? Or maybe it's a woman. Why do we assume that boaters are men?"

Robertson didn't respond to the invitation to discuss the gender of boaters, but he did provide one additional piece of information.

"There was a fishing pole in the boat. Looked new. I'm not sure it had ever been used. No bait, though. Or tackle box. Nothing, in fact, except the pole. Maybe he planned to pick up some bait here, but he never did."

When Carol left the marina she still did not know who left the fishing boat there the previous Tuesday, much less whether he—or she—had had anything to do with the Brae Loch murder. But her conversation with Ben Robertson had not been a total waste of time, for it had planted a tiny germ of suspicion in her mind. She thought long and hard about that suspicion en route back to Cumberland. When she pulled into the parking lot behind the sheriff's department, she knew of something she was going to have to do. Sooner rather than later.

CHAPTER 22

It was Saturday morning, and Kevin was staring at the wall calendar beside his desk and feeling out of sorts. The calendar told him that it was mid-August, that only two weeks remained before he would have to head back to the city and the fall semester at Madison College. It had been a hectic summer, by far the busiest he had experienced since buying the cottage on the lake. Of course he had no one to blame but himself. The opera had been his idea, and it had been considerably more demanding than he had anticipated. It would have been worth it had those weeks of rehearsing and coping with the difficult temperaments of his small cast culminated in a successful production. But Harley Gerlach's murder had denied him that pleasure, and now he was left with a not very satisfying consolation prize, helping Carol Kelleher catch Gerlach's killer.

It wasn't that he didn't want to help Carol. He had found over the two previous summers that he enjoyed his role as an unofficial, off the books, member of the sheriff's team as it investigated the crimes that had shattered the normally peaceful vacation season on Crooked Lake. But the deaths of John Britingham and Sandra Rackley had had nothing to do with him; seeking their killers had been almost like a game, a matter of matching his wits to theirs. And doing it as he and Carol had discovered each other and become lovers.

The summer now drawing to a close had been different. First the opera had been a thief of his time with Carol, and Gerlach's murder, unlike that of Britingham and Rackley, had had a lot to do with him. In all probability it would never have happened had he not decided to stage an opera and recruited the members of the company, including the murder victim and, almost certainly, the murderer. He had had no way of knowing that some of the people he had chosen to participate in his opera would harbor such strong animosities toward each other, but by bringing them together he had created the volatile mix which had ended in murder.

117

It had been less than a week since the discovery of Gerlach's body had derailed the opera and started the search for his killer. Yet it was already apparent that there would be little time for the shared end-of-summer evenings he had envisioned with Carol. If preparation of the opera had limited their time together over much of the summer, it looked as if the investigation into Gerlach's death might have that same effect for what remained of it. They had had dinner at The Cedar Post on Thursday and supper at his place on Friday, but Carol had spent only three nights at the cottage in nearly a week, and it didn't appear as if her schedule held out greater promise for the days and nights ahead. She didn't like to take her work home with her, but in recent days she had found herself doing just that. It was, Kevin thought, a commentary on my marginalized role in her investigation of Gerlach's murder. But what bothered him most was that while the summer was winding down, their relationship seemed to be losing some of its romantic excitement.

He shook off these unpleasant thoughts and got up to replenish his coffee. In spite of the fact that he had so far been only marginally involved in the investigation, Carol had agreed that he should concentrate on obtaining information on the other women pictured in Gerlach's photo album. Of these the late Helen Conklin was most important, but there had been two other unfamiliar women whose pictures had been taken in Gerlach's living room, meaning that they were among his relatively recent conquests and presumably lived in the area.

Kevin decided to go to Geneva and see what he could learn about Helen Conklin. When she had died, how she had died, anything else that might shed light on her relationship with both her husband and Harley Gerlach. There would, of course, be no mention of Gerlach in Helen's obituary, but Kevin intended to do what he could to track down acquaintances who might know more.

The other two women posed a much more difficult problem. One of them, according to the name under her picture, was Linda; the other was Lauren. But Linda who? Lauren who? How does one go about locating someone when the only clue is a first name? In cop shows on TV the police were always going around asking people if they recognized a face in a photograph. But there was always a reason why they asked those people—they were neighbors or relatives, or they worked for the same company, or they were known to have been at a party with the deceased. Linda and Lauren were a very different story. Would he have to show the picture to tellers at all of the area banks? To clerks at the checkout counters of supermarkets?

Happily, Helen Conklin would be a simpler problem. He temporarily put Linda and Lauren out of his mind and got ready to drive over to Geneva.

In her interview with Arthur Conklin, Carol had elicited from him the information that he had lost his wife roughly a year ago, which meant that Kevin needn't spend hours looking for her obituary in the *Finger Lakes Courier*. She could have pursued the matter and pinpointed the exact date, but hadn't done so. No matter. When he pulled into the newspaper's parking lot, he was confident that he would have the information he was seeking within half an hour.

It actually took only fifteen minutes, thanks to a cooperative staffer who guided him through the paper's morgue and to plain old good luck. It was a fairly long obit, reflecting either Mrs. Conklin's importance in the community or simply the paper's practice of catering to the morbid interests of a small-town readership. The obituary was accompanied by a picture which confirmed what he had expected. The woman in the photo labeled Helen in Gerlach's album was indeed Helen Conklin.

By the time he had finished reading the obituary, he had decided that its length was not due to Helen Conklin having done anything truly remarkable, but rather that she had been what is commonly called a pillar of the community. She had apparently been a member of important local service organizations, had served on the school board, and sung in the Methodist church choir. Her academic pedigree was noted, as was the fact that she had been a tournament bridge player. Her survivors included her husband, whose civic reputation was lauded, and three children, now all grown and successful.

What interested Kevin the most was the cause of her death, and the obituary had little to say about it except that it seemed to be related to a fall from which she had never fully recovered. He was disappointed but not surprised by this. He had been curious about it ever since he had overheard Conklin tell Janet Myers that his wife had passed away and confessed her affair with Gerlach on her deathbed. There was no mention, of course, of either Gerlach or a deathbed confession of infidelity in the obituary. But it was possible that someone in the community, someone other than Conklin, had been aware of Helen's relationship with Gerlach. Kevin's inquiry into the private lives of the Conklins was just beginning.

He located the address of the Conklin residence and drove through town and into an upscale neighborhood of well-maintained old homes, all with large wraparound porches and most with an old-fashioned widow's walk. The cellist's house had been painted an attractive Williamsburg blue and cream, and whomever he had hired to take care of landscaping had done an outstanding job. There was no car in the driveway, and no sign that Conklin was at home, but Kevin had no intention of talking with him anyway. It was the neighbors in whom he was interested.

He drove down the street a ways, parked, and took out his cell phone. He listened to the phone ringing in the Conklin home. Six rings and still no answer. Finally, an answering machine kicked in, informing him that the owner was unable to come to the phone and inviting him to leave a number, which Conklin promised to call back. It was only then that Kevin got out of his car, crossed the street, and walked back to a neighboring house with a well-polished Cadillac in its driveway.

"Hi," he said to the woman who opened the door. "I'm sorry to bother you like this, but I'm interested in your neighbors, the Conklins. There doesn't seem to be anyone at home."

The woman, a tall brunette who might have been any-where from 35 to 50, regarded him with the half smile of someone who wants to be polite but isn't quite sure just what to say.

"No, I think Mr. Conklin left an hour ago. He lives alone."

"What about Mrs. Conklin?"

"I'm afraid she died about a year ago," the neighbor said, and then, obviously worried about the effect of this news on the man at her door, offered the opinion that Mrs. Conklin had been a wonderful person and was much missed by everyone who knew her.

"I didn't know," Kevin said in what he hoped was a tone of voice which expressed both shock and sadness.

It was time to introduce himself, or at least the person he was pretending to be.

"I'm a second cousin of Helen's, and happened to be in the area and thought I'd stop by to say hello. A year ago, you say? She's been dead a year and I'd never heard. I guess we'd pretty much lost touch."

"Do you care to come in, Mr.—I don't think I got your name."

"No, of course not. Sorry. It's Peter." He'd try to finesse the family name, figuring that the woman would tell Arthur Conklin about this visit from Helen's second cousin. It was possible that Conklin wouldn't know anything about a second cousin, much less that person's last name. But the less said about himself the better.

"Hello, Peter. I'm Sherri. Please come in. I feel badly, being the bearer of bad news."

"That's very kind of you. I won't stay but a minute, but perhaps you can tell me a bit about it."

Kevin followed Sherri into a parlor which didn't look to be much used. She offered him a seat on an overstuffed couch and suggested coffee, which he gladly accepted. If he sipped it slowly and Sherri was not averse to gossip, he might learn more about Helen's death and the cuckolded husband.

"Thank you," he said, accepting the coffee and waving off the cream and sugar. "May I ask what happened? I mean what caused Helen's death?"

"The official word is that it was the result of complications from a fall she suffered. She was in the hospital for awhile. It looked like she was getting better, but then she suffered a relapse and died. I don't pretend to know anything about her medical condition, but that's what people were saying. Arthur said so, too."

"Where did this happen?"

"Right in the house. It seems she lost her footing at the top of the stairs and fell, hitting her head on a marble column at the bottom."

"How terrible. She's one of the last people I'd have imagined taking a tumble like that. If you'd told me she'd left Arthur and run off with another man, I wouldn't have been as shocked as I was when you said she was dead. Life can take some strange turns, can't it?"

Kevin had no idea how Sherri would react to this conversational gambit. She might see it simply as an overly dramatic way of saying that he couldn't believe the news that Helen was dead. On the other hand, she might interpret it as a maladroit admission that he had suspected his cousin of having affairs with other men.

For a long moment she said nothing. When she spoke, her response told him that perhaps she did know something about Helen Conklin's infidelity.

"I guess you're right—I mean about life taking strange turns. Do you know something about the life she was leading?"

"No," he said. "It's like I said, we'd been out of touch for a long time. More than two years, I think. Why—were she and Arthur having problems?"

"I don't know. She and I weren't close. But you know how it is with women—well, probably you don't know. It's a matter of intuition. Little things that are said, those unexpected silences that occur in a conversation."

"Helen was a more complicated person than she appeared on the surface," Kevin said. "At least that was my impression. I always wondered what she and Arthur saw in each other."

Sherri considered her coffee cup, weighing what she ought to say about the relationship between the Conklins to Helen's second cousin.

"After the accident," she began, having apparently decided to share local gossip, "there was talk that maybe it wasn't an accident. You know, that they'd been quarreling and Arthur pushed her."

"Really?" Kevin's surprise was genuine.

"For two or three days after her fall, the police were over at their house. It didn't make much sense. The rescue squad, of course, but why the police? Anyway, nothing came of it. Arthur talked to me briefly a couple of times when he got back from the hospital, and then one day she was gone. I remember that day. He wasn't a demonstrative type, but he looked like he was fighting back tears."

"So you don't know if he was ever under suspicion?"

"No," she said, and Kevin had the impression that she might have regretted having to answer in the negative.

It was at this point that his hostess must have decided that she'd said enough. She cleared her throat and smiled.

"I'm sorry. I have no business going on like this. I really know nothing about the Conklins. They were nice neighbors, minded their own business—oh, and he still does."

She got to her feet and put the coffee cups, neither of them empty, on the tray. She looked ready to take them to the kitchen. The little tete a tete with Arthur Conklin's neighbor had come to an abrupt end. Kevin thanked her for her kindness and understanding, urged her to say hello to Arthur, and took his leave.

He turned at the sidewalk to wave before crossing the street. She was still standing in the doorway, tray in hand, watching as Helen Conklin's second cousin made his way back to his car.

CHAPTER 23

While Kevin was discussing the Conklins with their neighbor over in Geneva, Carol was visiting the late Harley Gerlach's ex-wife in Southport. She would have preferred to be following up her conversation with Ben Robertson about the fishing boat that had been left untended at his marina dock, but she had made an appointment with Janet Myers for Saturday morning and felt obligated to keep it. And talking with Myers again was also important in view of what she had learned from Francis Farris, the man with the telescope. In fact, there were many important things she ought to be doing, things that she preferred to do herself rather than delegate them to Sam or her other officers. They were also things that she could not ask Kevin to do.

The Myers woman had provided them with the vaguest account of her whereabouts on the day of Gerlach's death of any of the members of Kevin's opera company. Driving about the hills and dales of Cumberland County for much of that fateful afternoon, she had said. If she needed an alibi, this one wouldn't do. And now, thanks to the voyeuristic Mr. Farris, it was known that Myers had not simply been driving around aimlessly. She had driven to her former husband's home on the bluff. Why had she done that, when it appeared that she still hated the ground he walked on? And why had she not mentioned it during the interview that evening at Brae Loch College?

They had agreed to meet at a coffee shop in Southport. It appeared that Mr. Myers would be at home, and his wife preferred to have her conversation with the sheriff somewhere else. Carol did not know what Janet Myers' husband knew about Gerlach. He surely knew that she had once been married to him, and was presumably aware that their divorce had not been amicable. But did he know that Gerlach was now living on Crooked Lake? That he and his wife had both been members of the cast of *Gianni Schicchi*?

Carol circled the town square in Southport, finding a parking spot across from the post office. She left the patrol car and took a seat on a bench near the bandstand. It was a pleasant day, not yet August hot, and she forced herself to relax and enjoy people watching. She was intentionally early.

At precisely 9:30 by the clock on the bank building, Janet Myers entered the coffee shop. Carol got up and made her way across the square to join her.

"Good morning, Mrs. Myers," she said, adopting a tone of voice that she hoped was disarmingly cheerful. "What a beautiful day—much more pleasant than the one when we met."

That day, less than a week ago, had also been sunny and warm, but they both knew what Carol was referring to.

"It's nice to see you again, Sheriff," the Myers woman said. It was doubtful that she meant it.

They found a table, ordered coffee, and quickly turned to the business of the day.

"Mrs. Myers," Carol began, "as I'm sure you know, I'm still trying to piece together what happened last Tuesday. And I'm glad you live close. Most of the rest of you people in the opera have scattered, so it's harder for me to follow up with them."

She had no intention—or need—to 'follow up' with most of the members of the opera company, but saying so might leave the impression that the conversation they were about to have would be merely routine.

"Like I told you the other evening, Sheriff, I'm glad to be helpful if I can," Myers said.

"I appreciate that," Carol assured her. "I hope you'll understand if I ask some of the same questions I asked when we talked over at the college. It was such a hectic night, so many people to interview. What I was trying to do was find out what everyone was doing during the time Mr. Gerlach must have been killed. So why don't you tell me what you were doing that afternoon."

Janet Myers sighed and affected a wan smile.

"I just drove around for a couple of hours."

"Go anywhere in particular? See anyone? Talk with anyone?"

"No. It's like I said before, I was just trying to relax, get myself ready for the dress rehearsal."

"So you didn't stop anywhere that afternoon?"

"Stop? No. But wait, I guess I did stop once. There's that lookout site on the road to Yates Center. I pulled over there, got out for a few minutes."

Carol was disappointed, but not surprised. Apparently nothing had happened since Tuesday to change Janet Myers' mind about the story she'd tell the sheriff.

"I think I remember that you mentioned driving out on that road along the crest of the bluff. Were you going anywhere in particular?"

"No, just enjoying the peace and quiet. It's a lonely road. Not much of anyone lives up there."

True enough, Carol thought. But one of the people who does live up there is Harley Gerlach. Make that did live up there.

"What if I told you that you were seen that afternoon at your former husband's house out at the end of the bluff?"

This was something that Janet Myers had not expected.

"But that's impossible. I can't imagine who told you that, but they're mistaken." Her voice was firm, but her face betrayed her anxiety.

"Perhaps, but I doubt it. The man who saw you gave me a very accurate description of your car and of you. He tells me that you parked behind Harley's house. That you walked around the house, tried the back porch door, and eventually drove away. And that this took place somewhere around 1:30."

"I'm sure it was someone else. Why on earth would I go to Harley's? I wouldn't be caught dead there."

"No, I'm sure you wouldn't. But it seems you were caught alive there. My informant happened to have been watching the house through a powerful telescope. It brought everything, including you and your BMW, up so close that you could almost see the time of day on your wristwatch."

Janet Myers visibly winced as she absorbed this information.

"You've had someone stalking me with a telescope? For God's sake, why me?"

"I haven't been stalking you, Mrs. Myers. I didn't even know the man who saw you until one of my officers realized that someone was watching Harley's place. He wasn't keen on admitting he was spying on your ex-husband, but I convinced him that he'd be better off if he told us what he'd seen. And what he'd seen was you, poking around Harley's on the afternoon when he was killed down at Brae Loch. Now what were you doing there?"

The Myers woman busied herself with her coffee, showing no inclination to answer the sheriff's question.

"I do not see how you are helping yourself by refusing to admit you were there. That is not in dispute. Really, it isn't. You may have a perfectly reasonable explanation, and I'd like to hear it."

Myers resolved her inner conflict in the only way now open to her.

"Yes, I did go to Harley's that afternoon," she finally said in a quiet voice. "I didn't want to tell you because I knew you'd jump at it as evidence that I meant to kill him."

"Why would I reach that conclusion, Mrs. Myers?"

"Well, he'd been killed and you'd be sure to find out how much I detested him."

"The way I hear it, many people detested him. Including a fair number of people in the opera company. So why would I assume it was you who meant to kill him?"

The paper napkin in Janet Myers' hands had been wadded and squeezed into a small ball.

"It wasn't a big thing," she said. "I mean being at Harley's house. I'd never been there. But then I found myself on that upper road and I remembered that he lived out near the end of the bluff. It just seemed like it would be interesting to see what kind of place he lived in. So I drove around until I found the turnoff with his name on the mailbox. It was stupid, I know, but it was just curiosity, nothing more."

"You could have saved yourself some trouble by telling me that in the first place," Carol said.

Janet Myers put the napkin down. Her face brightened.

"But then you tried to get into the house, didn't you?" Carol asked "Why was that?"

The worried ex-wife picked the napkin up again. Her ordeal wasn't over.

"Well, it was clear he wasn't there, so I thought I might get a peek at the inside."

The sheriff didn't comment on this further explanation of Mrs. Myers' actions on Tuesday afternoon. When she spoke again, she raised another question.

"So I assume that when you found the house locked, you drove to the college. Is that right?"

"On, no," was the answer. "I went back home. It was way too early for the dress rehearsal."

"Which means that you were home from, say, 2:15, 2:20, until early evening?"

"Yes, I was."

The woman had lied to her twice, refusing to acknowledge the visit to Gerlach's house. She might have gone directly home as she claimed to have done. But she could as easily be lying when she denied stopping at Brae Loch. She only had Janet's word for it that she had visited his house out of curiosity. What if she had gone there with the purpose of seeing her ex-husband, of talking to him? Or killing him? After all, if Harley Gerlach was not at home, the most obvious place for him to be was at the college.

In any event, Janet Myers' credibility was now in tatters. When she bade her good-bye, Carol knew that she would have to make the acquaintance of the husband and the neighbors. She would have to ask them whether they had seen her or her BMW in Southport on Tuesday afternoon. Especially during those crucial hours when the forensic evidence indicated that Harley Gerlach had been strangled.

CHAPTER 24

Before Carol had an opportunity to talk with Janet Myers' husband or her neighbors, much less pursue the lead suggested by the unattended fishing boat at Ben's Marina, she was confronted by an unexpected wrinkle in the Gerlach case. It was Kevin who brought it to her attention.

His phone call caught her at the office late that Saturday afternoon.

"I need to see you," he announced, "and the sooner the better. Any chance that you can join me for dinner tonight? Better yet, that you can stay over at the cottage? I know you're up to that lovely neck of yours in the Gerlach case, but that's one of the reasons I need to see you. I've learned something you ought to know about."

"Let's hear it."

This wasn't what Kevin had hoped to hear, and he said so.

"I was hoping you'd let me tell you at my place, tonight. The phone isn't my favorite medium, Carol. You know that. And you've got to eat anyway—and sleep. Why not do it here? You know, kill two birds with one stone."

"Why do I have the feeling your agenda has nothing to do with Gerlach? Or less to do with Gerlach than coaxing me into the sack?"

"Carol! I'm shocked that you should even think such a thing. I'm quite able to keep my priorities straight."

"Of course you are," she said, the smile in her voice reflecting the smile on her face. "And I know just what your priorities are."

"So, are you going to come over?"

"What choice do I have? How about six?"

"Great. Believe me, you'll be interested in what I have to tell you."

"I'd better be."

The dinner Kevin had whipped up would not have rated stars in any food critic's review, but it filled their stomachs and put them in the mood to talk about the Gerlach case.

They traded reports about their visits to Janet Myers and Arthur Conklin's neighbor, Sherri somebody, and then Kevin got down to what it was he'd told Carol she ought to know about.

On his way home from Geneva, he had decided on the spur of the moment to turn off on the upper bluff road and drive down to the late Harley Gerlach's house. There had been no particular reason for doing so. But he had no plans for the afternoon, and something about the house and its collection of opera memorabilia beckoned. And so it was that he had found himself parked behind the now empty house a little after noon, observed, no doubt, by Francis, a.k.a. Jeff, Farris.

Kevin would not have been there had he not pocketed a set of Gerlach's keys he had found in a bedside table drawer the day he and Carol had visited the house. He hadn't expected to use them, and he had neglected to tell Carol that he had them. But now they provided entree into the house on the bluff, and he intended to make use of them. He considered going around to the front of the house, the better to enter without being seen by Farris. But why should he worry about being seen going into Gerlach's house? Farris had certainly seen him clearly through his telescope when he and Carol had been there together, and must therefore assume he had some sort of official status. And if he didn't, so what? The sight of someone, familiar face or stranger, entering the house of the recently murdered Harley Gerlach would make his day.

So Kevin had boldly marched up the steps to the back porch and extracted the keys from his pocket. He had selected the key that looked to be the one most likely to fit the lock when he noticed that the small glass pane in the lower right-hand corner of the colonial-style door was missing. He had felt an instant frisson of excitement. The pane had not been missing the previous day, of that he was certain. He bent down and looked closely at the now empty square. Someone had used a glass cutter to remove the pane. It had been done so deftly that he had almost failed to notice it. A broken pane would have been much easier to spot. In fact, had the sun been lower in the sky or had it been an overcast day, he might have missed the evidence that someone had broken into the house. Whoever had done so had been very careful.

The door was locked, but was easily opened by reaching through the empty square where the glass had been. Kevin had gone on in, and begun looking immediately for some sign that an intruder had been in the house at some time during the previous 24 hours. Very probably at night. The most obvious reason for the break-in was theft—a dark and vacant house, some distance from its neighbors, an easy target. It didn't take long for Kevin to conclude that if theft was the motive, it had not been a common, garden-variety thief who had broken into the Gerlach house. None of the big-ticket items which would have tempted most thieves had been removed. None of the pictures and posters decorating the walls was missing, although some of them might have brought a tidy sum on the *Antiques Roadshow*. The bookshelves were similarly untouched, or appeared to be. Kevin had made no effort the previous day to examine Gerlach's books for first editions or other rarities, much less spend the time to undertake even a crude inventory of the collection. It was possible that one or two books had been stolen, but there were no gaps on the shelves and Kevin doubted it.

He went through all of the drawers in the desk, the file cabinet, the bedside tables. Carol had done the same thing the previous day and found nothing that looked interesting, but Kevin did it all again, trying to think like a thief with a mission. He found nothing, but that, of course, could be because the thief had beaten him to it. The same was true of the darkroom. There had been lots of photos, but the only ones that had interested Carol and him had been the ones in what he thought of as the harem album, and they had taken that with them.

No, he thought, whoever broke into the house had a very specific reason for doing so, and it wasn't to make away with valuable loot. What might that reason have been? Was there something in the house that he—or was it she—wanted? Something that might incriminate him—or was it her—in the death of Harley Gerlach? Kevin realized that he was assuming that the break-in and Gerlach's murder were related, and that was a very large assumption. But it would have been quite a coincidence for the man to have been killed and his home broken into, all in one week, by two very different people with two very different motives. And he knew that Carol was always telling him that she didn't put much stock in coincidences and that he shouldn't either. So Kevin chose to stick with his assumption that what had happened at the house was related to what had happened at the college.

He spent another quarter of an hour scouring the house for anything that might offer a clue to the identity of the burglar. There had been no burglary, of course, but for lack of a better term Kevin continued to think of whoever had broken into the house as a burglar. He tried to be careful around surfaces which might contain fingerprints, although he doubted that someone who had been so meticulous in removing the pane of glass on the back door would be so careless as to leave a trail of prints. Crawling around the floor in the study, looking for what, he wasn't quite sure, the thought occurred to him that he looked for all the world like a caricature of Sherlock Holmes. All he needed was a magnifying glass and a deer stalker hat. When he finally decided to call it a day, the only thing he had found was a small sliver of silver paper that looked like a piece of the wrapping for a stick of gum. He slipped it into his pocket, took one more quick look around, and left the house to the ghost of the late Harley Gerlach.

Carol agreed with his initial assessment that this was something she ought to know about.

"Interesting, isn't it?" she said. "Quite a lot of activity at the Gerlach mansion, considering that the owner hasn't been home. First there's Janet Myers, poking around there the day he's killed. Then there's somebody else—or is it Myers again?—sneaking in, uninvited, three days later. I'd figured that what mattered was what happened at the college. Now it's beginning to look as if Gerlach's house is a veritable crime-scene annex."

"I'm sorry I couldn't turn up anything that points to somebody as the killer."

"Don't be so sure of that. There's that piece of paper. And I'm sure it's from a gum wrapper. That makes two gum wrappers, one in the bathroom wastebasket at Brae Loch, the other in Gerlach's study. Harley could have chewed gum himself, in which case the gum-wrapper clue goes out the window. But what if it's from one of the other members of your little company?"

"I take it you don't have a record of who in the *Gianni Schicchi* crowd chewed gum," Kevin said. It was a statement, not a question.

"No, not yet. I guess I've been assuming it was Heather Merriman who'd left the wrapper in the wastebasket. You know, chewing gum is the sort of thing young girls do. But I can't picture Merriman breaking into Gerlach's house. Anyway, Bridges has been questioning all of your opera people."

"And now they'll be on their guard. They'll think that you suspect the killer of being a gum chewer. Crazy, isn't it? A stick of gum turns out to be the smoking gun."

"Come on, Kevin," Carol said. "You don't believe that, and neither do I."

"I wonder what kind of gum Heather chews." Kevin did not expect an answer to his non-question.

By the time they retired to the bedroom they had ceased speculating about who chewed gum and who might have broken into the murder victim's home. Kevin was relieved that Carol had not chastised him for going back to Gerlach's without consulting her. When they climbed into bed, both of them were relieved that there was more, much more, to their relationship than tracking down a killer on Crooked Lake.

CHAPTER 25

It was Kevin who was up and about on Sunday morning, while Carol was still under the covers at 9:10. The smell of coffee had not awakened her. The rattling of dishes in the kitchen had not disturbed her sleep. Kevin knew that she would be angry with herself for sleeping in so late. She might even be angry with him for not rousing her. She was entitled to a lazy day, but she would not see it that way. There were crimes and misdemeanors awaiting her attention, especially the murder of one Harley Gerlach five days previously, and Carol would not want to treat Sunday as the proverbial day of rest.

He made up his mind. Reluctantly. Leaning over the bed, Kevin planted a kiss on her forehead. He would have preferred to have kissed her on the lips, but she was buried under the sheet and that was impossible. Of course he could have shaken her or simply called out her name, but such an approach seemed cruel. Slow and easy does it, he thought.

Carol burrowed deeper into the bedding, muttering something unintelligible. He was about to give it up and go back to the kitchen when she suddenly bolted upright in the bed.

"What time is it?" It was a wide-awake voice, and the question hinted at panic.

"And good morning to you, too," he said, ignoring her question.

"Really, what time is it?"

"You've got the whole day in front of you. It's only a little after nine."

"Nine?" Carol practically leaped out of bed. She grabbed her robe and hurried down the hall to the bathroom. In less than a minute the shower was running. There would be no leisurely breakfast at the cottage this morning.

"I hate to eat and run," she said not much more than ten minutes later as she slid into a chair in the breakfast nook, "but I've got to get going. This is the trouble with staying here with you. It's too damn comfortable—I forget I'm a working girl."

"But it's Sunday morning, for God's sake. You don't actually have an appointment, do you? Or are you going to quiz somebody during the sermon?"

Carol busied herself spreading some marmalade on her toast.

"What I'm going to do is talk with some people, see if I can't get some straight answers about who was where last Tuesday. In my experience, Sunday's a good day to do it, at least in the morning. Which is why I'm taking a pass on the bacon and eggs."

"Who specifically do you have to see?" Kevin wanted to know.

"Your Gianni Schicchi wannabe, Rosetti. The man who was fishing, or so he says, while Gerlach was being strangled. And the Myers woman's neighbors. Somebody who can shed some light on where she was when she wasn't casing Gerlach's house. Then there's Redman. I still haven't talked to her since she admitted to spending time with our murder victim."

"All of this in one day?"

"Which is why I can't sleep in or have a second cup of coffee. Look, I love you and I'd love to stick around, but I've got a murderer to catch, and since you haven't been able to finger the culprit for me, I've got to go out and hassle some suspects. Excuse me while I brush my teeth."

Kevin watched her disappear down the hall. You're crazy, but I love you, he thought.

"I'll drop by on my way home, let you know what if anything I've learned," Carol said as she took out her keys and turned to give Kevin a quick kiss before leaving.

"I know you get a kick out of this," she said, pausing briefly at the door, "but don't you get a little tired of what seems to be our annual murder? I know I am. If it hadn't been for the death of your prima donna, I'd be suggesting we go back to bed."

"Primo uomo, Carol, not prima donna."

"You're changing the subject, aren't you?"

"No, just correcting your Italian. And if you promise to come back after talking to all of these people, I promise to go back to bed. Is it a deal?"

"I'll give it some thought. And I really do have to go."

She blew him another kiss as she backpedaled out of the door. Kevin stood there, coffee cup in hand, thinking about the fact that they had known each other for almost exactly two years, during which time their lives had been changed—and changed dramatically—by three murders on normally tranquil Crooked Lake.

———

Carol had been giving a lot of thought to Paolo Rosetti since her brief conversation with Ben Robertson at his marina. Kevin had identified him as one of the members of his cast who might have been Gerlach's killer. Rosetti had wanted to play the eponymous hero of the opera, and had, according to Kevin, been disappointed when the part went to Gerlach. In point of fact, he had been more than disappointed. He had obviously felt that there had been a grievous miscarriage of justice, that he was much better qualified to sing the lead than Gerlach. He had made no effort to hide his feelings about the matter throughout rehearsals and, after Gerlach's death, had been quick to suggest that the opera could still be saved—and saved by none other than Paolo Rosetti, who could step into the title role and thrill an appreciative audience at Brae Loch College.

But he was adamant that he hadn't killed Gerlach. He'd been fishing that afternoon, or so he said. Kevin had thought that strange, inasmuch as none of the people he knew went fishing during the middle of the day. Carol had initially given the matter little more thought, figuring that Rosetti probably didn't fish much and didn't have any idea when they'd be biting. And then she had learned that a fishing boat had been tied up to the dock at Ben's Marina and left there unclaimed for several hours. Of course there were literally hundreds of boats on the lake similar to the one that had annoyed Ben, and it could have belonged to the owner of any one of them. But the marina was but a short three-quarters of a mile above Brae Loch College and almost directly across the east arm of Crooked Lake from Rosetti's cottage.

The more she contemplated these facts, the more she began to wonder if the boat might belong to Rosetti. Suppose he had decided to go to the college but keep his presence there a secret. Driving and parking his car there would be risky. So would going by boat and leaving it at the college dock or on its beach. But why not take the boat, leave it at the marina, and walk to the college. The opera company wasn't supposed to assemble until early evening, and he was unknown to the students and faculty whom he would pass on the campus. Whatever his mission, it was unlikely that anyone would be able to prove that he had been at Brae Loch that afternoon.

And what might that mission have been? To kill Harley Gerlach? In view of his animus toward the man who had preempted his own claim to the role of Gianni Schicchi, that was a possibility. But how would he have known that Gerlach would be on campus? If their meeting had been the result of pure chance, there would have been no reason for his surreptitious arrival. On the other hand, perhaps Rosetti had overheard Gerlach say something that made it likely that he would be at the college that afternoon. Or perhaps the meeting had been prearranged. Carol had considered this possibility. Why would either of them have invited the other to meet on campus that day when they had rarely spoken to each other all summer and then only in words dripping with sarcasm?

Carol decided to set aside the question of why Rosetti and Gerlach had met and concentrate first on whether they had met. That meant pursuing Rosetti's claim to have been fishing and the possibility that it had been his boat that had been left at Ben's Marina. Her first step would be to visit the Rosetti residence and have a conversation with the sometime fisherman.

The cottage was small, nothing like Harley Gerlach's hillside mansion on the bluff. It looked much like its neighbors on Merchant's Point, some three miles south of Yates Center. These people were, for the most part, locals who provided goods and services for year-round residents and summer vacationers. Rosetti, she had learned when interviewing him the evening after Gerlach's murder, worked out of his home, providing tech help for people whose computers were misbehaving. Self-employed, he had the flexibility to participate in the production of *Gianni Schicchi* and otherwise indulge his interest in music.

Carol saw no sign of a car, which meant that her trip might prove to be a wild goose chase. But Mrs. Rosetti answered the door and explained that her husband was not at home. She volunteered no information as to his whereabouts, but quickly overcame her surprise at the presence of the county sheriff and invited Carol in for a cup of coffee.

"I'm Christina," she announced as she handed the sheriff her coffee mug. "I suppose you are here about that terrible thing that happened over at Brae Loch last week."

"I'm afraid so," Carol said, anxious to adopt a tone which didn't imply that Christina's husband was under suspicion. "It was really a double tragedy—a man killed and the opera cancelled. I'm sure it has been a great disappointment to your husband."

"Oh, yes. He'd been looking forward to it so much. He just loves to sing. And he's really good—he sings around the house, even while he's working, if you can imagine that. But of course we're so sorry about that poor man. Gerlach, isn't it?"

Carol was sure that Christina Rosetti knew exactly who that poor man was. Paolo would undoubtedly have held forth at great length about the opera and the man who was singing the title role, the role he believed he should have had. She wondered if Rosetti had said too much to his wife and now regretted it. She'd try to find out.

"I came over to talk with your husband, but maybe you can help me. In cases like this we have to talk with lots of people, see if they can help us piece together what happened. I had a chance to talk with Mr. Rosetti right after Mr. Gerlach's death, but it was just a brief chat. Everyone was so upset, you know. I thought it would be a good idea to pay a visit to the members of the cast of the opera. I'm hoping to find out what they may have seen or heard which could help us get to the bottom of this crime."

"I'm sure I don't know anything about it. Anything, that is, except what Paolo has told me."

"That's okay. For starters, can you tell me whether your husband was at home or at the college last Tuesday afternoon?"

"Was that the day that terrible thing happened?"

"Yes, that's the day," Carol said, trying to remember that she should call Gerlach's murder that terrible thing.

"I'm afraid I don't know."

"You weren't at home that day?" Carol asked, trying to be helpful.

"I was here, out in the kitchen, all day. I was putting up some jam. It's been a good summer for fruit."

"If you were here, you must know if your husband was here, too."

"I suppose I should, but I don't. He doesn't tell me where he's going. We both sort of do our own thing, you know."

This is going to be frustrating, Carol thought. Two people, living under the same roof, yet unaware of each other's presence. Or absence.

"Do you suppose he went fishing that afternoon?"

"Fishing?" She made it sound like an unfamiliar word, one she would have to look up in Webster's.

"Yes, fishing. There's a fishing boat on the beach," Carol said. She could see it through the front window from where she was sitting.

"I don't think Paolo does much fishing. He bought himself a pole awhile back, but I don't think he's ever gotten around to using it. Why, do you think he went fishing that day?"

"I don't know—it was just a thought." Carol decided not to mention Rosetti's alibi. Either he hadn't told his wife about it, or for some reason of her own, she had chosen to pretend that he hadn't.

Carol's efforts to get Mrs. Rosetti to talk about her husband were going nowhere. It was hard to believe that she knew so little about what he did and when, but she stuck to her line that they led separate lives, at least during the day. She had no idea whether they shared a bed at night.

It was while they were bogged down in another conversational cul-de-sac that the missing husband drove up and joined them in the living room.

The sheriff's presence had been given away by the official car in the driveway, but Rosetti still seemed surprised to see her sitting in his living room, sharing a cup of coffee with his wife. He didn't look as if the sight that greeted him as he walked in gave him any pleasure.

"What's this all about?" he asked, and then, remembering his manners, said hello and gave the sheriff a little bow.

"I wish I could say I'd come by to tell you we've solved Mr. Gerlach's murder, but that's not true. I was just following up on our conversation of last week, going over the same ground again with members of the cast. Your wife has been kind enough to let me have a cup of coffee, and in your absence she's been answering some of my questions."

Rosetti tried to pretend that what he had just heard didn't bother him. He was unsuccessful.

"Questions?" he said, his eyes narrowing as he spoke. "I'm sorry I wasn't here. Christina doesn't know anything about this."

"She's done her best to fill me in," Carol said, somewhat disingenuously.

"What did she tell you?" he asked, and then before the sheriff had a chance to answer, he turned to his wife. "What did you tell him?"

Carol chose to let Christina go first.

"Well, not much. We don't talk a lot, do we, so I couldn't be very helpful. She asked about you going fishing, and I said I didn't think you fished much. Was that all right?"

Christina Rosetti actually looked frightened. The look she gave her husband said as clearly as words that she hoped he wasn't angry with her for what she had said or not said to the sheriff.

"You really shouldn't have been badgering my wife," Paolo said. "I already told you what I know, which is nothing. If you have more questions, you should save them for me, not bother Christina with them."

Before Carol had an opportunity to comment on her conversation with Mrs. Rosetti, her husband dismissed her.

"Why don't you run along, dear." It wasn't a suggestion so much as an order. "I know you've got a lot to do."

Christina was out of the room in a matter of seconds. She was obviously accustomed to obeying her husband.

"Now," he said, "maybe you can tell me why you're here."

"It's like I said. I'm still asking questions of people who were in the opera company, and Sunday seemed like a good day to come and see you. In your case, it's the story about going fishing that I'd like to talk about."

"So? What's the question?"

Rosetti was not being belligerent, but he was moving in that direction.

"You told me you were fishing the afternoon Mr. Gerlach was killed. I wondered if you stopped off at Ben's Marina that day?"

Paolo Rosetti did not dissemble well, Carol thought. He hadn't liked the question.

"Why would I do that?"

"One of Ben's people said you tied up to the dock over there on Tuesday afternoon. He thought maybe you were coming in for bait, but you left the boat for several hours and never did get any bait."

No one at the marina had connected the fishing boat to Paolo Rosetti, but Carol was determined to push the envelope.

"That's ridiculous," Paolo said, and now he was angry. "I never stopped at any marina. Somebody's made a mistake. A big one."

"Well, it happens, I suppose. So you were fishing. Catch anything?"

"No, not a damn thing."

"Probably the wrong kind of bait. What did you use?"

"Sheriff, I'm tired of this." Rosetti's already florid face had turned a darker hue. "I had nothing whatsoever to do with Gerlach's death, and I don't take kindly to you and your damn questions. I suggest you leave me and my wife alone and start looking for whoever did it."

"Of course, Mr. Rosetti. That's what my officers and I are already doing. Twenty-four seven. And we intend to keep at it until we catch him."

Carol let herself out. She had not learned whether Paolo Rosetti had been on the Brae Loch campus on the afternoon of Harley Gerlach's death. But she had learned that he still did not have a persuasive alibi and that he should be treated as a prime suspect. Moreover, she thought, as she drove off in the direction of Southport, I do not like the man.

CHAPTER 26

Carol hadn't decided whether her next order of business was to seek out Janet Myers' neighbors or to drive over to Ithaca to talk with Mercedes Redman. Either way she would have to drive down East Lake Road for several miles, so she turned in the direction of Southport when she left Merchant's Point. It was not until she reached the junction where the road to Ithaca branched off to the east that she made up her mind to make the Myers stop first. Whether that decision would have made a difference in Redman's life will probably never be known.

As it happened, the sheriff wasn't the only person who wanted to talk with Mercedes Redman that Sunday in August. Heather Merriman had been thinking about Kevin's advice regarding her twin problems with Carpenter and Redman ever since their impromptu meeting on Friday. It was the violin teacher she respected most and wanted to hurt least, so she decided that a face-to-face conversation with her would be preferable to a phone call. As a result of that decision, she climbed into her car on Sunday morning and headed for Ithaca.

Heather was still unclear in her own mind what it was that Mercedes wanted from her. If it was to encourage and facilitate her career as a singer, she would be flattered. She whould welcome her as a mentor, taking advantage of her experience and her contacts. But why should it be necessary to transfer to a new college, move to Ithaca, and share her mentor's apartment? She'd given it a lot of thought, but concluded that she wasn't ready for such a major change.

Not even if Mercedes had no ulterior motive. But what if she did? Heather had tried to banish the thought that her would-be mentor desired a physical relationship with her. There had been no tangible evidence that she did, no casual touching, no expressions of affection. But there had been something, something which her French teacher would refer to as 'je ne sais quoi.' For some reason, the notion that Mercedes Redman was a lesbian anxious to have an affair with her would not go away. And Heather knew that she could not put herself in a position where she would have to rebuff her if and when she made her intentions clear.

Professor Whitman had urged her to finesse the issue by finding ways to be unavailable when Redman beckoned. He would probably have counseled her not to take the trip she was now taking. But Heather had convinced herself that the courteous if difficult thing to do was to have a frank face-to-face talk with Mercedes. She expected to be having that talk in another half an hour.

The clock above the stove said that it was almost 11:30. Unaware that she would soon have company, Mercedes Redman was sitting at her kitchen table. On the table in front of her were a half-full cup of cold coffee and a brief typed note. Mercedes had long since memorized the five words which constituted the note. She had been considering their meaning and their importance ever since the note had arrived in the mail Saturday afternoon. Normally a sound sleeper, she had spent a restless night worrying about the note, trying without much success to think of a way to find out if her hunch as to the note's author was correct.

She picked the note up for perhaps the tenth time since pouring her third cup of coffee of the morning. The words hadn't changed. They still occupied a place roughly halfway down a piece of inexpensive paper, intended for use with an inkjet printer. The paper still revealed the fact that it had been refolded to better fit the envelope it had come in.

Mercedes spoke the five words aloud, as if by doing so she might better decode the message.

Leave her alone! Remember Gerlach!

The key word among the five was 'Gerlach.' It made it virtually certain that the note came from someone who had been involved in the Brae Loch opera project. The author of the note was obviously warning her to have nothing to do with a woman who presumably had also been a member of Kevin Whitman's ill-fated company. Mercedes told herself that her relationships with the other women in the company had been exclusively professional—conducting the orchestra of which they were a part or coaching the singers among them. But deep down inside she knew that this was a lie. There was one woman who meant more to her than the rest, one woman with whom she had sought to cultivate a closer relationship. That woman was Heather Merriman. But how would another member of the company have known that? She doubted that she had spent more time talking with Heather than she had with Sandy Temple or other members of the orchestra's string section. Or with Janet Myers, for that matter. But she had to acknowledge that the nature of her conversations with Heather had been different.

Someone other than Heather was aware of that difference. The more she had thought about it, the more convinced she became that that someone was Sean Carpenter. His interest in Heather was no secret. And it was widely assumed among members of the company that his interest in her was more than platonic. He had become conspicuously protective of her as rehearsals progressed, even lashing out at Harley Gerlach on more than one occasion for his condescending treatment of Miss Merriman.

In all probability there had come a day when he was in his protective mode and Heather had confided in him that she believed that she had another suitor. Carpenter would have coaxed a name from her, leading in a matter of days to the note which lay on her kitchen table. In spite of its brevity, it was an angry note, and the phrase 'remember Gerlach' constituted either an attempt to scare her or, far more seriously, a threat on her life. Was Sean Carpenter suggesting in that brief unsigned note that he had killed Gerlach and was prepared to kill again? No, she thought, that would be the height of foolishness, and Carpenter was much too smart to give himself away so carelessly. More probably he was invoking Gerlach's death to demonstrate how seriously I should take his demand to leave Heather Merriman alone.

Mercedes got up to deposit her now empty coffee cup in the dishwasher. It was time to take a shower, to wash away these troubling thoughts. Perhaps she was overdoing her anxiety. Maybe the note was not from Carpenter. Maybe it had nothing to do with her interest in Heather Merriman. It might even be a prank. She doubted it.

As the noon hour approached, Mercedes Redman went into what she called her music room, took out her violin, and began a familiar ritual. She would relax by playing a favorite unaccompanied piece by Bach. It was while she was tuning up that the doorbell rang. It couldn't be Marcia, back from what she had said would be a long bike ride, because Marcia had her own key.

No students were scheduled, and Sunday was not a day on which solicitors or pollsters typically came to the door. Mercedes was annoyed at this interruption in what she viewed as an opportunity to exorcise her worries about the note.

To her great surprise, the person at the door was Heather Merriman. Under normal circumstances, Mercedes would have been delighted to see her. But not today, not with the threatening note still on her mind, not with Marcia due back in another hour or two at the most.

But Mercedes was genuinely fond of the girl and still interested in developing a personal relationship with her. It never occurred to her to send Heather away.

"What a nice surprise," she said. "I've been hoping you might find time to visit me, but I never expected to see you today. Come on in."

"I should have called first, I know. But I was over this way, and it seemed like a good opportunity to take you up on your offer to see your apartment."

"There's not a lot to see, as you'll see for yourself," Mercedes said as she led Heather into the living room.

The apartment was a small one, and her statement that there wasn't a lot to see was technically correct. In addition to the living room and kitchen, there was but one bedroom, a single bath, and a room which could have served as a study or a guest bedroom but which Mercedes had turned into a studio where she gave lessons and herself practiced the violin. But in another and more important sense there was quite a lot to see.

Heather asked if she might look around, but she had already started a self-guided tour before Mercedes could respond. She did it out of an innocent curiosity, but it immediately became apparent that what was interesting about the apartment was not the paucity of rooms but what those rooms contained. Especially the bedroom. It had not been straightened up yet, and the result was an unreconstructed snapshot of the personal lives of Redman and someone else. And that someone else was obviously another woman.

Heather stood in the doorway, with Mercedes behind her in the hall, looking at an unmade bed with two sets of pillows, each with the impression of the head and shoulders of whoever had slept there the night before. The closet door stood open, the clothes on their hangers revealing that two very different people with very different tastes shared the room. Some of those clothes were similar to what Redman had worn during rehearsals at Brae Loch, simple, with subdued colors and eminently practical. Other clothes, occupying their own section of the closet or draped over the room's only chair, were flamboyant in both color and style. Beneath the dresses and slacks on the hangers were two contrasting sets of footwear. There were at least three pairs of knee-high boots, two of them in dramatically bright colors. The pairs of low-heeled black and brown walking shoes next to them paled by comparison.

Heather turned away from her cursory appraisal of the bedroom, suddenly aware that there were little indicators everywhere that told the same story: She had been correct in her suspicion that Mercedes Redman had a lesbian partner.

"Let me make you some coffee," Mercedes said, steering Heather back into the living room. The damage had been done, as she knew it would be the moment she saw Heather at the door. It would no longer be possible to pretend that she lived alone. It might no longer be possible to persuade the girl to move in with her, to take Marcia's place. In all probability, such a relationship had never been in the cards. Nonetheless, Mercedes experienced a moment of almost painful regret.

Heather Merriman had made the trip to Ithaca to tell Mercedes that she would not be changing colleges or accepting the offer to share the older woman's apartment. But now that she was there, now that her suspicion had been turned into fact, she realized that she was less comfortable saying what she had come to say than she had expected to be. She was even embarrassed to be there, an intruder into someone else's private life. Someone she barely knew, someone who had been kind to her and whose kindness she may have misinterpreted. How could the woman have been coming on to her when she already had a partner?

"I promise not to stay long," she said in response to the offer of coffee. "But I'll have one cup with you before I go."

She waited in the living room while Mercedes tended to the coffee in the kitchen. The bookcase across the room from the couch interested her. Most of the books seemed to be about history, with an emphasis on the age of enlightenment. History was not one of her better subjects, but reading the titles of these books increased her respect for Mercedes. She was in the process of taking a biography of Rousseau off the shelf when the coffee arrived.

"You're welcome to borrow anything there that you like," Mercedes said as she set Heather's cup on the coffee table.

"Thanks. Maybe I will."

Having decided not to talk about what she had planned to talk about, Heather was relieved to have something else to discuss. She apologized for being historically illiterate and listened attentively while Mercedes spoke about the influence of enlightenment philosophers on America's founding fathers. Heather found herself thinking that her own professors had rarely made their subjects sound so fascinating.

Not surprisingly, the conversation soon turned to music, and Heather had just asked for an opinion on Mozart's operas when the door opened and a woman wearing biker's gear walked in.

"What's going on?" she asked as she took off her helmet and put it on top of the bookcase.

"Marcia, I'd like you to meet Heather Merriman. We were together in that opera production over on Crooked Lake. Heather, this is Marcia Kane."

Mercedes made no attempt to explain who Marcia Kane was or why she was in the process of making herself at home in the Redman apartment. But it was quite obvious that this was the woman who lived there with Mercedes, the woman who wore the colorful outfits now hanging in the bedroom closet when she wasn't dressed for bike riding.

"Miss Merriman," she said, acknowledging the stranger on the couch. She turned immediately to her partner.

"I thought you'd be ready. The show, remember? We're going to the matinee."

"There's plenty of time," Mercedes said. "Why don't you go ahead and shower. It won't take me long."

"I hope so. I can't stand to be late."

Heather had been listening to this brief colloquy with interest. The woman named Marcia had not exactly been unpleasant, but neither had she been particularly friendly. Or cordial. Heather wondered if she had been witness to a typical exchange between the two women or if the hint of tension in the air was due to her own presence in the apartment.

Ms. Kane disappeared into the bedroom without another word, only to reappear in a robe a few minutes later and head for the bathroom.

Anxious to minimize any feeling of uncomfortability on Mercedes' part, Heather got to her feet and said she'd have to be going. Redman made the polite disclaimer, but didn't try to stop her. She did remind her about the book she was going to take, but didn't urge her to come back.

It had been the briefest of visits. Mercedes had never mentioned the note that she assumed had come from Sean Carpenter. Heather had never mentioned the reason she had come to Ithaca. And neither of them had commented on the fact that Marcia Kane had made no effort to conceal the fact that she was unhappy to find a strange woman having coffee with her partner on this Sunday afternoon in August.

CHAPTER 27

Carol's attempt to learn more about Janet Myers' whereabouts the day of Harley Gerlach's murder had been a disappointing failure. Moreover, it had taken several hours of her time on Sunday afternoon, making it necessary to defer the conversation she had hoped to have with Mercedes Redman until another day. Most of the neighbors were at home, but they had nothing to add to Janet's own account of what she had done and when the previous Tuesday. She had said nothing to any of the neighbors about her plans, and no one had seen her either drive away or return home. The Myers house itself had been empty, and once again no one in the neighborhood knew where either Janet or her husband was. Somebody, she thought, will surely tell them that I was asking for them. She wondered what they would make of that news. It would depend, of course, on whether Janet had visited the Brae Loch campus the afternoon Gerlach had been killed. And on whether she had told her husband the truth about what she had been doing that day.

By Monday morning Carol had more or less gotten over her frustration with what had largely been a wasted Sunday. She had even set aside the Gerlach case for the moment to catch up on other business in her in-basket. It was while she was listening to Officer Grieves trying to justify how he had handled an angry motorist over the weekend that her secretary announced a visitor who wished to talk to her about the murder at Brae Loch.

The young man who came into her office gave his name as Christopher Ellis, a student at the college. He acted nervous and it took a few minutes before he summoned the courage to tell the sheriff what had prompted his visit to her office.

"I'm not sure that what I'm going to tell you is something you don't already know," Ellis said, "but I figured I ought to say something. You know, just in case."

"We always welcome help from our citizens," Carol said. She wondered how this young man, who claimed to be a business major at the college and an assistant in the provost's office, could be in a position to provide useful information regarding Gerlach's murder, but she was willing to listen.

"It's like this," he began. "Last Tuesday—that's the day the man from the opera was killed—last Tuesday I had to go down to the boathouse, and when I did I saw one of the people from the opera down on the beach. His name is Carpenter. I thought I should say something because the rest of those opera people weren't around, just this guy. There wasn't anything going on they needed to be there for, not until that night."

"Why do you assume this might be important?" Carol asked.

"Well, I couldn't imagine any of us killing that man. You know, any of the college people. I mean, why would we? It probably had to be one of the opera people, and here was one of them, hanging around near where it happened."

"I can see you've given quite a bit of thought to this," Carol said. "And what you say makes sense. We looked at it just the way you did. We asked all of the men and women in the opera where they'd been that afternoon. Now let me ask you another question. How do you know this man you saw on the beach was someone named Carpenter?"

Ellis looked flustered. It was a question he hadn't expected.

"I think I'd heard someone call him that. Maybe I've got it wrong. But it was someone from the opera. I'd seen him around."

This was an unsatisfactory explanation, and it was obvious that Ellis knew it.

"Mr. Ellis," Carol said, "I'm glad you came by. Your information may be important. But I don't think you got the man's name wrong. I think you know it was Mr. Carpenter, and I want you to tell me how you know that. Did you talk to him? Did someone point him out to you?"

"I'd met him before," Ellis said.

"Oh, and how was that?"

Reluctantly, Christopher Ellis told of his earlier encounter with Heather Merriman and Sean Carpenter on the beach, explaining that it was Miss Merriman who had introduced them.

"That's better. Now here's another question, and once again I'd appreciate an honest answer. Was Miss Merriman there on the beach with Mr. Carpenter when you saw him again last Tuesday?"

"I guess so."

"I'll take that as a yes," Carol said in her sternest voice. "But that's not what you said a moment ago. You said that Carpenter was the only member of the opera company you saw that day. But there were really two people, weren't there? Why didn't you mention her, too?"

"I didn't want to get her into trouble." It was, at last, a straightforward answer, and the one Carol expected.

"As it happens, Mr. Ellis, Miss Merriman had already told me she was on the beach most of Tuesday afternoon. In fact, as I suspect you know, she spent many rehearsal afternoons on the Brae Loch beach this summer. So what I've learned this morning is that you don't want me to suspect that Miss Merriman had anything to do with that murder over there, but that you are willing to let me believe that perhaps Mr. Carpenter did. You like Miss Merriman, don't you? And you don't much like Mr. Carpenter because he likes her too? Isn't that about right?"

The Brae Loch business major denied that this had been his motivation, but it was not a convincing denial.

Before he left, Carol had softened her criticism of Ellis and again thanked him for coming forward with what might be useful information. After he had left she considered the fact that Heather Merriman had readily admitted to the fact that she had been sunbathing at Brae Loch while someone was strangling Harley Gerlach in nearby Wayne Hall. But she had said nothing about the fact that Sean Carpenter was with her that afternoon. Did this mean that she was more interested in Carpenter than she had admitted? More interested, and hence more protective of him?

It was now imperative, she said to herself, to have a serious talk with both Merriman and Carpenter. Not together, but one at a time.

CHAPTER 28

The summer had gone by too quickly, thanks to the demands of preparing for the presentation of Puccini's opera. Kevin's usual swimming regimen had been one of the casualties of those hectic days from June until mid-August. In less than two weeks he would be heading back to the city, and if he were to do any swimming there, it would have to be at the health club. He had a membership, had had one for several years, but he didn't much enjoy the chlorinated pool and typically found that he swam less regularly there than he did at the lake. There was no way to make up for lost time, but there was nothing to prevent him from taking full advantage of the few days that were left before Labor Day.

The investigation of Gerlach's murder had given him little to do. In the week since it happened he had done only two things that might be construed as contributions to the solution of the case. He had visited Gerlach's house twice, first with Carol and then by himself. On the first occasion he had found the album containing pictures of the women Gerlach had entertained since moving to Crooked Lake. On the second he had found a scrap of gum wrapper that might or might not be important. His second contribution, the importance of which was also not proven, was the result of his conversation with Arthur Conklin's neighbor. He had learned that Conklin had briefly been under suspicion of having caused the death of his wife—the wife who had confessed to an affair with Gerlach.

It was fairly early on Monday morning that he set off on what he thought of as his long swim, one that took him to the end of Blue Water Point and around the bend into Mallard Cove. The lake was almost entirely free of boats at this early hour in the morning, so he could concentrate on the question of who had killed Harley Gerlach rather than worry about close encounters with careless boaters. He swam at a moderate pace, testing muscles too little used of late, and enjoying the cool water.

Kevin was frustrated, and his swim had become a form of therapy, helping him cope with his bad summer. First no opera.

And then no real opportunity to help solve the crime that had brought the opera to its untimely end.

He felt better for the exercise when he finished his swim, but he was still discouraged about the way the summer was ending. He wanted to be doing something to help Carol, but the one thing he had agreed to do, tracking down the unknown women pictured in Gerlach's 'harem album,' looked like a mission impossible. Where would he start? He had no better idea now than he did when he first saw their pictures.

The hell with it, he said to himself, as he finished toweling off. He'd forget about the murder investigation and go into Yates Center to stock his depleted larder.

It was nearly an hour later, and Kevin was pushing a cart down an aisle marked household supplies at Jacob's Supermarket. He tossed a box of garbage sacks and some dishwashing soap into the cart and consulted his shopping list. When he looked up, he saw that he was about to run into another shopper turning into his aisle.

"Sorry," he said, disengaging his cart from hers. "I wasn't paying attention."

"No problem. Neither was I." The woman spoke in a deep voice and gave him a pleasant smile. It was a lopsided smile. He knew he'd seen it somewhere before. Warm, friendly, one corner of her mouth turned up more than the other. It's rude to stare, he thought, but he couldn't take his eyes off the woman's face, a near perfect oval under nearly jet-black hair. He was sure he knew who she was, but he couldn't place her.

They went their separate ways, and it was while he was pondering the choices in the cereal aisle that Kevin remembered where he had seen the woman with the lopsided smile. Her picture had appeared in Harley Gerlach's album. He left his cart in the aisle and hurried to the front of the store. He quickly scanned the checkout lines, finally spotting her just as she was making her way to the exit.

Kevin wanted very much to talk with her, but he faced a problem with no apparent solution. He could catch up with her, ask to talk with her, and then be rebuffed the minute he mentioned Gerlach's name. What would he do if she simply got into her car and drove away? And that is almost certainly what she would do. He realized that he had been so sure he wouldn't be able to locate either of the two unknown women in Gerlach's photos that he hadn't given any thought to what he would do if he did find them.

But now that he had serendipitously—and quite literally— bumped into one of them, Kevin was determined not to let her get away. He'd think of a way to talk to her, the questions he'd want to ask her. But first he had to find out who she was and where she lived. So he followed her out into the supermarket's parking lot, keeping his distance, until she reached her car, filled the trunk with her groceries, and got ready to leave. He then walked toward the car, positioning himself so he could see the license number when she backed out of her parking space.

As soon as she drove off, Kevin took a crumpled receipt from the nearby dry cleaners out of his pocket and wrote down the number of the license plate on the back of it. He was still unsure what he would say to the woman, but he knew that he would soon be talking with her.

———

With the help of the sheriff's department and the motor vehicle administration, the task of turning the number on the car's license plate into a name and an address proved to be easy, and it was just ahead of noon that Kevin pulled off the road at a house on the outskirts of Yates Center. The house faced the lake and was surrounded by a white picket fence, a well-manicured lawn, and a variety of attractive rosebushes. The car with the familiar license plate was sitting on a recently resurfaced driveway, which made it likely that the woman with the lopsided smile was at home.

Kevin was still uncertain as to exactly how to approach the woman, but he felt better about doing it here than at the supermarket. Now if only the husband was not at home. He was sure that there was a husband, for she had been wearing a wedding band during their brief encounter on aisle 5. But in all likelihood the husband was at work. He'd soon find out.

She answered the door on the first ring of the bell, and recognized her caller immediately. She flashed him the lopsided smile.

"Well, hello. My friend from the supermarket. What brings you here? Did I drop something?"

It had not yet dawned on her that the man at her door would be unlikely to have known where she lived.

"Not that I know of. No, I just thought I'd take advantage of this beautiful day to stop by and say a proper hello. I don't usually meet people by banging into their shopping carts at the supermarket. Mind if I come in for a minute?"

The lopsided smile disappeared. She didn't look unfriendly, just puzzled.

"Well, no, of course not. Come on in."

"I'll only be here a few minutes," Kevin said, politely declining the offer of iced tea. He had avoided the use of the woman's name, Lauren Helman, knowing that his knowledge of who she was would alarm her. But there was no way he could long delay explaining his presence in her home. He got to the point as soon as he had taken a seat in the Helman living room.

"You have probably heard about what happened over at Brae Loch College last week—the murder of one of the members of the cast of the opera they were going to perform. The man who was killed was named Gerlach. Harley Gerlach. He lived down at the end of the bluff, had lived there more than two years. I hear that you knew Mr. Gerlach."

There was no trace of a smile on Lauren Helman's face now.

"You're mistaken. I don't know anyone with that name."

"Then perhaps you can explain this."

Kevin had made a quick trip to the sheriff's office in Cumberland after his chance meeting with Helman in the supermarket, and Carol had entrusted him with the 'harem album.' He opened it to the page containing the picture of Lauren and Harley and set it down on the coffee table in front of her.

Mrs. Helman must have known such a picture existed inasmuch as she had obviously posed for it. And willingly. But she could not imagine why it was in this stranger's possession. Or why he was sitting in her living room, asking her about a relationship which she had ended nearly two years ago and which she very much regretted.

"Why don't you tell me what this is all about," she said, her voice cold. "I don't even know your name."

"I'm sorry," Kevin said. "I'm not trying to be mysterious. The name is Whitman, Kevin Whitman. I was in charge of the production of that opera at Brae Loch, the one in which Mr. Gerlach was singing. I'm sure you can appreciate that I have something of an interest in his death. It led to the cancellation of my opera. I am finding that to understand why he was killed I need to know something about the life he lived. What I'm learning is that he had a way with women. That's probably not the best way to put it, but I'm sure you know what I mean."

"Okay, so I can't deny I knew him. I remember when he took that picture. He had a way of setting up the camera and then coming back and getting into the picture himself. But it was a long time ago. I learned the hard way that he wasn't a very nice man. He didn't end the relationship. I did."

"I guess you know you weren't the only woman in his life. He sort of collected them. Like a hobby almost. Do you mind telling me how he did it? I mean, how did you happen to start seeing him?"

"It seemed innocent enough," she said in a wry voice. "They have these occasional chamber music concerts around the lake, and I went to one. It took place at one of the wineries as I remember it. He was there, and we got to talking at intermission. He was interesting. Smart. He knew a lot about music—really about a lot of things. And he acted as if he was interested in me. I mean he didn't just talk. He listened. Most men don't do that. Anyway, one thing led to another and then we were meeting at his house. My husband never knew. He still doesn't, and I hope he never does. It was a dumb thing I did. Dave—that's my husband— isn't flashy like Gerlach, but he's really a rock. You know, the kind of person you don't really appreciate until something like this happens."

The other question that Kevin would have liked to ask of Lauren Helman was where she was the previous Tuesday afternoon. But it was Carol who'd have to ask that question. He couldn't imagine that something had rekindled Helman's anger with Gerlach and that she'd killed him. He certainly hoped that her husband would never find out about the relationship she'd had with Gerlach. In any event, it wasn't his place to treat her as a suspect in the murder at Brae Loch.

True to his word, Kevin did not stay long. Nor had he learned much. Mrs. Helman's account of how Gerlach had insinuated himself into her life was very similar to Mercedes Redman's. So Gerlach's modus operandi had now been fairly well established. But Kevin was more interested not just in what had happened on the afternoon of the dress rehearsal, but also in what Gerlach had been doing in the months and years before that, including his time with the Metropolitan Opera chorus. Much as he hated to lose any of the remaining days of summer at the lake with Carol, he decided he should take a short trip to the city and speak with the Met's archivist. He might even go tomorrow.

CHAPTER 29

The short flight to the city had been uneventful. Rather than take along a novel or the Berlioz book he had borrowed from Gerlach's library, Kevin had pulled out a pad to jot down the questions he wanted to be sure to ask of the Met's archivist. She had been very pleasant on the phone and had assured him that she would be available when he arrived. She even remembered Gerlach, but nothing in her remarks or tone of voice suggested how she or the Met had felt about him.

Instead of making notes for his conversation with the archivist, however, Kevin spent most of the short flight thinking about Carol and reflecting on their discussion of the previous evening. She had been less convinced than he was that the trip to the city would be worthwhile, and she was definitely disappointed that he would be gone for a day and possibly two. But she wished him well and extracted a promise that he would return to the lake for a long weekend as soon as he had launched his fall semester courses.

The apartment felt cold and impersonal after the cottage, and he realized that he wasn't looking forward to living in it for yet another academic year. He was glad that on this trip at least he'd only be sleeping at the apartment. He'd take his meals out. The cab took him uptown to the Met's offices, and before noon he was sitting across the desk from a white-haired woman whose name was Jenny DeAngelo. She was the one who had agreed to help him gather information on Harley Gerlach's years in the chorus.

"It's been a few years now since Harley left us," she said. "Haven't seen him since. How's he doing?"

"Not well," Kevin replied. He had not thought it necessary to mention Gerlach's death when he'd made the appointment. Better to share bad news when he saw her. "In fact, he's dead."

"When did this happen?" she asked, her voice still in neutral.

"A week ago today. I'm afraid he didn't die of natural causes. Somebody killed him."

This news finally produced a reaction in Ms. DeAngelo.

"Good gracious, that's awful." She leaned back in her chair and gazed out of the window at the skyline. "What did he do to deserve an end like that?"

It was an interesting way to put it. Jenny DeAngelo had obviously not thought highly of Harley Gerlach.

Kevin filled her in on the Brae Loch opera project and reported that the local authorities still had no clue as to the identity of the person who had strangled Harley. Even as he used the expression 'local authorities,' he thought of it as a wholly inappropriate way to describe Carol.

"I'm not here in any official capacity," Kevin said. "I'm a friend of the local sheriff up there, and she knows I'm here. We don't expect that anything in Mr. Gerlach's past will help explain what happened to him. For me he was just a talented singer. But we think it's important to learn what we can about him."

"Well, I suppose I'm the person you want to talk to. Me and maybe a couple of the old-timers in our chorus. Where do you want me to start, Mr. Whitman?"

"I know how long he was with you, give or take a year. But I have no idea why he left the Met. Or how he was thought of by the company and by his peers."

"He didn't leave of his own accord, that I know. I'm a record keeper, you understand, not a keeper of company secrets. But it was a big enough deal that it would be hard not to know what happened."

"Why a big deal?"

"Because he was good. The Met doesn't can people on a whim, especially the mainstays. He wasn't only a very good chorister. He could act as well as sing. He was good enough to be asked to take an occasional comprimario role. Oh, I'd better explain—a comprimario is—"

"That's okay. I know. I teach opera at Madison College when I'm not vacationing in the Finger Lakes."

Ms. DeAngelo looked at Kevin with a newfound respect.

"I see. Well, then, let me cut to the chase." Which she proceeded to do.

"There were three problems, as I understand it. Not that big at first, but eventually they became intolerable. At least that's what my friends in the chorus tell me. He started coming to rehearsals drunk, or nearly drunk. And late. You just can't run an opera company if the people you rely on don't take their responsibilities seriously. I'm sure you know stories about some of the big names, always cancelling at the last minute, making impossible demands. They may be a big drawing card, but they drive management crazy. That's why the company had to dismiss one of its superstars, Kathleen Battle. I'm sure you remember that."

Kevin nodded, telling her that he did.

"Well, Mr. Gerlach was like that. At first it was just the occasional bad day. But it became a habit."

"I'm not surprised to hear this," Kevin said. "He did the same thing to us this summer. It sounds as if getting fired down here didn't shake him up, persuade him to change his ways."

"I didn't know him personally," Ms. DeAngelo said, "but people who did were convinced that he was a borderline alcoholic when he left the Met. Anyway, that was just one of his problems. Every year the Met holds auditions for new choristers. Got to bring in infusions of new blood, you know. People move, retire, get sick. There's always turnover.

"Anyway, the panel that conducts these auditions always includes one or two members of the chorus. It's a plum job. The chorus master wouldn't tap you for the panel unless he thinks you're really special. Gerlach served on the panel for several years back in the '90s. Rumor has it that it worked out fine for awhile, but than something happened to his judgment. It seems he became kind of erratic, voting against candidates the rest of the panel thought were just fine. I don't suppose it's easy to get complete agreement all the time. Too subjective. But Gerlach was apparently odd man out a lot, and really stubborn about it. Stubborn and nasty, too. He was finally dropped from the panel."

"Was there any talk that his votes had anything to do with personal bias?"

"I wouldn't know," she answered. "Archives is a kind of insular place, hardly where the action is."

Kevin thought that Ms. DeAngelo had been privy to quite a bit of gossip for someone who worked in an insular component of the Metropolitan Opera.

"Then there's the clincher," she continued. "I think Mr. Gerlach might have survived the drinking and his votes on the auditions if it hadn't been for the violence."

"Violence?" Kevin had not been surprised by the news of Gerlach's drinking or the intimation that he could be cruel and dismissive of fellow singers. But violent?

"Yes, violence. He was involved in fisticuffs with other men in the chorus on at least two occasions, and he was the instigator. I heard about it from a friend in the chorus. She said he attacked another chorister after rehearsal once, and then went after him another time during a rehearsal while the director was trying to talk them through some stage business. Of course this happened quite a few years ago, but I remember it because it was so unusual. You hear a lot about temperamental divas, but not about choristers."

"Did your friend ever say what these altercations were about?"

"Women, I think. Word had it that Mr. Gerlach was a skirt chaser, and that the women tended to be other men's wives. I guess he got too close to the wives of some of his colleagues in the chorus, they took offense, and he got physical. Whatever the cause, the company just couldn't have one of its members brawling onstage."

"Can you give me some dates? When Gerlach was hired, when he was fired—even when he participated in the auditions."

"Sure," she said. "Just give me a few minutes."

Jenny DeAngelo had provided Kevin with information about Harley Gerlach's behavior without ever consulting any files. But she didn't have dates in her memory bank, which necessitated some research. It took all of three minutes.

Gerlach had joined the Met chorus in 1989 and had left the company in 2002. His membership on the panel evaluating auditions had lasted from 1997 until 2001. Kevin quickly did the math. Gerlach had been a valued member of the company in good standing for roughly a decade, but then things began to go bad, and they had gone bad in a hurry.

Ms. DeAngelo gave him the names of three members of the chorus who had been contemporaries of Gerlach and might be able to elaborate on what she had told him. She expressed her willingness to be of further help if he needed it, and bade him good-bye.

Kevin debated calling the members of the chorus whose names she had given him, only to decide that he had learned enough. It was much as he had expected, consistent with the

Harley Gerlach he had come to know over the summer. He couldn't see how any of it could help track down the Brae Loch strangler, but at least he had done what he could to fill in some of the blanks in his picture of the man who was to have introduced *Gianni Schicchi* to prospective opera fans on Crooked Lake.

CHAPTER 30

"So, what do you know now that you didn't know twenty-four hours ago?"

Carol had been doubtful that Kevin's trip to the city would bring them closer to an answer to the question of who had killed Harley Gerlach.

"Not much," he answered truthfully. "But I do know why his career at the Met was cut short. It's an interesting case, a cautionary tale of what not to do if you want to make your way in the world. Talk about great examples of talent wasted."

Having decided not to pursue members of the Met chorus who could document what the archivist had told him, Kevin had returned to the lake late the same afternoon and was now enjoying a glass of one of the better local Rieslings with Carol. The evening promised to be much better than the one he had been contemplating in his city apartment.

"I wish there was something you could do to help me up here," Carol said. "And I'm not talking about breaking and entering."

"I didn't break into Gerlach's house, Carol. Like I told you, someone had done it for me, taking that pane of glass out of the back door."

"So you said. Anyhow, there's a dozen or more things I've got to do, things I don't want to hand off to Sam or my other officers, things you can't very well do. I've got to talk with Redman about Gerlach. And Carpenter—why did he lie to me about being at Brae Loch Tuesday afternoon? Not to mention Merriman. She never said he was with her. Another lie. Why? I've got to see Myers' husband, see if he can corroborate her story. Where the hell is he, anyway? Never seems to be home. Then you tell me that Conklin was suspected in his wife's death. That means I need to talk with the police chief over in Geneva. And Conklin's nurseries. He said he was there on Tuesday, but I haven't had a chance to check it out. I've got a feeling I'm spinning my wheels."

"You sound beleaguered. I like the optimistic Carol much better."

163

"I'll be optimistic when we get a good lead. Or when somebody has a crisis of conscience and confesses to strangling Gerlach."

"Anything yet on whether any of my people chew gum?" Kevin laughed, shaking his head. "Crazy, isn't it? We're supposed to be looking for a murderer, but what are we doing—trying to find out who chews gum. Spearmint at that."

"Sam's on that one. He'll probably tell me that half a dozen of your cellists and sopranos all chew. My bet is that that wrapper you found was Gerlach's."

"Can't be. He was dead by the time I found it."

"Maybe. Or maybe we just overlooked it when we went through the house."

Over a second glass of wine they agreed to talk about pleasanter things. Unfortunately, with Labor Day and Kevin's return to the city looming, there weren't a lot of pleasant things to talk about. But it was a beautiful evening, and Kevin snapped them out of their funk by suggesting they take the canoe out. There would be no need to talk. They could simply relax and enjoy the sight of swallows darting about over the lake's surface in the gathering twilight.

The moon had risen high above the bluff across the lake by the time they retired to bed. Kevin and Carol were no closer to solving the Gerlach case than they had been several hours earlier, but they slept soundly. Tomorrow would be another day.

———

It was Kevin who started the coffee in the morning, but it was Carol who moved most quickly to get dressed, have breakfast, and set off on the day's business.

"My agenda didn't shrink while I was sleeping," the sheriff said, "but I've got to start somewhere and it's going to be with little Miss Merriman. I've got to stop at the office, have a word with the men, and call Sean Carpenter. I need to set up a meeting with him, this afternoon or tomorrow if possible. But I want to get Merriman's story—her revised story—first. I think there's more to their relationship than she'd have us believe. Of course she'll probably call him and tell him about our meeting before I see him, but there's nothing I can do about that, and I don't want to see them together."

"Why not?"

"Not sure. Just a hunch. Anyway, I think I'm more likely to get a straight answer from her than from him."

"I take it you think we should consider him a suspect in Gerlach's death. I don't see it. He strikes me as someone slipping into middle age who's taken a fancy to a pretty young woman. I don't see how that fits in with Gerlach's murder. I know he took offense at the way Gerlach talked down to Heather during rehearsals, but come on, how does that become a motive for murder?"

"I don't have a favorite suspect," Carol said. "Fact is, I can't really imagine any of your opera company strangling Gerlach. Several of them seem to have had good reasons to be pissed off at him, but most people don't go around killing someone just because they don't like him."

"Hate him is more like it," Kevin said. "I'll be interested in whether you get a feeling that Carpenter hated Gerlach. Like Myers did, or Conklin. Even Rosetti."

"You'll be the first to know. But I've got to run. You can clean up the kitchen, make up the bed, make yourself useful. And have supper ready for a tired sheriff. How's six o'clock sound?"

"You're becoming more like 'she who must be obeyed' every day."

Carol gave him a big hug and a kiss, and was gone. Kevin still had to decide how he'd spend the day.

Heather Merriman arrived at the sheriff's office shortly ahead of eleven. She had caught a nasty summer cold, with the result that her summer tan gave way to a less attractive red around her nose. Carol commiserated with her on the cold and inquired as to whether she'd like coffee.

"Thanks, but no thanks," she said, pulling a Kleenex from a pocket and wiping her nose. "Sorry about this. It would have been a killer if we were still doing the opera."

"It's such a shame about the opera. I'm sure you were really looking forward to it. I've never heard you sing, but I hear that you have a lovely voice. Are you planning on a musical career?"

"Yes, I am. It's my major in college. I was so thrilled when Professor Whitman gave me the part in the opera. He's been awfully good to me. So have the others—well, most of them. It was a good experience, even if we didn't get to do it."

Carol knew nothing about Merriman except what she had heard from Kevin. And from Bridges, who had interviewed her the night after Gerlach's murder. She was appraising her as they talked. Very young. Attractive if one discounted the runny nose. She looked like someone perfectly suited for what theatre people call ingénue roles. There was a kind of youthful innocence about her, yet she had attracted the attention of Sean Carpenter, a middle-aged, married man. And she had lied about his presence at Brae Loch during the afternoon when Gerlach was strangled.

"I asked you to come over so I could ask a few questions. I know my deputy probably went over the same ground with you last week, but please bear with me. Okay? I understand that you were at the college the afternoon Mr. Gerlach was killed. Sunbathing, I think."

"That's right. I spent a lot of the afternoons over there. Unlike most of the cast, I didn't have a job to go to. Besides, my kid brother couldn't bug me like he does at our place."

Carol had never had a kid brother, but she could imagine what it might be like.

"I'm sure you know that we have to account for where everybody was when the murder took place. And you were on the beach. Was anybody else from the opera group on campus then?"

"I can't say for sure. But I never saw anyone."

"Miss Merriman, you should know that someone saw you on the beach that afternoon and said that you weren't alone. He said you were with Mr. Carpenter."

Carol left it at that, letting this challenge to the young woman's veracity sink in. Heather took out another Kleenex and blew her nose before saying anything.

"Who told you this?"

"It doesn't matter. There's no reason to believe that it isn't true. So I think we have stories that contradict each other. Why don't you tell us who was with you?"

Heather Merriman seemed to shrink into her chair.

"I made a promise I wouldn't tell."

"And why did you do that? Surely you don't think that lying to the sheriff in a criminal investigation is a very good idea."

It was now clear to Heather that her cold was far from her principal problem.

"Okay. It was Mr. Carpenter. Please don't tell him I told you. He's a good man. I think he was just worried that if you knew he'd been at the college that afternoon you'd blame him for Mr. Gerlach's death."

"Why should I do that? You were at the college, and I haven't blamed you for Mr. Gerlach's death. To tell you the truth, lying makes him look more suspicious than admitting he was there. And it doesn't make you look good, either."

The young woman was now close to tears. Carol decided to adopt another approach.

"What exactly is your relationship with Mr. Carpenter?"

"Relationship?" She made it sound as if she weren't sure what the word meant.

"Yes, your relationship. I realize that you had a relationship with him as members of the cast in the opera, but that's not what I have in mind. You and he were together on the beach that day, and according to what I hear, the two of you often spent time together there. Do you want to tell me about it?"

Heather blushed through her tan.

"It was nothing like what you're implying. It was just about singing. You know, about the opera. He was an experienced singer, and he was helping me learn my role. That and little tricks about using my voice. He's really good. He could have been in the Metropolitan Opera chorus, just like Mr. Gerlach was. He auditioned for it a few years ago and says he really should have made it. It's a shame he didn't."

"I hadn't meant to imply anything, Miss Merriman. But I'm sure you know that there was talk that Mr. Carpenter might have been romantically interested in you."

"Yes, I know. But it's not true. I don't date men my father's age."

No, I'm sure you don't, Carol thought, but that doesn't mean that men your father's age might not want to have an affair with you. Happens all the time, even on Crooked Lake.

"I shall have to talk with Mr. Carpenter and ask him about last Tuesday. If he denies being at the college that afternoon, I'll have to tell him that there is another witness who says he was. It may not be necessary to tell him that you broke your promise to him. But if necessary, I'll have to tell him what you told me. Like I said, this is a serious matter, and getting at the truth is more important than keeping promises. I'm sure you understand."

"You really don't think he did it, do you? I mean, why would he? He wouldn't have any reason to, and anyway he's not that kind of man."

"At the moment we have no idea who killed Mr. Gerlach. But the more people we talk to, the more questions we ask, the closer we get to an answer to that question. I appreciate your coming over to Cumberland today. If you think of anything else we should know, tell me. Right away."

Heather Merriman left the sheriff's office with her cold still bothering her and more things to worry about. Carol, armed with what she had learned from Merriman, got ready to leave for the drive to Rochester and the visit with Sean Carpenter.

CHAPTER 31

As it turned out, Carol did not drive to Rochester. Instead, she was sitting in her office staring out of the window and wondering why she had agreed to Carpenter's offer to meet her in Cumberland. She could think of two reasons why he might have wanted to make the 140-mile roundtrip when he could more easily have stayed at home. The first was that he could pay a visit to Heather Merriman while he was in the vicinity of Crooked Lake. The second was that he wouldn't have to worry that the sheriff might bump into his wife and ask her potentially awkward questions.

It was now a quarter to three and too late to change plans. Carpenter would be arriving at any minute. Besides, she had put the extra time to good use, tidying up the loose ends in another case that she had neglected in the days following Harley Gerlach's murder.

Carol busied herself, rearranging things on her desk. They didn't need to be rearranged, but she was uncharacteristically nervous and it gave her something to do with her hands while she waited for Carpenter. Would Merriman have contacted him, warned him that the sheriff now knew that he had been at Brae Loch the afternoon of the murder? And if she had, so what? The reason he had given Merriman for denying he had been there was a logical one, the lie a small and probably inconsequential one. What she was looking for was something more dramatic, something that would give her a real lead. She doubted that her conversation with Sean Carpenter would produce much of a lead.

JoAnne Franks, the young woman who was trying very hard but with limited success to fill Ms. Maltbie's shoes as Carol's secretary, announced that Mr. Carpenter had arrived. He looked very much as he had when she had interviewed him the evening of Gerlach's death, but Carol thought he seemed older. The reason was clear. It had been only a few hours earlier that Heather Merriman had sat in the same chair, and in view of the talk that Carpenter was romantically interested in her, it would have been difficult not to have noticed the obvious disparity in their ages.

169

They exchanged small talk for a few minutes, Carpenter because he seemed anxious to avoid whatever the point of this meeting might be, Carol because she had decided to let him take the lead. Which he finally did.

"I'm sorry, but I'm not quite sure just why I'm here. When you called you said you needed to talk to me."

"That's right, I did," Carol said. "It's been a week now since Mr. Gerlach was killed. I'm sure you've thought a lot about it, you and everyone else in the opera company. Got any ideas?"

"Ideas? About who killed him?"

"If you do, I'd like to hear them."

Carpenter looked puzzled, unsure whether she was merely inviting speculation or coaxing him into some revealing—and perhaps damaging—remark.

"No," he said tentatively, "I guess not. It still seems like—well, just unbelievable."

"You were there, working with the cast for—what was it?—two months, give or take a week or two. How did the cast feel about Mr. Gerlach? Were you aware of anything? Maybe it was something small at the time, but now, as you look back on it, do you remember anything that in retrospect might be important?"

"There were the usual little disagreements, I suppose. But I can't think of anything like what you're talking about."

"How did you and Mr. Gerlach get along?"

Carpenter would have assumed that this would be among the sheriff's questions.

"Okay. He was good. Of course he knew it. He had a big ego. I expect everyone would agree on that."

"But did you and he get along?"

"Well, sure," Carpenter said, clearly uncomfortable as the sheriff's questions became more personal. "We weren't drinking buddies—never would have been. Just putting on a show."

Carol remembered Kevin saying that there had been some sort of contretemps involving Carpenter and Gerlach. Something to do with Harley's criticism of Heather Merriman. She decided to let it pass and turned to the subject of who had been where on the fateful afternoon.

"Let's talk about last Tuesday, the day of the dress rehearsal. The day Mr. Gerlach was killed. Where were you that afternoon?"

Sean Carpenter's expression told her that he was surprised by her question. And perhaps worried.

"I already told you," he said. "That night. You were questioning us about what had happened, and I said I'd been at my office up in Rochester. Remember?"

So, Merriman had apparently not called him to report on her conversation with the sheriff. Either that or he was prepared to leave the impression that, for whatever reason, Heather had lied.

"I remember. But I've been wondering whether you might have thought about it, decided that maybe you were at the college that afternoon."

Carpenter was no longer surprised by the sheriff's questions. He was angry.

"Are you accusing me of killing Gerlach?" he asked.

"Of course not, Mr. Carpenter. I'm investigating his murder. All I want everyone to do is simply answer my questions truthfully. This is how we do it."

He looked somewhat mollified.

"I didn't mean to be unpleasant, but you seemed to be doubting my word."

"I was doubting your word. You see, I happen to know that you were on the campus of Brae Loch College last Tuesday afternoon. We have an eyewitness who swears you were there. So I think you can see why I am giving you a chance to change your story."

"Who told you I was there?"

Carol had not mentioned Merriman, but figured that Carpenter suspected it was she who had betrayed him. It was time to set the record straight.

"One of the students at the college, a young man who's an assistant to the provost, saw you that day. You were on the beach, talking with Miss Merriman. He recognized you because she had introduced you to him not that many days earlier. I asked Miss Merriman if it was true that you had been there that day. She seemed reluctant to say so, but when I pressed her on it, she did. So I guess you could say that there are three people who know firsthand that you were there—the provost's observant assistant, Miss Merriman, and you yourself."

To say that Sean Carpenter was an unhappy man would have been an understatement. Not only had he been caught out in a lie, a lie he had angrily repeated. But he had also learned that the young woman he admired and trusted had gone back on her promise to support his lie.

"I thought it might look bad—Gerlach being killed and me being there when it happened. It was stupid, I know, but it made sense at the time to act like I hadn't been at the school. And then it would have looked funny if I changed my story."

"Forgive me for being confused, Mr. Carpenter, but I don't understand why you thought I'd be suspicious of you if I knew you were at Brae Loch when Mr. Gerlach was killed. You just told me that you and he had had no problems. Gotten along fine, just doing your job putting on an opera, you said. People don't go around strangling someone without a reason, and you don't seem to have had a reason. Why would I be suspicious of you?"

There didn't seem to be anything Carpenter could say to that, and he didn't.

It was time, Carol decided, to bring this conversation to a close. Just one more question.

"How would you describe your relationship with Miss Merriman?" she asked.

He'd been asked this question more than once. He had seen the question, unasked, on the faces of a number of people in the Brae Loch opera company. He was not about to be drawn into a defense of his interest in the young woman.

"We had a good professional relationship. She was my fiancée in the opera, so we sang together. It was a pleasure working with someone with her promise as a singer. I'm only sorry we didn't get to do it before an audience."

After Carpenter had left, Carol reviewed what he had said and not said. And what she had asked and not asked. She had learned that Merriman had not warned him that the sheriff knew he had been seen at Brae Loch on the afternoon of the murder. Which heightened her respect for the young woman. She had not learned anything about Carpenter's failed attempt to become a member of the Metropolitan Opera chorus. It was probably unimportant, but he had told Heather that he believed his rejection constituted a miscarriage of justice. And Kevin had reported that Harley Gerlach had been among those judging auditions for the chorus for several years and that his verdicts had increasingly been viewed as irrational and biased. What if Gerlach's vote had helped to sink Carpenter's aspirations, and what if Carpenter knew that?

172

There were many things that Carol had to do in her quest to identify Gerlach's killer. One of those things was to determine whether Gerlach had participated in Carpenter's Met audition. And if he had, whether Carpenter knew that Brae Loch's Gianni Schicchi had been responsible for his rejection by the Met.

CHAPTER 32

While the sheriff was talking with the parties to the ambiguous Carpenter-Merriman relationship, Kevin was sitting on his
deck feeling restless and just a bit sorry for himself. He could, of
course, offer Carol advice, both solicited and unsolicited,
regarding the Gerlach case, but he was much too close to the
members of the late opera company to be playing a conspicuous
role in the investigation, a role which might imply suspicion that
they had had something to do with Harley's untimely demise.

It was too early in the day to open a bottle of beer and not
quite close enough to the Labor Day weekend to start packing for
his return to the city and the academic year at Madison College.
So Kevin decided to take a drive. It was a beautiful August day, a
bit cooler than usual with a bright blue sky above, so he opted for
a trip over the nearby hills to Bari, a small hub town some twenty-
five miles west of Crooked Lake. It was a drive he always
enjoyed, and the trip might restore his sagging spirits.

He turned off West Lake Road at the West Branch inter-
section and headed up the hill, the first of a series of hills that
made a roller coaster of the secondary road between West Branch
and Bari. As he drove, he found himself wondering at the origin of
the town's name. Bari. Had it originally been settled by
immigrants from the Italian city on the Adriatic coast? Perhaps a
prominent early resident had given the town its name. Kevin
himself knew no one named Bari. Barry, of course, but not Bari.

As he drove westward, his mind drifted, inevitably, back
to the Gerlach case and the sad ending to the Brae Loch opera
adventure. He still found time to admire the countryside,
especially the miles of state forest preserve that flanked the road
for much of the way. And the rows of small, white cumulus clouds
that dotted the afternoon sky invited speculation as to what or
whom they looked like. As usual, once he had formed an opinion
about a particular cloud—Abraham Lincoln's profile or an
oversized ice cream cone—the prevailing currents would destroy
the illusion and create a new challenge for his imagination.

But it was Harley Gerlach's murder that was the focus of most of his thinking. The murder and the people he had gotten to know over the summer who might be the murderer.

Their names and faces popped into his mind in no particular order. Not alphabetical. Not based on their importance to the production of *Gianni Schicchi*. Certainly not in any ordering from least to most likely suspect, because Kevin had formed no opinion on that. Indeed, he found it hard to think of any of the company members as a murderer. As someone who had not simply killed Gerlach in a moment of anger, but had taken a length of piano wire and deliberately strangled him while he slept off too much liquor or beer in the big bed on the Wayne Hall stage.

There was Paolo Rosetti. A man whose ego was arguably as big as Gerlach's. If he was a suspect, it was presumably because he had coveted the leading role in the opera, the role that had gone to Gerlach. He had made it abundantly clear that he would make the best Schicchi. He'd told Kevin that on the day they had met, and he had never missed an opportunity to make the same claim during the weeks when the opera was in rehearsal. Moreover, he had sought Kevin out shortly after Gerlach's death to argue that the opera should go on as scheduled and that he should take over the lead. He hadn't said so in so many words, but he obviously believed that in the end, however unfortunate Gerlach's death may have been, Brae Loch would now have the Schicchi it deserved.

But how could the fact that Gerlach, not Rosetti, had been chosen to play the lead in the opera have been a motive for murder? Improbable? Absolutely. Inconceivable? That might be something else. Kevin didn't pretend to know what made Rosetti tick. And even if the man had wanted Gerlach dead, could he have killed him? He claimed to have been fishing that afternoon, something he almost never did, something no one had seen him doing. And Carol seemed to be convinced that he had left his boat at a marina within walking distance of the college on that fateful Tuesday. If so, he could have killed Gerlach. Kevin was skeptical. There were too many ifs.

He had come to a place where the road dipped sharply into a depression between two hills. There were no cars in sight, no houses, no barns, no sign of life, just a long ribbon of road unspooling down into the valley below. High above there were six, eight, maybe more buzzards circling lazily in the sky. As they soared on the afternoon's thermals, they rocked back and forth in the manner characteristic of their species. Kevin slowed the car, the better to watch them for a moment, then refocused his eyes on the road and his mind on the Gerlach case.

If not Rosetti, then perhaps Arthur Conklin. His motive, at least to most men, would presumably be more compelling than Rosetti's. His wife, by his own admission, had had an affair with Gerlach. And Conklin had apparently reacted angrily to what had happened. Why else would the Geneva police have been suspicious of Conklin when his wife died? Helen Conklin commits adultery, Conklin finds out about it, she dies an unnatural death, and nothing comes of the effort to implicate Conklin in his wife's death. Still.

And then who should come into his life but the man who had seduced his wife. Both of them together on an almost daily basis during the summer, a constant reminder of Helen's betrayal and Gerlach's role in it. Had the result been a rekindling of strong emotions, culminating in murder? Of course Conklin had an alibi or claimed that he did. He had been checking up on his string of nurseries. But to the best of Kevin's knowledge Conklin's presence at the nurseries had not been confirmed, and it was unlikely that every minute of those crucial hours could be accounted for in any event. In view of the proximity of the nurseries to the lake and the college, the alibi looked thin.

Kevin's thoughts turned to Janet Myers. He wanted to drop her from the short list that was taking shape in his mind, but he couldn't quite bring himself to do it. Unlike Rosetti and Conklin, whose quarrels with Gerlach were of recent vintage, hers went back quite a few years. If she had felt a need to avenge herself for his philandering, why hadn't she done it when the wound was new, before the scar tissue of time and a second marriage had grown over it?

Kevin was trying to imagine Myers as a killer when a fox emerged suddenly from the thick stand of trees on the right side of the road and darted across his path. Had he taken his eyes off the road at that moment he would have contributed to the seasonal toll of roadkill that littered the highways and byways of Cumberland County. He didn't much care for foxes, which had been making a much commented on comeback in the area. But they were handsome animals, and he breathed a sigh of relief that he had missed this one.

He was now close to the fork in the road that gave him a choice between Bari and Centerville. The turn made, he started thinking about Janet Myers again. Her divorce from Gerlach may have been, relatively speaking, ancient history, but that she still harbored a strong dislike for the man had been demonstrated on at least two occasions over the summer. The first had taken place back in June when she had demanded that he be dropped from the cast of *Gianni Schicchi*. The second had been much more recent, only days before his death, when she had exploded in anger in what Kevin remembered as the ugly bed episode. Even had he been willing to dismiss these outbursts as the venting of a volatile woman, her behavior on the afternoon of Gerlach's murder was enough to keep her on his list of suspects. She had been seen at her ex-husband's house, and had otherwise driven around aimlessly, leaving nobody to vouch for where she was or what she was doing. She could easily have stopped at the college. Rosetti's and Conklin's alibis were weak. Hers was essentially nonexistent.

Kevin had no business to conduct in Bari. He was just out for the ride, and it was now time to turn around and head home, this time with the sun at his back. He fully expected to see the buzzards again, perhaps even more of them. There would be carrion in the woods, drawing a crowd of scavengers. He usually spotted two or three hawks, often perched in dead trees along the roadside. He had seen none on the drive over, but it was the rare trip over this little-traveled road that he didn't make at least one sighting. Unlike buzzards, they were beautiful birds, much more impressive in flight. He hoped to see one on the way home.

Kevin had largely exhausted his list of suspects in Gerlach's murder. He had asked Carol to be the one to interview Myers, Conklin, and Rosetti the evening after the discovery of Gerlach's body. He had done so because these three were the company members who seemed to know Gerlach best or had had the most contentious relationship with him during rehearsals. There had also been a fourth, Sean Carpenter. He had been on the list for Carol because he had been conspicuously angry with Gerlach for his treatment of Heather Merriman. Now, on reflection, he wasn't sure Carpenter should be thought of as a suspect. His motive, if it could be called that, was much weaker than those of the others. Moreover, he insisted that he had been in Rochester all afternoon the day Gerlach was killed. Carol was going to talk with him today—she might even be doing so at that very moment. Unless she learned something that changed the picture dramatically, Kevin was inclined to drop to the bottom of his list this middle-aged man who seemed to have a thing for the opera's much younger Lauretta.

As he crested the last hill and headed back down the road into West Branch, Kevin gave a minute's thought to Lauren Helman. Perhaps it should be Lauren and Linda, two local women, one now identified, the other still unknown, who had been singled out by Gerlach for seduction and a privileged page in his photo album. It was useless to speculate about X, but he knew that Mrs. Helman had a husband who, unlike Arthur Conklin, did not know of his wife's affair with Harley Gerlach. Quite understandably, she didn't want him to know. How far would she go to prevent him from discovering this secret in her recent past? Kevin couldn't imagine that she would have killed Gerlach to protect her secret. Besides, she hadn't even know about the incriminating photo in the harem album until Kevin showed it to her, and that was after Gerlach's death. And if she thought Gerlach posed a threat to her marriage, why wait until a Tuesday afternoon in August to silence him? No, Kevin thought, I think I'll cross her off my list.

When he pulled into the drive behind his cottage, Kevin was glad he had taken the drive but still unhappy to be a marginal player in the search for the person who had spoiled his opera. Puccini's opera. Nor was his effort to put the candidates for Gerlach's killer into a more logical order very successful. If he were to be completely honest with himself, he knew no more at the end of the day than he had the day of the murder. But at least he had finally seen a red-shouldered hawk. It hadn't made his day, but it had briefly buoyed his spirits.

CHAPTER 33

Not having gone to Rochester for her meeting with Carpenter, Carol was free for the evening earlier than she had expected to be. She had changed out of her uniform and traded the official vehicle for her old Buick. It was a quarter of six when she let herself into the cottage.

"Hi, anybody home?"

Of course Kevin was there, as she knew he would be. He was dicing vegetables at a kitchen counter.

"Just me and that pork loin roast. You don't look nearly as harassed as you did this morning. Must have been a good day."

"Not bad. I'd like to tell you about it. How about the canoe?"

There hadn't been that many opportunities for the canoe rides which had become their favorite form of recreation. But it was early, dinner would keep, and Kevin was only too happy to say yes to Carol's proposal.

"Let me get into my shorts," he said.

Carol followed him into the bedroom, where she sat on the bed and watched as he changed.

"I remember when you were more modest," she said. "Like I'd arrest you for indecent exposure."

"That was back in the day, Carol. Way back. Let's go."

He slid into his sandals, and they headed for the beach.

As was their habit, Carol sat in the bow facing him, the better to carry on a conversation. She enjoyed paddling as much as Kevin did, but not when they had something they wanted to talk about. Today she had quite a bit that she wanted to talk about.

"You go first," Carol said, as they turned south toward Mallard Cove.

"There isn't much to tell," Kevin said. "All I did was go looking for hawks and buzzards."

"Hawks and buzzards?"

"That's about it. I gave some thought to who might have killed Gerlach, but there weren't any eureka moments. Let's say I had an uneventful day. But I want to hear about what you did. I've got a hunch you learned something important."

"Not sure how important, but there's one thing in particular you'll be interested in."

Carol proceeded to fill Kevin in on what Merriman and Carpenter had told her, with emphasis on their reluctant admission that he had been at Brae Loch during the afternoon of Gerlach's murder, much as Chris Ellis had said he was. They discussed how the two of them, especially Carpenter, had handled the sheriff's questions. And they spent several minutes expressing their interest in and frustration with the mounting evidence that too many of the opera company's members had trouble with their explanations of what they were doing—and where they were doing it—the day Gerlach was strangled.

But it was Carol's report that Carpenter had tried out un-successfully for the Metropolitan Opera chorus that really caught Kevin's attention. As she knew it would. She hadn't pursued the matter with Carpenter, having decided it would be prudent to approach the subject armed with hard data. Such as whether the Met kept records of who had auditioned and when, and who was on the auditions' panel when they did.

Kevin was visibly excited. He could once again be playing an active role in Carol's investigation of Gerlach's murder. Just that afternoon he had been downplaying Sean Carpenter as a suspect. Now it looked to be possible that he might have a real motive for murder.

"Let's not get carried away, Kevin," Carol said. "We don't know that Gerlach blackballed Carpenter. And if he did, we don't know that Carpenter knew it."

"I know," Kevin said, making an effort to rein in his new-found enthusiasm. "But it shouldn't take much to get an answer to your first question. And if Gerlach was on the panel that rejected Carpenter, I can't believe he wouldn't have jumped at the chance to rub it in when he came face to face with him again this summer."

"When was Gerlach participating in those auditions?"

"The woman who works in the Met archives said it was from 1997 to 2001."

"Let's assume that we can find out that Carpenter audi-tioned sometime during those years. Do you think he'd have remembered Gerlach after that long a time? Or if he did, that he'd know it was Gerlach who cost him the job? Or turn it around. Do you think Gerlach would have remembered Carpenter? I don't know how many people audition for that chorus in a year, but I'd imagine it's quite a few. And Gerlach would have seen Carpenter just that once before this summer. I don't know about you, but I doubt that I'd recall a face in those circumstances."

"Not just a face, Carol. The voice, too. Anyway, it's possible Carpenter mentioned to Gerlach that he'd auditioned, and that could have got Harley to thinking. Then he remembers. And being the kind of guy he is, he can't resist telling Carpenter that he's the one that did it to him."

"Okay, like you say, it's possible. Why don't you talk to that woman you saw at the Met, see if there's any reason to pursue this. You wouldn't have to go down to the city again, would you?"

"I doubt it. I'll try Mrs. DeAngelo—she's the archivist. I might even call some of the choristers whose names she gave me. I'll do it tomorrow."

It was going on seven o'clock when they beached the canoe. Kevin busied himself with dinner while Carol leafed through a recent issue of *Opera News* on the living room couch, wondering if she would ever be a real opera fan. Probably, if Kevin had his way, although her feelings on the subject were mixed at the moment.

The phone rang. It was Kevin who answered.

"It's for you," he said, leaning into the living room. "Want to take it in the study?"

Who, Carol asked silently, her mouth framing the word.

"Sam Bridges," he said, not bothering to cup his hand over the phone.

If she had to go out to deal with some emergency, it was too late where the roast was concerned. It would be ready in about fifteen minutes. Fortunately for both their evening and the roast, Carol did not have to leave until morning.

"I can't do anything until tomorrow," she said as she returned from Kevin's study, "but Mercedes Redman is dead."

Kevin nearly dropped the pot in which he had been steaming vegetables.

"Mercedes? My God, I can't believe it. What happened?"

Dinner no longer seemed very important. Kevin turned off the oven and the flame under the pot on the stove top and joined Carol in the living room.

"There was a call from Doug Owens, the police chief over in Ithaca. Sam was in the office, talked with him briefly. They don't know much yet, but Redman is definitely dead. In her apartment. Owens says the call reporting this came from a woman named Kane, who apparently shares the apartment with Redman. She told Owens that she got home from work around five and found Mercedes lying on the bedroom floor. Tried to revive her but it was way too late. She had no idea what happened to her, said she'd been fine when she said good-bye to her in the morning."

"I can't believe this," Kevin said. "She was so full of energy, a real take-charge person. And now she's dead."

Two members of his little company, dead in a matter of just nine days. One of them unmourned by his peers, the other much respected, even loved by them. Then the obvious question struck him.

"Why did the police chief call you?"

"I was getting around to that. Owens and his people looked around the apartment, of course, and it seems they found a piece of paper with a note on it. Short note. All it said was 'Leave her alone! Remember Gerlach!' The roommate found it on Mercedes' music stand in what was apparently the room where she gave violin lessons."

"Remember Gerlach? What's that supposed to mean?"

"Wish I knew. Anyway, the note sounded, you know, threatening. So Owens asked the Kane woman if she knew anything about it. And she said it had come in the mail on Saturday, and that they had talked about it. Mercedes had told her Gerlach was one of the people in the opera that she had been involved in over on Crooked Lake, and that he had been killed just last week.

"Not surprising that Owens seized on this information. Redman dead, having just received a threatening note mentioning Gerlach, who'd just been murdered. I suppose he immediately started thinking that maybe whoever wrote the note had killed Redman, although there seems to have been nothing to indicate her death was the result of foul play."

Kevin had shaken off the shock that came with the news that his chief assistant in the production of *Gianni Schicchi* was dead. His mind was now focused on the connection to Harley Gerlach's murder.

"The note said to 'leave her alone,' right? Who does 'her' refer to?"

Carol started to say something, but Kevin held up his hand.

"Sorry, just a rhetorical question. But that's got to be important. Her. The roommate? That makes no sense. What would Kane or whatever her name is have to do with Gerlach? Another of his conquests? Not likely."

"Maybe there's no connection between Gerlach's death and Redman's. No connection to the opera. Except that whoever wrote the note knew what had happened to Gerlach and knew that Mercedes knew it, too. In other words, the reference to Gerlach may have been just a way to tell her that what happened to him could happen to her."

Kevin had taken a seat on the couch and waved his hand in the general direction of Carol. She got the message. He was thinking and wanted a moment to order his thoughts.

"Wait a minute," he said. "Mercedes was being told to leave the woman alone. Why? How about because Redman was viewed as a threat by the note's author. If you look at it that way, who might Redman have been threatening?"

"I'm listening," Carol said.

"How about Sean Carpenter? He was obviously interested in Heather Merriman. According to Heather, so was Mercedes Redman. I can imagine Carpenter telling Mercedes to leave Heather alone. He wouldn't even have to have a thing about lesbians. He just didn't want to have competition for Heather's affection."

Carol considered this, then put forward another idea.

"Let's suppose it isn't Redman that's the threat. Suppose it's Heather. And who does she threaten? The roommate. I'm assuming, of course, that Kane is more than a roommate. I know that's a big assumption. But what if she's Redman's lover? And what if Redman talked about Heather, gave off signals that this attractive young musician was somehow more important to her than just another member of the Brae Loch opera project. I can imagine that Mercedes' partner might not be happy about that."

"I like my idea better," Kevin said. "But if you're right, maybe Kane didn't just find Redman's body. Maybe she killed her in a fit of jealousy, something like that."

He shook his head and laughed.

"You know what? I don't think we have a clue what we're talking about. As far as we know Redman's not a lesbian, Kane never heard of Merriman, the note is just a prank, somebody's idea of a bad joke."

"So we give it a rest, at least until I talk with Owens tomorrow. Right? At the rate we're going, we'll have Redman or Kane killing Gerlach. Let's eat."

That proved to be harder to do than they expected. The oven had been turned off before the roast was done. The veggies were cold and soggy. Carol and Kevin settled for scrambled eggs.

CHAPTER 34

Was it his imagination or did the face that stared back at him from the mirror look older than it had just twenty-four hours earlier? Kevin paused in the act of shaving a day's growth of stubble from his face and leaned closer to the mirror for a better look. It was all in his mind, but he was prepared to swear that the news of Mercedes Redman's death had accelerated the aging process. He had to admit that his reaction to Gerlach's death had been less sorrow at the loss of a fellow human being than a painful sense of disappointment that his opera would be stillborn. Redman's death was another matter. He had not been close to the woman, would probably never have been close. But he had respected her. For her professionalism, her patience, her invaluable help in turning a group of variously talented individuals into a passable ensemble. After the collapse of the Brae Loch opera, he had doubted that he would ever see her again. Now that he knew he would never see her again, he realized how much he would miss her.

Sheriff Kelleher's thoughts about Redman's death were of a different sort. She remembered her reaction back in June when Kevin had told her he was going to share the task of whipping the orchestra into shape with a violinist named Mercedes Redman. Carol had never met Redman, had not even heard of her until that day. But she had experienced a small twinge of jealousy. Now the woman was dead, and it sounded as if her death might be related in some way to the death of Harley Gerlach and the friction that had led to the demise of Kevin's plans for staging an opera on Crooked Lake. It was in her capacity as enforcer of law and order that she would now be thinking about Mercedes Redman.

She had arrived at her office early, had called Chief Owens, and was anxiously awaiting his return call. She had put out of her mind the conversation regarding Redman's death which she and Kevin had engaged in the night before. In the morning's light it looked like what it was, premature speculation. Better to wait until she had spoken with Owens. Or better yet, until she had gone over to Ithaca and taken stock of the situation herself.

Why hadn't the police chief called back? She had been told he would be back to her in ten minutes, but it had now been fifteen, going on twenty. Carol was trying to make good use of her time, but she found it hard to concentrate. It was while she was looking at the clock for the umpteenth time that Diane Franks, her new secretary, buzzed to report a visitor.

"I can't see anyone now. I've got a very important call coming in at any minute. Get a name and say I'll be in touch just as soon as I can."

"I'm sorry, Sheriff, but I think you should see her now. It's about the Gerlach case."

Carol cursed under her breath, but she went to the door separating her office from that of Miss Franks. The woman who was sitting in the reception area was tall, slender, casually dressed, her hair still damp from the morning's shower.

She got up and walked toward the open door and past the sheriff's secretary, whose expression said that she felt guilty about what was happening but had no choice in the matter.

"I'm sorry to come barging in, unannounced, like this. But I've been terribly worried, and I thought you ought to know about Janet."

Carol, of course, had no idea what this stranger was talking about. She motioned her into her office, offered her the chair across from the desk, and took her own seat behind it.

"I don't believe I got your name," she said.

"No, I don't suppose I told your secretary. It's Pederson, Sonia Pederson. I'm here to talk about my friend, Janet Myers. I think you know her. That's what I want to talk about."

Janet Myers. The former wife of Harley Gerlach. The woman who had, according to Francis Farris, the telescope man, visited Gerlach's home the day he was killed. And then what? Driven back to the college and killed him? Gone home? No one seemed to know.

Carol was a firm believer in putting things into some kind of logical order. First things first.

"I'm glad to meet you, Mrs. Pederson. Perhaps you should tell me how you know Mrs. Myers."

"Yes, of course," the woman said. She spoke quickly, whether to get to the point or because it was her normal speaking manner, Carol did not know. "I've known Janet since college. We were sorority sisters. Good friends. Since then, we'd sort of drifted

186

apart—you know, like people do. Then she surprised me one day a few years back, calling to tell me she'd been divorced, was at loose ends. I could tell she needed a change of scene, so I invited her up to spend some time with me. Anyway, one thing led to another. She met a Southport man, Charles Myers. They seemed to hit it off, and in due course they got married. I think what appealed to Janet was that he was the polar opposite of her first husband. Charles is what you'd call solid, or maybe steady. What you see is what you get."

Mrs. Pederson paused, as if to reflect on what she'd said, to see if it adequately described what had happened.

"But then," Carol said, "Mrs. Myers discovered that her former husband was also now living up here on Crooked Lake. Right?"

Carol was recalling her interview with Myers the evening after Gerlach's murder. So far, she'd learned nothing she didn't already know.

"That's right. It really bothered her, but I think she coped with it pretty well until the opera thing came along. Then they were back in each other's lives, every week, sometimes—"

The buzzer interrupted Mrs. Pederson's story. Miss Franks said that Chief Owens was on the line.

Carol briefly considered asking her visitor to step outside while she took the call, but decided it might be better to hear her out and then get back to Owens. Her decision was more a matter of courtesy than conviction that she'd learn anything important from Pederson. She'd try to hurry her up, say good-bye, and turn her attention to the matter of Mercedes Redman's unexpected death.

"Sorry about the interruption, Mrs. Pederson. I'm going to have to return that call right away, but I do want to let you finish what you have to say about Mrs. Myers. What is it you wanted to tell me?"

"Well, a funny thing happened. Janet could hardly bear to be in the same room with her first husband, but at the same time she seemed to find him fascinating. Does that make any sense? I'm not sure it does to me, and I know it troubled Janet. But it became obvious to me that she was developing a kind of love-hate relationship with him. Not that she did anything about it. And I'm sure she never said anything about it to him. She kept saying nasty things about him whenever we talked, but something was going on in her head.

"She and Charles got along okay, but things changed. Janet started giving off little clues that she found Charles boring. She talked less and less about him and more and more about Gerlach. It finally dawned on me that she was comparing them, and that it was the first husband who came off better in the comparison. The way she talked made him sound exciting. A lot of what she said was still negative, but you could sense that there was something about him that intrigued her. Unlike Charles, he had charisma, a kind of irresistible vitality. I'm not saying this very well, but I'd swear that she came to regret that she'd divorced him. And married Charles. It's too late to do anything about Gerlach, but I'd be willing to bet her marriage to Myers won't last. They seem to be going through the motions of marriage these days."

"Why are you telling me this, Mrs. Pederson?"

"Because Janet says you've been questioning her—I think the phrase she used was hounding her—about Gerlach's death and where she was and what she was doing when it happened. She thinks you suspect her of having killed him. That might make sense if Janet hated her ex-husband. But I'm sure she loved him. In a strange way, of course, but then love is a funny thing, isn't it? So how could she have killed him?"

Nothing the Pederson woman had said ruled out Janet Myers as a suspect in Gerlach's death. But it did put things in a somewhat different light. It might help explain why Myers had been poking around Gerlach's home the previous Tuesday. Or would it? It was possible that Pederson had misinterpreted Myers' behavior and words. In fact, Carol couldn't recall Pederson quoting anything Myers had said about her first husband.

"Did Janet ever tell you that maybe she still loved Gerlach? Not necessarily in so many words, you understand, but something that made her feelings for him stronger than mere impressions."

Sonia Pederson thought about the sheriff's question for a moment.

"She never used the word love," she said. "But I remember once, just last week, after he died, she made a comment about wishing she'd known him better. And on a couple of occasions she told me that there was a lot more to him than just those other women."

"I know you're her friend, but I wonder, do you think she would be capable of killing someone?"

"Goodness, no. Even if she hated him as much as she must have when they divorced, she wouldn't have killed him. But what I'm saying is that she didn't still hate him. Like I said, I think she believes divorcing him was the worst mistake she ever made."

When the office door closed behind Sonia Pederson, Carol sat quietly behind her desk, thinking about what she'd just learned. She wondered if Janet Myers would be willing to discuss this alleged change of heart about Harley Gerlach. Probably not. Even if it were true, she'd probably see it as unbelievable, a phony attempt to gain sympathy, to deflect suspicion.

It was while these thoughts were running through her mind that Miss Franks buzzed her on the intercom.

"Weren't you supposed to call Chief Owens?" she asked.

CHAPTER 35

Carol had finally spoken with Ithaca's chief of police, and they had agreed to meet at Redman's apartment at one o'clock. Owens said he would call Marcia Kane and tell her he wanted her present when the sheriff arrived. He had little to add to what he had told Bridges the night before, other than that Kane had made it clear that she had lost the love of her life.

Owens' instructions turned out to be less precise than she had expected, with the result that Carol didn't arrive at the apartment until nearly a quarter past one. She was mildly annoyed that the police chief of a small city could not have provided her with better directions, but she had found him cooperative in a case with jurisdictional issues during her first year as Cumberland County's sheriff, and was disinclined to complain about his role in her tardiness. It was he who let her in; the woman named Kane, who was the tenant and might have been expected to come to the door, remained seated during introductions.

Owens took Carol on a brief tour of the small apartment, showing her where Redman's body had been found in the bedroom. When they got to the room where Redman had given lessons, he took the threatening note from his pocket and somewhat melodramatically placed it on the music stand where he had found it the previous day. Carol studied it, but found nothing of interest other than those cryptic five words.

"I went over this with Ms. Kane last evening, Sheriff," he said as they took seats in the living room. "But I know you'd want to hear it all from her yourself. Especially due to that note about this man Gerlach."

Carol planned to get around to that, but first she wanted to talk about Mercedes Redman.

"Tell me, Ms. Kane, how long and how well have you known Ms. Redman?"

"I've known her for nearly four years. We're a couple, as you presumably know. I guess I'll have to amend that to were— we were a couple. We loved each other very much. I'm old

190

enough to have had my share of bad days, but yesterday was the worst. I still can't believe she's dead."

"You have my sympathy," Carol said. "How would you describe your relationship? What I mean is, many couples in love share many things, but still have separate lives. Different jobs, different responsibilities—things they don't talk much about. Did Ms. Redman share her life as a musician—the violin lessons, the opera she was involved in this summer?"

"Sure. We discussed it over dinner sometimes. She'd tell me about her day, me about mine."

"Did she talk about the opera, you know—" Carol fumbled for the name, pretending she couldn't think of it. "Sorry, I'm not an opera person. I can't seem to remember the opera she was doing. Help me out."

"I don't think I ever heard her mention it."

"That's okay," Carol said. "You told Chief Owens that Ms. Redman had received this peculiar message, a message that mentioned someone named Gerlach. The message that was on the music stand when you got home yesterday. Well, Gerlach was participating in this opera with Ms. Redman. And he was killed. Just about a week ago. I'm in charge of the investigation into his death, and when his name pops up in a message to Ms. Redman just days before her death, I'm naturally interested. What did she tell you about Gerlach?"

Marcia Kane thought about it. Surely Chief Owens asked you the same question, Carol said to herself. Don't you remember what you told him?

"Not very much, I guess. She mentioned that he had been killed, but she was more interested in the rest of the note."

"The rest of it? The part about leaving her alone?"

"Yes, that's it."

"Leaving who alone?" Carol asked. "Did she tell you whom the note referred to?"

"I don't think so. We didn't really talk about it. Well, not much."

"I'm sorry, but I thought you said that Ms. Redman was more interested in that part of the note—the part about leaving somebody alone, not the part about Gerlach."

Chief Owens was watching this exchange with interest, making a mental note that Marcia Kane looked flustered.

"I think she didn't understand it. She said it sounded threatening, but she couldn't imagine why anybody would be threatening her."

"Did she ever mention an envelope? You know, something with a return address? A postmark?"

"I don't think so."

Owens, who had been a silent witness to this interrogation, spoke up.

"We searched the apartment for it. It was in the trash basket under the kitchen sink. No return address, and the postmark was badly smudged. It looks like it begins with an S, maybe Sa or So or Su."

"It probably doesn't matter," Carol said, thinking to herself that it might matter a lot. "Anyway, you and Ms. Redman didn't really have much of a discussion about the cryptic message, did you?"

"Not really."

"You've known Ms. Redman for—what did you say?— four years. You must have gotten to know her pretty well. Can you think of any reason why somebody would be warning her? Threatening her? Any idea, however crazy it may seem, who she was supposed to leave alone?"

"I wish I could help you, but I can't."

Or won't, Carol thought.

"Let me toss out a name or two. Then you tell me if you ever heard Ms. Redman mention either of them. Okay? One is Sean Carpenter. Does it ring a bell?"

"Carpenter," Kane repeated the name. "I don't think so. Does he have something to do with this Gerlach person?"

Carol ignored the question.

"The other name is Heather Merriman. How about that one?"

It isn't always easy to read a face, even if you are an experienced law enforcement officer. But Carol would have sworn that this wasn't the first time Marcia Kane had heard of Heather Merriman.

"No again. Are these people Mercedes knew? People in that opera over on Crooked Lake?"

Once more Carol ignored the question, this time changing the subject.

"I've tried not to stare at your face, Ms. Kane, but it looks like you've been in an accident."

And indeed it did. There were ugly red scratches on both cheeks and her nose had been cut, marring what was otherwise an attractive face.

"I know. Like I told Chief Owens, I had an accident coming home on my bicycle yesterday. A dog ran into the street right in front of me, and I couldn't stop. Pitched right onto the road. There was a lot of gravel and it messed up my face. I probably would have treated it better, but when I got home, there was Mercedes, lying dead on the floor. My face didn't seem very important right then."

"No, I'm sure not. I hope it clears up soon. Look, I've taken a big chunk out of your lunch hour. I better let you go. It looks like Ms. Redman had a fatal heart attack or something like that. A terrible thing for one so young. I feel badly about raising all these questions about the opera business, but like I said, I'm investigating a murder over on Crooked Lake, and when Chief Owens mentioned the note about Gerlach, I knew I'd have to talk with you. I want to thank you for your cooperation. And tell you how sorry I am about Ms. Redman."

"That's very kind of you," Ms. Kane said as she showed them out.

———

Back in Owens' office, Carol and the police chief chatted for another twenty minutes.

"It was all pretty much what I expected," he said. "She didn't add anything to what she told me yesterday. Except maybe that she was uncomfortable talking about what she and Redman talked about. Did you get the feeling that they didn't have much in common? I mean other than a physical attraction. You saw the bedroom. They say that opposites attract, and I think that Kane and Redman prove the point."

"When do you expect the autopsy report?"

"Never can be sure. This one doesn't look that complicated. I'm no MD, but I'd bet on a heart attack. Maybe that threatening note had something to do with it. Or maybe it was just one of those things that happen, who knows when or why."

"You're probably right," Carol said. "But there's something I'd like you to talk to the medical examiner about. Something I'd like him to look at."

"It's her. Sharon Levine. What is it?"

"Did you notice that the only scratches are on her face? If you had a sudden fall from a bike, a fall hard enough to mess up your face like that, wouldn't you expect to have hurt your hands, too? I'd think one's instinct would be to use the hands to help break the fall. But her hands didn't look like she'd had a close encounter with any roadside gravel. And her bike, which stood in the hallway just outside the apartment door, it didn't have a scratch on it. I could be wrong. Probably am. But I wouldn't be surprised if Marcia Kane didn't fall off her bike. I think she may have had an altercation with Mercedes Redman. It got physical, and Redman scratched Kane's face—dug her nails into her face, leaving those nasty marks."

"That's interesting. No, I didn't notice that her hands showed no signs of trauma. But why would she and Redman be having a fight?"

"Jealousy, Doug, jealousy," Carol said. "Just between us, at least for the time being, I know that Redman had developed an interest in another woman. The one I mentioned to Kane—Heather Merriman, one of the cast of the Crooked Lake opera. If Kane found out about it, it would be possible that she confronted Redman and—well, one thing led to another."

"That would mean that Kane wrote the threatening note."

"Perhaps. But not necessarily. It was obvious that she knew almost nothing about the opera Redman was involved in. I doubt that she'd heard about Gerlach until after the note arrived. No, I think someone else wrote the note. But that's another story."

"Are you telling me that you think Kane killed Redman?" Owens asked, now aware that what he had thought of as a sad but uncomplicated death might in fact be homicide.

"No way of knowing. You're probably right that it was a heart attack, or a fatal seizure of some other kind. Let's hope the autopsy helps clarify matters. But why don't you ask the medical examiner to look for bits of skin under Redman's fingernails. I hope she doesn't find any, but I wouldn't be surprised if she does."

CHAPTER 36

It had turned into another beautiful late summer day. There was nothing he had to do, so Kevin took a leisurely swim after breakfast and was toweling himself off on the dock when he heard the phone ringing. He had timed it on several occasions and knew that the phone would ring seven times before he could make it back to the cottage. Knowing this, he had deliberately arranged for his voice mail to kick in after the eighth ring. But many callers came to the conclusion that he wasn't home and hung up before that. This morning's caller was more patient.

"Hello, this is Kevin," he said somewhat breathlessly.

"Oh, Professor Whitman, I'm glad I caught you. This is Sandy Temple. Remember? I played viola in your orchestra."

The call came as a surprise. He could picture Temple, of course. The orchestra had been too small for its members to remain anonymous over the course of the summer. But he doubted that he had spoken with the woman more than three or four times since she had auditioned for him back in May. He remembered that she played the viola, not only in his small orchestra but in a Finger Lakes string quartet along with Arthur Conklin. Why would she be calling him now, more than a week after Gerlach's death and the disbanding of the opera company?

"Yes, of course. How are you, Ms. Temple?"

"I'm okay, but I'm calling because I need to see you."

Kevin could not imagine what she needed to see him about.

"Well, of course. Is there something I can do for you?"

"Not exactly," she said. Needless to say, those words made Sandy Temple's call even more puzzling.

"Would you like to come over to my place?" Kevin couldn't remember where Temple lived, but he assumed that it was within relatively short driving distance of the cottage.

"I'm sorry, but I can't do that. I have several students coming in today, and there wouldn't be time to get over to the lake and back between lessons. I was wondering if you could possibly

195

meet me at my house. I know it's an imposition, but I really need to talk to you."

So, like the late Mercedes Redman and presumably a great many others, Temple earned a living by teaching her instrument to young aspiring musicians. Or perhaps she supplemented her income from another job by taking students. Musicians, like teachers, were notoriously poorly paid, he thought. Unless, of course, their name is Joshua Bell or James Galway. Or Placido Domingo.

"I suppose so," Kevin said, somewhat reluctantly. He didn't relish the idea of making the trip, but he was curious as to what Ms. Temple needed to see him about. "Where is it that you live?"

"It isn't all that far. I'm over near Latham. You just go up through West Branch and follow county road 27 until you get to the junction of 27 and 9. Turn right and it's about fourteen miles to Latham. When you see the sign telling you you're entering our town, watch for Foxridge Road on your left. We're the fifth house from the corner. It's a white colonial with black shutters."

Sandy Temple recited these directions as if she had never doubted that he would agree to her request. She either thought of him as someone who would go out of his way to help others or as someone whose curiosity would dictate a positive response.

"When did you have in mind?"

"How about three o'clock? I'll just have finished with Betty Rice."

————

And so it was that Kevin set out for the tiny village of Latham at 2:30, still wondering what Temple wanted to tell him. Or wanted him to do. The trip was as easy as she had said it would be, and it was almost exactly three when he punched her doorbell.

Betty Rice, a red-haired, freckle-faced girl who looked to be about ten walked past him as he entered the house. Temple, he realized as she invited him to have a seat and asked if he'd like coffee or tea, was somewhat younger than he had remembered. Probably in her middle thirties, certainly no older than forty. She was wearing a sweatshirt which would have been much too warm for a summer day except for the fact that the air conditioner had been turned way up. Kevin doubted that the temperature in the room was above 65, if that.

They sipped tea and for a brief moment engaged in small talk, including words of regret about the cancellation of the opera. It was Temple who steered the conversation to the reason they were sitting in her living room.

"I have another student coming soon, so I think I'd better tell you what's on my mind. It's about Arthur Conklin. Arthur's a good friend. We belong to a quartet, as I suppose you know. But I've been worrying about the investigation of Mr. Gerlach's murder, and I'm sure that the sheriff is going to be thinking of Arthur as a suspect. The affair between Gerlach and Arthur's late wife is no secret, and I'm sure the sheriff is aware of it. Arthur made no bones about how he felt toward Mr. Gerlach. You remember that first meeting we had, the one where Arthur made that unfortunate remark calling Mr. Gerlach a nigger in the woodpile."

"That isn't quite what Mr. Conklin said, Ms. Temple. He never mentioned Gerlach."

"I know. But that's who he was referring to, and it didn't take long for everyone to understand that. Anyhow, Arthur isn't that kind of person. He's really very kind. And he doesn't use words like that. I think he was just in shock that Mr. Gerlach was going to be in the opera. But I'm worried that the police are going to be looking for reasons why someone would have killed Mr. Gerlach, and the first person they'll think of is Arthur. But it couldn't have been Arthur."

"Why do you say it couldn't have been Arthur? Was he with you when it happened?"

"No, nothing like that. I mean Arthur couldn't have killed Mr. Gerlach because he's not that kind of person. He couldn't kill anyone."

"I'm sure we all believe that our friends couldn't be killers. That's a natural feeling, isn't it?"

"Yes, but I know Arthur. Let me explain. When he learned that his wife had been having an affair, he was devastated. He blamed himself. He said he'd been too busy, too selfish. That he hadn't held up his end of the marriage. He didn't blame Mr. Gerlach or his wife, he blamed himself. In fact, at first he didn't even know whom Helen had been having an affair with. And then when Helen had her accident, he was devastated all over again. He kept insisting it was his fault."

"Are you saying Mr. Conklin told you he was responsible for his wife's fall? For her death?"

"No, no," Temple said, sounding horrified that he would have thought such a thing. "He had nothing to do with her accident. But she fell because she had been drinking heavily, and Arthur knew that that was because of how he had handled her infidelity."

"I don't understand," Kevin said. "I thought you said the affair with Gerlach had devastated him. Now you say that she took to drink after he found out. That's counterintuitive, isn't it? I'd have thought he'd express his regrets for neglecting her, that he'd start courting her again. Why would she turn to the bottle?"

"You don't know Arthur. He's—well, he just has trouble knowing how to go about something like that. He's not a naturally warm, cuddly person. Too cerebral, if you know what I mean. He wouldn't really know how to show Helen how he felt. He'd try to talk about it, to reason with her, with himself. And she must have been a troubled woman—angry with herself for what she'd done, puzzled about Arthur's reaction, worried about what would happen next. She'd always liked a drink. But she started drinking more, and it became a way out of her problem, or so she probably thought. But it got out of hand, and then, tragically, she took that awful fall one day when she was drunk. We know she survived for awhile, was even conscious from time to time. One of those times she seems to have confessed to Arthur that the man she'd had the affair with was Mr. Gerlach. But she didn't make it. And now, after Arthur had begun to put his life back together, he becomes a prime suspect in Gerlach's death."

"Haven't I heard that the police once considered Mr. Conklin a suspect in his wife's death?"

"Oh, that's nothing," Temple said. "I think they typically consider the possibility of domestic violence in cases like that. They probably have to because there seems to be so much of it these days. But nothing came of it. There was no history of that sort of thing between Arthur and Helen, like we all told the police. And of course there was no evidence of foul play. I mean, how could there have been? It was just a tragic accident."

"I'm still confused about what Mr. Conklin said about Gerlach—that nigger in the woodpile remark. You say he's not like that. Okay, I'll buy that. But why, months, a year after he learns of Gerlach's affair with his wife, after you say he's put his life back together, why does he suddenly, out of the blue, say something that implies that he *still* blames Gerlach for this tragedy in his life? He sure didn't sound like somebody who's forgiving, who's forgotten."

Sandy Temple looked upset, and it was obvious why. Kevin had been playing devil's advocate, but she was interpreting his questions as a rejection of her portrait of Arthur Conklin as a decent human being for whom killing would be unimaginable.

"I considered going to the sheriff," she said. "But I thought you would understand what I've been telling you better than she would. I'd hoped you would sympathize with this poor man who's had such a rough time. That you'd want to help. I thought you would talk to the sheriff, convince her that Arthur is a victim, not a killer."

"Please, Ms. Temple. Rest assured that I do not doubt that you are sincerely concerned about Arthur Conklin and that you are convinced that he had nothing to do with Harley Gerlach's death. I shall share this information with the sheriff—all of it, and I won't edit it. I'll tell her exactly what you've told me. But I don't have the responsibility for investigating Mr. Gerlach's death. The sheriff will do what she believes she must do to bring his killer to justice. I hope that it turns out not to be Mr. Conklin. In fact, I would prefer that it not be any of the many people who worked so hard with me to produce Puccini's opera."

Whether this little speech would help Sandy Temple to sleep better that night, Kevin did not know. But he doubted it.

CHAPTER 37

Much as he wanted to jump in the lake and cool off when he got home, Kevin decided to wait until Carol arrived. Instead, he would put in the call to the Metropolitan Opera's archivist and learn what he could about whether Sean Carpenter's audition had taken place during Harley Gerlach's tenure as an audition panelist. He took a beer from the frig, pulled out a chair at the kitchen table, and punched in Ms. DeAngelo's number on his cell phone.

The resulting conversation was brief and disappointing. The Met kept no record of unsuccessful aspirants for a place in the Met chorus. Ms. DeAngelo could not remember a tenor named Carpenter; in fact, she was never informed about the names of those who auditioned. Only successful candidates had their names entered in her files, and then not until they formally joined the company. She once again suggested that he might want to call one of the chorus members whose names she had given him. But she warned him that none of them had served as audition panelists. They might be useful only because they were chorus veterans who could be privy to backstage gossip.

Kevin took her up on her suggestion this time and tried two members of the chorus. Surprisingly, they were available. They were also polite. They both remembered Gerlach unfavorably. But neither of them recalled any scuttlebutt about a tenor named Carpenter. Too long ago, they said.

He resigned himself to the fact that if Gerlach and Carpenter had ever crossed paths at the Met, he would learn of it only if Carpenter himself admitted it or had told someone else about it. He very much doubted that Carpenter would now volunteer such information in view of the fact that it would give him a motive for killing Gerlach. However, he might well have shared this bit of personal history, back before Gerlach's death. The obvious candidate was, of course, Heather Merriman. He would have been anxious to impress her, and one way to do that would have been to tell her he could have been a member of the Met chorus except for the shameful bias of Harley Gerlach.

The more he thought about it, however, the more Kevin doubted that Carpenter had ever met Gerlach before this summer. What were the odds, after all, that he had auditioned nearly a decade before on a day when Gerlach happened to be among those evaluating his performance? Carol would have to ask Merriman what Carpenter had told her about his unsuccessful quest for a place at the Met. There was nothing more he could do about the matter now.

Kevin took his beer with him and went into the study to check his e-mail messages. He realized as soon as he entered the room that his laptop wasn't in its accustomed place on the desk. He stopped, looking puzzled. It was always on the desk. Right in the middle of the desk, directly in front of the desk chair. Well, not always. Occasionally he took it out onto the deck when he was working on an article. But he couldn't recall doing that for weeks. He hadn't been writing an article; it was something his dean would ask him about when he got back to the city and attended the first faculty meeting of the fall semester. He started to formulate the excuse he would offer, but immediately set that thought aside and refocused on the laptop.

It wouldn't be there, but he would have to look. Kevin went out onto the deck where, as he knew would be the case, there was no laptop. There was no point in checking the other rooms, but he did it anyway. The laptop was gone. He was not usually a forgetful person, and he could not imagine what he might have done with the laptop in a rare forgetful moment. He finally faced the fact that he would have to consider the possibility of theft.

For as long as he had been coming to Crooked Lake, Kevin could not recall a single reported case of theft. None of his neighbors and acquaintances locked their doors. At first Kevin had reflexively locked the cottage at night and whenever he left to run errands. After all, he was a city boy, and no one in the city would dream of leaving doors unlocked, a standing invitation to thieves. But gradually he had adopted the more casual habits of the locals. His doors, front and back, had not only been unlocked when he set off for his meeting with Sandy Temple in Latham; the backdoor had not even been closed.

Once Kevin had admitted to himself that theft, no matter how unlikely, was still possible, he began to think about what else might have been taken. This necessitated a careful scrutiny of the contents of the several rooms of the cottage. A missing laptop

201

suggested an interest in electronic equipment. But his stereo and CD player were where they always were. So was his recently purchased high definition flat screen television. He turned to the shelves where he kept his collection of CDs and DVDs. Nothing had been disturbed.

What else was of value? His books were in place. He had no jewelry and his watch, a cheap Fossil, was on his wrist. He quickly went through his desk drawers. The only thing that might have attracted attention was his checkbook, and it was right where he had left it after his last trip to the bank.

The sight of the checkbook reminded him that the most accurate record of his finances was on his Quicken program, but that had disappeared with the laptop. Was it possible that someone wanted access to data on his several accounts? He couldn't imagine why. Could there be someone who wanted to steal something he was writing and publish it under his own name? If so, that person would be very disappointed.

Kevin soon gave up this unproductive speculation and dialed the sheriff's office to report the theft of the laptop. He could have waited until Carol arrived, but what if the thief had been breaking into a number of houses along the lake? Carol's people would want to get started on the search for the thief right away. Besides, he didn't want her to arrive for a swim and dinner and immediately have to turn her attention to a law enforcement issue.

She pulled in around 5:30 and headed immediately for the bedroom to get into her bathing suit. There was a lot to talk about, but it would have to wait until they had enjoyed a refreshing dip in the lake. Now that Carol was spending her nights at the cottage again, the evening swim had become something of a ritual. Except, of course, for those rare days when they took the canoe out. They had created rules about this. Rule number one was no discussion of the Gerlach case while swimming. There would be time later for that. But they were to put everything out of their minds except the pleasure of sharing a few moments in the lake waters, which even in the heat of late August were typically at least ten to fifteen degrees cooler than the air.

A half an hour later they were sitting on the deck, still wearing their bathing suits, nursing a glass of Chardonnay. For awhile they said little, enjoying instead the sight of flags flapping limply on their poles at the end of nearby docks and the sound of small waves lapping at the beach. It was relatively quiet, the only other sound coming from the occasional boat moving up or down the lake.

"I hate to break the mood," Kevin said, "but we're going to have to call out for pizza. Unless that is you want to try that roast we ruined last night. I'm trying to clean out the fridge, not add more to it before I have to leave."

The thought of his leaving was difficult for both of them, and neither wanted to talk about it. Kevin had brought it up, but quickly changed the subject.

"As your staff will tell you when you get to the office tomorrow, I've been visited by a thief. Someone stole my laptop while I was out this afternoon."

"You're serious?" Carol sounded as if she was more likely to hear about a drive-by shooting than a common, garden-variety theft.

"Afraid so. No need to talk about it. Your man, I think it was Barrett, said he'd get on it right away. It's not the end of the world. But you may have to rethink the conventional wisdom that Crooked Lake is free of thieves."

"You're forgetting that break-in at Gerlach's," Carol said.

"That wasn't theft. Nothing was stolen."

"A technicality. So you lost your laptop," she mused. "Anything else?"

"Not that I can think of."

"That's odd, don't you think? Sounds like whoever it was isn't the usual thief. Somebody who was specifically interested in your computer. Any idea why?"

"None. I've been all over this. It's a real mystery."

Carol suddenly straightened up and turned toward him. Kevin admired the way the movement showed off her figure to good advantage. He realized that he'd fallen in love with her before ever seeing her in a bathing suit, much less with no clothes on, but he felt a small thrill of pleasure to be reminded of what a great body she had. Almost as good as her mind.

"Wait a minute," she said. "I've got an idea. Thieves don't usually make off with just one item when there are other goodies lying around. Not unless that one item is what they're after. If you rule that out—meaning the laptop wasn't the reason for the theft, how about somebody stealing it to cover up the real reason for the theft?"

"I'm not sure I follow you."

"Think," she said. It sounded like an order. "Is there anything here that someone might want, something you'd not think to look for because you're focused on the laptop? On a conventional theft?"

"Not that I know of. I've been over everything."

"Probably not everything, Kevin. Remember up at Gerlach's house the other night you took a biography of Berlioz out of his bookcase. If it were your house, you might not even think to look for that particular book after a burglary because you wouldn't know that the thief broke into the house for one reason only: to steal Berlioz."

"What you're saying is that my thief took the laptop to confuse me. Which maybe he did. Maybe he was after something else."

"Right. Something that he was sure was in your cottage, something you wouldn't think to look for when you discovered the theft of the laptop."

"And what might that be?"

"I don't know. But think about it."

"I'm thinking, and nothing comes to mind."

Suddenly it was Kevin's turn to straighten up in his chair.

"Go back a minute. You mentioned Berlioz and Gerlach's cottage. You meant it as an example, but we did steal something besides the Berlioz biography. Well, we didn't really steal it. But we took it with us. Remember? Gerlach's harem album."

"Yes, but that's in my office, not your cottage."

"No it isn't. I borrowed it from your office when I went to visit the Helman woman, the one I bumped into at the supermarket. I knew right away that she was one of the women in the album, and I wanted to show her the picture, get her to admit she'd had an affair with Gerlach."

"Are you telling me you still have the album?" Carol did not sound pleased.

"I intended to bring it right back, but—"

"No buts, Kevin. That album could turn out to be important evidence. Where is it?"

"I tucked it into a shelf in that bookcase in the living room. Over by my stereo."

They both came out of their chairs at the same time, bumping into each other as they hurried through the door into the living room.

"Which shelf?" Carol asked as she knelt in front of the bookcase.

"The bottom one, I think. Not sure."

In a matter of less than a minute all of the books and assorted files had been pulled from the bookcase and strewn across the floor. The album with photos of Harley Gerlach and the women in his life was not among them.

"Maybe you put it in another bookcase. Maybe you were even clever enough to put it under lock and key in a file cabinet."

"My file cabinet doesn't have a lock and key," Kevin said, acutely aware that Carol was being sarcastic. "And I'm sure it was this bookcase."

"We'd better look in the study anyway."

By the time Kevin finally placed his call for pizza, they had reluctantly acknowledged that Gerlach's harem album was no longer in the cottage.

CHAPTER 38

There was more to talk about than a stolen laptop and Gerlach's photos of his conquests. A lot more. They both realized that nothing would be gained by indulging in recriminations over the missing photo album, and by mutual agreement they focused on other matters over their pizza. Those other matters included Sandy Temple's unsolicited defense of Arthur Conklin and Sonia Pederson's tale of Janet Myers' second thoughts about her divorce from Harley Gerlach. Not to mention Carol's report on her meeting with Marcia Kane. Thursday had been a busy day.

The one thing about which they were in complete agreement was that it was way too soon to cross Conklin and Myers off the list of suspects. They both thought it interesting that Temple and Pederson had come forward on the same day to proclaim the innocence of two members of Kevin's opera company. But Carol, who was notoriously skeptical of coincidences, was prepared to accept the fact that in this case there was no other explanation for it.

Temple's defense of Conklin had been based on nothing more than her conviction that he was a nice man who had been devastated by his wife's infidelity and death. Appearing and sounding devastated could be a calculated act as well as a deeply felt response to a crisis in his life. Myers' case was somewhat different. Carol had no reason to believe that Pederson had fabricated the story of Janet's ambivalence about Gerlach, but the old college friend obviously did not know whether Myers had discussed her feelings with her first husband, and if so, how he had reacted. What if he had laughed in her face?

She had known that she would have to speak with Janet Myers again. Now she would have to talk with Sandy Temple as well. And she had yet to discuss with the Geneva police their investigation of Helen Conklin's death. Was their suspicion of her husband simply a matter of routine procedure, as Temple had assumed, or was there something in the circumstances surrounding her death that raised a red flag?

There didn't seem to be enough hours in the day to deal with all of these issues, she thought.

They had spent more time discussing Mercedes Redman. In spite of the 'remember Gerlach' note, Carol was of the opinion that Sean Carpenter had had nothing to do with Redman's death. Indeed, there was no reason to think that she died from other than natural causes. Carol would wait until the autopsy report came in before questioning Carpenter again. If it confirmed that there had been no foul play, she might simply let the matter of the threatening note drop. But she would have to pursue with him the issue of his failed effort to join the Metropolitan Opera chorus. Was his rejection due to Gerlach? If so, when had he learned about it and from whom?

They talked about Marcia Kane and Carol's suspicion that she might have had a physical altercation with Redman. Hopefully the autopsy would answer that question. But that was a matter for the Ithaca police to deal with, not the Cumberland County sheriff's department. Carol fervently hoped that neither the autopsy nor Chief Owens' investigation would produce evidence that Sean Carpenter was in any way involved in Redman's death. Bad enough that he was under suspicion for Gerlach's murder.

They had been kicking these issues around for a couple of hours when Carol yawned and admitted to being tired.

"What time is it anyway?" she asked, suddenly aware that she didn't have her watch on. It was then that she was reminded that they had never changed out of their bathing suits. They had gradually dried in the warm evening air, and both Carol and Kevin had become so preoccupied with their dissection of new developments in the Gerlach case that they hadn't thought to change.

Kevin looked at his blue trunks.

"I guess murder has a way of taking your mind off your wardrobe," he said. "Oh, and by the way, to answer your question, it's not much after nine o'clock."

"I'm sure you'll forgive me if I call it a night," Carol said. She stood up and started toward the bedroom. "Just gotta change into my nightgown."

As he watched her, Kevin experienced a sensation in his chest so strong it could have been mistaken for angina. He was contemplating the end of summer, just days away, and another eight months of separation from Carol.

"Wait," he said as he, too, got to his feet. "You can do whatever you like, but I'm going to change into nothing."

He calmly stepped out of his trunks.

"Nice," Carol said, her face breaking into a smile. "But don't you think you ought to turn off that light? I like the show, but you do have neighbors, you know."

As she said it, she started to peel off her bathing suit. They came together in a tight embrace, all worries about Harley Gerlach's murder and the missing harem album temporarily forgotten.

CHAPTER 39

Sam Bridges made sure his coffee was secure in the cup holder, backed out of his drive, and set off for the Cumberland County sheriff's office. It was 7:35 on a warm and humid Friday morning in late August. The drive was one Sam had made hundreds of times; barring a disaster the like of which he could not remember in all of his 43 years, it would take no more than ten minutes. He made a bet with himself that he'd arrive before the sheriff did. When Carol Kelleher became sheriff of Cumberland County four years earlier, she had made it a practice to come in early and stay late. Rare was the day when she was not already at her desk when the first of her fellow officers drove into the parking lot. Even rarer was the day when she was not the last to leave. It had taken only a few days before Sam and his colleagues got the message and adjusted their schedules in an effort to look as conscientious as their new boss.

But in recent weeks, and more particularly in recent days, the sheriff had taken to arriving later and leaving earlier. And everyone in the department knew that she was arriving from the cottage of Professor Kevin Whitman, where she had spent the night, and leaving to return to that cottage, where she would spend yet another night. No one, least of all Bridges, was prepared to argue that she was shirking her duty. But some of the men were worried that she might be losing her focus.

Sam knew she wasn't losing her focus. What he was worried about was that she was letting Whitman become a de facto member of the force, the person she turned to when it came time to brainstorm a problem. Which might have been all right if she did not already have a deputy sheriff. His name was Sam Bridges.

Sam had not been particularly happy with an assignment he had been given on the Gerlach case. He had been told to check out the local restaurants and find out which ones had served spaghetti and meatballs for lunch on the day that Gerlach had been killed. Apparently the autopsy had determined that that had been the victim's lunch before he was strangled. Sam knew that it made a certain amount of sense to find out where he had dined. But a couple of the men had kidded him about his meatball assignment, and he had come to see it as a demeaning task. Nor was that all. Ever since he had reported the contents of Wayne Hall's bathroom wastebasket, he had spent an inordinate amount of time talking to the various members of the opera company. Who had started to write a note and then tossed it away unfinished? Who wore hearing aids? Who chewed gum? Which of the women had been having her period? He understood the potential importance of the note. But why did he have to discover who had tossed out a hearing-aid battery or a gum wrapper, or who had disposed of a used maxi-pad?

It wasn't that these were difficult assignments. Well, locating the author of the unfinished note had proved impossible. But he now knew who had hearing problems and who chewed gum, and he felt that he had invaded the privacy of a couple of the women in the company. He also knew where in the area you could get a meal of spaghetti and meatballs. And in the meanwhile, Kelleher and her friend Whitman had no doubt been occupied with more important aspects of the case.

It was roughly eight and a half minutes after leaving home that Sam pulled into the small parking lot behind the building which housed the sheriff's department. To his surprise, the sheriff's car was there. He touched its hood as he walked past it. It was slightly warm, but not hot. She had obviously arrived at least ten minutes before he arrived. What did this earlier than usual arrival portend? Had Sam been a fan of Sherlock Holmes, he might have said to himself that perhaps the game was afoot. In any event, he shoved aside his thoughts about the sheriff and her lover, or whatever Whitman was, and hurried into the building.

Carol approached the usual morning meeting in a business-like manner. She willed herself not to think about the pleasures of the night before, just as she had willed herself to get up early and leave Kevin to eat breakfast alone. She was already on her second cup of coffee when the last of her team strolled into the squad room.

"I think we may be approaching a moment of truth in the Gerlach case," she announced. As she ticked off recent developments, she began to have doubts as to whether that assessment was in fact an accurate one. But she was determined to create a sense of urgency, so she forged ahead.

"Sam, you've been working at tying down some loose ends. What do you have for us?"

This was the moment Sam had dreaded. He would rather have shared his findings quietly with the sheriff, rather than share them with a room full of his colleagues. He'd try to do it quickly.

"Two people in the company chew gum. One of them is a young woman named Lisa Tompkins. No surprise there. You always see young women chewing gum. The other one's a bit of a surprise—Paolo Rosetti. He thinks it helps keep his teeth a perfect white. The only member of the company who wears hearing aids is George Kulakowski. He uses a 312 battery, the kind we fished out of the wastebasket. The maxi-pad could have been Heather Merriman's or Grace Overton's. I didn't think you'd want me to pursue the matter further. I'm still coming up blank on the note."

There, he'd said it. He looked around the room, half expecting to see an ill-concealed smirk on somebody's face. But they all wore expressions of rapt attention, as if Sam had just announced that he had coaxed a confession from the orchestra's flutist.

"That's good," Carol said. "We can forget about the hearing-aid battery and the maxi-pad, I think, but the chewing gum may be important. How about Italian meatballs on somebody's luncheon menu?"

Sam wasn't surprised that the sheriff dismissed as unimportant his report on the people who had a hearing loss or were having their period. He couldn't imagine why who chewed gum was any more important, but she'd share her reasons when she was ready to do so. He turned to the meatballs.

"Several restaurants put spaghetti and meatballs on their menus from time to time, but there are three who did so for lunch a week ago Tuesday. One is Bartoli's in Yates Center. You can get it there any day, any lunch or dinner. They're Italian, you know. The Cedar Post also had it on their menu that day, both lunch and dinner. In fact, they offer it almost as often as Bartoli's. Finally, there's the Hilltop. So Mr. Gerlach could have eaten spaghetti and meatballs at any one of those places. I suppose he could have gone to some place down in Elmira or up in Geneva, too, but I concentrated on restaurants around the lake."

"Good. That gives us a place to start. I'm going to want to show a picture of Gerlach around at these restaurants, talk to waiters, bartenders, anybody who might have seen him. We can ask about credit card records, too. At the moment, we don't have a snapshot of Gerlach, but I expect to get one today. Then we start finding out who served our murder victim his last meal."

Carol then turned to Officer Grieves. To her chagrin, she had discovered that not only had she not assigned him the task of locating Gerlach's car, she had completely forgotten to give that assignment to anyone. She had corrected her error earlier in the week, with the result that Grieves had been looking for the car as well as working his normal beat. It should have been an easy assignment, inasmuch as everyone assumed the car was somewhere on the Brae Loch campus. Gerlach had been found dead at the college, so surely his car would be found there as well. But finding the car was proving to be more difficult.

"It's still the same old story," Grieves said, sounding frustrated. "They don't have a parking system—you know, students here, faculty there, guests in a special lot. I've gone over the whole area several times. They assure me they haven't towed anybody since Gerlach was killed. I suppose the car could have been stolen, but that would have been tough inasmuch as the keys were in Gerlach's pants pocket. In any event, no car. Which is weird. It's not like looking for a needle in a haystack after all. It's a small campus."

Gerlach's car's whereabouts was a comparatively minor issue, but Carol found their inability to find it irritating. She didn't like loose ends, and this was an annoying loose end.

"Maybe Gerlach, like Rosetti, didn't drive right onto campus that day. Have you looked along the lake road, say a dozen or so cottages either way? Can't imagine why he would have parked somewhere like that, but who knows what went on in his mind."

"I'll check it out," Grieves said in a voice that lacked conviction.

Carol eventually doled out the day's assignments, giving Sam Bridges one which she suspected would go a long way toward making him feel better about himself—and about her. She had become conscious of the fact that his nose was out of joint, something she correctly blamed on her relationship with Kevin. It was time to ask him to tackle what would look like a more important task than finding out where one could get a spaghetti and meatballs lunch or who chewed gum. She detained him at the end of the meeting and explained the need to have a good chat with members of Geneva's police department. Just what had been their thinking during the investigation of Helen Conklin's death?

Was there ever a real question of Conklin's guilt? And if there was, what ultimately persuaded the police to drop that line of inquiry? Sam was tenacious. He'd get answers.

She and Kevin had agreed that he'd go over to Gerlach's house on the bluff and see if he could find a photo of Gerlach. If he'd taken better care of the harem album, they could simply crop one of the pictures of Gerlach and his women and circulate it. But Kevin insisted that finding another picture of Gerlach would be no problem. He promised to deliver that picture into Carol's hands by noon.

———

The missing pane of glass in the back door to the Gerlach house had been replaced, the doors and windows had all been locked, and a large sign had been stapled to the back door announcing that, on orders from the sheriff, trespassing was forbidden. Kevin took the keys Carol had given him and let himself into the house.

There might be pictures of Gerlach in his desk, but Kevin headed for the darkroom first. It took all of thirty seconds for him to find half a dozen photos that would serve Carol's purpose. The poses were different, as was Gerlach's choice of clothes. But one thing was common to all of them: the man looked very pleased with himself. If one were to put a caption to any of the pictures, it could well read 'I've got it made.'

Kevin looked around the house for no other reason than that he had accomplished his mission and was in no hurry. He was tempted to 'borrow' another book or two, but he decided against it. When he let himself out, he wondered if Mr. Farris had seen him. And if he had, what he had made of Kevin's presence there.

It had been Kevin's plan to take the upper road back to the end of the bluff and from there to Cumberland. But as he started out on the return journey, it occurred to him that if he took the lower road along the west arm of the lake he would go right by Heather Merriman's home. Carol had made no mention of having told her about Redman's death, and she would surely have said so if she had. Kevin decided that Miss Merriman was owed the courtesy of a report on this piece of bad news, so he changed course and dropped down to the lower lake road. Unlike the open road that ran along the crest of the hill, the one on which he soon found himself was narrow, the overhanging trees creating the illusion that he was driving through a green tunnel.

The Merriman house was only about two miles north of the end of the bluff. Kevin anticipated no problem locating it, having just driven Heather home after her swim across the lake the previous week. Nor was there a problem. He pulled as far off the road as the terrain permitted, and walked down a short flight of wooden steps that led to the house and the beach. His knock on the back door was answered promptly by Heather herself. Once again she was wearing her bathing suit, and once again he was reminded of how attractive she was. And how young.

"Professor Whitman! What are you doing here?" The question reflected pleasant surprise, not anxiety.

"Do you mind if I come in for a minute?"

"Of course not. I'm the only one here—we won't be bothering anybody."

The Merriman house was modest by any standard, especially when contrasted with the Gerlach home he had just left. They went out onto the porch, from which he could see the beach some twenty feet below, accessible via another flight of wooden steps. The neighboring cottages were close by, but the tree cover created a sense of privacy.

Kevin declined the offer of something to drink. There was nothing to be gained by putting off his news of Mercedes Redman's death, so he got right to the point.

"I'm afraid I'm here to share some bad news with you," he said.

Heather said nothing, but the look that came over her face told him that she was steeling herself for whatever it was he had to tell her.

"Mercedes Redman is dead," he said. "She died sometime on Wednesday, just two days ago."

Heather closed her eyes and seemed to sink down into the cushions of the Adirondack chair on which she was sitting.

"That's terrible. I don't believe it." Obviously she did believe it, but desperately wanted not to. "She was only my mother's age. What happened?"

"Nobody knows, not yet. It looks like she had a heart attack, but the Ithaca police are investigating."

"Things like this don't happen. I guess I mean they shouldn't happen. Not to nice people like Ms. Redman."

Was it Kevin's imagination or was Heather tearing up?

"I know. I've known about it since Wednesday evening, and I still can't believe it."

"I was over there, talking with her, just last weekend. She didn't look sick or anything."

Kevin hadn't known this. Neither had Carol.

"You visited her in Ithaca just a few days ago?"

"Yes. Remember, we'd talked about my being worried that she might have wanted to have a relationship with me. I'd given it a lot of thought, and finally decided that I'd better level with her—tell her I just couldn't move in with her. We had a nice talk, although I have to admit I never got around to my real reason for going to see her. Her roommate came in, and somehow conversation became awkward."

"So you met Ms. Kane?"

"Do you know her?"

"No, but the sheriff went over there and met with her and the Ithaca police chief. It seems that Kane is the one who discovered the body. She said she found her when she came home from work on Wednesday."

"I'm pretty sure that Ms. Kane is Ms. Redman's partner. Or was her partner. There was just the one bed, so I guess my hunch about Mercedes' interest in me was right. You know, she probably did want to take me as her lover."

"I don't think her interest in you was only physical, Heather. She was a pretty discerning woman, and I think she really admired you and hoped to help you realize your potential."

"You're probably right. But it doesn't matter anymore, does it?" There was now no question about it. Heather Merriman was crying. She excused herself and went inside to get a Kleenex.

"What was your opinion of Ms. Kane?" Kevin asked when Heather came back onto the porch.

"I didn't get a chance to form an opinion. She only got home a few minutes before I left, and she had to change. They were going to a matinee or something like that."

"But surely you must have had some impression."

"It's funny, but I got the feeling from what little I saw of her that she was jealous of me. That probably sounds self-serving of me, saying that I might have been a threat to her. Of course, I wasn't, but she acted like she wasn't happy to see me there, talking to Mercedes."

"Do you have any reason to believe that Mercedes had ever talked about you to Ms. Kane?"

"I wouldn't know. When she introduced us, she didn't say something like 'this is that woman from the opera I've told you about.' It's a pure guess, but I don't think my name had ever come up before that afternoon."

"I have to be going, but now that I know you were at the Redman apartment on Sunday, there's one more thing I'm curious about. Did Mercedes say anything about receiving a threatening message in the mail?"

"No, she didn't. What's this about a threatening message?"

"It's my understanding that she received a letter last Saturday. It wasn't really a letter, just a short one-line message. It said 'leave her alone, remember Gerlach.' She didn't mention it?"

"Absolutely not," Heather said, but her facial expression and body language made it clear that she didn't like what she heard. "Who was it from?"

"The sheriff doesn't know. There was no signature, no return address on the envelope."

Was it his imagination, or did Heather relax in her chair?

"But that's a weird message," she said. "And it does sound like a threat. Mercedes was supposed to leave someone alone or what happened to Mr. Gerlach might happen to her. And now she's dead, just like Mr. Gerlach. What do you make of it?"

"I'm mystified. But until we learn otherwise, she died of a heart attack, so the comparison with Gerlach is a non-starter."

The conversation drifted back to the terrible fact that Mercedes Redman had died. Heather asked about a memorial service, but Kevin didn't know about any plans for one. They soon ran out of anything more to say about the death of this woman who had raised such conflicting feelings in Heather Merriman's mind, and Kevin said good-bye and set off for the sheriff's office.

He had learned more than he had expected to. Heather had visited Redman in Ithaca; she had met and formed a tentative and apparently negative opinion of Marcia Kane; and Mercedes had not shared with her the fact that she had received a cryptic and threatening note only days before. Kevin was certain that at that very moment Heather was reflecting on news of the note and trying to work out in her mind just who had written the message and to whom it referred. He did not doubt that she would have it figured out quickly.

CHAPTER 40

Carol had been giving a lot of thought to the fact that Brae Loch College still had no use of Wayne Hall. She had insisted that it be treated as a crime scene, and had had it locked, the keys in her possession. But she was having trouble conjuring up future developments which could justify her retaining control of the building where Harley Gerlach had been strangled to death. It was Friday morning after the staff meeting that she decided to turn the keys over to the school's provost.

She had Miss Franks call Armitage's office to make an appointment, and learned that he would see her as soon as she could get there from Cumberland, if that was convenient. He's really impatient to take down the yellow tape and the posted signs, she thought. He wants to freshen the place up before the fall semester starts. Or, more probably, he simply wants to reassert his authority, putting the unpleasant interlude of a misbegotten opera production, murder, and official lockdown behind him. Well, I'll accommodate him, and I'll do it now.

Thirty-five minutes later, Carol was sitting in Jason Armitage's office, ready to negotiate the terms of her surrender to Brae Loch College.

"I'm glad you are prepared to let us have our auditorium back," Armitage said, smiling at his witticism.

"And I appreciate your patience with us," Carol said. "I regret that we couldn't turn the keys back to you sooner. Of course it's only been a week and a half. I've heard of cases where it was weeks before things could return to normal after a murder. There was a theatre in the city which was blacked out for nearly two months after a well-known dignitary was found stabbed to death in the balcony."

Something like that may have been true, but Carol had made it up, trying to assure the provost that what he and Brae Loch had been through was not unusual.

"I hope you are about ready to make an arrest," the provost said.

"I wish I could tell you an arrest is imminent, but we're not there yet. You always hope that the guilty party will make a mistake, or that somebody will remember something important—some snatch of conversation, for example. That hasn't happened yet. But we're making progress."

"Do you think you'll want to stage one of those reenactments of the crime here at the college?"

Carol studied Jason Armitage across his big desk. He had obviously read a lot of mysteries, especially the ones where sleuths like Hercule Poirot assembled the suspects at the crime scene, walked them through their steps leading up to the fatal moment, and then dramatically announced the identity of the culprit. She doubted that anything like that would be happening this time.

"That is highly unlikely," she said.

"Well, you know that you have my promise of cooperation in case you need to do it," he said. He went on to tell the sheriff how important it was to have Wayne Hall ready for the drama club to start work on its fall play.

"What play will they be putting on?" Carol asked. She was mildly curious.

"*A Midsummer Night's Dream*," the provost said proudly, obviously pleased to report that Brae Loch staged Shakespeare rather than some piece of inferior fluff. "Last fall we did Ibsen."

"I hope it's a rousing success," she said. Better than *Gianni Schicchi* she considered adding, but thought better of it.

Remembering how worried he had been about the impact on recruitment of a murder on campus, she asked how things were going on that front.

"Too soon to know," Armitage said, "but I'm more optimistic than I was at first. We're still getting applications for spring term, and registration for this fall is pretty steady."

"That's good."

It was time to move on, to let the custodial staff get started on Wayne Hall, to let Armitage get back to whatever problems had piled up on his desk. Carol thanked him again for his understanding of any inconvenience she may have caused the college. He told her she could expect to see him at the trial of whoever had killed the opera's leading man.

Would there be a trial? That would depend on where her investigation led. At the moment it was going nowhere fast.

———

While she was waiting for reports from Bridges on his conversation with Geneva's police chief, from Barrett on what he had learned at the restaurants Gerlach might have visited for his last lunch, and from Owens on the result of the Redman autopsy, Carol had to decide on her own next move. There were several people she needed to see. Myers, to find out whether her friend Pederson had been right about her change of heart regarding Gerlach. Merriman, to find out whether Sean Carpenter had said anything about the reason for his failure to become a member of the Metropolitan Opera chorus. Conklin, to discuss his wife's death and his shaky alibi for the afternoon of Gerlach's murder. Rosetti, to question him about breaking into Gerlach's house.

She'd have to wait for Bridges' report before seeing Conklin. It would make more sense to speak with Merriman after she had learned what the medical examiner had to say. This left Myers and Rosetti. Myers would be the easier of the two to talk with, although that was no guarantee that she would be more truthful. Rosetti would be predictably unpleasant, but unlike Myers he could not stake out an ambiguous middle ground. He could either deny that he had broken into Gerlach's home or admit that he had.

Carol chose to approach Rosetti first. After her experience with Sean Carpenter, she had decided that it was probably better to question people in her office than on their own turf. For one thing, it meant that she had control over who else was present. For another, it gave her a psychological edge. Or at least she believed it did. Whether it would do so in Rosetti's case, she wasn't sure.

Rosetti worked at home, or so he had told her, and so she expected him to be there when she called. The phone rang six times before Paolo himself answered.

"Yes?"

"Mr. Rosetti, this is Sheriff Kelleher. How are you to-day?" Carol didn't much care how he was today, but she hoped he would reciprocate if she were pleasant. He didn't.

"To what do I owe the pleasure of your call?"

"I'd like to talk with you, and I'm calling to ask you to come over to my office so we can have a chat."

"This is Friday, Sheriff. It's a workday. I can't just drop everything. If you need to ask me a question, why don't you do it over the phone, then we can both get back to work."

"I don't think this is something we can do over the phone, Mr. Rosetti. It's very important. I really do need to see you."

"I can't do it. My wife has the car. She went shopping, and you know how women are when they go shopping."

Rosetti could simply be commenting on his experience with his own wife, but she doubted it. In all probability he subscribed to a lot of negative generalizations about women. It wouldn't surprise her if he were a thorough-going misogynist.

"When do you expect her back?"

"Who knows?"

"Look, Mr. Rosetti, it's only 10:45. I doubt she'll be away all day. And I plan to be in my office all day. So any time will be okay with me. I'm looking forward to seeing you."

Carol hung up the phone before he could protest further. She could imagine him fuming. And perhaps worrying about what her agenda might be. But she was confident that he would be there.

She was momentarily pleased with herself for handling the conversation in such a way that Rosetti would have no choice but to make the trip to Cumberland. It took but a few seconds, however, to realize that she had trapped herself. She would now have to remain at her desk until he arrived, and heaven knew when that would be. She only hoped that it wouldn't be so late in the day that she'd have to call Kevin and tell him to hold dinner. She resisted the temptation to call Rosetti back, and turned her attention to her in-basket.

She pulled out the photos of Gerlach that Kevin had brought back and spread them out in front of her. She was glad that he had not settled for a single photo; Barrett might have to leave one or more at the restaurants if the people on duty weren't the ones who had been on duty a week ago Tuesday.

The pictures reminded her that Gerlach had been a handsome man. He looked a bit like a film star who, as he aged, had acquired wrinkles that spoke of experience and wisdom. The mane of white hair enhanced the image. Carol wondered, not for the first time, why he had favored middle-aged women when he might well have spent his mature years seducing women in their 20s and 30s.

Rosetti arrived shortly before two o'clock, by which time Carol had made a few phone calls, dictated some correspondence, and consumed a takeout lunch which she had prevailed on Miss Franks to pick up at the Rustic Inn.

"Ah, Mr. Rosetti, I'm so glad you were able to make it."

"You didn't give me much choice. What seems to be the trouble this time?"

Carol had no intention of revisiting his dubious story that he had been fishing while Gerlach was being strangled. Nor did she intend to ask him where he had been the previous Friday night, the night of the break-in at Gerlach's house. That would have given him the opportunity to say he had been at home with the wife who spent all her time shopping. No, she would come right out and tell him that she knew he had broken into Gerlach's residence on the bluff.

She did not know whether he had been anywhere near the house. But she did know that he chewed gum and that a gum wrapper had been dropped on Gerlach's living room carpet the night of the break-in. It hardly constituted strong circumstantial evidence. After all, lots of people chew gum. Carol was sure it had not been Lisa Tompkins, the other member of Kevin's company Bridges had identified as a gum chewer. For that matter, the break-in could have been the work of someone unconnected with the Brae Loch opera project. Nevertheless, Carol was prepared to act as if she knew that Paolo Rosetti had paid a surreptitious visit to his late rival's house the previous week.

"I want you to tell me why you broke into Harley Ger-lach's house last Friday night. What were you looking for?"

Rosetti looked stunned, as well he might. Usually in control of what he said and how he said it, this time he fumbled for words.

"But I didn't break into his house." It was a weak denial. "What makes you think I did?"

"You left a calling card, Mr. Rosetti."

"A calling card? I don't carry calling cards."

"I used the word figuratively. You dropped something that belonged to you."

"But I'm sure I didn't drop—" Rosetti caught himself too late.

"Why don't you tell me what you were after?"

"What was it?" He still was having trouble believing that he had left something incriminating behind in Gerlach's house.

Carol resisted the temptation to turn on a smile that said she had won this round.

"Nothing big. Just a gum wrapper. The fingerprints are yours."

The wrapper had not been tested for prints. It might or might not have any, but what mattered was that Rosetti believed that it did.

"It's not what you think," he said. The pompous air which came so naturally to him was nowhere in evidence. "I wasn't after anything. I was just curious."

"Curious? About what?"

"About Gerlach. His house, his life. I knew he was dead, so the house would be empty. I thought it would be easy to get in and look around. I just wanted to get a feel for the man. You can usually learn a lot about someone by seeing where and how he lives."

Carol was prepared to indulge him in his attempt to explain himself. Whether his reason for breaking in was curiosity, she didn't know. It was possible that there was something in the house, or something he thought might be in the house, that he wanted.

"What was your impression?"

The expression on Rosetti's face suggested that he wasn't quite sure how to answer the sheriff's question.

"Well, it was clear that he had money. I don't know where it came from, but there was expensive stuff all over. I didn't like the art, but he was a pretty good photographer. It was obvious that opera was a big part of his life."

"Did you kill Mr. Gerlach?" Carol asked.

The question was not what Rosetti expected, but this time he didn't fumble for an answer.

"I did not!" he snapped. The anger she had encountered when she spoke with him at his house on Sunday had returned.

CHAPTER 41

As Sam Bridges pulled into a visitor's parking space at the Geneva police department building, he was struck by the number of patrol cars in the lot. He counted nine, and in view of the fact that it was a weekday, he assumed that there would be at least that many and probably more out and about on the city's streets. He wished the Cumberland County Sheriff's Department had a fleet of comparable size. Carol had called ahead to alert them to the fact that her deputy was coming and to explain the purpose of his visit. The police chief himself was on vacation, but a knowledgeable veteran on the force had been tapped to meet with Sam and answer his questions.

Sam enjoyed these opportunities to sit down with his counterparts in other upstate jurisdictions. It gave him a chance to talk shop and swap stories about law enforcement problems. He had never gotten the sense that Cumberland County and its nearby cities and counties were competitors, seeking to one-up each other. To the contrary, a spirit of cooperation seemed to prevail, whether the issue was the occasional inter-jurisdictional car chase or a need to share data. Toby Jensen, the officer who sat across the desk from Sam on this morning in late August, was a representative example of this cooperative spirit.

They chatted amiably for the better part of half an hour before getting down to the business which had brought Sam to Geneva. Jensen had heard of Harley Gerlach's murder, but knew little about the case, which gave Sam an excuse to regale him with the story of the failed Brae Loch opera project and the gallery of personalities who were now the object of their investigation. Most of this information was not strictly necessary, given the limited nature of Sam's mission, but he enjoyed the chance to show off his command of the issues, and Jensen was a good listener.

At the appropriate point in the story, Sam segued into the matter of the death of Arthur Conklin's wife Helen.

"You see, Mr. Conklin is being treated as a suspect in the case. We have no idea at this point whether he had anything to do with Gerlach's death, but seeing as Gerlach had an affair with his wife not long before her death, I guess you could say that he had a motive. We know that he knew it was Gerlach who'd been carrying on with his wife. He admits she told him before she died. But we don't know much about what happened to her, what caused her death. Rumor has it that you people may have suspected Mr. Conklin for a time. Want to tell me about it?"

"Sure, though you might get a different version depending on who you talk to. She had a fall, a pretty bad one. She took a tumble down a flight of stairs in their house, got banged up pretty bad. But the worst of it was what it did to her head. She was in the hospital for quite awhile, in and out of consciousness. You'd have to see the medical records if you want to know the details. Anyway, just when it looked like she might be going to make it, she had a relapse and died."

"If she had a bad fall, where did Mr. Conklin fit into the picture?"

"Well, he reported her accident. Called 911. Of course we have no idea whether he called right away or not. In the beginning, there didn't seem to be any reason to suspect it was anything but what he said it was, a fall down the stairs. But when she got to the hospital they found quite a bit of bruising, and not all of it looked like it could have been caused by the fall. I mean some of the bruises were older. That's the sort of thing that starts us thinking about spousal abuse. So we talked to Mr. Conklin. Of course he denied ever having abused his wife. Some of his neighbors got worried when they heard we'd been questioning him. They assured us he was a kind man, someone who'd never hurt his wife. But it was when we talked to neighbors that we learned about the wife's infidelity. Conklin hadn't mentioned it. So naturally we started to wonder if maybe he had a reason to mistreat her. Maybe even try to kill her.

"One of the guys who was looking into it got this idea that a simple fall down those stairs couldn't have hurt her that badly. He got it into his head that she might have been pushed. Or even that Conklin followed her down the stairs and slammed her head against the floor or a marble column that stood there on the landing. She was questioned about it, of course, but all she said was that she'd fallen. Said she'd been careless. But she wasn't very coherent, so we never did know whether she was telling the truth or covering for her husband. Anyway, there wasn't anything we could do. You can't arrest a husband for assault or attempted murder when the wife denies he'd done anything."

"Who's the guy who thought she might have been pushed?"

"Name's John Freitas. But he's not with us any longer. He moved to California back in the spring. Most of the guys didn't buy his argument. We couldn't figure why the wife would deny she'd been deliberately pushed if that's what had happened. She was in bad shape, but I thought she was lucid enough to remember something like that."

"The way I hear it, she'd been drinking heavily. That could have affected her balance, explain why she fell."

"You hear wrong. They checked her blood alcohol level when she got to the hospital. She hadn't been drinking at all. Zero. Nada."

"Really?" Sam was surprised by this information, which contradicted what Sandy Temple had told the sheriff's friend.

"Really. She was stone cold sober. That's one of the reasons Freitas was suspicious about Conklin's story."

Why had a close friend of Conklin's claimed that his wife's fall had had something to do with her drinking? If he remembered the sheriff's summary of Whitman's report correctly, the Temple woman had not simply assumed Mrs. Conklin had been drunk when she fell. She had reported it as a fact.

"I assume that there was a lot of local interest in Mrs. Conklin's death," Sam said. It was a question, but he treated it as if he already knew the answer.

"Yes, indeed. The Conklins have been important local figures for years. The local paper gave the accident and Mrs. Conklin's condition prominent coverage. It got quite a bit of attention on the TV station, too."

"Do you remember if there was any talk in the media about her being drunk at the time of the accident?"

"I'm sure there wasn't. Like I said, she was sober, and the hospital wouldn't give out information about a routine blood alcohol level test to a reporter. No reason for my department to talk about it either, especially when she wasn't drunk."

"Then why would a close friend of the Conklins be saying that Mrs. Conklin fell because she was drunk?"

Sam thought he knew the answer to that question. Arthur Conklin had told her his wife had been drunk. And if he had told

Temple, he had probably told others. Or assumed that Temple would spread the word. Why?

On the way back to Cumberland, the deputy sheriff went over in his mind what he had learned about the possible relevance of Helen Conklin's death to that of Harley Gerlach.

Gerlach's affair with her still gave Conklin a motive for killing him. His conversation with Toby Jensen had neither strengthened nor weakened that motive. Or had it?

CHAPTER 42

Officer Jim Barrett had inherited Sam Bridges' spaghetti and meatballs assignment. He had kidded Bridges about it, but now that it was his, he was enjoying the task of tracking down the place where Gerlach had taken lunch on that fateful Tuesday. He had started at Bartoli's, using the investigation as an excuse to have lunch there. The lunch had been good, but nobody recognized Gerlach's picture and the owner assured him that he had no staff other than those on duty that day. The Hilltop also produced a blank. That left The Cedar Post, one of the favorite eateries of the officers in the sheriff's department, although most of them spent more time at the bar than at the tables. They frequently patronized the bar after work, and much as they enjoyed the beer, they enjoyed admiring Ginny Smith, the bartender, more. She was not always on duty, of course, and Barrett and his colleagues typically settled for just one beer when they discovered that Ginny was not there.

Barrett would have been happy to stop by The Post on any day that Ginny was on duty. But today promised to be even better than usual. Not only would she be there (he had checked on her schedule on his way over to Bartoli's), but now, by process of elimination, there was an excellent chance that it was The Post where Gerlach had had his last lunch. And Ginny was noted for being observant and having a good memory as well as a cheerful personality and a great figure. When Barrett entered the restaurant at 1:25, he was in a very good frame of mind.

Most of the lunch crowd had departed, and there were several empty stools available at the bar.

"Hi, Ginny," he said as he slid onto one of the stools. "How are things?"

"I don't know about things," she said, a welcoming smile on her face, "but I'm just fine. How about you?"

"Not bad. I'm glad you're here today, because I'm hoping you may be able to help me."

"Help you?"

"Right. Why don't you pour me whatever you've got on draft, and I'll tell you what's on my mind."

He watched her as she walked down to the taps, admiring the way she looked in her tank top and short shorts. When she turned to bring him his beer, he looked away, seeking to create the impression that he had not been staring at her. Ginny, of course, knew better.

"So, you need to talk to me. Personal business or official business?"

"Official. Sheriff's orders."

Ginny had expected that to be the case. Barrett was probably the most laconic member of the sheriff's department. She had long ago divided the frequent visitors to The Post's bar into three categories: the talkers, the oglers, and the talkers and oglers. Jim Barrett was an ogler, albeit one who tried to pretend that he wasn't.

"You know me, always glad to be able to help you people out. What's on your mind?"

"It's about that murder over at Brae Loch College," he said. "The man who was killed was someone named Harley Gerlach. You've probably heard his name, or read about him in *The Gazette*. Anyway, there's a chance he ate over here at The Post now and then. I'd like you to look at his picture and see if you recognize him as someone who's been in here."

"Sure, I'll give it a try."

Barrett brought a folder he'd been carrying up onto the bar and took out a couple of the photos Kevin had removed from Gerlach's darkroom. Ginny held them up so she could get a better look at the man's face. There was no hesitation.

"Oh, yes. I've seen him in here a number of times. I don't remember him sitting at the bar, but he had lunch here fairly often this summer. He liked that table over in the corner."

Ginny pointed to the table which Gerlach had apparently favored.

"The next question is tougher," Barrett said. "Do you remember if he had lunch here last Tuesday? I mean a week ago Tuesday."

"I don't live here 24/7, Jim," she said, still examining the photos. "Some days it's early, but more often I come in at five and work the evening hours. And I really do have the occasional day off. Let me check my schedule for this month."

She left the bar and went through a swinging door to what was presumably a small office. She was back in less than a minute.

"It looks like I was here Tuesday a week. For lunch. But I don't know whether I could tell you he was here that day. If you'd asked me last week, I'd probably have been able to tell you, but after awhile all the days begin to look alike."

Damn! Barrett said it under his breath, but Ginny knew he was disappointed.

"Can you think of anything that might help me focus on that day?" she asked. "The weather, for example?"

Barrett wasn't coming up with anything when Ginny's face suddenly lighted up.

"Wait a minute," she said. "Did Gerlach have lunch with someone else that day?"

"I don't know. Maybe the sheriff knows, but she didn't mention it."

"I asked because one day last week Gerlach had lunch with someone. Just a second."

Ginny disappeared through the swinging door again, only to reappear seconds later.

"I'm not thinking straight today," she said, sounding annoyed with herself. "Don't know what's the matter with me. I wasn't here for the lunch hour on Monday, and Gerlach was killed Tuesday afternoon. So the only day I could have seen him here was Tuesday. And I know he was with somebody last week on the day he had lunch here."

Barrett breathed a big sigh of relief. But immediately realized that he now faced another problem. The sheriff would want to know who the other person was, but there were no photos of anyone but Gerlach in his folder.

"Can you remember what the other person looked like?" he asked hopefully.

"Let's see. A man, obviously. Average height and weight. Brown hair, but graying. He wore glasses, wire rims as I remember. He came over to the bar several times to get a refill, so I did get a fairly good look at his face. I'd guess he was in his fifties. He's probably a businessman or a professional, you know, someone not familiar with manual labor."

Ginny's bar customers were primarily men who could be described as manual laborers of one kind or another, but there was nothing in her voice to suggest reverse snobbery. Barrett was amazed at the mental picture she had drawn of someone she had, in all likelihood, seen only once.

He didn't know who Gerlach's luncheon partner might have been. He had had little contact with members of the opera company, and for all he knew this man had not been involved in that project. If he had been, the sheriff would probably have know who he was from Ginny's description. Even Bridges might have known. But at least he would be able to report that Gerlach had eaten his meal of spaghetti and meatballs at The Cedar Post. The sheriff could take it from there.

One other question occurred to him. He knew it was important, but it also gave him another few minutes with The Post's attractive bartender.

"Do you remember if Gerlach had much to drink that day?"

"Indeed he did. He usually drank heavily when he came in. That's one of the reasons I remember him so well. But last week he really outdid himself. Usually he came to the bar, got his drink, then went back to his table. This time the other man got his drinks. I'm not sure just how many scotches he put away, but it could easily have been five. His partner had something, too, a gin and tonic I think, but just the one."

"Did Gerlach act drunk when he left?"

"I wasn't paying attention, I'm afraid. I happened to look up as they were on their way out the door, but it was too late to see how he was doing. Not that I cared at the time."

"By the way," Barrett said as he gathered up his change and placed a tip for Ginny on the bar, "do you remember who waited on them?"

"I'm pretty certain it was Jill Fenton. She's not in today. Should I tell her you want to talk with her?"

"That's probably a good idea. She might have picked up something from their conversation that the sheriff would be interested in."

When Barrett left for the trip back to Cumberland, he was pleased with himself. He had a good, solid report for the sheriff, and he'd enjoyed the opportunity to spend half an hour with Ginny Smith. He liked to think that she thought of him as a friend.

———

The sheriff was out having a late lunch when he got back to Cumberland. He could have given his report to Bridges and set off on his routine task of pulling over speeders and otherwise policing the highways of Cumberland County. But he wanted to present the report himself, so he pulled out a chair in a corner of the squad room and turned his attention to a copy of *People* magazine that had somehow found its way into the building.

He didn't have long to wait. Carol came in just ahead of three, her face registering her surprise to find him there, engaged in what didn't look like official business.

"Jim," she said, leaning across the squad room table, "what's going on?"

"I've been waiting for you to get back from lunch so I could fill you in on what I learned at The Cedar Post. I think you're going to like this."

"Gerlach had his meatballs at The Post?"

"He sure did. And he didn't dine alone either. According to Ginny Smith—she's the bartender there—he had lunch with another man and had a helluva lot to drink."

Carol knew full well who Ginny Smith was, and was privately amused that Barrett felt it necessary to identify her as The Post's bartender, as if this would be something only men would know.

"Who's the other man?" she asked, addressing the most important revelation in Barrett's report.

"She didn't know." He sounded slightly defensive on Ginny's behalf. "But she gave me a pretty good description."

He proceeded to describe the man who had lunched with Harley Gerlach. Carol listened intently. Her initial reaction was one of disappointment. There was nothing really distinctive about the man Barrett was describing. He could have been an old friend, a neighbor, any one of dozens of people about whom she would know nothing. He might even have been a member of the opera company, although Carol doubted this in view of the fact that Gerlach had apparently been disliked by everyone in the company. She realized that she had been hoping that Gerlach's companion would turn out to be somebody who'd been involved in the *Gianni Schicchi* project.

Barrett started to provide more details about Gerlach's consumption of scotch when Carol interrupted him.

"Wait a minute, Jim. Tell me again what Ginny said about this man. Everything she said, even if it seems irrelevant."

Barrett repeated what he had said before. He was sure he had left nothing out.

This time Carol concentrated on comparing Barrett's description with the people she had come to think of as prime suspects in Gerlach's murder. It could not have been Janet Myers for obvious reasons, and it didn't sound the least like Paolo Rosetti or Sean Carpenter. Arthur Conklin was another story. In fact, the more she thought about it, the more she saw Conklin in Barrett's verbal portrait.

Carol knew better than to jump to the conclusion that Gerlach and Conklin had, for whatever reason, lunched together at The Cedar Post the day Gerlach was killed. She'd have to give it more thought, speak with Ginny Smith herself, and eventually have another talk with Conklin. But when Barrett left to patrol county roads and she returned to her desk, Carol had trouble suppressing the feeling that her investigation might have turned a critical corner.

CHAPTER 43

It was the time of the year when the Weather Channel typically focused on late summer heat waves and the hurricane season. But on the last Saturday in August, with Labor Day just over a week away, a cold front had passed through New York and New England, dropping temperatures precipitously and threatening to set records in the Finger Lakes region. Carol and Kevin had paid little attention to the forecast, and when they finally crawled into bed around midnight on Friday, they had no inkling of what the morrow would bring.

Carol was up first, and it was when she ventured out onto the deck to fill her lungs with fresh morning air that she first realized how dramatically the weather had changed. The thermometer told the story. It was a chilly 45 degrees. She was wearing the light summer robe which had served her well since she had moved some of her clothes to the cottage. Not this morning.

She borrowed a warmer robe from Kevin, and over breakfast they talked about the weather, making the predictable jokes about global warming. They had discussed the new developments in the Gerlach case the previous evening until there was literally nothing more to say. Neither of them was in any hurry to start doing the things they had agreed needed doing, although the list was long. But by the time ten o'clock rolled around, Carol announced that she was going to take a shower.

"If I don't get a move on, we might as well kiss today good-bye."

"Just when I was thinking about going back to bed," Kevin said.

"Well, if you do, you're not going to have any company. I want to make the rounds of Arthur Conklin's nurseries and pay a visit to Miss Merriman. What are you going to do for the good of the cause?"

"I promised to talk to the Helman woman, remember? She's my candidate for the thief who relieved me of Gerlach's photo album."

"Tell you what. Why don't you get ready and come with me while I try to find out what Conklin was doing a week ago Tuesday. Then we'll split up. I'll take Merriman and you see if Helman swiped the album. Okay?"

It was, and by eleven o'clock they were on the road.

"I should have followed up on Conklin's alibi sooner than this," Carol said as they turned onto the interlake road east of Yates Center. The closest of Conklin's nurseries, according to directions they had obtained over the phone, was just over a mile south, next to the Summerwind Winery.

On the way from the cottage to the nursery they had revisited their tentative conclusion of the night before: It was probably Conklin who had lunched with Gerlach on the day of his death. But why had he done so? And after lunch had he gone on to Brae Loch and strangled Gerlach to death? The trip to the nurseries would not answer the first question, but it might help to answer the second.

The one question they were quite sure they had answered was who had started to write a note and then crumpled it and tossed it, unfinished, into the wastebasket in the bathroom in Wayne Hall. It had read 'How about Tuesday noon? We could—' and then nothing more. They had assumed that the author of the note hadn't finished it because he—or was it she?—had spotted the person for whom the note was intended before finishing the message, and had simply communicated whatever was on his mind orally. And what had happened on Tuesday noon? Gerlach and somebody, probably Conklin, had met at The Cedar Post. The message would then have read, if finished, 'How about Tuesday noon? We could meet at The Cedar Post for lunch.'

All of this had been speculation, of course, but it made sense. What didn't make sense was why Conklin would want to meet Gerlach for lunch. Or, if the roles had been reversed and it had been Gerlach who wrote the unfinished note, why would Gerlach have wanted to meet Conklin for lunch. Perhaps they would learn something useful at the nursery they were now approaching.

Neither Carol nor Kevin had done much gardening, at least not in recent years. Carol had had little or no time for it, and Kevin was frankly disinterested. They had not visited any of Arthur Conklin's three nurseries. If they had, they would have known that these were not your typical nurseries, stocked with the usual assortment of annuals, perennials, and floral arrangements. Instead, Conklin's Nurseries specialized in what might be called yard and patio design. When they drove into the interlake nursery, they were greeted by an impressive array of outdoor fountains, stone lanterns, a koi pond, and a dry sand and rock garden which Kevin recognized as copied from Kyoto's famous Ryōan-ji garden. There were, of course, a variety of shrubs, plants, and flagstones of various sizes, but the principal business of this nursery was obviously to create elegant landscapes for upscale customers.

Carol parked the car and left Kevin to stroll through the artfully arranged display while she sought out the manager. She half expected to find Conklin himself somewhere on the property, but was quickly disabused of that idea when she located a man who appeared to be in charge. He was sitting in a spacious office, the walls of which were covered with beautiful photos of some of the gardens which the nursery had designed. On the wall behind his desk was a framed photo of the owner. It was a good likeness of Arthur Conklin, standing in the midst of a display of bonsai trees and smiling at the camera.

"Good morning," Carol said as she approached the desk. "Is Mr. Conklin in, by chance?"

She hoped he wouldn't be, for that could make it more difficult for her to get a candid answer to the question of whether he had been at the nursery on the Tuesday afternoon when Gerlach had been killed. But she needn't have worried.

"I'm afraid not," the man behind the desk said. "But I'm his manager, and I'd be glad to help you."

"Silly of me to expect him to be here," Carol said in an apologetic tone. "He's entitled to his weekend, isn't he?"

"Mr. Conklin is hardly ever here at the nursery," the manager said. "He handles the business; we do the design work and sales. His office is in his home, up in Geneva. Did you need to see him? I could give you his phone number, although I think I'd wait until Monday to call."

"No thanks, that won't be necessary."

Carol was considering the information that Conklin could rarely be found at the nursery. And presumably that meant any of the three nurseries.

"That would explain it," she added. "I came by last week, I think it was Tuesday, asking for him, but I was told he wasn't here."

"Well, that's a coincidence," the manager said. "You just weren't lucky. He happened to stop by a week ago last Tuesday, first time he'd been here in several weeks. But he was here for only about five minutes. I think he wanted to check the price on a lantern a friend of his had asked him about."

"Can you believe it," Carol said, shaking her head, "we must have just missed each other. When did he stop by?"

"It must have been around three. Something like that."

"That doesn't make me feel so bad. I came by in the morning."

Carol felt a small twinge of guilt that she had once more resorted to a lie. It seemed to be coming more easily to her.

"Is there something I can help you with?" The manager seemed to have decided that they had devoted enough time to this customer's unsuccessful efforts to see Mr. Conklin.

"No, not now. I'm waiting for my partner. He's been looking at your koi pond. I think someone is already helping him."

Another lie. Now they'd be expecting Kevin to get into a serious discussion of koi ponds, their cost, what happens to the koi during the winter, and so on. She'd better get them out of the nursery and on their way to Geneva and nursery number two.

The other two nurseries were farther away from Crooked Lake, one on the northern outskirts of Geneva, the other several miles west at a major thruway exit. If Conklin had paid a visit to either one on Tuesday afternoon, no one at either nursery had seen him. The resident manager in each case said essentially what the manager at the interlake road nursery had said: The owner never— well, almost never—stopped by. When he held a meeting with his managers, they occurred at his home in Geneva. Their contacts were almost exclusively by e-mail. He ran a tight ship. Business was good. But he didn't interfere with the week to week running of the nurseries, and the managers agreed that that was a good thing.

It was at the second nursery, which like the first had the picture of Conklin and the bonsai trees in the manager's office, that Carol had an idea.

"Would you mind if I made a copy of that picture on the wall?" she asked. "I have a friend who always talks about dressing up her place with bonsai. Maybe I could steer her to you people. Could you possibly slip that picture out of the frame for just a minute and make a copy for me?"

The manager seemed surprised at the request, but could think of no reason why he shouldn't be obliging. So Carol left the nursery with the picture of Conklin which she intended to show Ginny Smith and the waitress at The Cedar Post. The price she had paid was yet another lie. Three in less than an hour. If it wasn't necessary to identify Harley Gerlach's killer, she'd probably be ashamed of herself.

On their way back to the lake, Carol decided to put Kevin to work.

"Conklin's alibi for that Tuesday afternoon is that he was visiting his nurseries. We now know that he rarely visited them, and the only one who could corroborate his alibi was the manager of the interlake road nursery. Let's find out how many minutes it would take to drive over there from Brae Loch. Then double that, add in five or at most ten minutes at the nursery, and we'd know how hard it would be for Conklin to fit a murder into his afternoon schedule. Or how easy. I've got a pretty good idea about the time, but we need to be as precise as we can. So why don't you take your car and time the trip from Brae Loch to the nursery and back. In fact, why don't you, while you're at it, figure the time from The Cedar Post to the nursery and then back to Brae Loch. I'll try to pin Ginny down on when Gerlach and Conklin left The Post."

"You're asking me to do this at today's inflated gas prices?" Kevin asked with a smile. "Just kidding. I'll do it as soon as we get back to the cottage and my car. But you're still assuming it was Conklin who had lunch with Gerlach. We don't know that."

"We'll know, one way or another, after I show Conklin's picture to Ginny. I'm betting it is Conklin, although I'm damned if I know why they'd ever sit down to break bread together."

————

By shortly after noon, they knew two things. One was that a roundtrip between Brae Loch and the interlake road nursery, at five miles per hour over the posted speed limit with a ten-minute stopover at the nursery, would take 46 minutes. The second thing they knew was that it had indeed been Arthur Conklin who had lunched at The Cedar Post with Harley Gerlach. Neither Ginny

Smith nor Jill Fenton, their waitress, had any difficulty identifying him.

"I'd recognize him even without all those funny little trees," Jill said.

CHAPTER 44

The fact that Conklin had dined with Gerlach the day of the latter's murder did not suddenly transform the nursery-owning cellist into Carol's prime suspect. Quite to the contrary, it might suggest that he didn't belong on the list of suspects at all. The fact that they had gotten together for a midday meal at The Cedar Post could indicate that they had decided to let bygones be bygones, that they had been brought together by the passing of time and a common love of music.

Carol wasn't sure just how she felt about this mysterious luncheon 'date.' One thing she was sure of was that she couldn't now give her other suspects a pass and concentrate exclusively on Conklin. One of those other suspects was Sean Carpenter, whose grievance with Gerlach might be more recent than Conklin's. She would have to speak again with Heather Merriman and see if Sean had said anything to her about Gerlach having played a role in denying him a place in the Metropolitan Opera chorus. Supportive of Carpenter as the young woman had tried to be, she was more likely to tell her the truth than Sean himself.

"Miss Merriman," she said when Heather answered the phone, "this is Sheriff Kelleher again. I'm sure you must be tired of hearing from me. I thought maybe you'd already gone back to school. The college semester seems to start much sooner than it did when I was in school, even before Labor Day."

"I guess I'm lucky. We don't have to be back until the sixth. But I don't suppose you called to talk about college."

"That's true, although I'm glad you can squeeze a few more days out of the summer. Something's come up that I need to talk with you about. Don't worry; it has nothing to do with you. But we do need to talk. And once again I'm not in a position to drive over to your place. I was hoping you could drive to Cumberland. This afternoon would be fine, but if that doesn't work, could you come tomorrow?"

"If it has to be, I'd rather get it over with. When would be convenient?"

"How about two? I'm working at the office. If you like, we could go across the street to Mayes and get coffee. Or ice cream."

"That's very kind, but I'd rather just answer your questions and head back home. I've got a date tonight."

"So be it. I'll see you at two."

A date? She hoped it wasn't with Carpenter. The thought that it might be troubled her right up to the time that Merriman arrived at her door.

In spite of the fact that she had assured Heather that their discussion would not be about her, the young woman looked uncomfortable. Even nervous?

"I propose to keep this brief," Carol began. "I know that Sean Carpenter spent a lot of time with you this summer."

"Only at Brae Loch when we were rehearsing," Heather interrupted. She was obviously anxious to make it clear that their relationship was limited to the opera.

"Well, yes, that's what I meant. And I assume that the two of you talked about many things."

"May I ask you a question, Sheriff?"

"Of course," Carol replied, curious about what the question would be.

"You want to ask me about the note that Mr. Carpenter sent to Ms. Redman, don't you?"

Carol was about to say that, no, that wasn't what she had in mind. But she bit her tongue.

"Did you want to tell me about it?"

"Professor Whitman mentioned it when he told me about Ms. Redman's death, as I suppose you know." Heather had apparently figured out that the professor and the sheriff were more than casual acquaintances. "I've been thinking about it a lot ever since. The professor didn't say Mr. Carpenter wrote the note, but it doesn't take a genius to realize that he did. It bothers me that he wrote that note. It bothers me a lot. I mean what kind of a man would do something like that? Threaten another person, someone who'd never done him any harm, just because he thought she was in love with me. There was nothing between me and Ms. Redman, nothing at all. But Mr. Carpenter was jealous of her. Can you imagine that? Jealous of a nice woman who happened to be a lesbian and had maybe wanted me to be her partner. I say maybe, because we'll never know, will we?"

Carol listened, fascinated, to this revealing monologue. The Heather Merriman of Wednesday morning, so anxious to keep a promise to Sean Carpenter, had disappeared, her place taken by someone who had clearly lost all respect for him. She had even repeatedly referred to him as Mr. Carpenter, as if to distance herself from him.

"You know, Heather, we don't know that Carpenter wrote the threatening note."

"Well, maybe you don't, but I do. Don't get me wrong, Sheriff. I have no proof. But he warned me to stay away from Ms. Redman, told me that all she wanted was to lure me into her bed. I suppose I worried that he might have been right, but when I heard about the note, it all began to fall into place. He was the one who wanted to lure me into bed. This married man who was willing to cheat on his wife was actually jealous of a woman he saw as competition. I'd been flattered by his attention, I guess, even if I knew nothing would come of it. But now I find it disgusting."

Heather sounded disgusted, but she looked relieved to have shared her feelings with the sheriff.

"Do you think that Carpenter could have killed Ms. Redman?" Carol asked. "That if he was the one who threatened her, he then carried out his threat?"

"I thought she died of a heart attack," she said. "But, yes, I think he could have killed her. He just wasn't behaving rationally."

There was no point in pushing that issue further. It was time to turn to the reason Carol had asked Heather Merriman to come over to Cumberland.

"I think we'll know soon enough what really happened to Ms. Redman," she said. "Actually, the reason I wanted to talk with you wasn't that note. It's about a conversation you had with Mr. Carpenter. When we spoke earlier in the week, you mentioned that he'd once auditioned for the Metropolitan Opera chorus and that he'd told you he should have been accepted. I'd like to hear more about what he said to you about that."

Carol anticipated that Heather, in her newfound disappointment in Sean Carpenter, would have no qualms talking frankly about what he had told her.

"What is it you want to know?" Heather was trying to adjust to this new line of questioning.

"I can understand that he was unhappy about being rejected. But did he ever tell you why he thought he didn't make it?"

"Yes, he did," she replied. "He said that Mr. Gerlach was among the people conducting the audition, and that he had voted no."

"How did Mr. Carpenter know this? I mean did he learn it at the time he auditioned? Or did Mr. Gerlach say something just this summer?"

"I'm not sure what happened at the audition. But I didn't get the impression that he'd ever met Mr. Gerlach until this summer. Anyway, something must have happened to remind Mr. Gerlach that he'd heard Sean audition. Do you mind if I call him Sean? Mr. Carpenter sounds like someone I hardly know, when actually I know him too well."

"Whatever you wish," Carol said. "So I take it that Gerlach told Carpenter that he'd had a hand in keeping him out of the Met chorus. Gerlach, being Gerlach, was rubbing it in."

"That's what Sean said. He was really pissed. Here he was, years after the audition, being reminded of it by the man who cost him a job he really wanted."

"You didn't mention this when we spoke the other day, Heather."

"We were talking about Mr. Gerlach's murder, weren't we? And who might have been at the college that afternoon. If I had said something about Mr. Gerlach having screwed him, that would have given Sean a motive for murder. So I thought I'd better be quiet."

"But you're telling me about it today. It still could give Carpenter a motive for killing Gerlach, couldn't it? I asked you if you thought Sean could have killed Ms. Redman. Do you think he could have killed Mr. Gerlach?"

"I don't want you to think I'm accusing him of Mr. Gerlach's murder when I tell you what he said about the audition," she said, weighing her words carefully. "So, no, I don't think he killed Mr. Gerlach. But the other day I was protecting him. Today I think he should look out for himself."

You should have let him do that from the beginning, Carol thought. But she could appreciate the young woman's dilemma. Or what she had perceived as her dilemma before she found out about Carpenter's note to Redman. That had been a rude wake-up call.

Carol thanked Heather for her candor and once again said that she should keep an open mind regarding the cause of Redman's death. She promised to let her know if the autopsy clarified things.

"You said you had a date tonight," Carol said as Heather got up to leave. "When you mentioned it, I have to confess I hoped it wasn't with Carpenter. I think you've been telling me that I needn't have worried."

"It's with a boy you've met, Chris Ellis. The guy who's an assistant to the provost at Brae Loch."

When she left, Heather Merriman was wearing a broad smile.

CHAPTER 45

Had Kevin only lost a laptop, it was unlikely that he would ever see it again. But he had lost both the laptop and Harley Gerlach's photo album, which immediately reduced the number of possible thieves to a much more manageable number. In fact, he was convinced that he knew exactly who the thief was, and he was determined to pay her a visit and demand the return of both items. She had been clever, masking the theft of the album by taking the laptop as well. But she had been too clever by half. There were others who might have had a motive for stealing the album. But he could only think of one person who knew that the album was in his possession, and she would even have been wrong about that if he had returned it to the sheriff's office as he should have. Her name was Lauren Helman.

After a leisurely Sunday breakfast, Carol had had a small crisis of conscience and dealt with it by going to church. It was the perfect opportunity to pay Ms. Helman a visit. If she, too, had gone to church, he'd wait for her. Kevin was in no hurry. His problem was how to regain possession of the album and the laptop without arousing the curiosity of Mr. Helman. Much as he was annoyed with the woman who had violated his home and his property, he could appreciate her fear that her husband would discover her infidelity. As he drove toward Yates Center, he formulated a plan that he hoped would allow him to recover the album and the laptop without inadvertently revealing Mrs. Helman's secret to her husband if he happened to be at home. En route he stopped at a roadside stand and picked up some sweet corn and tomatoes.

It was nearly eleven o'clock when he pulled into the now familiar house on East Lake Road. Two cars were in the drive, which meant that both of the Helmans were home. It was Mrs. Helman who answered the door. The look on her face gave her away. She was frightened, as well she might have been.

Kevin spoke quietly but firmly.

"Please step outside and close the door."

She did as he asked.

244

"I have come for my laptop and for a photo album which you stole from my cottage last Thursday. I would rather that you not waste my time pretending that you weren't anywhere near my place. If you are afraid that your husband may wonder whom you're talking to, tell him that I am stopping by to bring you some produce from a roadside market. I have some corn and tomatoes in my car. Just bring me the album and the laptop and I'll be on my way."

"But this is—"

Kevin gave her no time to say whatever it was that she was about to say.

"Don't say anything," he said, making no effort to disguise the fact that he was angry. "If you don't want your husband to hear of your relationship with Harley Gerlach, you will do as I ask. The laptop is mine and I want it back—now! And you will be in real trouble if you don't give me the album. It is potential evidence in a criminal matter, and the sheriff wants it back immediately. Tell your husband anything you wish, but get me the album and my laptop. Do I make myself clear?"

Lauren Helman, now afraid to speak, motioned toward Kevin's car. He got the message. He collected the corn and tomatoes from the backseat, and handed them to her. She disappeared into the house and returned three minutes later, carrying a roll of newspapers.

"It's in here," she said as she gave him the papers. "The picture of me is gone. I tore it out and burned it."

"That wasn't a very good idea," Kevin said. He unrolled the papers enough to make sure that the album was there, as she had said it was. He briefly thumbed through it, satisfying himself that the other photos were intact.

"And now where's the laptop?"

Mrs. Helman looked anxiously over her shoulder, but Mr. Helman had not appeared at the door. He was either preoccupied or not especially curious.

"It's in the trunk of my car," she said. She went over to the car, unlocked the trunk, and removed the laptop, hiding it with her body as she transferred it into Kevin's possession. It had all taken no more than four minutes.

Kevin slid behind the wheel of his car and leaned out the window.

"I don't know how you managed to enter and leave my house without any of my neighbors seeing you. And I don't want to know. I trust that you won't be doing things like that again. You are a very lucky woman that your little escapade hasn't had more serious consequences. The sheriff will be most displeased when she finds that the picture is missing. She may want to pay you a visit herself."

"What do I owe you for the vegetables?" she asked.

"Enjoy them. There's no charge. And no, I won't be pressing charges for the theft. Like I said, you're a lucky woman."

Kevin pulled onto East Lake Road and headed north. Lauren Helman was still standing in the driveway, clutching an empty roll of newspapers and watching him drive away.

———

They had agreed that if he was able to recover Gerlach's photo album, Carol would take it with her and have a talk with Janet Myers. Of course she might not be at home, in which case the meeting would have to be postponed to another day. But it turned out that Janet would be at home, so after a quick lunch with Kevin, Carol left for Southport. She wanted to know whether Sonia Pederson had been right about Janet's change of heart about Gerlach. Perhaps the album could help her answer that question.

Carol had thought a good deal about what Pederson had told her, and, quite frankly, she had had trouble crediting it. How could Myers welcome back into her head, and maybe even her heart, a man who had not only carried on with other women when he was married to her but had also apparently continued to do so over the years since their divorce? She did not strike Carol as a patsy, a weak woman who could put up with this kind of emotional abuse. Indeed, as recently as the night after Gerlach's death during Carol's first interrogation of the woman, she had made no bones about the fact that she disliked him heartily. Kevin had cited incidents which added to the picture of a woman who had had her fill of the womanizer to whom she had once been married.

But at the same time, Carol found it hard to believe that Sonia Pederson had imagined everything Myers had shared with her. It was possible, of course, that Pederson was by nature a romantic, someone who was concerned that Charles and Janet Myers were falling out of love, someone who was unconsciously overreacting to a word or two here, a wistful expression there, in order to satisfy her own conviction that love will find a way. It wasn't likely, but it was possible.

Carol hoped that showing Janet the photos in Gerlach's album might stimulate responses which would clarify her role as a suspect in Gerlach's murder.

Once again, Charles Myers was not at home. Janet explained that he was at the office. On Sunday?

"Yes, he always seems to be behind in his work. He puts in dreadfully long hours. He has become a workaholic. His health has become a worry."

Carol did not want to talk about Charles. She wanted to talk about Harley Gerlach.

She had carefully removed the photo of Janet and Harley from its place on page one of the album before leaving Kevin's cottage. She set that photo down on the coffee table in front of the couch where they were sitting, sipping their iced tea. Janet leaned forward, studying this snapshot of their life back in the days before their divorce. She left it there on the coffee table for several seconds, although it seemed like much longer, during which time she said nothing.

"Where did you find this?" she finally asked as she picked it up and settled back on the couch with it. Janet's face had registered nothing, neither antipathy nor pleasure, as she studied the picture.

"It was in Harley's house up on the bluff," Carol responded.

"Why?" Janet asked, but she wasn't addressing the question to Carol. "Our relationship ended years ago."

For a moment neither of them said anything. Then Janet asked a question. This time it was intended for Carol.

"Do you think it looks like me?"

"Oh, yes. What drew my attention to it was that I recognized you. You'd done something else with your hair, and of course you were a bit younger. But it's still an unmistakable likeness."

Janet Myers continued to look at the picture.

"I do look younger, don't I? But of course. Can you believe that Harley and I were in love back then?"

Carol wished that she could read minds. Was Janet experiencing nostalgia for another, more innocent time? Was she thinking about her own lost youth, or were her thoughts focused on Harley Gerlach? Was she reflecting on what might have been? It was time to pull out the album and let her look at the other pictures.

"The picture you've been looking at was part of an album of pictures we found in Mr. Gerlach's home last week. As a matter of fact, the first picture in the album was the one of you and Harley. I'm not sure whether he had given it pride of place or simply put it first for chronological reasons. In any event, I thought you might want to see the album."

She removed the album from her briefcase and laid it, unopened, on the coffee table.

"It looks like a scrapbook," Janet said.

"Well, in a way it is. Harley was keeping a record."

Janet set her glass of tea on the table and opened the album. She quickly flipped through it without pausing to study any of the photos. Page after page were devoted to pictures of Harley and different women, most of whom meant nothing to her. With three exceptions. Printed beneath each picture was a name. There was a Gwyneth, a Lauren, a Helen, and several others. The last picture identified the woman as Mercedes.

While Janet looked at these pictures, Carol looked at Janet. Her expression, so inscrutable while she was studying her own picture, underwent a dramatic change. Initially she looked shocked. And then color spread across her face. When she flipped back to the photo of Harley and Mercedes, her face was red, her jaw clenched. A blood vessel was pulsing in Janet Myers' forehead.

"This is Mercedes Redman, isn't it? And these are pictures of Harley's women, going back to me?"

"That's what we think. We know for a fact that at least two of the women pictured had affairs with him, the ones named Lauren and Helen."

"Redman, too?" Her tone suggested that the idea struck her as preposterous.

"We'll never know, but I doubt it. I suspect that he would have liked her to be one of his conquests, but she died before she could tell us what, if anything, happened."

"She's dead?" Janet's surprise was real.

"I'm afraid so. It was a heart attack or something like that. Last Wednesday."

Janet stared at the photo of Gerlach and Redman, both of them now deceased.

"I can't believe it. In fact, I don't think I can believe any of this. But I suspect you're right about the purpose of the album. This woman Gwyneth was the one who led to my divorce—at least one of the ones. Can you believe that he would have kept a photographic record of his conquests? The egotistical bastard."

To say that this was a different Janet Myers than the one who had so pensively studied the photo of her younger self with Harley Gerlach would have been a large understatement. Three minutes earlier it was hard to know what she was thinking. No more. Carol doubted that she had ever seen such a sudden transformation.

"I think you have answered my question—the question I intended to ask," Carol said. "Whether you had ever seen this album of photos before."

"No, never. But I've never been in his house on the bluff, as I think I told you, so I couldn't have seen it. And he was never so crude as to bring it to our rehearsals."

A sudden thought seemed to have crossed Janet's mind.

"I suppose you think this proves that I could have killed Harley, don't you? You set me up, didn't you? If you could get me to tell you how I hated him, then you'd know I could have strangled him."

"But you'd already told me you hated him, way back when we first met. Remember? And you told Professor Whitman that you hated Gerlach and didn't want him in the opera, even before the rehearsals had begun. No, Mrs. Myers, if there is any reason to suspect you of killing your first husband, it isn't because of how you reacted when you viewed the photographic evidence of his relationships with women."

Later, while she was driving back to the cottage, Carol reviewed what she had witnessed and heard in the Myers' living room. It had been an inconclusive afternoon, but it actually tended to bear out what Sonia Pederson had said about Janet Myers' feelings towards Harley Gerlach.

CHAPTER 46

Monday of the last week of summer before Labor Day brought with it a return of seasonable weather. The cold front had moved on to the east, and Carol and Kevin took their breakfast out onto the deck.

"Do you remember when we had our very first conversation? It was right here. We were probably sitting in these same two chairs."

It was Carol who was recalling the morning they had met, two years earlier, on the day that Kevin had returned from an early morning swim to discover a dead man on his dock.

"I sure do. And I was nervous as a cat, thinking you'd suspect me of having killed Britingham."

"Well, what was I to think? I'd never met you, and there you were, telling me you'd been taking a swim at five o'clock in the morning. I thought you were nuts."

"Don't you wish every story had a happy ending? Like ours did." Kevin was enjoying reminiscing, remembering the relationship which had grown out of such an inauspicious beginning.

"Has our story had a happy ending?"

Carol immediately regretted the question. They had now been in a relationship for two years, but it was a relationship which faced the same problem every Labor Day. For that was when he had to close up the cottage and return to the city to take up his duties as professor of music at Madison College. And that meant that they would be living many miles apart through autumn, winter, and spring, a separation interrupted occasionally by all too few and all too brief weekends together. This year's separation would begin in one week.

"Sorry, Kevin, I didn't mean to bring it up."

They both knew that a happy ending was at best problematic if they continued to live separate lives for so many months out of every year. The summer just ending was to have changed things. The opera Kevin was staging at Brae Loch College was supposed to have led to an invitation to a year's visiting appointment there. That had never been guaranteed, but any prospect that it could happen disappeared the day Harley Gerlach had been murdered and the opera cancelled. By tacit agreement they had agreed not to dwell on it, but it had been hard to banish it from the back of their minds.

"Enough of the long faces," Kevin said. "How about one more cup of coffee before we face the day?"

"Sure. I'll have another Danish, too."

They gradually changed the subject of the conversation to the next steps in the investigation of Gerlach's death. It was 8:50 when Sam Bridges called. The sheriff was once again proving his point that her relationship with Whitman was affecting her morning arrival time.

"Good morning," he said cheerfully. "I thought I'd catch you at the professor's."

Carol wished he wouldn't refer to Kevin as the professor. She'd told him as much, but it hadn't made a difference.

"Chief Owens just called from Ithaca," he said. "He's got a report on the autopsy of that Redman woman. Says to call him back at your earliest convenience."

"Thanks, Sam. I'll do it right now. I may need to go directly over to Ithaca, depending on what he tells me. If I do, I'll let you know. One way or another, you take the morning briefing. And thanks for holding the fort."

She experienced a brief pang of guilt. Had she been letting her team down? She knew the answer was 'no,' that her many discussions of the case with Kevin had helped the investigation along in important ways. But she wasn't sure that Bridges and the others saw it that way.

"I've got to put a call in to Owens," she told Kevin when she hung up. "Autopsy report at last."

Two minutes later she was talking with Ithaca's police chief.

"It's pretty much what we thought," he said. "Redman did have a heart attack. I guess they can come sometimes without warning. This one did. No previous history. Unfortunately, she was alone and apparently couldn't call 911. Anyway, she didn't, and she was dead when her partner, Miss Kane, got home. According to the autopsy, she'd been dead for as long as seven or eight hours when Kane called for help and the rescue squad arrived."

"Damn shame," was Carol's sincere reaction to the news. "Anything on my theory that Redman and Kane had been fighting?"

"You were right on the money on that one. No question about it, there was stuff under Redman's fingernails—pieces of skin, like you said. We've already verified that it was Kane's. She started to raise a fuss about her rights, but she came around. Of course that doesn't say anything about Kane causing the heart attack. There's no way to prove that Redman was so traumatized that her ticker failed her."

"Do you know when they had their fight, or what it was about?"

"All we have to go on is what Kane tells us. She says they got into an argument the night before, which is convenient, I suppose. It'd be easier to see a connection between the fight and the heart attack if it had occurred just before Kane went to work the morning Redman died. And maybe it did. But no neighbor heard anything."

"And what about their argument?"

"Same story. Kane says it was just a disagreement about her pulling her weight around the apartment. I guess Redman was neat, Kane was sloppy, and their odd-couple relationship finally blew up in their faces."

"I don't buy that for a minute, Doug. I'd bet money that Kane thought Redman was enamored of another woman, challenged her, and it led to pushing, shoving, scratching. It probably got real nasty, ending in Redman's heart attack. And I think it happened Wednesday morning."

"We'd never prove any of that, Carol," Owens said.

"Probably not. But I know the young woman I think Kane saw as her rival for Redman's affection. And she's pretty credible. It's not my jurisdiction, and my hands are full of the Gerlach business—our Brae Loch opera murder. You'll have to decide if it's worth pursuing."

"I'll take that under advisement. By the way, Kane vehemently denies writing that threatening note to Redman."

"I think I'd believe her on that one. Like I told you when we met in the apartment, that 'remember Gerlach' line doesn't sound like Kane. She didn't know much of anything about our Crooked Lake murder. Gerlach isn't a name that's likely to have popped into her mind if she wanted to threaten Mercedes. It's my guess that the author of that note is someone who was involved in the opera over here. Lucky for him it looks like Redman's death can't be laid on him."

"Do you want to read the medical examiner's report?"

"No thanks. Your summary's good enough for me. Thanks for fixing it, so I don't have to worry about a two front murder investigation."

"You're welcome, as always."

Carol filled Kevin in on what Owens had told her, or at least what he had not been able to figure out from overhearing one end of the conversation. They would like to have spent the rest of the morning dissecting the case, but Carol was anxious to get back to the office and demonstrate to her troops that she was still very much in charge of Cumberland County's law enforcement team.

Before she left, however, they had reached an agreement that they would have dinner at The Cedar Post and travel together to Rochester the following morning. Sean Carpenter would not welcome their visit.

CHAPTER 47

"Why so insistent on dinner here tonight?" Kevin asked as they took their seats at a corner table at The Cedar Post.

"I thought you liked it," Carol replied. "It's the scene of some of our best evenings, isn't it?"

"Well, yes, but you seemed especially anxious to get away from the cottage. Getting tired of my cooking?"

"Never. If you ever want a second career, you could try being a chef."

"Thanks but no thanks. By the way, do you realize that I've hardly ever had one of your meals? It's always me or places like this."

"It's called division of labor, Kevin. I work a long day while you swim and goof off. And maybe do a bit of writing every once in awhile. So you cook to even things out."

The banter went on for a couple of minutes until a waitress came by to take their order.

"I'd love to try a recipe on you. Ever try calamari?" Carol said when the young woman moved on to another table.

"Indeed I have. There's a nice seafood place about two blocks from my apartment in the city. We should try it when you come down."

"Damn, I'd hoped I could expand your culinary horizons a bit." Carol gave Kevin a big smile and looked across the room to where the waitress was waiting for the bartender to set up their beers. The bartender was Ginny Smith, and the fact that she was on duty was the reason Carol had been anxious to dine at The Post.

"I'm going to put a couple of questions to Ginny," she said, "as soon as the beer arrives."

When Carol got up to talk with Ginny, Kevin busied himself observing his fellow patrons. By the time she came back, his beer was gone and their steak sandwiches had arrived.

"Dig in before it gets cold," he said.

"It was an interesting conversation. I got a pretty precise time as to when Gerlach and Conklin left after their lunch. More importantly, Ginny was pretty sure that Gerlach was drunk, almost out on his feet. She didn't get a good look at them when they left, but she had the impression that Conklin was holding him up. Her report gave me an idea. What if Gerlach didn't drive when he left here? What if he couldn't? Suppose Conklin drove him to Brae Loch and—"

"Tucked him into bed and strangled him." Kevin finished her thought.

"Maybe, maybe not. But what if Gerlach's car is still here at The Post? We've been looking for it for a week. We know it isn't at his house, and it doesn't seem to be at the college. How about it never left here that day?"

"But surely someone would have noticed that a car hadn't been moved for days. Somebody would have complained."

"I don't know. Their parking area is kinda strange. Some of it's paved, then there's that grass area out back, plus a couple of places beside the shed where they keep their cordwood. You've seen it. Bar's open late, staff comes in and out at all hours. This isn't a valet parking kind of restaurant."

"So let's look," Kevin said. "You hold the table and I'll do it."

"Your steak will be cold. I suggest we eat and then go walk about."

"Sorry. I can't put my curiosity on hold. I'll be back in five minutes."

"Okay, then I'm coming with you. I'll have the waitress hold the table and keep the steak warm."

They were gone only three minutes. Gerlach's car was indeed at The Post, tucked away in a corner of the grass plot behind the restaurant. It was covered with a layer of dust and grass clippings that had been thrown up by a mower.

Back at their table and digging into steaks that were not as rare as they had ordered, Carol and Kevin were discussing next steps.

"I think it's time to confront Conklin. Like tomorrow."

"Agreed," Carol said. "We've got that appointment with Carpenter tomorrow morning. Glad I insisted it be early. We should be back by noon, which gives me plenty of time to talk with Conklin."

"Wait a minute," Kevin said. "Are you saying that you want to see him alone? I'm going along to Rochester, why don't I come with you when you see Conklin, too?"

"It's not like Carpenter. In his case, you're the one who has the contact at the Met. You can sound knowledgeable about their recruitment practices, make Gerlach's role sound convincing. But Conklin would just wonder why you're with me."

"Let him wonder. I'd be your silent partner if you like, let you ask the questions."

"Are you kidding?" Carol asked, a hint of a smile on her face. "You wouldn't be able to stay out of it. I know you too well."

They might be close to the end of the chase, and Kevin didn't want to be left out.

"Suppose I came with my mouth taped shut," he said.

"That would really have Conklin wondering what we were up to," Carol said. "All right, you can keep me company. But remember, the way he sees it, I'll be investigating Gerlach's murder, and you'll be a music teacher who tried to put on an opera. Let's not confuse him."

That problem settled, Kevin asked about the car.

"What are you going to do about Gerlach's car?"

"I'll turn it over to Jack Grieves. He's been spinning his wheels looking for it in the wrong places, so I'll give him a chance to bring it in. I can't imagine we'll learn anything from it, but he can give it a thorough going over. He can pick it up tomorrow."

En route back to the cottage, Carol was wondering out loud whether Arthur Conklin had suddenly become her number-one suspect.

"It's likely he took Gerlach back to the college, and it's likely that Gerlach was in no shape to defend himself. If Conklin wanted to kill him, he couldn't have had a better opportunity."

"*If* he wanted to kill him," Kevin said. "That's a big if."

"I know. To be honest about it, I find it hard to believe that any of my so-called suspects have what looks like a compelling motive for killing Gerlach. I've disliked a lot of people in my life—well, at least a few. But I don't remember ever considering killing any of them. What about you?"

"I try not to dislike people, Carol, much less think about killing them. Either Gerlach's strangler came unhinged for some reason or the killer had a much more serious grievance than we know about."

"Maybe Conklin's had more on his mind than his late wife's affair. We'll see if he unburdens himself when we confront him about his luncheon with Gerlach. The one thing we know for sure is that he never mentioned it when I interviewed him the night we discovered Harley's body."

Tuesday promised to be a very busy day.

CHAPTER 48

Carol had insisted that they be on their way by 8:20 at the latest, which had the effect of depriving Kevin of the early swim he had dreamed of off and on all night. But Sean Carpenter would be waiting for the sheriff at his office in downtown Rochester at 9:45, and she was determined to be there early if possible and on time at the latest. They would be coming into town during rush hour, and MapQuest had indicated that there would be quite a few twists and turns before they reached the parking lot of Carpenter's firm of CPAs.

But the trip was pleasant, the roads lightly traveled for the first three-quarters of the way. They had gone over the questions they would ask the night before, and chose to spend the drive drinking a second cup of coffee and listening to one of Kevin's CDs, an opera by Britten. Carol had reluctantly agreed to hear it, but by the time they had reached the city limits, she had decided that it was probably not a good introduction to opera for a novice. Kevin had inferred as much from her facial expression, or lack thereof, and turned it off before she asked him to. Next time he would go back to Mozart, or perhaps Verdi.

In spite of the traffic, they pulled into a lot next to a building identified as The Ontario Complex at almost exactly 9:45. The directory in the lobby told them that Winston, Laidlaw, and Carpenter, CPAs, was on the fifth floor. The office was directly across from the bank of elevators, and a white-haired woman of approximately 70 years of age invited them to take seats and offered them coffee. Kevin said yes, Carol no, and the woman disappeared momentarily. When she reappeared with his coffee, Kevin thought he detected a hint of suppressed curiosity. She must have known who they were, or at least who the sheriff was, but it was doubtful that Carpenter had told her why they had made the appointment. Kevin wondered if Sean had ever discussed with her what he had been up to during the summer when he left the office early for the trip over to Crooked Lake. Probably not.

Carpenter and his colleagues had separate offices, so the conversation Carol and Kevin would be having with the man who was to have sung Rinuccio in Puccini's opera would be a private one. Carpenter himself came out to greet them, and they soon found themselves in a simply furnished room, sitting around a large walnut desk, their backs to shelves lined with rows of official-looking books which were apparently the guide to complex tax laws for CPAs.

"You've come quite a distance. And so early," Carpenter said. "Naturally, I'm hoping you are here to tell me you've arrested Gerlach's killer."

"I wish we were," Carol said, "but I'm not there yet. I still have questions. I brought Professor Whitman along because he's in a better position than I am to talk with you about one of those questions."

She turned to Kevin and asked him to go ahead.

"Sean—do you mind if I call you Sean? After all those weeks of rehearsing our opera, Mr. Carpenter would be much too formal, don't you think?"

"Of course. I'm Sean, and you're Kevin."

"Good. I remember that when you first met with me, back when I was casting the opera, you told me how much you loved opera. You said something about wanting to be a world-class tenor in your next incarnation. Well, I can't comment on reincarnation, but you have a naturally lovely voice. It's a shame that the good people of Crooked Lake never got a chance to hear you."

"That's very kind of you."

"I mean it," Kevin said. "But I sometimes wondered why you didn't pursue a career in opera. Like Mr. Gerlach did. He had a good voice, but no better than yours. And, of course, you're a tenor, and we know how much in demand good tenors are. Anyway, as you know, I teach music down in the city, and I know some people at the Met. I was talking with someone there not that long ago, and we got to discussing how people were chosen for the Met chorus. It was just an academic conversation, but we soon found ourselves talking about the process. And that led to this man sharing an anecdote that involved Harley Gerlach back when he was in the chorus."

Kevin paused to take a sip of his cooling coffee. He was watching Carpenter, who was listening intently, his posture rigid.

"It seems that the Met has a chorus member or two serve on panels that audition candidates for the chorus. Gerlach did that for several years in the late '90s. It seems he became somewhat erratic, even biased in his judgment. He finally had to be removed from the panel. There were stories about particular candidates that Gerlach voted down. One of them sounded very much like you. Of course the person I was talking with couldn't remember a name. Maybe he'd never heard the name. But when you told me about wanting to be an opera singer, I was reminded of that story. By any chance did you actually try out for the Met chorus?"

Kevin knew that he had stretched the truth, but he hadn't gone so far as to say that his interlocutor at the Met had told him that Gerlach had blackballed someone named Carpenter. The problem confronting Carpenter was whether to admit to auditioning for the chorus, and, if he did so, whether to acknowledge Gerlach's role in his failure to become a member of that chorus. In other words, would he tell them what he had told Heather Merriman or would he put his story in conflict with hers once again.

What Carpenter did was split the difference.

"I did audition for the Met chorus. It was many years ago, and I had pretty much forgotten about it. I did it as sort of a lark. If I'd been selected, I'd have had to take a big cut in income, relocate downstate. For whatever reason, I didn't pass muster. Not that it mattered. I couldn't have uprooted my family. It would have meant my wife giving up her job, the kids changing schools, the whole bit."

"Did they ever tell you why they didn't offer you a place in the chorus?"

"No. Just the standard 'thank you' for trying out."

"Did you know that Gerlach was on the panel?"

"I didn't know any of them. It wasn't like *American Idol*, where the panel members are celebrities themselves."

"And when you joined our opera company down at Brae Loch, did you recognize Gerlach as one of the panelists?"

"After all those years? I didn't pay attention to the individual panelists when I auditioned. I couldn't even tell you now how many were men, how many women. So no, I didn't recognize Gerlach."

Kevin's role in the questioning of Sean Carpenter had come to an end. He had not been aggressive. To the contrary, he had been polite, sympathetic. But the thrust of the questions would not have been lost on Carpenter. Now it was Carol's turn.

"I appreciate your candor," she said, well aware that he had not been candid. "Now I'd like to focus on something else. Or someone else. Have you heard about Mercedes Redman?"

"Redman? What do you mean?"

"She's dead, or hadn't you heard?"

"Dead?" It would have been hard for anyone to have feigned the look of absolute astonishment on Carpenter's face.

"Yes, I'm afraid that Mercedes is dead. She died last Wednesday. And you knew nothing about it?"

"Of course not. Why would I know about it? Has it been on national news? I don't look at the local news, and she's not from here in any event."

There was none of the matter-of-fact tone which he had used in answering Kevin's questions. Sean Carpenter was now on the defensive, obviously troubled that the sheriff should assume that he'd know anything about yet another death of a member of the opera troupe.

"I'm sorry to be sharing the bad news with you," Carol said. "Mercedes died in her apartment in Ithaca. When she was found, the police also found a note, and that is what I want to ask you about. It was a very brief note, unsigned. It had apparently arrived in the mail only a few days before her death. It said that Mercedes should leave her alone and that she should remember Gerlach. It didn't say who 'her' was. Naturally, the Ithaca police were interested in who sent the note because it had threatened Ms. Redman and now she is dead. Perhaps the writer of the note had killed her."

"But why are you telling me this?"

"Quite simply, Mr. Carpenter, because we believe you wrote that note."

"But that's absurd. Why would I be writing a note to Mercedes Redman? And why on earth would you suspect me of killing her?"

"I haven't said anything about you killing her. I only said that the police had a logical reason to infer that the note and Ms. Redman's death were related. That doesn't mean that the person who wrote the note did kill her. But I think you can understand why they might have thought so."

"But why would the police think that I wrote that note to Mercedes?"

"They didn't. I did. The Ithaca police didn't know who Gerlach was, and they had never heard of you either. But I knew who Gerlach was, and the fact that he was mentioned in the note started me thinking about the opera company to which both you and Redman had belonged. Let's think about it. Everybody in the company knew Gerlach, of course. But what member of the company also had a reason to warn Redman to stay away from another woman?"

Sean Carpenter suddenly looked very uncomfortable.

"It wasn't really a complicated deduction. The only woman Mercedes was known to have been close to by members of the Brae Loch opera troupe was Heather Merriman. And who was known to be more than professionally interested in Miss Merriman? That would be you, Mr. Carpenter. You had made your interest in Miss Merriman very obvious to everyone in the company. And surely you knew from day-to-day observation that Redman was interested in her, too. Others might have seen her interest in Heather as simply a matter of wanting to mentor her, to cultivate her talent. But you knew that there was more to it than that. You're an observant man, and you suspected, rightly, that Mercedes was a lesbian and that her interest in Heather was physical as well as professional. She was competition, potentially serious competition. So you wrote the note, warning her off."

"You can't prove that," Carpenter said.

"Oh, I think there's a pretty good chance that we can. But it may be beside the point. We now know that Mercedes Redman died of a heart attack. We also know that she had a physical altercation with her roommate—her partner, if you will—before her death. It would appear that the partner saw Heather as a threat, just as you saw Mercedes as a threat. It is unlikely that anyone will be indicted for having been involved in Mercedes' death. But that doesn't absolve you of responsibility for threatening her."

Carpenter now looked pensive, as of weighing the pros and cons of admitting that he had sent the message to Redman.

"Do you really think it's a crime to ask someone to stay away from someone else? I'll bet it happens all the time. I'm no lawyer, but it sounds like a free-speech issue to me."

"Perhaps," Carol answered. "But I am a lawyer, and I'd strongly recommend that you make it a policy not to threaten anyone, anytime, in any way. That's dangerous territory, and I don't think you want to test the limits of the first amendment. I also think we've touched on all the issues we came to talk about. We have to be getting back to the lake."

She and Kevin pushed back their chairs and got up. The handshakes with Sean Carpenter were perfunctory, even chilly.

"Do you really think you could indict him for that letter he sent to Redman?" Kevin asked on the drive home.

"It would probably not be worth the time or effort. There've been some recent cases, mostly involving the Internet, but the law is ambiguous. But I think he did write the 'leave her alone' note, don't you?"

"I'm as sure of it as I am that Conklin wrote the 'how about Tuesday noon' note to Gerlach," Kevin said. They both hoped to bring that issue to closure that afternoon.

CHAPTER 49

They arrived back at the cottage in time for a leisurely lunch before heading for Geneva and Arthur Conklin's house. There were two messages on Kevin's answering machine, one for him and one for Carol. Hers was from her office, his from Heather Merriman.

The message for Carol had to do with a problem other than the Gerlach case, so she called and left instructions for Bridges. Merriman wanted to see Kevin. He called her right back.

"Professor Whitman? Oh, there I go again—I know you don't like that. But look, I really need to see you, show you something. Or maybe I should say listen to something. I know you must have a CD player. Can I come over?"

"I'm going to be tied up for awhile this afternoon. Is tomorrow morning soon enough?"

"Of course," she replied. "I don't like to bother you, but it may be important. What's a good time?"

"I expect to be here all morning. Let's make it ten."

"Good. I'll be there."

"What's this, another revelation about our friend Carpenter?" Carol asked when he hung up the phone.

"No idea. I wasn't anxious to have her coming over later today, and I thought you'd be up and gone well before ten in the morning. Okay?"

"You don't think she'll want me to be here?" Carol asked.

"It didn't sound that way. She asked to see me."

"I hope that she hasn't decided to make a play for you now that she's on the rebound from Carpenter."

"That's sick, Carol."

"You never know, though. At least you're not married, and you haven't been sending threatening messages to anyone."

"Let's cut the comedy and have lunch," Kevin said.

After a minute or two of opening and closing cupboard doors and checking the refrigerator, Kevin spelled out the bad news.

"Not much here," he reported. "Salami, a few slices of swiss, peanut butter, and some cream cheese. No, scratch the cream cheese. That's for the bagels and breakfast."

Carol shook her head.

"I guess it'll have to be a peanut butter and salami sand-wich."

"Are you okay? I mean, what's all this smart-ass stuff?"

"I'm fine, just a little giddy. I've got this hunch that we're in the home stretch, that we'll have Gerlach's killer in a matter of days."

"Who's it going to be?" Kevin asked.

"I have no idea."

———

Conklin had agreed to meet the sheriff at his office, which was actually the converted family room in his home. On the drive to Geneva they found themselves discussing the fact that Carol had never had a one-on-one conversation with him since the night of Gerlach's death. Two people had given Kevin their impressions of him: a neighbor, Sherri somebody, and a fellow member of the string quartet, Sandy Temple. They had learned something of his whereabouts on the afternoon of Gerlach's death from people at his nurseries, and Ginny Smith, the bartender at The Cedar Post, had placed him at The Post during the lunch hour on that same day. But the result of these several conversations was a puzzle from which a great many pieces were missing. Conklin was a suspect because his wife, now deceased, had had a relatively recent affair with Gerlach, an affair which Conklin himself had readily acknowledged. The picture which emerged from the conversations with the neighbor and the violist was impressionistic and of limited value. The only thing that Carol and Kevin knew for sure, other than Helen Conklin's infidelity, was that Conklin had failed to mention his luncheon with Gerlach when Carol had interviewed him some two weeks earlier. And that had been the proximate cause of their trip to Geneva and to the elegant old house into whose driveway Carol was now turning her car.

Arthur Conklin was gracious. Whether he had been dis-turbed or not by the sheriff's request to talk with him, there was no evidence of it when they took seats in the spacious and beautifully furnished living room.

"I don't have anyone to help me with the amenities anymore, you know, but I can bring you iced tea or, if you prefer, coffee."

"That's kind of you, but no thanks," Carol said.

"Please just ignore me," Kevin spoke up. "I just happen to be with the sheriff this afternoon; we've been going over some loose ends regarding my use of Wayne Hall at the college."

"Glad to see you, Kevin. It's the first time since that dreadful day two weeks ago."

Carol gave Kevin a look which, however guarded, said that he was to let her do the talking.

"I'm sorry not to have paid you the courtesy of a call sooner than this, Mr. Conklin. The investigation has been going rather slowly, unfortunately. This is a busy time of the summer for my department—we seem to have a lot on our plate. Anyway, I do have a few things I'd like to talk about."

"Sure. Go right ahead."

Kevin was having trouble reading Conklin's face. His expression was opaque. *Either he has nothing whatsoever to fear, or he's a master at dissembling.*

"I might as well get right to my most important question. I have learned that, on the day Harley Gerlach died, you and he had lunch together at The Cedar Post, that restaurant up north of West Branch. When we spoke that evening after his body had been discovered, you never mentioned it. Why don't you tell me about it?"

Conklin smiled what looked like a rueful smile.

"I'm sorry about that, Sheriff. It really wasn't necessary for me not to mention it. I suppose I thought—subconsciously, you know—that you were just beginning your investigation and that you'd seize on anything that looked the least bit suspicious."

"But why would you have believed that I'd be suspicious? After all, we all eat lunch quite often with friends and colleagues. I can't imagine why I would have imagined any relationship between your lunch with Gerlach and his death later that afternoon."

"Like I said, it was wrong of me. Things were so hectic; we were all in shock. Rumors were flying."

"Rumors?"

"Yes. Everybody sitting there in the auditorium, no one knowing anything—it was natural, I guess, for people to start speculating about what had happened to Mr. Gerlach."

"Did you have a theory?" Carol asked.

"No. Not then or since."

"So you thought I might misinterpret an admission that you'd had lunch with Gerlach. Okay. But later, let's say sometime in the next day or two, after the confusion of that first evening was past, you might have called me to tell me about the lunch. Why didn't you?"

Conklin shook his head, again with a rueful smile.

"I guess that I just tried to block out of my mind what had happened that terrible day. You know, forget it, go on with life the best one can."

Not a very convincing explanation, Kevin thought.

"Let me go back to the lunch, if I may," Carol said. "My understanding has been that you and Gerlach were not friends. That's hardly surprising, inasmuch as he had had an affair with your wife. I would think that something like that would be hard to put out of your mind. So how does it happen that you decided to have lunch that day?"

Conklin straightened up and moved forward to the edge of the couch as if getting ready to give a speech.

"I'd thought long and hard about what had happened between Harley and Helen. It had hurt me, very deeply. I can't deny it. But it has been a year since it happened. Helen was gone. There was nothing I could do to bring her back. There didn't seem to be much point in carrying a grudge forever where Harley was concerned. He had moved on. Why couldn't I? There we were, both doing what we loved to do: playing and singing music. It was a shared pleasure. Somehow it seemed to me that it was time to forgive. So I asked him to join me for lunch, figuring we could make a fresh start. I didn't expect to become his friend, start playing poker with him or anything like that. But I thought we could talk like civilized human beings, put the past behind us, enjoy doing Puccini together."

"Had you broached the subject with him before that day?"

"No, that just happened to be the day when I finally decided to do what I'd been thinking about much of the summer."

"You had decided that Harley was no longer 'the nigger in the woodpile,' right?"

"Yes, and I regret that remark more than you know. I wish I could apologize to the members of your company, Kevin."

There's been lots of time to do that, Kevin thought. What stopped you?

"How did Gerlach take the olive branch you offered him?" Carol asked.

"Just fine. I think he'd been ready to do it for some time, but was afraid I'd rebuff him. In fact, he got all emotional. Almost maudlin. He drank a lot, as Kevin knows, and I think he was so touched by what was happening that he drank more than he should have."

"So you drove him back to the college after lunch?"

"I did. He didn't seem to be in any condition to drive. So I dropped him off at the college and went on home by way of my interlake road nursery. I'd have been glad to drive him home, but we had the dress rehearsal that night and he'd have been without a car to make it back to Brae Loch. And I did have to get to the nursery. When I let him out in front of Wayne Hall, it was the last time I saw him alive. I still can hardly believe that he died on the same day we'd said we'd let bygones be bygones. What a terrible thing. A real tragedy."

Kevin was waiting for Conklin to pull out a handkerchief, dab his eyes, and blow his nose.

Carol still wanted to go over the rest of Conklin's afternoon, so she reviewed his earlier statement with him, step by step. His answers to her questions were fairly consistent with what she had learned from the nursery managers. But they did not add up to an ironclad alibi that would have made it impossible for him to have killed Gerlach.

"What do you make of his story?" Carol asked as they headed back to the cottage.

"It's possible that it happened just the way he says," Kevin said. "Wouldn't that be something, Janet Myers and Arthur Conklin both trying to make up to the man who had messed up their lives. And doing it right about when Gerlach gets himself killed. But I'd be careful of Conklin. I was watching his face as much as I was listening to what he had to say. And his face was nothing but a mask."

"I think it would be a good idea to have a talk with that girl who waited on them at The Post. She must have overheard them, gotten some impression of whether they seemed to be burying the hatchet like Conklin says they were."

When they arrived at the cottage, neither Carol nor Kevin was convinced that Arthur Conklin had recently lost his new best friend.

CHAPTER 50

Carol had departed for her office in Cumberland at ten of seven, anxious to be in her seat in the squad room before any of her fellow officers came strolling in. She was well aware that there was talk behind her back about the 'Whitman effect,' and she had decided that this would be a good morning to demonstrate that she was still the same old sheriff.

Kevin, in the meanwhile, had not bothered to shower and dress until it was almost time for Heather Merriman to arrive. He had picked up the Berlioz biography after breakfast, and had lost track of the time until an unanticipated FedEx delivery reminded him that it was already 9:40. He had no need to try to impress Heather, but he didn't think it was a good idea for her to find him in his bathrobe, face unshaven and hair uncombed, at ten o'clock.

He had just tucked in his shirt and slipped into his sandals when the doorbell rang.

"Good morning, Kevin. See? I got it right. Do you know that none of my professors would like me to call them by their first names? You're special."

Kevin chose to take it as a compliment.

"My students don't usually call me Kevin," he said, "but our little Brae Loch company hardly qualified as students. Anyway, I've been called worse things than professor. So, what's on your mind? I'm curious."

"I'll tell you, but first could you possibly let me have a cup of coffee?"

"Of course," Kevin said. He ushered Heather to a chair on the deck and retreated to the kitchen to reheat the breakfast pot.

"Now," he said, as they settled into their seats, "to what do I owe the pleasure?"

"I just bought a recording of *Gianni Schicchi*, and I wanted you to hear it."

Kevin hadn't known what to expect, but this surely wasn't it.

"That's very thoughtful of you, Heather, but don't you suppose it'll take quite awhile? I'm afraid I have some things I have to do."

Actually there was nothing urgent on Kevin's agenda for the morning, but at the moment he found the prospect of listening to a recording of the opera he had so recently hoped to stage at Brae Loch depressing.

"Oh, I didn't mean the whole opera. I just wanted to play a part of it. Okay?"

At this point Kevin was more than a little curious. They took their coffee into the cottage, and Heather popped the CD into Kevin's player and forwarded it to the track she wanted him to hear.

"Now listen closely to this, please."

What followed was the brief passage in which Schicchi explains his plan to impersonate the old man. That passage finished, Heather shut the set off and turned to Kevin.

"Who does that sound like?"

"Like Schicchi."

"Yes, I know, but think about his voice. Does it remind you of anyone else who sings Schicchi's role?"

"Well, it doesn't sound like Mr. Gerlach did, if that's what you're getting at."

"You're right. Of course I knew you would be. I didn't really think much about it until I listened to my new CD. But when I did, I thought back to the day Mr. Gerlach died. And to the day I told you I heard him singing in that practice room backstage in Wayne Hall. But I'm sure it wasn't him."

"Can you slow down a bit? You're telling me that it wasn't Mr. Gerlach you heard that day?"

"That's right. At least I think it is. I've always known that different artists sing the same roles differently. My voice teacher tells me my sound is more like Kiri Te Kanawa's than Leotyne Price's. I think she's just trying to give a boost to my confidence, but I know what she means. Remember how people used to compare Pavarotti to Domingo, one voice called silver, the other bronze, or something like that. Even if they were both doing the same aria, like Nessun dorma."

"I'm with you. The voice you heard that day, there was something about it that makes you think it was somebody other than Gerlach."

"The problem is that when I heard Schicchi's music coming from the practice room, I just assumed it was Mr. Gerlach. After all, he was our Schicchi. Why would it be anyone else? And that room is partially sound-proofed, so it wasn't as loud or as clear as it might have been. But now I think I made a mistake. In fact, I'm really quite sure of it. And I knew I had to tell you."

"I'm very glad you did. It may be important. You are convinced that it was someone other than Gerlach singing Schicchi's music. Do you have an idea who that someone else was?"

"Yes, but I'm not at all sure. I'd never heard him singing Schicchi's part, and like I said, the sound was somewhat muffled. But there was something about that voice that was definitely familiar."

"That's okay, Heather. I'm not asking you who it was, only who you think it might have been."

"I think it was Mr. Rosetti."

"But as far as we know, he wasn't even on the campus that afternoon."

"Then I must be wrong. Maybe I thought of him because everyone knew he would like to have been Gianni Schicchi, although I guess that doesn't make much sense."

"But you said there was something in the voice that reminded you of Mr. Rosetti. You seem to have a very good ear. I'd recommend that if the sheriff asks you to tell her what you've told me, be honest with her. Say it sounded like Rosetti. Don't second-guess yourself just because you've heard that he wasn't there that day. You don't know that, and the sheriff may not be one hundred percent sure of it either."

"I don't want to get Mr. Rosetti into any kind of trouble."

"That's a noble sentiment, Heather, but it isn't you who would be getting him into trouble. It's like Mr. Carpenter. You didn't want to get him into trouble either, so you lied to the sheriff about whether he was with you that Tuesday. It's the same with Mr. Rosetti. If either Rosetti or Carpenter is in trouble, it will be trouble of their own making."

Before she left, Kevin asked Heather if he might borrow her CD of *Gianni Schicchi*.

"I'd like to play it through, just to see how a professional performance stacks up against what we sounded like. I'll get it back to you in a day or two. The Lauretta on the disc won't sound just like you, but I'll bet you hold your own with her."

"You're just trying to flatter me."

"It's always more fun when flattery is based on fact, Heather."

After she had gone, Kevin considered the significance of what he had learned so unexpectedly that morning. He was willing to bet that Heather Merriman was right about the owner of the voice coming from the practice room two weeks earlier. Which meant that Paolo Rosetti had been lying to Carol about what he had been doing that day. And that she might well have been right that he had left his boat at Ben's Marina and walked to Brae Loch the afternoon of Harley Gerlach's murder.

CHAPTER 51

While Kevin was absorbing the implications of Heather Merriman's second thoughts about who had been practicing Gianni Schicchi's music, Carol was seeking more information about the Gerlach-Conklin lunch at The Cedar Post.

Her call to The Post elicited the good news that Jill Fenton, who had been their waitress on that fatal Tuesday, was on duty again that very day. The lunch hour would officially begin at 11:30, so Carol planned to be at the restaurant at 11:15. Fenton would probably be setting up her tables. Carol could question her while she was getting ready for the lunch-hour crowd.

Ginny Smith was not working the bar that day, but Carol shared a cheery hello with the man who was on duty and quickly spotted Fenton, who was standing next to a service station and chatting with one of the other waitresses.

"Miss Fenton, may I have a word with you?" she said.

The young woman excused herself and followed Carol to a table on the far side of the room.

"Is there something wrong?" she asked. Jill Fenton had never had any trouble with the law, but here she was in the company of the sheriff of Cumberland County for the second time in a single week. The first time she had been asked whether the man in the picture the sheriff showed her was one of the two men she had served at a corner table on a recent Tuesday. She had found it exciting to be able to help the sheriff. This time she was uneasy. Had she made a mistake? Had the sheriff found out something which contradicted her identification of the man?

"No, no," Carol assured her. "We just need more information, and I hope you may be able to help us."

Fenton relaxed and told the sheriff she'd do her best.

"I know it's now more than two weeks ago that you served those two men we talked about earlier. But I'd like you to think back if you can to that day. What can you tell me about their conversation? Do you remember anything that was said, anything that might tell us whether they seemed to be in a good mood? Or maybe a bad mood?"

Jill Fenton's face took on a worried look again. She can't remember, Carol thought. Damn it!

"I don't think so," Fenton said after thinking about it for a moment. "We were busy, and I was trying to remember orders. Besides, the boss doesn't like us to eavesdrop, so I try not to pay attention to what people are talking about."

"I understand, and it's okay. But don't you have some feeling about whether the men were getting along? You know, sometimes two people sit and eat and hardly ever say anything to each other. Other times they carry on an animated conversation."

Another pause as Fenton considered Carol's question.

"I guess you'd say they talked quite a bit. I'm sorry I can't be more helpful."

Carol was ready to let it go when the waitress's face lit up. She'd had an idea.

"Maybe the Listers could help. They're a couple who come in here a lot, and I remember that they were having lunch that day at the table next to the men you're talking about. I don't know much about them, except that they're always very pleasant and leave good tips. Brady, he's the owner, might know how to get in touch with them. I think he's here. You could ask Jerry— he's the bartender."

"I think I will," Carol said. "Thanks for the suggestion. Have a good day."

Brady Traber was in the office behind the bar. Carol was surprised to realize that she had never met him or seen him mixing with the customers at The Post. She was wondering whether he was preternaturally shy or had simply chosen to let his bartenders be his glad-handers. But when he greeted her, she thought she understood why he might have spent most of his time out of sight in the backroom. He had a bad speech impediment, so bad that she had to concentrate to understand him. In all likelihood he was self-conscious about it.

But he rose to the occasion, telling her that the Listers' names were Bernard and Elaine and that they lived on the east side of the lake some five miles north of Southport. He was sure that their phone was listed in the small local directory. "Nice people," he said, "regulars in this place, always welcome."

The Listers were not at home, so Carol left a message asking them to call her, explaining that she would like to speak with them about somebody they might have seen at The Cedar

Post recently. She tried to sound matter of fact, but didn't leave any details. She didn't want them to have worried the issue and rehearsed what they would say when she talked with them. When she left for the office, she could only hope that they hadn't gone out of town. She wanted to see them just as soon as possible, preferably that very day.

A man who identified himself as Bernie Lister called the sheriff's office at a little after four. It was arranged that Carol would drop by at their cocktail hour, which meant 5:30 or thereabouts.

Carol rapped on the Listers' cottage door promptly at 5:30, and was invited into a pleasant if overly busy house. The walls and various surfaces were covered with framed pictures of generations of Listers, or people whom Carol assumed were relatives, past and present, of Elaine and Bernard Lister. It was the husband who answered the door, but it was Mrs. Lister who selected a chair for Carol and offered to fetch her a gin and tonic.

"It's what keeps us going on these days," she said. "Do you like yours with a wedge of lime?"

"No thanks," Carol replied. "It sounds good, but I'm on duty, so I'd better take a pass. I promise not to take but a few minutes of your time. By the way, it was Brady Traber down at The Cedar Post who gave me your names. He speaks very highly of you, was sure you'd be glad to help me with my problem."

"We certainly will do what we can," Mr. Lister said, "but I don't know what it is you think we can help you with."

"Of course not," Carol said, making mental notes about this seemingly affable middle-aged couple. Mrs. Lister had prematurely grey hair, and Mr. Lister, the shorter of the two, was nearly bald. But both of them appeared to be in good condition. She thought they looked like marathoners.

"It has to do with a lunch you had at The Cedar Post awhile back," she continued. "Two weeks ago yesterday to be exact. I know that it can be hard to remember a particular day, but I was hoping that you could recall that Tuesday and tell me a bit about two men I understand were sitting at an adjacent table."

She paused to see if either of the Listers might recall the day and their fellow diners without further elaboration on her part. It was Mrs. Lister who spoke up.

"I think I know who you're talking about. Would they be men about our age? One of them with white hair, but not really old? Am I right, Bernie, weren't they the men who spent the lunch hour quarreling?"

Carol waited for Mr. Lister to confirm his wife's memory. Or to question it.

"I think so. That was the man who got really vulgar, wasn't it?"

It looked as if the Listers were going to be helpful. Carol offered a couple of additional hints about the appearance of the two men, and their response made it clear that they were indeed talking about Conklin and Gerlach.

"You said that they were quarreling, even being vulgar. Would you care to elaborate?"

"Well," Mr. Lister began, "they weren't having an argument at first. Just talking. We weren't paying attention. I mean it was none of our business. But then the one with the white hair began to raise his voice. You couldn't help but notice. The other man tried to calm him down. They'd be okay for a minute or two, and then the conversation got loud again. It got to the point that it was embarrassing. Elaine and I tried to ignore them, but it wasn't easy."

"I think they were drunk," Mrs. Lister added. "At least the man with white hair was. His partner kept getting refills at the bar of whatever it was he was drinking."

"It was when the conversation turned vulgar that we thought we'd better be leaving. If we hadn't already just about finished our lunch, I'd have asked the waitress to change our table."

"When you say vulgar, what do you mean?" Carol asked.

"They started talking nasty. At least the white-haired man did. Not the kind of talk you usually hear in a restaurant."

"Can you be more specific?" Carol asked. She had no idea what the Listers' vulgarity threshold might be. Had they been troubled by a few 'damns,' or had Harley Gerlach pulled out all the stops? It might be important.

"It's not the kind of language we use," Mrs. Lister said. "It really burned my ears."

Burned her ears? Carol hadn't heard that expression in a long time.

"I'm sorry to keep asking," Carol said, "but I would really appreciate it if you could tell me exactly what was said. It would help me get a picture of just how angry they were, and that could be important to an investigation I'm conducting."

"Well," Mrs. Lister said, "it was like that awful remark the vice president made to a senator a few years ago. It caused quite a stir, although of course it couldn't be printed in the newspapers."

Carol had no idea what the woman was talking about. It occurred to her that she might be losing touch with the wide, wide world beyond Crooked Lake.

"I don't remember anything about the vice president being vulgar. Why don't you tell me what he said."

"Oh, for heaven's sake, Elaine, the sheriff will have heard worse." Mr. Lister turned to Carol and spelled it out for her.

"What the white-haired man said to the other man was 'go fuck yourself.' It was really quite shocking. I thought about mentioning it to Mr. Traber, but figured I ought to stay out of it."

"You were probably right. I'm not sure what Mr. Traber could have done about it. Anyway, I thank you for telling me, even if it was unpleasant. By the way, did you get a sense of what they were arguing about?"

"Not really," Mrs. Lister said. "Like we said, we try to mind our own business."

But Mr. Lister did have something to add.

"I overheard the word 'wife' several times. I'm not sure whose wife they were talking about, but I suspect they were quarreling about one of their wives."

Yes, Carol thought, that makes sense. And it would have been Helen Conklin, not the former Janet Gerlach, that was the subject of the lunchtime unpleasantness.

Carol thanked the Listers for their cooperation, told them it might prove important to a case she was working on, and wished them a pleasant evening after once again declining their offer of a gin and tonic.

Later, after a swim and a simple supper, Carol and Kevin retreated to chairs at the end of the dock and tried to make sense of what they had learned that day. It was another of those beautiful evenings which showed Crooked Lake at its late summer best. Almost too beautiful and relaxing for serious thinking about a brutal crime and an appropriate punishment.

It was Kevin who finally interrupted their increasingly unfocused musings about Harley Gerlach's death.

"We need to tackle things with a fresh mind," he said. "I may regret saying this, but I have a hunch that we're close to the answer to the puzzle of who killed Gerlach. Do you ever get the feeling that things that have been confusing are beginning to make sense? Of course you do. Just yesterday you told me you thought you'd have Gerlach's killer in just a matter of days. You said you didn't know who it would be, but something must have prompted you to say that. I don't want to go biblical on you, but I think the days of 'through a glass darkly' are coming to an end. What do you say that we set tomorrow aside for some serious brainstorming. A good breakfast, maybe a wake-up dip in the lake, and then we solve the crime that ruined my opera."

"Why this sudden surge of optimism? Have you thought of something that hasn't occurred to me yet?"

"No. Like I said, it's just a hunch. But I think we know everything we need to know. We just haven't put it all together in the right way. Can you let Bridges handle the other stuff? Then you and I could put the little grey cells to work."

"The little grey cells?"

"That's what Hercule Poirot used to say. It won't be a matter of finding new evidence. It'll be a matter of thinking hard about the evidence we already have. Putting the brain to work. Make that two brains."

"You're very persuasive. I hope you're also correct. I'll call Sam in the morning, tell him that I've decided to spend my day meditating. I'd rather not say I expect to have solved the Gerlach case by sundown."

"Oh ye of little faith," Kevin said. "Let's pack it in."

CHAPTER 52

The Thursday morning before Labor Day dawned humid and hazy. The alarm clock was ringing persistently, and Carol groped for it ineffectually. She had deliberately placed it out of reach the night before, knowing that she might shut it off and go back to sleep. Sam Bridges would have to be notified that he was to be in charge, and for her to sleep through the morning briefing would not only be professionally irresponsible. It would also serve to feed the gossip mill regarding her relationship with Kevin Whitman.

She threw off the sheet, got out of bed, and silenced the alarm clock. Not, however, before it had awakened Kevin.

"Too early," he said, trying to pretend that he would be able to sleep a while longer.

"I think not. You're the one who said that today's the day we solve the opera murder. It'll never happen if we stay in bed."

Carol pulled the sheet off him and hit him with her pillow. Kevin looked at his watch and groaned.

"Why must we start before seven?"

"Because I've noticed that the morning hours are your most productive. So come on, get up."

"Where did you get an idea like that? I'm a night person, or hadn't you noticed?"

"I'm talking about mental acuity, not physical prowess."

Carol picked up the pillow and pummeled him with it.

By 7:30 they had showered and dressed and were jointly tackling the task of making breakfast.

"I thought we were going to take a swim before we got down to work," Kevin said as he buttered the toast.

"Let's save it, make it a reward for solving Gerlach's murder. Assuming we solve it."

"You really are a pessimist, aren't you?" Kevin said.

"No. I'm a realist. I haven't seen any sign of a smoking gun, have you?"

"No, but I don't remember that we had a smoking gun two years ago when we solved the Britingham case. Or last summer when we figured out who killed Sandra Rackley."

"What you're saying is that nabbing criminals on Crooked Lake is dependent on your intuition. My men over in Cumberland will be thrilled to hear that."

But Carol said it with a smile. She knew that closing the two cases which had marked the tumultuous two years of their relationship had been the result of teamwork. But she also knew that Kevin's creative thinking had been indispensable in both cases.

It was nearly 8:30 when they settled into chairs on the deck and began to review and rethink what they knew about the murder of Harley Gerlach. And the possible role in that murder of four members of Kevin's small opera company: Sean Carpenter, Arthur Conklin, Janet Myers, and Paolo Rosetti.

"Let's start with Myers," Kevin suggested. "I don't think I've spoken with her since Harley's death. So what do I know? Only that she wanted me to sack her former husband and that she raised hell when he took that flying leap onto the stage bed. You're the expert on Janet. What do you think?"

"I'm hardly an expert on her. She strikes me as a complex person. There's no question that she disliked Harley. Disliked him heartily. She told you that almost as soon as you'd met her, and I think she meant it. She called him an egotistical bastard when I showed her his photo album. But I think the Pederson woman was right. Somewhere along the way Janet had begun to miss Harley. Maybe miss him isn't quite the way to put it, but she had begun to reflect on the days with him and see him in a less harsh light. You could see it in the way she looked, the things she said, when I showed her the picture of her and Harley that was taken when they were still a happy couple."

"But you said she still sounded angry with him, even after she knew he was dead."

"Yes she did, and that's why I'm willing to bet she didn't kill him. I suspect that her feelings toward him were ambivalent, right down to the time he died. It was as if she had come to realize that there were two Harleys: the charming lover and the unapologetic womanizer. She was seeing the charming lover when I showed her the picture of the two of them. But when she saw the pictures of him with the other women, she immediately became the angry victim of his infidelity. And what does that tell us? I think it says that she was in her 'missing Harley' mode until the photo album reminded her about what a rat he really was. Which means that she was still feeling nostalgic about him when he died. And that means that she didn't kill him. You don't kill someone you may have loathed but have begun to feel differently about."

"Sounds logical," Kevin acknowledged, "but what about her trying to get into his house the day he died? Her lack of an alibi for the rest of that afternoon?"

"I think they reinforce what I've been saying. She didn't go to his house in an angry, confrontational frame of mind. She wanted to talk with him, see if they might get back together. Or at least bury all the unpleasantness."

"And what do you suppose she was up to while she was driving around? Driving around with no one to vouch for her whereabouts?"

"I have no idea. She was probably doing just that—driving around, her mind on how she might make a fresh start with Harley. If you haven't committed a crime, you don't worry about having an alibi."

"So," Kevin said, his voice betraying a touch of skepticism, "you're writing Myers off as a suspect. Right?"

"No, it's too soon to do that," Carol replied. "I'm just saying that she's an unlikely suspect."

"More unlikely than the others?"

"Well, that's what we hope to sort out today, isn't it? How about Carpenter? If the case against him is based on what Gerlach did to ruin his chances of joining the Met chorus, you're probably in a better position than I am to make book on him as our killer."

"Are you kidding?" Kevin doubted that he was in a better position to assess the odds that Carpenter had killed Gerlach. "You're the one who caught him out in all those lies."

"Actually it was Miss Merriman who did that," Carol said.

"Anyway, I don't think his lies need to weigh that heavily against him. Everyone knew he disliked Gerlach, so I can understand why he didn't want to admit to being at Brae Loch the afternoon Harley was killed. And why he claimed to know nothing about Harley's role in costing him the Met job."

"I know, but he still strikes me as something of a weasel."

"The way I look at it, what makes me think he's innocent of Gerlach's death is that note he sent to Mercedes."

Carol nearly choked on her coffee.

"The note to Mercedes? What are you talking about?"

"I know. The threatening note is all about something else—Carpenter's fascination with Merriman. He was worried enough about Redman as a rival that he warned her to stay clear of Heather. But think about it. What was uppermost in Carpenter's mind all summer?"

"Merriman?" Carol asked.

"Right. Here he was, a married middle-aged man, behaving like a lovesick puppy. Infatuated with a girl barely out of high school. Why did he tell Heather about the business at the Met? To impress her. And he seemed to have assumed that she reciprocated his interest. Why else would he believe that she would keep his presence at Brae Loch that afternoon a secret?"

"But why would his interest in Merriman make him a less likely suspect in Gerlach's murder?"

"I could be wrong, of course, but I find it hard to imagine that a guy so wrapped up in cultivating a relationship with Merriman would also have been nursing such a powerful grudge against Gerlach. That sounds like a pretty crowded agenda to me. I'm no psychologist, but I'd bet that most people have trouble focusing on more than one big thing at a time. And Heather was Carpenter's one big thing."

"But what if something happened that Tuesday, something that really angered him—something that caused him to lash out at Gerlach."

"It's possible," Kevin said. "But it's unlikely. I just can't picture Carpenter suddenly deciding to strangle Gerlach. I know he was at the college, but he was busy courting Merriman. In his own way, of course. Thank goodness she finally decided she'd had enough of him."

"And so we have two down, two to go," Carol said.

"I'm not writing Carpenter off, any more than you're willing to cross Myers off the list of suspects. But there's still Rosetti and Conklin. You've got this scenario where Rosetti takes his boat to a marina, walks from there to the college, and kills Gerlach, all the while pretending to be fishing. Do you want to convince me?"

"This is where the guesswork comes in," Carol began. "You were the one who said fishermen don't do it during the heat of the day. And where was the bait? Pardon the pun, but his alibi sounds fishy. It would have been easy to cross the lake, tie up at

Ben's, and walk the short distance to the college. We know he was there. Heather Merriman's identification of his voice proves it. What would have been easier than slipping out of the practice room and strangling Gerlach while he slept off all the scotch he'd drunk at lunch?"

"Not so fast," Kevin interrupted. "You haven't confronted him with Merriman's story. I doubt very much that he'd corroborate what she told you. So all you've got is her ear. Good as it may be, I can't believe it would be hard for a good defense attorney to demolish her on the witness stand. And what proof could you offer that it was his boat at the marina? Or that he walked to Brae Loch? Any witnesses? Not that I've heard about."

"Like I said, we're in guesswork territory. But it's an informed guess. Besides, you could always take the stand and vouch for Merriman's ability to distinguish one baritone from another."

Kevin wanted no part of such a high-stakes role.

"Let's pretend that Rosetti did just what you think he did, and that Heather is right that he was the one she heard singing. Looked at from one angle, his behavior is highly suspicious. Why take such a roundabout way of coming to Brae Loch? And for that matter, why go to the college hours before the dress rehearsal? To kill Gerlach? But he wouldn't have known that Gerlach would be there, so that can't be right. How about to use the practice studio? According to Merriman, he did that. And he was practicing Schicchi's part. Aha! We have a motive for the killing. He had always wanted that role, and with Gerlach dead, he could take over. After a bit of practice, of course."

"You're making my case," Carol said.

"Maybe, maybe not. Think about it. If you've killed Gerlach, the last thing you would want to happen would be for someone to hear you singing in the practice studio, especially if you're singing Schicchi's music. Rosetti knows enough about such things to know that someone might recognize his voice. So, if he killed Gerlach, Heather would not have heard him singing. But she did, which means that he did not kill Gerlach."

Carol had been listening intently, acknowledging Kevin's logic with the occasional nod of her head. But when he had finished, she put forward one more caveat.

"We don't know which came first, Harley being strangled or Rosetti singing. Wouldn't that make a difference?"

"It would, but it's doubtful we'll ever know," Kevin said. "Not unless the killer provides you with a timeline. I wouldn't bet on that happening."

"What about Rosetti's phony alibi?"

"He thought he might need one if anybody claimed to have had heard him singing backstage at around the time Gerlach was killed. And what he thought was a good one came quickly to mind because he had come to Brae Loch by boat. At least as far as the marina. By the way, speaking of guesses, here's one. The Rosettis only have one car, and Mrs. Rosetti was using it that afternoon. Hence Paolo's use of the boat. It would be easy to check."

"I'll do that," Carol said, now aware that Kevin was once again proving his value as an unofficial deputy sheriff.

"If I'm right, we can stop worrying about Rosetti breaking into Gerlach's home. It was probably just what he said it was: simple curiosity about how the other half lives. Or lived."

"Which leaves us with Conklin," Carol said. "If you've got ice in the ice trays, I'm going to make myself some iced tea. How about you? Then let's tackle suspect number four."

It was now mid-morning, and they had relegated Janet Myers, Sean Carpenter, and Paolo Rosetti to the status of persons of interest, a step below that of prime suspects. Both Carol and Kevin were thinking the same thing when she returned with the iced tea: What if Conklin were also to prove to be a less-promising suspect than they had imagined him to be? Would they have to go back to the beginning and cast a wider net?

"Let's start with what we know," Carol began, "and one of the things we know is that Conklin was at the college about the time that Gerlach was killed. He admits driving him there after their lunch at The Post. Strange, isn't it? Rosetti was there, singing his little heart out. Carpenter was there, courting Miss Merriman. Myers could well have been there, too; at least she can't prove she wasn't. Considering that your dress rehearsal wasn't scheduled to start until 7:30, I'd say that the opera company was somewhat overrepresented on campus when Gerlach met his end. Wouldn't you?"

"It really was one of those coincidences you're always dismissing," Kevin said. "I'm sure they didn't gang up on Harley—you know, draw straws to see who'd get to strangle him."

Carol chose to ignore Kevin's attempt to inject some humor into their discussion.

"What's important is that we know Conklin was actually with Gerlach. He says he dropped him off at Wayne Hall. But he could as easily have gone into the building with him. It wouldn't have taken more than a few minutes to coax him into that big bed, grab a length of piano wire, and use it as a garrote the minute he closed his eyes. Then off to the nursery."

"And getting him into the bed wouldn't have been that hard if he was as drunk as he must have been, considering what the bartender told us. If Conklin wanted to strangle him, the bed would have been the perfect place to do it, and it would have been easy to lure Harley into the bed. I remember the proprietary interest he took in the bed the day it was delivered. He called it 'my bed.'"

"That's another reason to suspect Conklin, the fact that Gerlach was drunk," Carol said. "Ginny has it that Conklin kept getting him refills of his scotch all through lunch. There's a good chance he was deliberately trying to get him drunk."

"I don't believe Conklin or anybody else had to try to get Gerlach drunk. He did pretty well at it all by himself."

"I know," Carol said, "but Conklin doesn't seem to have tried to stop it. He never put his foot down, said that's enough. He dutifully ran off to the bar and got Harley one drink after another. He could well have been planning all along what he would do when they got back to the college. The only favor Conklin seems to have done for Harley is not to let him drive drunk. How thoughtful."

"So you're convinced that Conklin purposefully helped get Gerlach drunk so he could have an excuse to drive him to campus and kill him?"

"Not one hundred percent convinced, but it's hard to argue with that scenario," Carol replied. "Besides, what the Listers told me makes it clear that the lunch-table conversation between Gerlach and Conklin turned nasty. Real nasty. Nasty enough that it's not that much of a stretch to believe that Gerlach had goaded him to the point where Conklin wanted to kill him."

"Conklin told you that he had asked Gerlach to go to lunch because he wanted to offer him an olive branch. Put the past behind them. That doesn't square with what the Listers overheard."

"No it doesn't," Carol said. "Which means that Conklin lied to me. So instead of using lunch to make up with the man who had an affair with his wife, he used it to accuse him, to berate him. After all, he may have known *of* the man before this summer, but he didn't actually know him. But then he has a chance to observe him during rehearsals for the opera, and decides he's a real piece of work. The lunch is his opportunity to get some belated revenge."

Kevin was staring at his half-empty glass of iced tea, but his mind was elsewhere.

"What if Conklin invited Gerlach to lunch for the reason he gave you," he asked. "What if he actually expected to use the occasion to put the past behind them. And what if Gerlach just laughed at him. Don't you suppose that would really infuriate Conklin? I could imagine the conversation turning ugly in a hurry. It's one thing to remember being angry about something that happened a year ago, but it's another to be given a new reason to be angry—a reason which would seem inexplicable, simply perverse."

Carol thought about this line of reasoning for a moment.

"But why would Gerlach get nasty if Conklin was trying to be nice?"

"Who knows. Like I said, maybe he was just being perverse. Anyway, this takes me back to what I suspect is the more important Conklin lie. The one he told about his wife's death. Remember, he seems to have told friends that his wife took that bad fall because she was drunk. But the police claim that there was no evidence of alcohol in her bloodstream at all. Now, why would he have lied about that? The way I see it, he did have something to do with her death. Either he deliberately pushed her down the stairs, or he was attacking her and she accidentally fell. The police never charged him, but he was anxious to put an end to any rumors. So he tells people she fell because she was drunk.

"He knows he's responsible for Helen's death and that he caused it because he was furious with her for the affair with Gerlach. Now flash forward to this summer. He doesn't have a good opinion of Gerlach, of course—remember the 'nigger in the woodpile' remark. But as the summer goes on, he starts to think that there's no point carrying a grudge. After all, he seems to have blamed his wife for what happened. So he decides to make nice with the man who cuckolded him—that's a terrible word, isn't it?

287

But when he tries to establish some kind of friendship with Gerlach, something goes wrong. It backfires. Gerlach has had too much to drink; he gets mad, and he tells Conklin to shove it. Literally."

Kevin paused to finish his iced tea. Carol's reaction made it clear that she wasn't ready to embrace what sounded suspiciously like another of his wild ideas.

"I think I prefer my scenario. I had a professor in law school who liked to say that, other things being equal, the simplest, most obvious explanation is likely to be the right one. And the simplest, most obvious explanation is that Conklin went into lunch with a big chip on his shoulder. He lied to me."

"Could be," Kevin said. "But in my experience, other things are rarely equal. I won't be surprised to learn that Conklin's effort to bury the hatchet blew up in his face. Whatever touched him off, Gerlach lost it. Whether that made Conklin a murderer, I don't know. But it's a real possibility."

"Do you find this as exhausting as I do?" Carol asked. "I'm brain tired. Let's take a break and go swimming."

"Good idea," Kevin agreed. They changed and, five minutes later, took running dives off the dock, one after the other. The decision about what to do next had been put on hold for the time being.

CHAPTER 53

That evening, Arthur Conklin and Sandy Temple were sitting in Conklin's living room, awaiting the arrival of the Derwent sisters. Jane and Jean Derwent were the first and second violinists in the Prism String Quartet, which was about to hold its first rehearsal for the upcoming fall season. Conklin wanted to discuss Borodin's second string quartet in D, the music for which lay on the coffee table in front of them. But Temple, who had not seen the group's cellist since the collapse of the opera project, was more concerned with the status of the investigation into Harley Gerlach's murder.

"Tell me, Arthur, how are you doing? I mean, I'm worried about you. Worried that they'll be thinking you might have killed Gerlach."

It was clear from the tone of her voice that she really was worried about her colleague.

"Oh, I'm okay. It's nice of you to be concerned about me, but it's going to be all right. The sheriff has talked with me, of course, but she's very pleasant. There's no need to be worried."

"I guess I can't help it," Temple said. "I fear they'll zero in on Helen's affair and figure you've had it in for Gerlach ever since."

"That's history. It happened over a year ago."

"I know, but that doesn't mean that they'll see it that way. Besides, they don't know you like I do. They don't know you at all."

Conklin smiled. It was a sad smile.

"I mean no offense, Sandy. And I do appreciate your concern. But let's be completely honest. You don't really know me. None of us *really* knows each other. I didn't really know Helen, even if I'd lived with her for many years and loved her dearly."

"You know what I mean, Arthur. I talked with Professor Whitman last week. I wanted him to know that—"

"You talked with Whitman about me?" Conklin said, interrupting her. "Why did you do that?"

"It didn't seem appropriate to talk with the sheriff, but I thought I could let him know about you, and then he could share it with her."

"What do you mean? What was it about me you thought he should know?"

"That you are a kind, decent person, Arthur. That you couldn't possibly have killed Gerlach. That you couldn't kill anybody. Like I said, they don't know you. But I do—everyone around here does, and we have to stick up for you. Anyway, I'm worried. Whitman kept questioning me, especially about Helen. I assumed he'd be understanding, but he sounded—I don't know, doubtful. I have no idea whether he shared what I told him with the sheriff."

Arthur Conklin sat silently for a moment, staring at the Borodin score, but thinking about Harley Gerlach, Kevin Whitman, and the sheriff of Cumberland County.

"You're a good friend, Sandy. A loyal friend. I appreciate that. But I wouldn't want you going out on a limb for me—saying something, doing something you might later regret. I don't think there's anything you can do to influence the investigation into Gerlach's death."

"That's what Whitman said. He promised to talk with the sheriff, but he made it clear that it was her investigation, that she'd do whatever she thought she had to do. I guess he doesn't have much influence."

"I'm not so sure about that. There are rumors that Whitman and the sheriff are pretty close. That they're sleeping together."

"Really?" Temple was obviously surprised to hear this. But then she seized on it as evidence that her decision to speak with Kevin had been the right one.

"That's good, isn't it? I mean, she's more likely to believe what I told him if they're that close. She is, isn't she?"

Sandy Temple was beginning to have doubts. And Arthur Conklin's face took on that opaque look which Kevin had noticed when Carol had questioned him two days earlier.

"Sandy," Conklin said, "why don't we talk about the Borodin quartet? What the sheriff thinks and does is out of our hands."

And so they turned their attention to Borodin. The Derwent sisters arrived some ten minutes later, and the Prism String

290

Quartet was soon making music together. The quartet's cellist, however, was having a hard time concentrating on the score in front of him.

————

It was a few minutes after eleven the next morning when Sheriff Kelleher, Deputy Sheriff Bridges, and sheriff's department veteran Bill Parsons climbed into Bridges' patrol car and set out for Geneva. Carol and Kevin had talked late into the evening the previous day, debating what to do with the ideas generated by their brainstorming session. Carol had wanted to proceed cautiously. Kevin had argued for a more aggressive approach. In the end, they had agreed that Carol should arrange to meet with the D.A. the next morning, lay out her case, and then pay Arthur Conklin a visit.

For obvious reasons, there was no room for Kevin in the small party that set off from Cumberland for Geneva. This was official business, not something in which a professor of music should be involved. Which left him to spend the hours restlessly pacing around the cottage or trying to write his article for *Opera News*. He knew that he could not do either. Instead, he elected to take a long swim, the one which took him south along Blue Water Point and into Mallard Cove, the one which had ended in his discovery of a dead man on his dock two summers before. A discovery which had brought the sheriff of Cumberland County into his life.

At 11:12, Kevin dove into Crooked Lake.

At 11:51, Carol and her colleagues knocked on Arthur Conklin's door.

"Good morning, Sheriff," Conklin greeted the uniformed party. "Won't you come in?"

"Thank you, Mr. Conklin. If you don't mind, my colleagues can wait in here." Carol pointed to a small, formal parlor, apparently little used, across the hall from the living room.

"Would you like coffee? A soft drink?" Conklin asked.

"Thanks, but no thanks. Let's go in there," Carol said, gesturing toward the living room.

"You have presumably come to arrest me," their host said. "Otherwise, you would probably have come alone. It really wasn't necessary to bring along a posse, you know."

"Yes, I'm aware of that. It's simply standard operating procedure."

They took seats, Conklin on the couch, Carol on what looked like the most comfortable chair in the room, across a large coffee table from the couch. The books and magazines on the coffee table looked as if they had been carefully placed to make a statement regarding the taste of the owner.

"Am I correct that this isn't simply a social visit?" Conklin was affecting a light, almost jocular tone. But he looked tired, his face drawn.

"No, I'm afraid it isn't," Carol replied, although choosing not to confirm his assumption that she was there to arrest him. "I wonder if you have anything you might like to add to what you told me when I was last here."

"You mean, do I wish to change my story. Is that it?"

"If you wish to," Carol said.

"Sheriff, I am emotionally exhausted. This has been a very long and tiring two weeks. Or is it now closer to three weeks? In fact it has been a long and tiring summer. One might even say that it has been a long and tiring year if you go back to the day I learned that my wife had been having an affair with Harley Gerlach. That and her death shortly thereafter. I'm not much in the mood to continue the charade."

Carol had not known what to expect. She and Kevin had considered several scenarios, including one in which Conklin would angrily launch into a tirade against the sheriff. But it was beginning to look as if he might go to the other extreme and meekly confess that he had killed Gerlach. She patiently waited to see what he would say. What he would do.

"Gerlach has been on my mind for a long time, as I'm sure you can imagine. When I invited him to lunch, it was not because I was prepared to forgive him. It was because I knew that the opera that had brought us together would soon be over, and that before that happened I wanted him to tell me in his own words about his affair with my wife. I had no intention of doing him harm. I suppose that in a way I was seeking closure for a very painful time in my life."

Conklin paused. He reached out idly, rearranging a magazine which appeared not to be perfectly aligned with others in the pile on the coffee table.

"I had obviously underestimated the man. I had observed him over the course of the summer, and realized that he could be irascible and cruel in his dealings with people. And I had assumed that he would take some kind of perverse pleasure in telling me about his relationship with Helen. That he would enjoy my discomfort as I listened to him. He probably did. But when I ventured to ask him questions, he became agitated. And then belligerent. When I sought to calm him down, he lashed out at me. I saw this man at his unvarnished worst, this man who had seduced my wife and ruined my life."

Carol, who had listened without comment, finally interrupted.

"I take it he was drunk."

"He had had a lot to drink, yes."

"And I'm told by people at the restaurant that you kept buying his drinks."

"If I suggested he stop drinking, he just became more belligerent. It was easier to get him his scotch."

"And?" Carol wanted Conklin to resume his monologue.

"It became unbearable. I'm not sure at exactly what point it happened, but there came a moment when I knew that Gerlach did not deserve to live."

"Mr. Conklin," Carol spoke up, "I think it's about time I reminded you that you have a right to remain silent, and that anything you say may be used against you in a court of law."

"I know all about my Miranda rights, Sheriff."

"Then you know that you should call your lawyer."

"I do not need a lawyer. As I told you, I'm tired—very tired—of this charade. I killed Harley Gerlach that afternoon. It was almost ridiculously easy. The bed was there. In his condition he didn't have to be urged to climb into it. I suppose I could have strangled him with my own two hands, but the piano wire was convenient, and it meant that I didn't have to dirty my hands by touching his miserable neck. Three minutes and I was on my way to the nursery."

"I still think you ought to call your lawyer. You need to discuss your defense with a qualified criminal attorney."

"Defense?" Arthur Conklin said with a wry laugh. "I lost my wife, Sheriff. I was furious with her. But she was only weak. Gerlach was another story. He was evil. Pure, unadulterated evil. I killed him."

CHAPTER 54

As Carol explained it to Kevin later that day, Conklin had accompanied them back to Cumberland without an argument. He had confessed to responsibility for his wife's ultimately fatal fall. No, he hadn't tried to kill her, but he had been pushing and shoving her near the top of the stairs one day and she had lost her balance and fallen. Of course he had tried to cover it up, and while the police had initially been suspicious, they had eventually concluded that it had been an accident. While he had resented Gerlach, it was Helen he had blamed for her extramarital fling. Until this summer. Then he had had an opportunity to observe Gerlach up close for nearly ten weeks, and he had gradually come to the conclusion that he should have reserved his bitterness, his anger, for him.

"Why do think he decided to confess?" Kevin asked. "I thought you could have had a hard time making a murder charge stick."

"I'm not sure I know what was going on in his mind," Carol said. "But my impression is that he had begun to feel remorse about his wife. And I don't mean he only regretted how he'd treated her, or his role in her death. I think he was consumed with self-hatred. And then that hatred got transferred to Gerlach. Arthur had killed the wrong person, and he had to make it right by killing the one who really deserved to die. Somehow in the end he had simply lost the will to rationalize what he had done. He was tired. He just gave up."

"What's going to happen?"

"It's out of my hands," Carol said, and she sounded relieved to say so. "They may be discussing a plea right now. He faces jail, but I can't say what the charge will be—murder one, murder two, I just don't know. Nor do I know what the sentence will be. The only thing I know for sure is that his life has been ruined."

"So there won't be a big trial like there was last year in the Rackley case. Which means that Jason Armitage will be disappointed. He'll have to stay focused on being the provost of

Brae Loch College rather than sneak off to the courtroom to get his crime and punishment fix."

It was, they agreed, an unexpected ending to Crooked Lake's latest murder case.

———

Labor Day weekend. The end of the summer for many area residents, including Kevin Whitman. He was due back for the first day of classes at Madison College on Tuesday. Already he was feeling an anticipatory emptiness, settling back into his city apartment while Carol was hundreds of miles away. He had promised her that he would come back to the lake for a long weekend as soon as he had met his classes for the first time, but that would hardly compensate for the many months when they would be living separate lives.

The Festival of Lights would give them one final opportunity to share the lake and the cottage before he headed for the city. The previous summer, at Kevin's suggestion, Carol had used the July Fourth version of this tradition to try to trap Sandra Rackley's killer. This time they would share the occasion, placing flares along Kevin's beach and enjoying the spectacle of miles of lake shoreline glowing red in the dark of an early September evening.

After a simple supper, Kevin brought an armload of seasoned logs down to the beach and started a fire. In a matter of minutes the logs were burning brightly and sending tiny sparks into the night sky. At precisely nine o'clock, he lit his flares. They watched as neighbors and residents on the bluff across the lake did likewise. Kevin closed his eyes, imagining a similar sight in a far-off time when their Native American forebears celebrated the harvest season.

"Hey, let's take a look at this from the canoe," Carol said.

"Why not?" Kevin liked the idea. "Let me get that lantern on the deck."

Three minutes later, the lantern between them, they shoved off from the beach and were soon drifting along some twenty yards offshore.

"I love it, don't you?" Carol said.

"Especially when I can share it with you."

"You know, Kevin, I've been so caught up in the Gerlach case that I don't think I ever really told you how sorry I am that you didn't get a chance to put on your opera."

"Yes you did. I just didn't want to talk about it."

"Anyway, it had to be a terrible disappointment. You've been a good sport about it. Have you given any thought to doing it another summer?"

Kevin chuckled.

"No way. I doubt the powers that be at Brae Loch would let me within a mile of the place. Besides, I learned quite a bit about myself this summer. What was it you called me? An impresario? Well, I'm no impresario. I don't think I'm a very good conductor either. No, I think I'll stick to teaching."

"And sleuthing," Carol added.

They paddled quietly, parallel to the shoreline, enjoying the flares and the occasional beach fire.

"You haven't forgotten that you're coming back next weekend, have you?"

"I promise to be at the cottage next Friday night. Why don't you stay there this week. Keep the bed warm for me."

"I'd love to, but my place needs a thorough housecleaning. I think I'd better go back to Cumberland. But I'll be here when you arrive. Promise."

Neither one of them wanted to talk about what was uppermost in their minds: the many long lonely weeks between September and May.

They had reached the place where Blue Water Point turns into Mallard Cove. Just as the last flare on the point guttered out, a full moon started to rise above the crest of the bluff across the lake.

"Beautiful, isn't it?" Carol said.

"Oh, yes. Beautiful may not even do it justice." Kevin wasn't looking at the moon. His eyes were on Carol.